PENGUIN BOOKS

Lone Wolf

Lone Wolf

GREGG HURWITZ

PENGUIN BOOKS

PENGUIN BOOKS

UK | USA | Canada | Ireland | Australia
India | New Zealand | South Africa

Penguin Books is part of the Penguin Random House group of companies
whose addresses can be found at global.penguinrandomhouse.com

First published in the United States of America by Minotaur Books,
an imprint of St. Martin's Publishing Group 2024
First published in Great Britain by Penguin Michael Joseph 2024
Published in Penguin Books 2024

001

Typeset by Jouve (UK), Milton Keynes
Printed and bound in Great Britain by Clays Ltd, Elcograf S.p.A.

The authorized representative in the EEA is Penguin Random House Ireland,
Morrison Chambers, 32 Nassau Street, Dublin D02 YH68

A CIP catalogue record for this book is available from the British Library

ISBN: 978–1–405–95338–2

www.greenpenguin.co.uk

To the men and women who operate the printing presses and unstick the machinery. To the crews who mop the floors, clear the clutter, and allow space for productivity and focus. To the workers who keep the warehouses moving, the mail rooms running, and the supplies flowing. To the inventory managers who steward our tomes through the arteries of the industry so they can nourish the culture. To the editors and editorial assistants who are the first to believe and who shepherd the work from rough draft to bookshelf. To the copyeditors and proofreaders who fine-tune and triple-check. To the production editors who set the type and the designers who entice readers to judge our books by their covers. To the technologists who build the networks, debug the systems, and encrypt the ebooks. To the translators and sub-rights coordinators who search out new eyes and ears into which to deliver narratives. To the sales reps who traffic in enthusiasm, the coin of the realm. To the marketers and publicists who communicate the story of our stories so the world might receive them. To the human resourcers who replenish the departments with fresh minds. To the brains in finance and accounting who calculate the royalties, transform red to black, and aim the ship toward prosperity. To the legal counsel who protect the intellectual property and safeguard the copyrights. To the editorial directors, associate publishers, and imprint publishers who hold the infrastructure together. To the C-suite-ers, president, and publisher who keep a roof over the whole enterprise, navigate the rapidly changing landscape, and shine their vision throughout.

For devoting yourselves to this sacred undertaking and for creating the conditions for the word to go forth in all its ambition, imperfection, and occasional glory, you have my admiration and gratitude.

You are singular.

The world breaks every one and afterward many are strong at the broken places. But those that will not break it kills.

– Ernest Hemingway

Every man has a secret in him, many die without finding it.

– Stéphane Mallarmé

Prologue

The important thing wasn't how Evan got here, shirtless and blood-spattered in an underground bar, nor why he had half a human ear in his pocket, nor why the heavily perspiring bald bouncer proportioned like the Farnese Atlas seemed determined to twist Evan's head off his torso. The important thing, given the size of the manhunt massing for him on the streets outside, was what he did with the precious next few seconds.

1. Pale Nothingness

Evan stood where the long dirt road gave over to the desolate heat-miraged loam, staring at the double-wide manufactured home where the man who was presumably his biological father lived, the man Evan had never laid eyes on, the man he had reason to believe was currently inside those four dilapidated walls.

He had the taste of dirt in his mouth, sunbaked Texas mountain laurel. A taste of land foreign to him, the taste of another kind of life.

The taste of poverty was familiar, despite the fact that his own childhood indigence had been of the urban variety. He recognized something here in the cracking cement boards that spoke to drafts, the dimpled roof that let in rain, the pink paint faded to pale nothingness that no one would ever bother to patch. It was the kind of broke that looked right back into you, into your worst parts, and told you that what you saw around you was a precise reflection of just how worthless you were and would always be.

The mailbox spoke to drunkenness and disregard, its wooden post snapped by a wayward bumper.

Parked just beyond, at an arbitrary slant where in an alternate universe a front lawn might live, was a Ford F-150 not unlike Evan's, except this one was dark blue, with rusting wheel wells and a dent in the right rear fender.

The front door was shut against the sandpaper wind. A black trash bag that had replaced a windowpane thrashed back and forth and then fell still in the heavy heat.

Blooming in his stomach was a kind of dread he'd nearly forgotten, a dread of private stakes and private consequences, of opening a door that could never again be shut.

He stepped up onto the porch, the sagging boards rasping against the soles of his boots.

Once he knocked on that door, he could never undo it.

He searched for his breath, lost it, found it again.

He knocked.

A few seconds' delay spoke to surprise that an unannounced visitor would trek to this edge of civilization.

And then footsteps, approaching.

2. Same Old, Same Old

The surprising thing about compiling weapons was how fucking *expensive* it was. You'd think from the lamestream media that any inbred mouth-breathing reprobate desirous of a good rampage could just go assemble a personal armory.

But you gotta save up.

Five hundred and change for a pump shotgun purchased in Texas to avoid registration. Seventy-five bucks for a box of rifled slug cartridges times ten for a case of 250 if you're lucky enough to find it. Seven hundo for a semiauto shotgun bought at an Arizona gun show. Six fifty for a pistol, thirty bucks for each mag, and a hundred a pop per box of fifty hollow-point cartridges. Another fifty for a cleaning kit and one twenty-five for a supply of high-quality springs. Seventeen hundred fifty bucks for a box magazine-fed 5.56 mm NATO carbine, which he'd just picked up in Reno to circumvent California's restrictive gun laws. Fifty dollars for each magazine and a grand for one thousand practice-ball rounds. Another two K for a case of a thousand hollow-points, which were harder to find by the day, so by the time you're done gearing up to protect yourself you coulda bought a time-share in Palm Springs.

Hard to plan for when the only gig you can find is working minimum wage in a fucking warehouse twenty-nine hours a week, one shy of what you need to get health and benefits. The working conditions were for shit, too. Last week a foreman literally suggested they wear adult diapers on shift so they wouldn't waste time taking bathroom breaks.

American born, raised in the prosperous nineties, now forty-three years old, and this was what Martin Quinn had – twenty-nine hours of work a week and Depends. With no prospect to ever get anything more.

The world had stopped making sense to him.

It used to be that if you busted your hump and kept your head down you could make enough to cover rent and the cable bill and maybe take a girl out for dinner and a movie on the weekend. Used to be that a high-school graduate with some credits at community college could land a job that'd keep him above the poverty line. Used to be employers valued folks who spoke English and bothered to pay for car insurance. Used to be an American could keep his head above water even if he wasn't trained in the latest computing-whatever or hadn't inherited Daddy's business or couldn't cut the line because of what kind of anatomy he came packaged with or how much pigment he had in his skin. Not that it was a *right,* but it was a way of life the world he'd been raised in had taught him to expect.

He didn't have that anymore.

Now he just had resentment.

And fear.

It felt like he couldn't trust anything anymore. The news was all fucked up and screamy, and the internet was driving everyone insane, and as far as Martin was concerned both political parties could go suck a bag of dicks. Everything felt like guilt, guilt, guilt rammed in his face 24/7. When he was younger and dumber he'd done shit he'd never do now – pinched an ass or used a slur – but that wasn't who he was now and it felt like the world was just waiting to root out an old grudge and flatten him into all the worst parts of himself he'd ever been. When he turned on the TV, he didn't recognize any of the actors no more, and the movies were all about lecturing people, and it seemed like every last fool in the world was trying to be an influencer, which as far as he understood meant they had good abs or tits and could make arty-farty photos of themselves with kombucha balanced on their heads while doing yoga poses or fronting like a gangsta. Then there were the other types, the freaks demanding to be celebrated for being fat or having some mental illness or coming from a country somewhere no one had ever heard of. And you couldn't say what you thought anymore in public, and you weren't allowed to disagree with people, and you couldn't use words you'd used your whole life, and even the new words got updated every three minutes. The whole thing was confusing as hell, like walking barefoot through a maze of mousetraps, and if he was honest it made him feel like one of those old-ass Eskimos the tribe just shoves off on an ice floe because they're useless. Part of him deep down suspected that was the whole point. To show him that his time was over.

When the world shifted this far upside down, it meant it was about to break.

And he was gonna be ready for it.

If anyone came for him or pushed him too far, he'd be ready.

He arrived back at his tiny apartment in Panorama City, the only place he could afford, with a broken air conditioner hanging in the window, dumbbells on the ratty carpet, a pull-up bar across his bedroom doorframe, and two whores who lived next door and kept the walls thumping. The sole decoration in the entire shithole was the Sears photo of him and Maryanne from back in happier days with Joshy propped between them on Martin's knee, all fat and smiley. Martin had tacked it up by the gooseneck lamp set on the floor next to his mattress so it would be the last thing he'd see every night. A comforting reminder that there'd once been a time when the world had made any kind of sense.

Martin nestled the new 5.56 mm NATO carbine between the shotguns in the rack he kept in the closet. The big gun made him feel safe, protected, like he was still worth something after all.

Even if the world didn't have plans for him, he had plans for the world.

When he stood up to admire his weapons cache, he didn't see the feminine figure standing behind him, gripping a belt looped into the shape of a noose.

Martin Quinn dangled from the convenient pull-up bar, the tips of his Carhartt boots stretching to graze the ground. The stool had already been neatly placed, toppled just out of reach beneath him to the side. For the first few seconds he'd tried to hoist himself up to shake his head loose, but she'd greased the metal pole with petroleum jelly, so it hadn't been long before his arm muscles gave out. Now his weight sagged, the belt torquing his head to the left.

That always interested Karissa, which way the head tilted in a hanging. It abided by some weird natural law like wishbones and that groundhog in Punxsutawney. Her scorecard showed Left 6, Right 7, so she was pleased to even up the score.

Quinn gurgled a bit, his lower lip wet with drool. His face hadn't purpled yet but the blood was building up, like he was embarrassed, which he should be since she'd loosened his trousers and tugged them down to his shins.

Karissa preferred not to use guns, because guns could be traced, and she liked to choose different methods to obscure the connection between jobs. Just last month, she'd crossed 'fell asleep with a lit cigarette and died in a house fire' off her bingo card when dispensing with a perky accountant with a proclivity for embezzlement. This morning's gig, autoerotic asphyxiation gone awry, would likewise leave no fingerprints.

Especially once she disposed of Quinn's arsenal and plugged her USB Rubber Ducky drive into his antique laptop, where it would purge his search memory of anything to do with weapon acquisitions and implant a history of perusing vibrant S&M vids.

It had to go slowly, the strangulation, for the forensics to add up. Karissa needed everything to add up, because when the forensics added up that meant that she had never been here.

She stood before him, arms clasped at the small of her back, observing. It was a rarity in the human experience to watch someone die up close, and for her it held endless anthropological interest, like seeing peregrine falcons mate or an octopus crack a crab apart to get at the meat.

Quinn's bladder released, sheeting yellow down his bare inner thigh. To no avail his fingernails scrabbled at the edge of the leather band, gouging his throat. He strained to thrust his toes into the carpet and pull another sip of air through his constricted windpipe. His eyes pleaded with her. He made squeaking noises.

People said the weirdest shit before they died. Karissa collected dying words. Mostly folks were scared or regretful. Few were angry or defiant; almost everyone begged. The most common refrain was 'Wait.' That always amused her. Wait for what?

Quinn choked some more, his bluing lips trying to shape themselves to say something.

She was curious.

She heeled one of the ten-pound dumbbells off the baseboard and rolled it over toward him. His boots scrabbled for purchase and then found it, buying him a few inches' lift.

The words came so soft she had to step right up to him. At five foot four, she had to tilt her face up near his, close enough that she could feel his breath against her cheeks. She was flat-chested and tapered, gymnast-strong, and her power caught most everyone, Martin Quinn included, off guard.

He wobbled on his precarious perch, the dumbbell rolling beneath his toes. '. . . Joshy . . . tell . . . wish I . . . more time with . . . made it . . . right . . . him . . .'

More of the usual.

Karissa sidled a half step in, catching waves of heat from Quinn's body and the smell of urine. Their lips, almost close enough to kiss.

She placed the ball of her foot on the dumbbell, rolling it slowly out from under Quinn's toes. His eyes bulged. A blood vessel had given way, a lightning strike bleeding through the sclera. '. . . wait,' he creaked, his legs straining to hold the dumbbell underfoot. '. . . wait . . .'

Same old, same old, and besides, she had another stop today.

With a brisk nudge of her toe, she pushed the dumbbell free.

3. A Once-Brutal Man

Orphan X was missing.

It had been three days since Evan Smoak had blinked off the radar – or blinked *further* off the off-the-radar realm he inhabited – and Joey had kept herself busy being furious with him so she didn't have to be worried.

He wasn't answering his RoamZone phone, which had happened precisely never in all the time she'd known him, not once since he'd slammed into her on a mission way back and they'd gotten stuck with each other. X kinda sorta looked after her and she looked after him, too, because if left to his own devices, he would've fallen desperately behind when it came to digital intrusion (and, like, interpersonal skills). And besides, *someone* had to make sure the world's most dangerous assassin didn't embarrass himself.

Even though she was seventeen and he was, like, late-thirties old, they had some stuff in common, her and Evan, like that they were both recruited out of broke-ass foster homes into the full-black Orphan Program by three-letter-agency types intent on turning them into disposable weapons. Joey had washed out early on 'cuz turned out that while hacking was her love language, killing enemies of the state in violation of international law wasn't so much her jam. And X – after neutralizing boo-koo targets in boo-koo time zones – had proven to be not so disposable once he'd parted ways with the Program, so the joke was on the government asshats who thought they could take him down.

Not that they'd stopped trying.

Since Evan had been on his own, he took pro bono missions under the guise of the Nowhere Man, who (Movie Trailer Voice:) *Helped the Powerless and Downtrodden Who Had Nowhere Left to Turn.*

A secret phone number passed from one client to the next: 1-855-2-NOWHERE. When someone in the seriously worst moment of their life dialed the line, the call got split into digital packets and filtered through a host of encrypted virtual-private-network tunnels on various continents before it rang through to the RoamZone.

The one thing you could count on in this screwed-up world?

The Nowhere Man would answer.

Which is why, after seventy-two hours of him *not* picking up, Joey had finally caved in to her mounting concerns and broken into his place to see what the hell was going on. The front door, with its labyrinth of internal security bars, water core to deter battering rams, and murderers' row of next-level dead bolts, was a pretty good disincentive for mortals who were not her. She'd gotten through it before, though it had taken a half hour, two sizes of bump keys, a Dangerfield Z-wrench, a .023-inch-gauge half-diamond pick, and a copious serving of light-viscosity spray lubricant (insert gross dude joke here). So the next time she'd been over and Evan had retreated to meditate on his floating bed, she'd taken an impression of his key to save time in the future.

Now here she was, alone in the deserted penthouse.

She'd been standing frozen on the poured-concrete floor for maybe ten minutes trying to make her brain believe what her eyes were feeding her.

The RoamZone.

Sitting on the kitchen island.

Abandoned by X as surely as she had been.

She felt a weightlessness in her stomach, a roller-coaster drop where her body couldn't catch up to the rules of physics.

X was reliable.

X honored his word.

X had that phone on him always.

The Second Commandment decreed it: *How you do anything is how you do everything.*

Evan stuck to that edict with the same OCD meticulousness with which he kept his penthouse psychotically spotless and tidy.

The Nowhere Man didn't take breaks. He wasn't allowed to. The very thought was a perversion of natural law.

She realized she'd forgotten to breathe, and she gulped in a hunk of air and finally broke eye contact with the abandoned phone.

Like Evan, the seven-thousand-square-foot condo was designed for maximum efficiency. Slab, stone, stainless-steel fixtures. The floor-to-ceiling windows made the penthouse's floating starkness apparent, like a Scandinavian tree house hovering twenty-one stories above Wilshire Boulevard. With its discreet-armor sunshades and glass walk-in vodka freezer, it usually felt cool and contemporary.

But today it felt like a crypt.

Her legs were growing numb.

What the hell could have gotten to Evan? What made him disappear?

His last mission had been crazier than most. At its conclusion, he'd gone to Texas in search of the biological father he'd never known, a onetime rodeo cowboy named Jacob Baridon. Even though X had been resistant to the whole thing, Joey had tracked down the location for him behind his back.

Had he caught up to his father?

Was that what had pushed him over the edge?

Or was it something worse?

And if he *had* disappeared 'cuz of something to do with his bio dad, did that mean this was all her fault?

No. She wasn't gonna blame herself for Evan's choices. Not even if she felt panic bubbling up her throat at the thought of him going missing. Clearly he'd gotten back here safely enough to leave his phone behind. He'd probably wander in soon enough with some stupid excuse and get all brooding and moody when she tried to ask what happened.

She'd wait here, give him until nightfall. Not that she was happy about it. In fact, she was the kind of mad she could feel seething beneath her skin.

She stomped over to the RoamZone and with a few furious flicks of her thumbs changed his ringtone to something he'd find maximally embarrassing. Then she glared around at all the annoyingly dust-free surfaces, every last thing in perfect place.

Throwing open the cupboards, she rearranged the height-ordered glasses so they were all messed up. She interspersed salad plates with dinner plates, giving each stack a jagged rise that would make Evan twitchy.

The high midday light was starting to bleed into oranges and golds, the sun not really caring too much about the arbitrary deadline she'd given Evan to get back home.

Shoving her way into the glass-walled freezer, she took a pull of vodka straight from the bottle, some variety that cost more than the national median income and had been, like, filtered eleventy billion times through panda hide.

It tasted fine.

She paced some more.

Dusk was coming on.

She retrieved a box of paper clips from a kitchen drawer, then charged back to the master suite with the levitating bed held aloft by the push of neodymium rare-earth magnets and the pull of steel cables. After lining up the paper clips on the floor, she flicked them one by one into the magnetic field so they pinged invisibly onto the bed's Houdini undercarriage.

When she ran out of paper clips, she did missile dive-bombs onto the bed to see if she could get it to sway on its cables.

She couldn't.

In the north-facing window she could see the last reflections of light dwindling in the windows along the Wilshire Corridor as nightfall smothered the sky.

She couldn't imagine her life if X was gone for real. Even if he was stubborn and a colossal pain, he was the only person who *got* her, got the kind of rough she'd come from and the kind of rough she still was. Her brain couldn't compute the levels of lonely she'd feel if he'd finally gone and gotten himself killed.

Or if he'd taken off and left her like everyone always did.

Anger swelled up fast and familiar. She threw open the bureau drawers. His socks were folded tight like hand grenades and lined up with mathematical precision. She pulled them apart and shoved strays in his shirt drawer and threw others across the floor. Then she contemplated cleaning the toilet with his toothbrush, but she thought of that one look he got when his eyes crinkled at the edges and he couldn't help but be gentle as only a once-brutal man knew how to be.

Then she was bawling. Shit.

Ugly-crying, with snot and everything.

She allotted herself five minutes to be a mess. She only took three.

Then she moved through the bathroom, past the tempting

toothbrush and into the shower. Gripping the hot-water handle, she waited a beat for it to scan the vein pattern in her palm. It gave a nearly imperceptible vibration and then she twisted it the wrong way and swung open the secret door disguised seamlessly in the tile pattern.

She entered the Vault.

The Nowhere Man's inner sanctum, a hidden space he'd retrofitted to be the nerve center of his operations. No more than four hundred square feet filled with server racks, computer hardware, weapon lockers, and an L-shaped sheet-metal desk. Exposed beams matched the pattern of the public stairs to the roof above, the ceiling encroaching down on the forgotten storage area that had never even made it onto the building blueprint.

Aside from X, she was the only person who'd ever seen it.

Collapsing into his chair and clicking the mouse, she brought to life the hidden micro-OLED screens mounted to the three concrete walls that embraced the desk. Two of the walls featured pirated feeds from around the building, an intimate look at the spaces and corridors of the Castle Heights Residential Tower. The other showed the measly file Joey had compiled on Evan's 'father' – a few credit-card charges clustered around Blessing, the most Texas-sounding town in all of Texas.

A fresh swell of regret washed through her for pursuing Jacob Baridon when Evan had told her to leave it alone. The Fourth of the Ten Commandments X lived by – *Never make it personal* – meant he avoided telenovela drama like this at all turns. Not that he always could. A while back, he'd met his mother briefly and learned that he had a half brother, Andre Duran, who needed his help. Turned out Evan and Andre had actually been in a foster home together like a million years ago and had never suspected they were related. If Joey ever found out *she* had a half-sibling? She'd be all over that shit. But not X. After helping Andre, he hadn't been in touch with him even though the guy lived right here in Los Angeles and had a cute daughter and everything.

Never make it personal.

That was Evan.

And yet Joey had pushed him. Found an approximate location for his father. And led him right onto the only kind of terrain Orphan X wasn't trained for.

She rubbed her eyes. Then she felt someone watching her.

Evan's little aloe vera plant, Vera III, looked up at Joey from the desk, noirishly lit in the artificial light of the OLED monitors. Inhabiting her bowl filled with rainbow-colored glass pebbles, she was Evan's only companion here in the penthouse, probably because she placed as few demands on him as he did on her.

'I don't know where he is,' Joey told Vera.

Vera converted carbon dioxide to malic acid with seeming concern.

'Fine,' Joey said. 'I'll call Tommy.'

Tommy Stojack, a nine-fingered armorer with a workshop off the Strip in real Las Vegas, was Evan's most trusted contact. Tommy not only conducted R&D for government-sanctioned black groups but also machined ghost weapons for a few unsanctioned individuals, X included. Over the years, he and Evan had fallen into a cadence where they relied on each other.

Calling up videotelephony software she'd personally encrypted, she pinged Tommy.

Three rings, five, seven.

Then he answered, that bulbous nose looming large as he squinted at the screen like a Boomer. He was driving somewhere, his phone resting on one knee, jouncing around. A biker's mustache framed his upper lip, the bottom one pooched out with Skoal. 'Roadkill Spreads and Delicacies. Taking out or dining in?'

'Gross.'

He gave a double take, noted that it was Joey. His baggy hound-dog eyes looked happy to see her, even if his mouth didn't follow suit. 'What do you want?' he said, over a wash of engine noise from his rig.

'Evan's missing,' Joey told him. 'Three days.'

'How do you know he's missing? Insteada off being himself somewhere?'

'He left his RoamZone here at —' She caught herself. Evan's operational security protocols meant that not even Tommy could know where he lived. 'Left it behind.'

'What? He left the *RoamZone*? That thing's always stuck to him like shit on a shovel.'

'Thus my call.'

'And you think what?'

'I don't know,' Joey said. 'What if he needs our help? What if he's in trouble? What if he was killed in an extreme gender-reveal mishap?'

'Then at least we'd have something to laugh about.'

'Tommy!'

'C'mon, girlie girl. Tell me you wouldn't love to chisel *that* shit on his tombstone.'

'I think . . . I think he went to find his father.'

'Why do you think that?'

Guilt permeated her hesitation. 'I mighta dug up a location for him. Maybe whatever happened set him off.'

'You're so worried, why don't you just find him?'

'Oh, sure. Tracking down the Nowhere Man. That should be a snap.'

'You know him pretty good. Ask yourself what he'd get up to if he left his phone behind.'

'"*What Would Evan Smoak Do?*" Said: No one ever.'

'You check his safe houses?'

Joey hesitated a split second too long. '. . . *Yeah.*'

Why hadn't she thought of that? Her fingers were moving already, pulling up the internal surveillance feeds from the dozen or so safe houses Evan kept scattered around the greater Los Angeles area.

East LA: empty.

Westchester: empty.

Boyle Heights: empty.

Tarzana – holy shit.

There he was, sitting on the couch of the sparsely furnished bungalow, staring at . . . It looked like he was staring at nothing. And swaying ever so slightly. On the floor before him were several vodka bottles, which a quick zoom and image enhancement showed to be empty.

'Just spotted him.' Even to her own ears, her voice sounded dry and strained. 'I'll call you back when I get to him.'

'Bated breath, crossed fingers, thoughts and prayers.' Tommy spit a jet of tobacco juice through his gap teeth out the window and hung up.

Joey studied Evan some more, her mouth ajar with disbelief.

He was drunk.

Not quaffing two fingers of some vodka distilled by Amazonian warrior queens in northern Anatolia and then poured over a geode-shaped ice cube. But fucking hammered.

You shoulda seen him.

It was a disgrace.

4. The Kentucky Fried Fuck

Evan heard a pick set scratching at the front lock of his Tarzana safe house. When the door swung open, a cold, hard light fell across the bungalow, and his pupils contracted. The glare made his brain ache.

He had his ARES 1911 raised and aimed but was not as surprised as he'd have thought to see Joey stride inside, her angry walk with her Doc Martens stomping out ahead of her. The diamond pendant glinted at her chest, a concession to the elegant, striking a contrast with her flannel and scowl, both oversize.

'What the Kentucky Fried Fuck?' she said.

He lowered the pistol. 'Language.' His voice was cracked, desiccated.

She threw something at him. It struck his chest, not gently, and fell into his lap.

His RoamZone.

'You're not allowed to just *disappear* and not have the Nowhere Man phone on you,' she said. 'What if someone needed you and you didn't answer?'

Though she'd violently heeled the door shut behind her, he could still feel the aftereffect of the blast of daylight, an ice pick through his corneas. He shifted on the couch, his boot knocking over an empty bottle of Cîroc. It rattled noisily on the hardwood, describing an excruciatingly lethargic arc across the floor to stop at Joey's feet.

She looked down at it as if that just said it all.

Maybe it did.

Her hands were on her hips, rarely a good sign. 'It's not just you, you know. You have responsibilities to – to *people,* okay?'

The alcohol was wearing off, leaving a dull ache in Evan's cranium. He'd vomited once cleanly last night, the kind of avian regurgitation when the booze hits bottom and your stomach says, *Nope,* and sends it right back out in the form it came in.

He lifted his chin slightly to indicate the refrigerator. 'Saline.'

When she walked to the kitchen, her boots knocked the floor with slightly less vehemence, a promising development. She poked through the takeout by the sink. 'You,' she said, 'left shit on the counter. Isn't that one of the signs of the apocalypse?' She was joking, but the tremor of concern in her voice betrayed her. 'And besides, you shouldn't use plastic straws.' She held up the offending utensil.

The throbbing in his head intensified. 'It came in the bag.'

'As a proper La-La-Land-ian you should get your own, you know, made out of bamboo or steel so you don't, like, strangle turtles.'

'It came in the takeout bag,' he repeated. 'What was I supposed to do? Bring in a straw-sniffing canine?'

'Just look in the bag,' she said angrily. 'Take it out.'

'I'll send a check to the Turtle Anti-Strangulation League.'

'Is that a thing?'

'No.'

She leaned into the fridge, digging in the vegetable drawer and coming up with an IV bag. 'Tommy was worried about you, you know.'

'Tommy,' he repeated skeptically.

'Yes, *Tommy.* You don't just leave your phone behind like that. Ever. That's, like, the deal.'

She came over and tossed a saline pouch at him. It hit his chest with slightly less force than the RoamZone had.

He said, 'I also need the –'

She flicked her other hand. The infusion kit landed in his lap.

It took some focus but he spiked the IV bag, leaned with a groan, and hooked it on the knob of the halogen floor lamp to his side. He milked the juice down the line, cleared the bubbles, then poked at his arm for a good vein.

'What happened?' Joey said. 'Where were you?'

'Texas.'

He found a drained bottle at his feet, raised it at a tilt to see the tiny isosceles of vodka pooling at the base.

'Did you find your dad?'

He poured a few drops over the crook of his elbow to sterilize it, then ripped the top off the sterile catheter bag, uncapped the needle with his front teeth, and slid it into his vein. 'Nothing,' he said. 'I found nothing.'

'I don't know what that means.'

He leaned back, stared at the ceiling, waited for the drip to start. 'I don't either, Josephine.'

She hesitated. In the half-light, her irises looked translucent, nearly jade. Her long lashes blinked, eyes flashing. Her thick black-brown hair was shaved on the right side in an undercut, long locks flipped over to cascade down her cheek. An emerald stone punctuated her left nostril. She looked tough and beautiful and suddenly fragile.

She whipped out her phone. 'I'm calling Tommy.'

'Put the filters on.'

'I *know* how to make an encrypted call, X. *I'm* the one who made your encryption un-shitty.'

He felt the saline solution hitting his blood, the boost immediate. His headache evanesced, his veins swelling, bringing a flush of much-needed energy.

Then Tommy was in his face, peering out from the rectangle of Joey's phone in extreme close-up, his mustache ballooned to Teddy Roosevelt proportions.

'Jesus,' Tommy's mustache said. 'You look like the back a my balls.'

'I think he's having some kinda midlife crisis,' Joey informed Tommy. 'Which is . . . *unbecoming*.' She held the phone at her chest aiming out so they both stared at him.

'Okay,' Tommy said to Evan. 'So you caught up to Papa Smurf and now you feel like a can of crushed assholes. Lay it out for us cheap-seaters.'

Evan said, 'No.'

Joey rotated the phone briefly for her and Tommy to share a look of aggravation and then swiveled it back.

'I seen you drink more times than I can count without taking off my shoes,' Tommy said. 'But I never seen you drunk.'

Evan adjusted the roller clamp to increase the flow into his veins. His vision sharpened and he felt the first premonition of clarity in a day or so. 'I've never seen me drunk either.'

Joey's glare hardened. 'Whatever happened or didn't with your father, you need to compartmentalize that shit and deal with it on your own time.' She picked up the rugged phone beside him and flung it into his lap. 'You're *X*. Grow a pair.'

'Listen to sugarbritches,' Tommy said. '"N" I'm gonna spit some truth at you, too.'

'I'm not in the mood for –'

'No. Fuck that. A friend's a person who's right when they tell you you're wrong.' Tommy had inexplicably repositioned his phone camera so only a single eye peered out with speakeasy intensity. 'So listen up, honcho. Whatever's got you spunfucked, you gotta snap to and get back on yer feet. You know how, too. Start small.'

'Small?' Evan said. '"Small" doesn't happen around me.'

A sudden blare erupted from his crotch: *DONCHA WISH YER GIRLFRIEND WUZ HAAAWT LIKE ME?!*

The RoamZone, with a Josephine Morales-amended ringtone.

Her lips parted slightly to show the hair-thin gap in her front teeth.

He glared at her. 'You really thought it necessary to –'

DONCHA WISH YER GIRLFRIEND WUZ HAAAWT LIKE ME?!

Joey touched her fingertips to one ear. 'Sorry. I'm having trouble hearing you. Mayhaps you should pick up, as is your sworn responsibility.'

Miserably, Evan set the RoamZone on his knee and pressed SPEAKER. He tried to muster energy but his voice still came out flat. 'Do you need my help?'

'Yeah,' a young girl's voice said. 'My dog went missing.'

5. Loco

Joey stared at Evan. On her phone, Tommy's visible eye rolled and then the screen went dark as he cut the connection.

Evan sighed, the RoamZone heavy against his thigh. 'How did you get this number?'

'Duh,' the girl at the other end of the line said. 'It's Sofia. Andre's daughter.'

Sofia Duran, the eleven-year-old daughter of Evan's half brother.

The half brother who drank too much and – like most folks who'd grown up in the foster system – had a hard time staying out of trouble. The half brother Evan had saved on a prior mission and helped reunite with his daughter. The half brother whom Evan had largely and happily ignored since then.

Sofia lived with her mother, Brianna Ramirez, Andre's ex. Evan had met Sofia all of once, and as far as he knew, she had no idea that they were related. Despite coming up together in the Pride House Group Home, Evan and Andre had only learned of their blood relationship recently themselves. They'd reconnected in the midst of a homicidal onslaught, which might be strange for some people but for Evan was relatively normal.

Evan tugged the needle from his arm and stood up. 'Sofia, you can't call this number. It's not for you.'

'Why not? I heard Dad talking and *he* said it's for people who are upset –'

'It's not for people who are *"upset."*'

'– and Loco ran away and I can't find him.'

Evan pinched his eyes, his headache threatening a comeback. 'Loco.'

'Dad got him for when he can't be with me. He's my whaddayacallit? Volitional object.'

He bent his arm to put pressure on the puncture spot. 'Transitional.'

'He's not a *object* though. He's my dog and he ran away two days ago and I can't find him and what if a coyote or a hawk got him or someone took him.' Her voice wobbled and Evan thought, *Here we go.*

Joey's brow was intensely furrowed. Her expressions were rarely subtle, but her current display was silent-movie worthy.

Evan turned away from her and thumbed the phone off speaker. 'I'm not a dogcatcher.'

'But Dad said you help people.'

'I help people who really need help. Not kids with missing pets.'

'He's not a pet,' Sofia said. 'He's . . . he's my best friend.'

And then she was crying. Evan pressed the RoamZone tighter to his cheek in hopes of muffling the speaker, but when he risked a glance over his shoulder, Joey was standing with her arms crossed, her face brimming with disappointment.

'Look,' Evan said. 'I'm sorry. It's not what I do.'

But if Sofia heard him, she gave no sign, only sobbing broken by great shuddering breaths.

Evan stood a long time with the phone cool against his cheek and the sounds of Sofia. He clenched his eyes shut, bit his lip to trap the incipient profanity before it left his mouth. When he opened his eyes, his head was throbbing anew, the girl was still sniveling, and Joey was staring at him expectantly.

Joey threw her hands wide, fingers spread, and mouthed, *Start small.*

He mouthed back, *No fucking way.*

Joey grinned big, mouthed, *Language.*

Even in photographs, Loco was the ugliest dog Evan had ever seen. A trembling skeletal miniature pinscher–Chihuahua mix, he sported wiry thrusts of uneven hair, bat ears, and a psychotic snaggletoothed scowl. A bulging carbuncle riding the top of his tiny snout looked to be on the verge of explosion. Scrolling through digital pictures and videos with expert flicks of her thumb, Sofia charted the love story of girl and dog. Loco curled in her lap while she studied. Loco eating a French fry straight out of her lips. Loco dressed as a ladybug for Halloween, his terror-rictus undiminished beneath spring-mounted red poof antennae.

The dog loved her, that much was clear. He wobbled in her orbit in a fit of perennial anxiety, only calming when she picked him up and held him. His tiny misshapen head jerked around in constant rotation, bulging eyes on the lookout for imagined threats, and he made a guttural noise that sounded like a phlegm-intensive growl.

When Sofia blew gently into the mutt's face, which seemed a common ritual, he calmed and closed his eyes, basking in the faint breeze. The only other time he appeared to be in a nonagitated state was when he was sleeping atop her head on the pillow, scraggly hind and front legs framing either side of her face, an occurrence memorialized in myriad bedtime selfies.

For the past twenty minutes, Evan and Sofia had been sitting on the couch in the tidy apartment while Brianna bustled to and fro in the background, washing dishes, vacuuming, loading Sofia's lunch box for the next day, and then paying bills at the rickety desk in the corner. The amount of labor a single mother had waiting at the end of a workday seemed insurmountable, and yet Brianna kept at it, knocking down one task after another with a bowler's efficiency.

'Okay,' Evan told Sofia and her endlessly active iPhone finger. 'I think you've provided sufficient documentation to identify the dog.'

'Hang on.' Sofia's thumbs tapped expertly, bringing up another video. 'I gotta show you this time I snuck him inta the pool at the Y and he swam in circles 'cuz of his bum leg.'

The treasure trove of Loco's digital imagery was clearly inexhaustible. Sofia had had him for less than a year, and yet his personal archive seemed to exceed that of most United States presidents.

'The man *said* he's got it,' Brianna called over her shoulder from the desk. 'Don't everyone need to see endless footage of that crazy dog.'

A knock on the door and Sofia flew up from the couch. 'Dad!'

Brianna's head snapped up, reading glasses low on her nose. 'You invited your father here?'

'Uh, *yeah*,' Sofia said, gesturing back at Evan. 'He's *Dad's* friend.'

Evan cleared his throat. 'I wouldn't say we're exactly –'

Sofia pulled the door open and jumped up onto her father, who play-groaned, stumbling in under her weight. He collapsed onto the carpet with her.

'Don't play,' Brianna said. 'Someone's gonna get a tooth knocked out and you know who'll have to front the dentist bill.'

'Okay, okay.' Andre rose, straightened his clothes. A bit skinnier than Evan, he wore an oil-stained mechanic's shirt, and blue-white jeans low on his hips – not quite the sag he favored back in the day but enough to show off a band of underwear. 'How's my little girl?'

'I'll be better once Evan finds Loco.'

Evan stood. He and Andre faced each other awkwardly across the living room. "Tsup,' Andre said.

'Sup.' The reply slipped out of Evan's mouth before he could catch it.

Around Andre, Evan found himself dropping back into the street patter of their youth. Reminders of the past he'd left behind messed with his mental wiring. They hit his DNA, knocking old sensations back into his body. Taste of mold from the walls. Chafing of ill-fitting clothes. That awful gut-deep emptiness when the check from the state was late and there was nothing to eat for days but generic potato chips, the ones that came in white boxes with black block lettering. Worst of all was the shame burning beneath the skin at the wary looks they drew from clerks when a pack of them chimed a shop door to enter, at the sight of parents driving normal kids by in station wagons, at the chipped plates off which they ate their runny mac and cheese, and the cracked plastic glasses that leaked beads of water over their knuckles. Broke and powerless. Useless, too, except for Evan, who was lucky enough to get chosen for a program that created expendable human weapons no one cared about and no one would miss.

He'd won the lottery in Jack Johns, the handler who'd raised him from the age of twelve. Jack's philosophy – at turns pragmatic, sagacious, and blue-collar Zen – had been Evan's touchstone up to the moment of Jack's death. The toughest and finest man Evan had known, he was the first person to show Evan respect by placing exacting demands on him, by expecting more than Evan thought he had in him, by giving him a place in the world. And as sure as Jack had drilled into his young head marksman skills, hand-to-hand disciplines, and psyops techniques, he'd hammered home the most important lesson of all.

That the hardest part wasn't teaching Evan to be an assassin. The hardest part was keeping him human.

Every day was a fight between the two warring instincts – the push of perfection and isolation versus the pull of emotional contact with its endlessly confounding shades of gray. Evan felt it now in his repulsion for everything Andre's appearance had surfaced in him and in the drumbeat of guilt he felt at having pulled himself out when most everyone else from Pride House had wound up dead, or in a cell, or scraping by. His head, muddy from vodka and the aftermath of what he'd encountered in that prefabricated house in Texas, wasn't making any of this easier.

'Good on you for agreeing to do this,' Andre said.

Evan said, 'I didn't agree.'

'How do you know Dad again?' Sofia asked.

We had the same mom even if we never knew it.

'We knew each other from back when,' Evan said.

'What was Dad like as a kid?'

'He sketched a lot,' Evan said. 'And talked even more.'

Andre laughed. 'What you know, man? Running your skinny ass around the playground tryin' to not get it beat.'

Brianna had not risen from her desk. She kept her head down, scribbling away in a checkbook. Andre glanced over at her quickly and then once again.

'How you doing, Bri?' Andre said.

'You know,' she said.

'Nope. Why I'm asking.'

She put her pen down with a sigh. 'It was a lotta work when you brought that ratty dog over here –'

Sofia, arms crossed: 'He's *not* ratty.'

'– and it's a lot more work comforting this child day and night now that he ran away.'

Andre showed his palms, heeling away. 'Hold up, hold up. We're gonna get this fixed. Ain't that right, Evan?'

Evan felt his molars grind.

Brianna *mm-hmm*ed and went back to her work as Andre joined Evan and Sofia over at the couch. Sofia had dropped to the carpet in a perfect ballerina split. She was a dancer, always twirling and spinning, her hair fastened at her nape in a frayed bun.

Evan said, 'What else can you tell me about Loco?'

Sofia rotated slightly to second-position stretch, rainbowing one arm up and over her torso, an elegant taffy stick of a girl. 'He's allergic to apples, make him throw up –'

Brianna, still not looking up: 'On my carpet.'

'– and he's got this guilty face that's so cute when he tinkles by mistake –'

'On my carpet.'

'– and he curls his tongue when he yawns like –'

'Stop,' Evan said. 'I mean, did he go outside by himself? Did he ever run off? Did he go missing from here?'

'No. No. And no. We went over to Leela's house 'cuz we was going to the park. She lives in the fancy apartments across from Del Taco 'cuz her momma works at Disney – the studio, not like Space Mountain – and her momma's allergic to dogs so Loco couldn't come in so I tied his leash to the fat post thing at the bottom of the stairs and went up to get Leela and when I came out he was *gone*.'

'Was the leash gone, too?'

'No. It was there. And his collar. Just empty.'

'So he slipped the collar.'

'And that's got his tags and everything so no one's gonna

know how to call us.' Sofia sat up out of her stretch and hugged her knees, her cheeks flushing.

Moving quickly to avert a breakdown, Andre smiled big, clasped his hands, and rubbed them together like a waiter about to recommend the Parmesan-crusted sand dabs. 'So, Evil E. Where we gonna start?'

Evan asked, 'Is the dog chipped?'

'Nah,' Andre said. 'I found him on the street behind a dumpster.'

'Well, we should start at the pounds –'

'*Seriously?*' Sofia said. 'I've already checked them, like, a *hundred times*.' She side-eyed her father. 'I thought you said he was good at this.'

Evan pushed through: 'I'll go over to the apartments then and look around.'

'Hang on.' Sofia popped up in a single motion, a jack-in-the-box exploding. 'Mom had flyers made for me at work.'

Brianna, head still down: 'Though no one's gonna mention unsanctioned use of the office copy machine to Mr Olmeda at the holiday party.'

'Mom, come on. Let's get 'em from the car.'

Brianna shoved out from the desk and followed her daughter out. At the door, she looked back at Evan and Andre. 'Don't you two do anything dumb, you hear?'

The door closed, an awkward silence asserting itself. Evan glanced out the window. Debris littered the sidewalk across the street, a rusty shopping cart on its side, someone's life possessions spilled across the cracked concrete. The pandemic had been brutal for the city's residents, homeless encampments springing up all over, humans washed up beneath every underpass and scattered across every sidewalk. So much suffering forced to the surface, and yet he was here, in hot pursuit of a pet.

'You seem tense, man,' Andre said.

'I'm not tense.'

'You know who says that? Tense people, that's who.' Andre sucked his teeth, flicked his chin. 'You got to let go and let God, you know?' He tilted his head, studied Evan. 'What?'

Evan said, 'I forgot how quickly you annoy me.'

'Nah, man. The *annoying* Christians are the ones who've been Bible-thumping their whole lives. You wanna know if Jesus got anything interesting to tell you, find a fuckup like me who found God 'cuz he *had* to. See what *that* dude knows.'

'Leviticus 17:11?' Evan said.

'Huh?'

'Nuthin'.'

Andre's grin was so good-natured it made it slightly less easy to stay aggravated with him. 'Look, man. I wanna thank you, showing up for Sofia like this. That dog, man. He's everything to her. I got him for when I can't be around, you know? I'm busting tail, working three jobs, tryin'a make good. It's hard out there, man. It's hard.'

Evan said, 'Right.'

'And I'm still trying for Bri, but you know what she told me? She wouldn't get back with me if the world was flooded with piss and I lived in a tree.'

'Cold.'

'Women are like that, man.'

The front door flew wide and Sofia ran in cradling a phone-book-thick stack of photocopies. 'You can put them up for me.'

As Brianna resumed her position at the desk, Sofia thrust the flyers at Evan. He stared at them.

'I don't do flyers,' he said. 'You put them up.'

Brianna's voice floated over: 'She has a dance recital.'

Evan glared at Andre. Andre waved his hands. 'Hail no.

33

I'm driving Lyft tonight. They got streak bonuses starting at ten so I'm gonna be carting drunk white girls around hipster-ass Echo Park all night.'

Sofia kept her radiant focus on Evan. The smile she had screwed onto her face looked rehearsed. She had dimples. The proffered flyers hung there between them.

Evan said, 'I'll need the address of the place he went missing from.'

She tapped the stack. 'On the flyer.'

He looked down. There it was.

'Please, Evan?' she said. 'You said you're going there anyways.'

She worried her bottom lip with her teeth. There was an instant of pure vulnerability in her face. Evan caught a flicker of his own features in her expression and felt his heart stop.

My niece.

I have a niece.

He took the goddamned stack of flyers and walked out.

6. An Elegant Picture of Accidental Death

Anwuli Okonkwo was stressed the hell out.

When she'd been promoted to senior software engineering manager last year, her parents had thrown a party for her, though she suspected the motivation was less to celebrate her and more to showcase her promotion to various aunties and cousins. The old joke was that an Okonkwo had four career choices: lawyer, doctor, engineer, or don't show up at the family reunion.

To speed up existing big-data-analysis techniques, Anwuli had two spike teams pursuing approaches to building a revolutionary measurement engine at petabyte-per-minute scale to optimize predictive analytics for e-commerce consumer behavior. The new job meant interfacing with a lot of Chads in engineering and Chelseas in marketing, most of whom elaborately complimented her hair until she'd done the big chop to save time in the morning and to remove her head from contention as a conversation starter for overly exuberant 'allies.'

The work was challenging in all good ways, Anwuli's rise meteoric. Recently she'd been cleared to attend strategy meetings at the VP level, which meant elbow-to-elbowing with the best and brightest behind closed doors. Being invited to brainstorm over confidential company matters felt like finally being handed the keys to the kingdom, so there was no way she could say no, despite the untenable workload she was already carrying.

This all would've been manageable because she was an

Okonkwo and her parents didn't raise no *olodo*, but then Dad's Alzheimer's had kicked into high gear and then Mom had fallen and broken her hip. The next week her brother's shipping company in Lagos had gone under, putting him in hock to the wrong people. Now everyone was short on time and money and resources, and it felt like it was up to her to come up with more of all three.

Which is why she'd carved out forty minutes of Me Time after work today before Amar from accounting emailed over the capital expenditures report for her to review. Stone-resin bathtub filled to the brim, Butterball bath bomb from Lush, ERIMAJ's 'Conflict of a Man' bumping from her Samsung Edge. Relaxing into the soapy water, she took a single healthy hit of OG Kush from her vape pen just to loosen the screws a touch and nestled into her inflatable neck pillow. She'd lit a few chill-out candles on the counter, but her thoughts kept drifting back to the sheer volume of cash required to take care of both parents and bail her brother out. Her brain scrambled to hatch ideas for how she could generate a next-level payday.

Deciding she needed to go lights-out to give her overburdened brain a rest, she pulled a silk sleep mask over her eyes and sank into the bathtub until the warm water slid up to her chin.

That's when Karissa stepped into the bathroom holding a frayed extension cord.

She'd taken her shoes off in the foyer, her socks silent on the tile, an added precaution in case the music thumping from the Samsung Edge stopped. The bathroom smelled delicious – cocoa-butter bubble bath, and mint-vanilla wafting from the candles. Easing forward, she halted over the freestanding bathtub, her reflection drawing into rippling view in the lightly foamed surface of the water.

Okonkwo was rocking her head from side to side, lips moving with the lyrics. Her cropped haircut had taken both a hair dryer and curling iron out of contention, though Karissa probably wouldn't have gone for either these days; appliances had gotten trickier with their ground-fault interrupters. The most dependable *objet d'électrocution* was a toaster oven, but acute midbath Pop-Tart cravings weren't common enough for a coroner to buy the notion of a tubside toaster.

So here she was wielding a frayed extension cord. After the fact she'd plug the Samsung charging cord into the power strip, which would paint an elegant picture of accidental death: Mildly Stoned Soaking Executive Charges Phone, Disaster Ensues.

Karissa loved these moments. This proximity to another soul about to be extinguished. Watching the flare of the nostrils, the faintly heaving chest, each precious breath transformed into something momentous. The kind of concentrated power she felt inside, God trapped like a genie in her chest.

Okonkwo was humming a bit now, one set of toes emerging from the water to drum against the rim of the tub. Beneath the cloudy water, her clavicles and the tops of her arms were visible but the rest of her naked body faded away like a magic trick.

Karissa leaned over her. Closer, closer, until their noses almost touched. She felt Okonkwo's breath against her chin, tasted her mint toothpaste.

An adrenalized tickle came on deep in her stomach, in her loins. She could do anything. She could be anything. She was everything.

Slowly she straightened back up. Extended her fist, clenching the power strip, over the water.

The track stopped on Okonkwo's phone. With a squeak

of her heels against the bathtub, she slid up and shoved her mask to her forehead with the heel of her hand.

She clocked Karissa standing over her and started. Her eyes narrowed, pupils tightening, a hard intelligence concentrating in her stare. 'Who the fuck are you, and what are you doing in my bathroom?'

Karissa dropped the power strip into the water.

A faint fizzle.

And nothing else.

Karissa sighed.

With all the safety codes and regulations these days it was getting harder and harder to stage a basic accident. Arc-fault circuit interrupters, OSHA-approved wiring, surge protectors, and self-grounding outlets in wet and dry rooms alike. Some bathtubs were even plumbed with plastic pipe to reduce the likelihood of an electrical current.

It was like they were trying to put her out of work.

Okonkwo stared down at the power strip that had plopped between her legs, then followed the snake of the plugged-in cord over the lip of the tub. Her gaze rose to find Karissa's.

What fear it held was quickly overtaken by anger.

'Damn,' Karissa said. 'I'm sorry, sweetie. We'll have to go another way.'

Okonkwo's hands sloshed up in unison to grip the sides of the tub to hasten her rise.

Karissa moved in a flash, leaning over the water, cupping the balls of Okonkwo's shoulders and plunging her to the bottom. Clamping her neck would've been easier, of course, but that would leave bruises and bruises would leave questions.

A burst of Okonkwo's breath bubbled up immediately, scared out of her, which meant a quicker route to the desired outcome. Her hands rose to slap at Karissa's biceps and her knees windshield-wipered, spilling water over the brim.

There'd be some mop-up work, but not much.

Karissa took care to keep her grip even on the shoulders. She wanted no contusions, no fingernail scrapes.

Homicidal drowning was nearly impossible to prove and far less likely than the obvious story; a hot bath and marijuana had dilated Okonkwo's blood vessels, causing her to faint and slip beneath the surface.

Occam's razor was a helpful bitch.

Karissa's shirt was drenched, her sleeves plunged in to the elbows. Okonkwo bucked one last time, her back arcing. Her feet were still jerking but there was no power in her anymore, just her nervous system shuddering to a halt. The foam at the surface had cleared, allowing Karissa to stare straight down in Okonkwo's eyes. There was hatred in them and then an empty sort of peacefulness.

Tiny bubbles clung to her eyelashes.

Karissa held her under for a few more minutes. And then let go.

With filled lungs, Okonkwo's body did not rise.

Karissa sat back on her heels and caught her breath.

Now she'd ticked two out of three off her quarterly cleanup. She was pleased with her improvisation; preserving a staged accident was key for two reasons.

She didn't like patterns.

And she'd planned the next one as an evident homicide.

7. Orphan X and the Case of the Missing Dog

The picture Sofia had chosen for the flyer was patently ridiculous. Loco mounted in a front carrier over Sofia's sternum, his legs splayed as if he were parachuting. One enormous ear was enormouser than the other. Bulging wet eyes. Jaws parted slightly, the tip of his tongue hanging blissfully over the jagged row of his bottom teeth, which seemed rammed into the gums at random angles.

Evan pressed the flyer to a wooden post on the second floor of the apartment complex and hammered a staple through Loco's neck like a bowtie. Though far from extravagant, the complex leaned upper-middle-class with a furnished lobby, foreign vehicles in the carports, and smoked glass rimming the outdoor walkways. Packages from Amazon, Walmart, and Solventry were mounded on some of the doormats like Christmas gifts, which spoke to trusted building security. Given the block Sofia lived on, he understood why she'd called these the 'fancy apartments.'

Before approaching, he'd done a spot check of the building but hadn't bothered to memorize all the surrounding streets. It was a tiny erosion in the Third Commandment – *Master your surroundings* – but the past few days had put him through the spin cycle, and a missing dog was hardly a mission requiring maximum vigor.

He moved along the floating walkway, heading back toward the stairs. On the thoroughfare below, a Google Street View vehicle drifted by, its all-seeing 360-degree camera poking up from the roof like a periscope. Evan's lab-engineered shirt looked as plain as he did, but an adversarial pattern hidden in the design threw off machine-vision algorithms and thwarted facial-recognition software. Despite that, he turned away until the car coasted out of sight.

One of the windows at his side was open, the dinner party inside lubricated with red wine and Miles Davis. Evan reached the next post and stapled Loco's face to the wood.

A sandpapery voice issued from a dark patch farther down the corridor. 'Do you have clearance to post materials on privately owned property?'

Evan peered into the shadows. 'What sort of clearance?'

'Supermajority vote by the board.'

He moved close, an ancient woman's shape resolving from the darkness. She was so old she looked as if she'd never been young. Tight gray curls shellacked into a turtle shell around her face, body hunched into a shape like an inverted U, head floating where her shoulder should be. In one liver-spotted claw, she clutched a combo walking stick–chair contraption that looked like it came out of a Soviet lab in 1982. With a snap of her arm, she flung out the tripod base, and lowered herself onto the sturdy seat. The hem of her housedress fluttered low over swollen ankles, brushing the tops of black orthopedic shoes with Velcro straps.

Jack had instilled in Evan a respect for elders. Due to his distaste for ideology, Jack ensured that each of his lessons combined the strategic with the moral. *Preceding generations bequeathed you the world, despite all its imperfections and shortcomings,* he'd told twelve-year-old Evan. *For that they deserve an assurance that you won't make them irrelevant. If you do, you wind up fighting the past and destabilizing the present.*

'No, ma'am,' he answered. 'I don't have that clearance.'

'Who will clean them up?' She gestured at the flyers fluttering along the second floor and the visible posts downstairs.

'Who will repair the damage to the building edifice? And moreover, do you even live here?'

'No, ma'am, I don't.'

'Did you know that property crime has been precipitously on the rise in Los Angeles?'

'I did not, ma'am.'

'Did you know that vandalism causing property damage in excess of four hundred dollars is classified as a felony rather than a misdemeanor?'

'You seem to know a lot more than I do, ma'am.'

'I am a ninety-seven-year-old woman with her faculties intact. I basically know *everything*.'

He was uncertain of a reply that she might find suitable.

'Don't think I don't know what you're up to,' she said. 'I know how these robbery crews work. You come by under some pretense.' She gave a disdainful sneer at the stack of flyers in his hands. 'A missing puppy. But you're really sneaking around here casing these condos.'

'I didn't mean to make you uncomfortable,' Evan said. The stairs were a few paces beyond her provisional perch, so he started toward them.

She stiffened. 'I know your type, too, with your army boots and all. If you think you can intimidate me, you're sorely mistaken. I grew up in Brooklyn back when it was still Brooklyn, young man. I want you to look at me. Look me in the face and ask yourself . . .' She rose with more haste than seemed probable. 'Do I look scared?'

He never imagined that a version of his own words rendered through a nonagenarian could contain such menace. Giving her a wide berth, he slid past her en route to the stairs. 'You certainly do not.'

With crossed arms, she observed his descent before disappearing back inside.

Reaching ground level, Evan drew in a breath of night air. A breeze wafted over the scent of the deep fryer from the taco joint across the street. He looked at the line of telephone poles stretching up the block, flyers waggling on all of them like Most Wanted posters with countless renegade Locos staring out.

Orphan X and the Case of the Missing Dog.

What idiocy.

As he turned to leave, he caught a glint from beneath the second-floor walkway. Tucked beneath the overhang and nestled beside a swallows' nest was the black lens of a surveillance camera. It aimed directly down at the base of the stairs, capturing the newel-post onto which Sofia had hooked Loco's leash.

If he could identify the camera model, Joey should be able to hack the system remotely.

Tucking the remaining flyers beneath his arm, he started up the stairs once more. The wrought-iron railing had plenty of space between the bars. Nearing the top of the stairs, he stooped to peer through the rails. The camera was just out of reach, smudged from the mud pellets of the swallows' nest. He dropped to all fours on the second-to-top step and shoved his arm through to the shoulder, straining until his fingertips wiped off the offending mud.

Reverse white lettering caught the ambient light: IRONKLAD KAM.

Good news – IronKlad's system was Swiss cheese and he knew Joey had an exploit for it.

Pleased, he withdrew his arm, clamped down on the flyers, and prepared to rise.

He sensed movement above him.

He turned to look up.

The ancient woman loomed over him on the landing, her folded walking stick–chair drawn back like a cricket bat.

Before he could raise a protective arm, she swung it down at him, catching him just beneath the jaw with the pan of the plastic seat.

His heel slipped and he had a brief searing moment of what-the-fuck-itude before his shoulder blades hit squarely a few steps down, knocking the breath out of him. Through a squall of liberated flyers, he tumbled ass over teakettle, her backlit form swimming into view with each rotation, and then he hit the ground and saw nothing at all.

Evan blinked up at two faces peering down at him. The old lady, wearing a victorious sneer. And a middle-aged woman gone shapeless beneath an embroidered peasant dress that looked more utilitarian than bohemian.

'Mother, look what you did.' Resting her hands on her knees, the woman crouched over him, her big blue eyes tornadoes of aggressive empathy. 'Do you need me to call you an ambulance?'

As Evan pulled himself up to sit, an airborne flyer swooped up from the sidewalk, Loco's photocopied mug smacking him in the face. He crumpled it free and rose.

'Dear, oh dear. Don't stand up too fast. Do you need some water? You might have a brain hematoma.' A breathy, ethereal woman with pale skin and a seemingly perpetual nervous smile, she was damp and agitated, curlicues of baby hair embellishing her high forehead. She rubbed her hands together and then placed a palm on Evan's brow, inexplicably checking for a fever.

Evan shook free. 'I'm fine.'

'He got what was coming to him,' Mother said, wobbling forward on the post of her cane-chair.

Having underestimated her once, Evan took a wary step back.

'Mother, stop it *right now.*' An apologetic glance at Evan. 'She's been captured by cable news. Everything's a threat.'

'I'm standing right here, Doris,' Mother said.

Doris ignored her. 'I'm calling you a doctor at once.'

'A doctor! You should call the police.'

'No, no,' Evan said, rubbing his swollen jaw. 'No doctor.'

'My mom didn't really intend to hurt you –'

'I sure as hell *did.*'

'– and I really hope, we really hope . . .' Doris clutched her wide pink hands at her stomach, her lips trembling with concern.

'What?' Evan said.

'That you won't pursue legal action against us.'

A mini tornado of flyers twisted around them, and Evan snatched a few from the air. 'I'm not going to sue you. I'm fine.' He crouched to pick up another flyer, and Doris squatted next to him, sweeping up a few more. 'I have to go,' he said. 'I'm busy.'

'If you have to tell people you're busy,' Mother said, 'then you're not busy.'

Evan took the flyers from Doris and nodded at the old woman. 'Ma'am.'

He walked away, photocopies of Loco clustering at his boots like dead leaves.

Doris called after him, 'Don't forget to have someone wake you up every twenty minutes tonight in case it's a concussion!'

He trudged several blocks to his Ford F-150, climbed in, gripped the wheel, and released a breath through clenched teeth.

He checked his jaw in the rearview. It was comically red at the hinge, as if he'd been stung by a wasp. His left elbow was bruised, his cargo pants torn at both knees, and his shoulder blades felt as if they'd been massaged with a cheese grater.

He texted Joey the address of the building, information on the IronKlad surveillance cam, and what he needed. A half second later, an incoming video-call request blinked up. He threw the RoamZone at the windshield, where it stuck in place, the antigravity suction case adhering it to the pane. For a few seconds he debated not picking up. Then he knuckled the screen.

Joey's face appeared. 'X! Hold up. I'm on with Tommy. We were just talking about you behind your back.'

'I don't want —'

But it was too late, her chewed-to-the-quick black-painted fingernails flying beneath the lens. Within an instant, Tommy stared out beside her on the split screen.

Evan said, 'No need to talk right now to either of —'

'Wait a minute.' Joey leaned in, her head angled. 'What happened to your jaw?'

'Nothing. It's —'

'Looks like you got coldcocked,' Tommy said. 'Who the hell caught *you* off guard?'

'No one. Can we just —'

'Uh-uh,' Tommy said. 'I don't give a shit if a blind kid with a Wiffle-ball bat beat you like a piñata, there ain't no room for ego or pride on a mission, no matter how small. There's just ground truth.'

Joey nodded along vehemently. 'That's right.'

'So cough it out,' Tommy said.

Their faces were frozen in matching expressions of outrage and adamancy, Tommy's rugged and biker-mustachioed, Josephine's smooth and feminine. They waited on a response with more intensity than the occasion demanded.

Evan inhaled deeply. 'Fine,' he said.

8. Laughing

Joey and Tommy kept laughing.

9. The Man Himself

Finally home in Penthouse 21A, Evan lay supine on a training mat in the spacious great room. He'd tidied up the passive-aggressive mess Joey had left for him but was still finding objects out of place. He'd given up for the time being and worked out on the heavy bag, sweating the alcohol from his system. Now his torso and head were propped up by two yoga blocks, one on the middle height running vertically between his shoulder blades and the other on end supporting the back of his head. *Matsyasana* helped open up his throat, chest, and abdomen, splaying his rib cage up toward the ceiling and encouraging his shoulders to melt to the floor.

Under Jack's tutelage, he'd trained himself to relax through the initial discomfort and restlessness until his body recognized that this was a shape it was designed to embody, an arrangement of tendons and fascia and bones that could realign more than merely his physical self.

But aside from when that happened?

Meditation sucked.

As it did now. He felt unsettled, dysregulated, every scrape and bruise a needling distraction. His thoughts spun from Andre and Sofia to Mother and Doris to that ugly-ass dog named Loco. What the hell was he doing?

He'd abandoned his RoamZone.

He'd drunk too much.

He'd disregarded Jack's Ten Commandments for no good reason.

And in doing so he'd allowed a little old lady to knock him down a flight of stairs.

Ever since he'd entered that prefab in Blessing, Texas, he'd felt disconnected from his training, alienated from himself. He'd left what happened there in the rearview, but it wasn't receding.

That meant it was time to turn around and look it in the teeth.

Evan waited on the porch in the fifty-grit wind as a man's weight creaked the floorboards inside, approaching the closed front door.

Evan's shoulders were already squared, his spine erect, arms and hands loose at his sides. No nonverbal tells, no expectations, nothing he'd dare to call hope.

When the door opened and Evan laid eyes on Jacob Baridon, the first thing he registered was how little he felt. No flare of recognition, no spark, no surge of emotion.

He might have been looking at any other stranger in the front half of his sixties. Baridon was handsome gone to seed, salt-and-pepper stubble, tousle of hair showing beneath the brim of a beat-to-shit straw Stetson Gunfighter. The cowboy hat, cocked back on his head, looked a part of the man himself, as if he'd been designed for that very thing, molded into the most complementary form to fill it. Lanky and fit, he wore a denim shirt with pearl-colored buttons, dark blue 501s, and full-quill ostrich boots in a pecan brown that had been sun-beaten to a tawny shine at the toes. He smelled of cigarette smoke, dried sweat, and earth.

At six foot and a bit he was taller than Evan, but he hung his head in a loose-and-easy way that spoke to good-natured endurance in the face of all the shit life can throw at you. A closer look showed a touch of rot — skin sallowed on incipient jowls, smoker-yellow stalagmites climbing his incisors, a two-inch gap between the welt and the outsole of the left boot that could be fixed for five bucks or with a needle and thread and a modicum of care.

Average of build, not too handsome, Evan stared up at him. He did not feel defensive.

He did not feel defensive.

He did not feel defensive at all.

The man didn't speak first, that would have been too much of a concession, but his face was open and without anger.

'My name's Evan. I might be your son.'

He said it without need and with a touch of annoyance, as if he was just as put out to have arrived here at the edge of a state that was not his own as this guy might be from having someone drive up and pound on his door.

'Huh,' Baridon said with a lack of alacrity that seemed to suggest he'd acted his role in this script a time or two before. 'Okay. Well, come on in.'

He pulled the door further ajar and heeled back out of the way in a single smooth gesture that held a kind of masculine elegance.

Evan entered.

The double-wide was dilapidated but impeccably clean, a bizarre combination. Shoes lined neatly on a patch of torn-up carpet, chipped counter wiped clean, each threadbare pillow perfectly straight on the lop-sided couch.

Jacob turned around to face a mirror hung haphazardly in the middle of one paneled wall, pulled off his hat, and ran his fingers through his hair, examining his scalp.

Evan stood facing his back. 'This your place?'

'This? Nah. A lady I was knockin' boots with let me crash here when she moved back in with her old man. Lucky stuff – she inherited it after her mom had one of them strokes turns you into a vegetable.'

Baridon kept at his hair in the mirror and Evan realized: He was checking for thinning.

'Well?' Baridon said to his reflection.

Evan was silent.

'This is where you tell me who your mom is,' Baridon continued, not unkindly. He turned around briefly to favor Evan with eye contact.

'There was a lotta ass back then.' A bonding snap of the head. 'You been there.'

When Evan spoke his voice was perfectly steady. 'Veronica LeGrande.'

'Redhead?'

Evan's heart rate was nice and steady, he'd guess a tick above sixty. His pulse was normal. He was fully inside his body.

He said, 'No.'

Baridon settled the hat back on his head, lumbered over to the couch, and flung himself down in a Huckleberry sprawl. 'Come on then,' he said. 'Have a seat.'

Evan stared at him for maybe three full seconds. Then he walked over and sat in a ripped armchair opposite the couch. 'College girl,' he said. 'Went to Vassar. Bit of money.'

Now Baridon had his phone out and he was scrolling through messages. 'Don't really remember.' Now and then he flashed his eyes up at Evan. His attention was 80 percent on the phone, 20 percent on Evan. 'Wait. Maybe. Yeah. Yeah, yeah, yeah, yeah. Vassar girl. Okay. How's she doing?'

'She's dead.'

'Wow. Life, huh?' His focus went back to the phone and lodged there.

Twenty seconds passed, maybe thirty. When Baridon looked up, he did a tiny double take with his eyes as if he'd lost track of the fact that he had company. 'What?'

Evan said, 'You were on your phone.'

'Look,' Baridon said. 'It was really nice meeting you. I mean that, truly.' A pause. 'But I have a girl coming over. Gotta get the tail while the gettin's good. You been there, I'm sure.'

Evan said, 'Right.'

'I do want to talk more and all that, you just caught me at a bad time.'

The tight layout put the kitchen right on top of them. One of the cupboard doors was missing and Evan could see the dishes inside. The *plates were ordered by size and perfectly stacked, the cups lined up like soldiers, mugs arranged by height.*

'I understand,' Evan said.

'So come back some other time and I'll buy you a beer. How 'bout that?'

Evan rose.

He'd laid out five strides to the door and took them now, counting them off. His hand was on the knob when Baridon said, 'Wait.'

Evan turned around.

Baridon was standing boldly, feet splayed, stiffened legs pushed slightly forward to put his crotch on display. 'I hate to ask this. I mean timing and all.' A sheepish smile that looked jarringly youthful. 'Can I borrow twenty bucks? The ATM at the bar's shot and I promised her, you know, I'd take her for a burger. I mean I got it, I got plenty, but the ATM's out and I'm not gonna drive all the way to the bank.'

Evan felt his weight — even between both feet. His posture was solid, dignified. That was what he could do right now.

He reached into his pocket. Pulled out the inch-wide stack of folded hundreds, peeled off the top bill, and extended it to Baridon.

It took a moment for Baridon to reset himself in his boots. He sidled forward and took it, the gesture forcing him into a little bow. 'Hey, man. All right. Appreciate it.'

The exchange should have felt vindicating in a strategic or biblical sense, but it didn't. It didn't whatsoever.

Evan turned around. He walked through the door.

'Hey, I'll pay you back for sure.'

Evan kept on to the borrowed Wrangler.

'Next time you're around look me up!'

Evan drove away from the pink-painted double-wide with its dimpled roof. He did not look in the rearview.

The dirt road was long.

He drove for a good distance.

Then he pulled over onto the verge and vomited into the dirt.

10. Lupine Menace

Karissa abided by two rules when she required a getaway driver.

One: Choose someone wholly unconnected to her.

Two: Choose someone willing to do anything, because quite often on her jobs the need to do anything arose.

She preferred former military, since they'd already broken the seal to the real world; every last one of them had written a check with their life to have a job, food, health care.

The homeless encampment at the Veterans Administration in Westwood had spilled outside the gates and up along the San Vicente Boulevard sidewalk. There was an advantage to setting up on this side of the spiked wrought-iron fence; being off federal property put the shanties into the purview of softer 'community policing' – no drugs searches, no harassment, plenty of privacy.

The lineup of rugged gray tents sporting American flags was referred to in the media as 'Veterans Row' instead of 'Skid Row,' a fancy bit of language play to take the stink off the mini-slum that had sprung up a syringe's throw from affluent Brentwood cafés and boutiques. The encampment had a feeling of semipermanence to it – potted plants, couches, even a few rickety bookcases – and it was maintained with pride.

Sitting in a stolen black Chevy Suburban, Karissa watched the denizens working their shifts, collecting trash, sweeping the pavement. Two shirtless men played chess with soap carvings on an overturned Amazon delivery box. A woman with dusty hair sat on the curb, repetitively running her hands up the nape of her neck. A portly wizard draped in a regal gown of rags sat on a lawn chair smoking a blunt with Falstaffian aplomb.

They wouldn't be useful.

Through her Steiner tactical binoculars, Karissa singled out two of the homeless vets who'd been mopping up the porta-potties. One black, one white, muscular builds showing through army-green T-shirts, no signs of tooth erosion or caved cheeks from drug use. Working with focused efficiency and serious expressions, they retained their military posture, carrying themselves with dignity. As they moved back to their shared tent, the others parted deferentially.

Because of her current employer, money wasn't an issue, which meant she could proceed with speed and efficiency. Grabbing the Pelican laptop case off the console, she climbed out. Given her diminutive stature, she had to slide off the seat, jam her heels into the runner, and hop from there. The truck was lifted to accommodate bigger tires; she'd chosen it in the event a pursuit took her off road.

Hoodie pulled up, reflective Oakleys hiding her eyes, full-finger gloves made of tactical rubber. The night air smelled of car exhaust and the sickly-sweet stench of garbage. She disappeared into the human flotsam on the sidewalk, no one paying her any mind. There were various ruckuses – a shouted confrontation over a bottle, schizo nattering, someone sawing a piece of plywood.

Reaching the charcoal tent, she slipped inside.

The domed interior was more spacious than she would have anticipated. The men sat on opposing cots, one scrubbing his throat with a wet washcloth, the other reading. The latter wore a pair of wire-frame eyeglasses that looked oddly delicate on his weather-beaten face. The trapped air held breath and body odor, the smell of a den. When she rose to her full height, the tarp of the ceiling didn't brush the top of her head.

They alerted to her entry, chest muscles shifting as they swiveled their heads. They emanated a lupine menace that relaxed once they took her measure. Five foot four and female didn't represent a threat.

'You don't just walk into a man's home,' the reader said.

'Do you know how to drive?' she asked.

The white guy set down his washcloth on the cot next to him. 'I commanded an M1151 Enhanced Armament Carrier through three fifteen-month tours in Iraq. Do *you* know how to fucking drive?'

She looked back at the reader. 'How about you?'

'Yeah,' he said. 'I can drive.'

'Tactically?'

'Who the hell are *you*?'

To them? No one. In her jacket and sunglasses, she was nothing more than a drawn hood and a pair of bug eyes. She wasn't pretty enough to be striking and she was too pretty to be striking in the other direction, which made her perfectly forgettable.

Crouching, she set down the Pelican case, unsnapped the catches, and lifted the lid. The bundled stacks of Benjamins gave off the verdant smell of green. Though neither man moved more than his eyes, a disruption like an electrical current moved through the tent.

'That's a hundred,' she said. 'Another hundred for after.'

Of course there would be no need for a second payment. A key aspect of Karissa's continued success in the private sector was that she left no loose ends. The people who employed her paid for perfection and expected nothing less. When she needed a basic lookout or a wheelman, she found it helpful to find people who went unaccounted for, people no one would miss.

'After *what*?'

She reached beneath the currency straps and came out with two steel tent stakes. Seven inches long, with curved tops that fit neatly in the palm and pointed ends she'd sharpened to gleaming tips.

The reader pulled off his glasses. He sat up.

She stood over the open suitcase, one tent stake protruding from each fist between her index and middle fingers. 'The thing is,' she said, 'I only need *one* of you.'

With a flip of her hands, she reversed the stakes, clenching the pointed ends, the curved tops out. She straightened her arms left and right, a spike extended in the direction of either man.

Both of their feet were on the ground. They were equidistant from her. Their arms were bent slightly, hands pressed to the thin mattresses of their cots. To reach the tent stakes, they'd have to lunge.

They were trained soldiers and the tent stakes were sufficiently sharp to get the job done. No doubt there'd be some tumbling and shouting in the tight space, but that wouldn't be out of the ordinary for this stretch of tents, and battle-testing always carried some risk. She hoped that this, her first stop, would also be her last. She could use a one-and-done; the delivery date on her third target had been accelerated to tomorrow morning, and she didn't want to have to shop at tent city downtown or the homeless village in East Hollywood.

The tang of sweat intensified. Their nostrils were flaring. She could see their pulses beating in the sides of their necks. She waited and then waited some more.

The white dude cleared his throat. 'I am an American

soldier,' he said. 'I am a warrior and a member of a team. I serve the people of the United States and live the army values.'

His friend cocked his head at her, lips peeling back from clenched teeth. 'That's right,' he said. 'What the hell do you think we are?'

Karissa set the steel spikes back in the Pelican case, snapped it shut, and rose to leave. 'I think,' she said, 'you're not what I'm looking for.'

11. A Stolid Kind of Wisdom

Poured over the supporting yoga blocks, Evan's body finally released. There was no tension and no engagement, just himself and gravity. On the next exhalation, his intercostals let go, his shoulders fanning wide like wings, and his chest cracked open. He felt the vertebrae popping one by one, and the end of his breath came ragged and edged with a divine kind of aching.

Eyes closed, he lay there in an endorphin haze, at last primed for meditation.

From the darkness, a forest resolves – the Virginia oaks of his youth surrounding Jack's farmhouse. Evan is in a clearing, ankles deep in Halloween leaves. The tree trunks are gnarled, anthropomorphic, mutely observing with a stolid kind of wisdom. The sun shoots down in great columns of light stirred by living dust, and squirrels scrabble invisibly in the branches above.

He takes a full rotation, and when he comes back to where he'd started, Jack is standing before him. Preternaturally observant eyes, crow's-feet baked into his temples, that square bulldog face.

At this point for Evan, talking to Jack feels like playing chess against himself. Though Evan has bits and pieces from their shared time, their meditative engagements have become a blur of real memories and what Evan anticipates and fills in. Maybe that's what the memory of a person is once grief fades to a softer hue. The last trickle of immortality.

Jack spreads his hands. 'Well?'

'Well what?'

'You're the one who dragged me outta the grave to be here.' That familiar single-barrel voice, gravelly and smooth all at once.

Evan chews his lip, notices he is doing it, and stops. He feels like he is twelve years old again. 'I screwed up my approach to the apartment building.'

Jack just looks at him. In moments like this he doesn't seem to need to blink.

'The First Commandment,' Evan says. 'Assume nothing.'

'Like that an old bird could hand you your ass?'

'And the Third. Master your surroundings. I let that slip, too.'

'I seem to recall one in between,' Jack says. 'Funny you left that one out.'

Evan looks down at his boots sank into the autumnal carpet. The Second Commandment: How you do anything is how you do everything.

'You're lucky you learned your lesson at the end of a ninety-year-old broad's folding cane instead of from the muzzle of a .45.'

Evan feels an uncharacteristic need to explain himself. 'When I was in Texas,' he said, 'I met . . .' He can't figure out the right noun.

Jack says, 'I know.'

Evan is at a loss for what to say. In the brief time he'd known his mother, he'd created nothing more than a few tenuous strands of connection. With Jack dead and what he'd faced in Blessing, there is no longer even the possibility of someone else out there to represent provenance, righteousness, a last frontier.

'What'd you see in that double-wide?' Jack asks.

The breeze stirs the leaves between them, and in the boughs above, Evan hears birdsong and the whispery flitting of wings.

When he speaks, his throat feels dry. 'It wasn't what I saw,' he says. 'It's what I didn't see.'

Jack gives a faint nod. There is some warmth in it. Understanding, too.

Evan clears his throat. 'It's not about my father or where I came *from. I was fine not knowing. Not knowing meant at least that there* might *be something, some kind of human covenant for . . . I don't know. I don't know.' He felt infuriatingly inarticulate. He waved a hand listlessly at the trees, the woods, the world beyond. 'And without that? Without the* possibility *of that?'*

Jack waits with the patience of the surrounding trees.

'What's the fucking point, Jack?'

Jack's baseball-catcher head bobs twice, giving the question its due. It is respectful, his pause, a willingness to sit with what is. Evan can never see the gears turning in Jack's head, his opaqueness worthy of a onetime station chief with the Agency. But nothing about him seems furtive either. He regards Evan now with his still-waters-run-deep calm.

'Maybe that is,' Jack says, 'the point.'

Evan feels the fall breeze at his throat, the soft give of earth beneath his boots. Unhurried as ever, Jack watches the words work on him.

Jack scratches at his neck, one cheek bunching up. 'What if there's no one to fix anything?' he said. 'Except you.'

His lips twitch knowingly and the woods fade away and —

— Evan was back in his penthouse and off the yoga blocks lying on his side, cheek resting against the meat of his biceps, the forgotten Commandment pounding in his head.

He lay there for a time and breathed.

At the edge of the kitchen, Evan stood before the drip-fed vertical garden, breathing in the rich scent of soil. The living wall rose above and around him, dwarfing him. Twined along its lower third was a passionfruit vine. He tested the ovoid offerings, fingertips brushing the wrinkled dark purple hulls until he found one with precisely the right give.

He plucked it.

Walking over to the kitchen island, he selected a teaspoon he'd pocketed at the Savoy Hotel in London and a steak knife fabricated from German stainless steel. He set the passion-fruit on a wooden cutting board and sliced a quarter-inch cap of leathery rind off one end. The aperture was just wide enough for him to poke the spoon through the pith to reach the pulpy seeds.

With a minimum of scraping, he gathered the first bite, a clump of black seeds bound by sacs of juice. He brought the spoonful to his mouth, closed his eyes.

Tart and tropical, a faint acidic wash along the sides of the tongue.

He paused and set the teaspoon down on the cutting board next to the passionfruit. With his knuckle he nudged it until it was even with the knife, both parallel to the sides of the cutting board, which was in turn aligned with the edges of the island.

He chewed.

He swallowed.

How you do anything is how you do everything.

12. An Odd Bit of Black Magic

Evan could scarcely believe what he was seeing on the surveillance footage.

A smooth-edged delivery robot the size and shape of a small refrigerator trundling along the sidewalk on six rugged wheels. With its cool aquatic-blue coloring and the Solventry logo – a smiley-face daisy bobbing cheerfully on a stem – emblazoned on the side, it looked unthreatening, adorable, neotenic.

Sitting at his sheet-metal desk in the Vault, Evan observed the future of e-commerce delivery playing out on the OLED screens coating the concrete walls before him.

Life-size Joey floated on the screens to his right, MC'ing the fruits of her hacking whilst masticating her third taco from Henry's in Studio City, an odd bit of black magic given that it was 8:00 A.M. and Henry's didn't open until ten. 'They're like the Solventry mascots,' she said, gesturing at the robot. 'They're named FWIPs. Cute, right?'

'Which stands for?'

'FreeWillPower.' She glugged down some White Pineapple Monster, produced another taco from the white bag, dumped hot sauce over it and most of her fingers, then lapped the side of her hand like a caribou going at a salt lick. 'That's the name of Solventry's AI division.'

'The Orwellian wordplay boggles the mind.'

'Inferior minds are readily boggled,' Joey said, through a full mouth.

Vera III seemed to smirk at that one, her serrated leaves spread with amusement.

On the big feed covering the front wall, Evan followed the FWIP as it approached a familiar apartment building, nonplussed pedestrians and spooked dogs clearing out of its way. A trio of teenage girls paused to shoot an iPhone video of it.

'How it works is, delivery vans drop a bunch of FWIPs off in a neighborhood,' Joey said between mouthfuls. She seemed to have cut out the middleman of chewing, skipping straight from biting to swallowing. 'They have to follow pedestrian laws, can't go over ten miles per hour. Range is an eight-mile radius and – most important – they can fit a sixteen-inch pizza.' She made excited pizza hands, indistinguishable from jazz hands but for context. 'You use an app to unlock the secure cargo compartment with your stuff. They run all their routes and meet up at shift's end to get transported back to the warehouse or industrial kitchen or HQ or whatever.'

'Solventry has a food division?'

'Solventry's like Amazon or Apple or Google,' Joey said. 'They have a *everything* division. Now check *this*.'

A clickity-clack of her remote fingers changed the surveillance angle to that of the second-floor camera that had nearly vanquished Evan. Down at the base of the stairs, he spotted a familiar homely canine – Loco, leashed to the newel-post as Sofia had said. He tugged at his collar, sniffed the ground, lifted his scrawny leg, and peed on the sidewalk.

From the edge of the frame, the FWIP rolled into view, and Loco froze, leg lifted, urine cut off midstream. As the robot halted obediently at the base of the stairs, a heavyset woman lumbered into view, presumably one of the first-floor residents. Breaking from his trance, Loco barked and snapped at the cuffs of her pants, and she shooed him with a closed-toe wedge shoe.

At the recorded barking, Joey's Rhodesian ridgeback, clev-erly named Dog, stuck his head up into the side-wall feed next to Joey, head cocked, forehead furrowed, tortilla-chip ears perked. His hound lips formed a vague circle and he made a noise low in his throat like a practice woof, unsure yet if the threat was sufficient to draw a full-throated response. Joey kissed his enormous head, shoved him away, and returned her focus to the surveillance footage.

The woman tapped at the screen of her phone, and a moment later a sleek door in the side of the robot slid open in response. She crouched and removed a thick flat package. When she turned to walk past Loco once more, the dog went crazy, snarling and bouncing on his hind legs, the tension of the leash turning him bipedal.

As the FWIP's door started to close, Loco slipped his collar. He shot over and dove into the cargo compartment. The door shut after him. The FWIP rolled away, the unwary passenger trapped in its belly. The whole thing took less than three seconds.

'Yeah,' Joey said. '*That* just happened. I'm thinking he smelled someone's lunch in there.'

Evan rubbed his eyes. 'This mission gets better and better.'

'I know, right? Oh, Evan? I meant to ask . . .'

'What?'

''Member that one time you got beat up by an old lady with a cane?'

Not the first round of this particular line of joking.

'Yes, Joey,' Evan said wearily.

'Oldilocks hit you *jussst* right.'

'Clever.'

'I mean, it was nearly a granicular homicide.'

'Can you just show me what else you found?'

'Fine.' Joey's hand dug in the white bag, rooted around,

and came out with yet another taco. The bag was like a clown car, endlessly replenishing. She halted, alarmed. 'Hang on. Wait – *hang on*.' More foraging in the bag. Then she sagged in her gamer chair, boneless with relief. 'There's gotta be a German word for that feeling of soul-elevating joy when you find that *one extra hot sauce* in the taco bag.' She poured liberally. '*Saucenfreude?*'

'Joey.'

She licked each fingertip individually, a grooming ritual worthy of a house cat or a five-year-old eating Cheetos. '*Fremdsäucen?*'

'Joey.'

'*Backpfeifengesalsa?*'

'Josephine.'

'Okay, fine, allow me to speed us along.' A theatrical throat clearing. 'Autonomous delivery robots have specific routes that can be traced. As a marvel of raw talent and prodigious learning, I already determined that this particular FWIP ran an internal service route for employees of Solventry. The drop-off you just witnessed was a notary-public logbook delivered to a paralegal. While Solventry's digital security is literally the best in the world next to Google and the NSA, the FWIP doesn't even have a TPM, so a few hours ago I kidnapped the robot on its regular route –'

Evan said: 'You kidnapped a *robot*?'

'– stole its firmware, and pulled everything off the disk and RAM. Then I noted the next stop and hacked into various surveillance cameras from surrounding commercial and residential security systems, which yielded . . . this.'

The front wall lit up with new surveillance footage, granting a wide view encompassing three entrances to a row of modern town houses on a busy street.

'Aaand *action*,' Joey said, snapping her fingers.

The FWIP rolled up to the middle town house and halted. A moment later, a portly middle-aged man wearing wide corduroys, loafers, and a cardigan over a button-up emerged and lumbered down the steps. Erudite face, jet-black sponge curls, woolly beard. A metal chain secured rimless rectangular glasses around his neck.

'Dr Benjamin Hill,' Joey said.

With a practiced wag of his head, Hill donned his glasses, and then poked at his phone. A secure cargo compartment popped open, and he withdrew a manila document envelope. The door slid shut.

Then the FWIP began to rattle on its six wheels. It looked as if it were suffering from indigestion or contemplating an eruption. Hill stared down at it, mildly horrified. Then another cargo door popped open and Loco came flying out.

The crazed dog turned to attack the FWIP, which promptly fled. Then he pawed the pavement a few times with his back legs, sat down, and vigorously licked his anus, his curlicue tail providing ready access. Rising to all fours, he peered around, terrified and trembling and panting, looking like any other deranged collarless stray.

Benjamin Hill studied him. Then squatted and extended his hand tentatively.

Loco inched forward, sniffed his fingertips.

Then bounded into Hill's arms.

Holding him with an endearing gentleness, Hill carried him back into the town house, and the door shut behind him.

The screens blinked black, and then all of a sudden Joey was on all of them, surrounding Evan. With grappling-hook fingers, she conveyed the last bite of taco over her maw and lowered it in.

'Is it humanly possible for me to deliver you a more

complete win?' Joey asked. 'I mean, put a bow on it. Signed, sealed, delivered. Served up like Five Guys fries. So c'mon, X. Give it to me.' Lips pooched out, she nodded and kept nodding, beckoning with four fingers.

Evan sighed. 'Joey is the Empress of all Realms Known and Unknown.'

She made some elaborate empressy hand gesture. 'Any other questions?'

'Why the hell are there paper clips under my bed?'

'Why the hell are you *looking* for paper clips under your bed?'

He grimaced. 'You win this round, Josephine Morales.'

'If there's nothing else then.' She bolted forward. 'Oh, wait. I forgot to ask you the most important thing.'

'What?'

''Member that one time you got beat up by an old lady with a cane?'

Evan ended the call.

13. Rough Treatment

Evan was ready.

ARES 1911 snugged in his appendix holster.

Extra mags in the streamlined inner pockets of his tactical-discreet cargo pants.

Strider folding knife in his left front pocket.

Adversarial-patterned shirt with fake show buttons and hidden magnetic catches that gave way in case he needed to quick-draw straight through his shirt.

Original S.W.A.T. boots laced tight, mostly hidden by the cuffs of his pants.

He'd surveilled the neighborhood, checking windows, rooftops, and parked cars. He'd charted multiple escape routes and left his customized Ford F-150 a half mile away on a side street with no parking restrictions.

He'd hacked into City Hall's land registry and pulled blueprints for the town house – three stories, grand foyer, elevator from a subterranean garage that rose directly to all floors.

He'd compiled a basic dossier on Benjamin Hill – Oakland native, applied physics and engineering major at Howard, Ph.D. in bioinformatics from UCLA. Multiple high-level jobs cementing his place as a leading expert in artificial intelligence, culminating in a post as the principal deep-learning scientist at Solventry. His wife, deceased five years. Seventeen-year-old daughter, Jayla Alexis Hill, a junior at the Ramón C. Cortines School of Visual and Performing Arts, aka Grand Arts.

All this for a dog.

Approaching a man who by all accounts seemed like a

decent human being hardly seemed treacherous. But the travails of the past days had brought Evan full circle back to the Ten Commandments and the operational precision that had kept him alive for three decades and counting.

He walked past the row of town houses once more, head lowered, hands shoved in his pockets. Then he cut through the alley behind them, with its neatly ordered trash bins and sliding garage gates leading to the less swanky neighboring apartment buildings. The windows of Dr Hill's town house were tinted, giving nothing back but a reflection of the gray clouds stacked overhead.

The complex constituted a patch of gentrification in LA proper just below where the 101 doglegged south. Freeways twined every which way around the neighborhood, overpasses and exits, and there were auto salvages, rail yards, and restaurants to the west butting up against the dry concrete channel of the Los Angeles River. A tent city had sprung up several blocks to the north, and vagrants begged on street corners and camped in doorways of buildings worth millions of dollars. The wealth gap cranking wider, ready to snap.

Circling back, Evan scanned the surrounding balconies and cast an eye along the metered spaces for any parked cars that had their exhaust running. All clear.

Up five concrete steps to the narrow porch. Head cocked at the door, listening for sounds of barking or psychotic growling from within. Nothing.

Evan raised his fist to knock.

Something inside crashed over. Loud and perhaps accidental, like a dropped tray of dishes or a china hutch overturning.

He lowered his fist. Listened some more.

Silence.

He tried the doorknob. Unlocked.

Easing the door open, he stepped into a vestibule with a side table and a Tunisian tapestry of woven wool.

The first thing to hit his senses was the smell. Metallic and minerally, the scent of danger and the hunt, of disgust and arousal. Immediately it skewered him with pinprick memories – a death gurgle in a lampshade shop in Gaza, a crimson-slick stone ledge in a São Paulo bathhouse, an Estonian bleeding out on the floor of an abandoned textile factory.

A chain reaction of muscle memory commenced – from the blood scent to a surge of alertness to the reach for the holster. Evan's ARES was in hand, his shirt still broken open from the draw for an instant before the magnetic buttons resealed the front with a nearly inaudible clack. The air of the vestibule pressed a slight tackiness against his cheeks. A few cautious strides brought him to the three-story foyer, the scent growing hotter, the town house gaping high and wide. The tall central opening gave the interior a dollhouse effect, catwalks with clear panels, wide doorways, and glass-walled rooms putting much of the space on display. A modern imperial staircase branched up the middle of the place, two symmetrical rises on either side interrupted by landings. The design centerpiece of the town house, the stairs appeared to float, glass tread with no risers curving up through the space like ribs.

White, airy, glass-intensive – it reminded him of his own penthouse. An orderly retreat from the chaos of the world, a home base from which a doctor of bioinformatics might make wild intellectual forays.

Which made the violation of the place all the more jarring.

Pictures had been torn from the walls, drawers dumped, the cushions of the leather sectional slashed.

There was Loco. The ridiculous animal had wedged

himself into the corner of the sofa. His ears, adorned with tufts of batting, flared wide like antlers. His ribs quivered beneath steel-gray wiry hair and his bulging eyes seemed ready to pop. Black lips wrinkled back from those snaggly teeth, his tremors reaching epileptic proportions.

A new-looking alarm pad to Evan's side had been jimmied off the wall, its wires snipped. From the third floor, the sharp edge of daylight knifed through a sliding glass door, its black curtains raked aside on fat wooden hoops resembling napkin rings. The slider let out onto a balcony with wide-set rails that Evan had observed from the alley and – given the setback of the upper floors – he could partially see from the foyer.

He took all this in as if with the peripheral vision of his mind, his primary focus given to the obvious: Dr Benjamin Hill lying prone on the Berber carpet underpinning the sectional. Zip ties bound his wrists at the small of his back, his ankles secured in like fashion. His hands, purpled from lack of circulation, stubbed upward like a grotesque tail. The suit he wore was rumpled at the knees, his cuffs and sleeves hiked obscenely from the rough treatment he'd received. Neck torqued, chin stabbed into the floor, Adam's apple on shiny display.

The entrance wound near the top of his head was small and neat, and there was no visible exit wound. Blood trickled from his parted lips to feed a widening spot in the rug. Open eyes stared back at Evan. The left bottom lid fluttered, but Evan knew it was just a trick of the nervous system.

A faint movement on the third floor drew his eye, spiking his adrenaline. As his gaze jerked upward, a compact human form swathed in black peeled away from the swept-back column of black curtains, differentiated abruptly from the matching backdrop.

Benjamin Hill's killer, still in the house.

14. Desecrated

Aiming up the three stories of the foyer, Evan pinned the black form in the high-profile Straight Eight sights of his 1911. The black fleece balaclava hood covered all but a crescent of face – feminine bone structure and piercing eyes that held no panic. The dead steadiness of the return gaze told him this wasn't an average robbery-in-progress. She was a seasoned operator.

She was backlit against the sliding glass door. As she shifted, something glinted at her right hand; since he'd caught her off guard, she hadn't had time to lift her weapon. He couldn't be sure from this distance but he guessed it was a .22 revolver, which would have two advantages. A revolver would leave no incriminating shells to pick up. And a .22 wouldn't provide enough bullet velocity for the round to exit the skull, leaving it to bounce around, scrambling the brain. He thought of that neat entry hole atop Dr Hill's head auguring the damage within.

'Move forward,' he said.

She took a moment, but despite the three floors separating them, he had her, and she knew he had her. With a single elegant stride, she eased to the waist-high panel wall of the catwalk. She was short, maybe five three.

'Drop the gun over,' he said.

Robotically, she moved the revolver over the railing, careful to hold it sideways so as not to draw fire. She stared down, gauging him, and he stared back.

He jerked his muzzle once: *Go.*

She let the gun fall.

It tumbled through the core of the town house, plopping onto the sectional across from Loco. The tiny dog bolted upright and snarled at the gun. Evan let his eyes dip, confirmed that the revolver was a .22. A low-end choice of weapon for an operator of her composure unless she was staging a crime scene: home invasion gone wrong.

Evan said, 'If you move, I'll put a round through your face. Understand?'

The ninja-like mask dipped in a nod.

ARES steady, keeping her in his sights, he moved forward cautiously, foot over foot. Up the first flight of stairs, his boots peeling off the glass tread with a faint suctioning noise, his body rotating to hold target acquisition. The crisp modern space desecrated with death and damage, the streams of sunlight, and the abattoir smell turned everything to a dream.

She didn't move. Didn't seem to breathe. Just a band of face staring down at the bore of his pistol as he drew himself carefully to the landing of the second floor. To one side, an open door into a bedroom; to the other, a modern kitchen with a butcher-block island.

Now only one floor separated him from the intruder. 'What's your business here?' she asked.

His breathing steady, his hands steadier, he started up the second flight of stairs on the left, the town house seeming to spin as his twisting rise shifted the perspective between them. Again he felt that dizzying sensation, the world spiraling around the fixed point of his muzzle, the frozen woman above rotating with painstaking cinematic slowness, everything controlled, a surface tension that refused to pop.

She took a step back toward the sliding glass door, and he said, 'No.'

She halted. To her left: the elevator doors, a bedroom with

lavender walls, and the facing flight of stairs. To her right: him, rising.

He was halfway to the third floor, aiming up at her across the atrium, each step bringing them closer to level. If she blinked he did not notice.

Another step. Now he could note the rise and fall of her chest. She was compact, strong, her posture aligned.

'What are you going to do when you get to me?' Her tone was calm, even slightly bored. 'Citizen's arrest?'

'We'll figure that out,' he said.

Her eyes swept the open space below her, and he sensed her calculating a leap onto the opposing stairs, a swing onto the second-floor catwalk, a plummet to the couch below.

None were great options, and he had a clear enough sight line to hit her no matter which way she broke.

She floated back a step so smoothly he barely registered it, easing herself toward the elevator, the raked-aside black curtains.

His boot set down on the next glass step, everything so still he heard the rubber sole crinkle as it bent. 'Lace your hands behind your head. *Now.*'

She obeyed.

Eight more steps would bring him to the third floor, across the landing from her.

'Looks like you got your prize,' she said. 'Now come unwrap me.'

Steady hands cupping the 1911, no wobble, no shake. He lifted his boot, prepared for the next step.

A mechanical click shuddered the building, and then came the deep vibration of the elevator. Her backup, rising to the rescue?

The black fabric over the woman's mouth shifted into what he guessed was a smile. 'Uh-oh.'

His eyes flicked to the floor indicators. *G* for *garage* was lit up. Then *1*.

The rumbling kept on. The woman was close enough to the elevator doors that she could have reached out and knocked on them.

Now *2* was illuminated. The glow faded, the car in the space between floors.

Arms tensed with a slight bend at the elbows, he padded swiftly up a few steps, acquiring more of her critical mass and putting her body between him and the elevator. If one of her partners opened fire from the car, she'd absorb the rounds first.

Her back was pressed to the bunched curtains, her shoulder blade nearly touching the frame of the elevator doors.

He stayed four steps down to cut his profile from the elevator's vantage. He was merely a head, the top of a torso, two arms aiming a gun. That was all of him they'd have. And yet they'd be clumped neatly before him. Once the doors parted, he could aerate her and the elevator with a tight grouping.

Now the third-floor indicator glowed.

A ding.

A forever delay before the doors peeled wide.

Evan took the slack out of the trigger.

A teenage girl stepped out.

The very motion brought her to the edge of the catwalk. Alarm in her eyes, staring down at the wreckage below. And then a single word muffled by emotion: '*Dad?*'

Evan said, 'Get ba—'

The woman sprang behind Jayla Hill, wrapping her up with an arm across her throat.

Jayla cried out. Her head twisted back, the intruder's face hidden behind hers. She had braces on her teeth, a spotting of acne on her chin. Seventeen years old.

The intruder's shoulder dipped as she reached behind her and entwined a hand in the curtain. Gripping it in a gloved fist, careful to keep Jayla between herself and Evan, she moved slowly across the face of the sliding glass door, pulling the curtain from the rod, each wooden hoop giving way with a ping.

Evan came up another step, iron sights level, front post pegged on the rear notch, both aligned with the slender edge of the woman's forehead peeking out just above Jayla's shoulder. The woman was precise, leaving little of her to hit.

More curtain rings gave way: *Ping. Ping. Ping.*

'Steady,' he told the woman. 'She's a kid. She's just a kid.'

Ping. Ping. Ping.

The girl was breathing hard, hyperventilating.

'Let her go and I'll let you go,' he said.

The woman kept on, leaving no separation between herself and the girl, moving with greater vigilance yet.

Ping.

Ping.

Ping.

The curtain tore free, heaping on the catwalk with a sigh of fabric.

The woman unlocked the sliding glass door and flung it open behind her. The November chill crawled inside, curled itself through the interior, wound itself around Evan on the stairs.

Twisting her hand, the woman took up the fabric around her forearm.

Evan sensed the gears turning, a premonition of what she was about to do, but he couldn't catch up to it, not all the way.

'Hang on,' he said, as much to himself as to her.

The woman remained skillfully hidden behind Jayla, Evan

tracking the visible parts of her with his pistol. A flash of elbow, a sliver of leg, and then the woman's hand flared up into view, holding a flex-cuff prepped in a loop. The noose lowered over the girl's head, fastened around her throat, and zippered tight, the noise strident.

Jayla cried out, a strangled wheeze, flecks of saliva flying from her mouth. Her fingernails dug at the strip of plastic that had embedded in her throat, cinching off her airway.

Evan had a split second of denial, of disbelief that the woman was willing to sacrifice the girl to enable her escape.

With a whoosh like a flung cape, the curtain whipped out and around Jayla's midsection in kimono-belt position. The effort brought the woman's head barely visible to the side of Jayla's head – two inches of the edge of that balaclava hood.

Evan fired.

A burst of red exploded from the side of the hood, black fabric flapping, glittering flesh showing beneath. The woman grunted once low, animalistic. The force of the round knocked the balaclava askew, the torn section widening the eye gap and exposing most of the woman's face. Plain, clean features pinched with pain. Twisting in her grip, Jayla looked up at her with bulging eyes.

For a single suspended instant they were face-to-face in an intimate tableau vivant, the assassin's identity laid bare.

Staggered from the shot, the woman tumbled back onto the balcony holding both ends of the curtain, pulling the band of fabric tight against Jayla's midsection.

And then she slid backward gymnastically, tipping onto one hip, slipping straight through the wide-set rails, and whisking out into the open air above the alley.

Evan sprang up onto the third-floor landing. A frozen instant as Jayla stared at him with parted lips, face lurching with dry heaves, suffocating. Behind her a sense of whistling, of falling, of slack being taken out of the line.

And then the curtain pulled tight around Jayla's waist and ripped her backward off her feet across the threshold and onto the balcony, slamming her against the railing.

Evan flew forward. The air was vibrating, metal rungs singing like a Tibetan bowl from the impact of Jayla's shoulder blades. The girl was wedged against the railing in a sitting position, flex-cuff crushing her throat, band of fabric biting into her stomach. The woman swung somewhere below on the ends of the curtain, her weight pinning Jayla in place.

There was no choice but to cut the woman free. Evan grabbed for his Strider, hooking the shark fin atop the blade on the edge of his left pocket and snapping the knife open as he drew it. Skidding forward on his knees, he dug the knife into the slender stretch of curtain between Jayla's side and the railing. The curtain gave way, the fabric popping loose, ripped away through the rails. Below he heard a crash of the woman landing on something – car hood? trash can?

Jayla toppled into him, arms contorting, head thrashing, oxygen gone. Redness came up beneath her dark skin, rouging her face. Fingernail gouges marred her neck where she'd tried to get at the flex-cuff.

But the woman had yanked it tight, burying it in the soft skin too deep for Evan to get the tip of the Strider beneath without slashing the girl's throat in the process. She pawed at his shoulder, eyes staring up pleadingly.

She was going to die in his arms and there was nothing he could do about it.

Over the wail of wind through the alley below, he heard the sound of sirens closing in.

15. Human Matter

Jayla Alexis Hill.

A junior at Grand Arts High School.

Same age as Joey.

Shuddering in Evan's arms, lips guppying, trachea cinched shut. Oxygen all around with no way to get it into her body.

Two stories below, her father lay sprawled, his gray matter annihilated by lead, his killer relentless enough to destroy his daughter calmly and tactically in order to escape.

Jayla's lashes, curled and long, parted wide. Evan could see his reflection in her deep brown eyes. He hadn't reacted for one full second, perhaps two, and there was no more time to not react.

His body was moving before his brain caught up to the plan, gathering her up in his arms, racing back in off the balcony, banging his shoulder on the edge of the sliding glass door. Sprinting down the stairs, their body heat mingling, Jayla jouncing against his chest and staring up at him with a stunned calm that felt like surrender. The sirens sounded closer now, right up the block. Too fast a response for his gunshot – a neighbor must have alerted to the crashing sounds earlier.

He nearly tripped on the second-floor landing, kept his boots beneath him, stumbling into the kitchen. Raking an elbow across the island, dumping her onto the butcher block. Flinging open drawers – silverware, steak knives, spices, and then there like a miracle, an aluminum drinking straw.

Snatching it up, back over to Jayla, her head rolling from

side to side in an ecstasy of pain. He ignored her suffering. It would get in the way of what had to be done.

He pressed his fingertips to find her larynx, just below the band of embedded plastic. Easing his touch down, finding the gentle give of the cricothyroid membrane. As the Strider blade came up, Jayla's eyes flared with terror at the sight of it and she began thrashing anew. With an elbow, he pinned her forehead down – 'Got you, I got you' – and pressed the tip of the blade to her soft skin. It dimpled for a moment and then broke, Jayla stiffening on the butcher block.

Red and blue lights strobed the foyer now, compounding off the endless panes of glass and reflecting through the wide doorway of the kitchen. They mapped phantasmagoric shapes across the surfaces, making the room crawl.

Blood washed across the knife tip, glossy rivulets. With a measured jerk of his wrist, he sliced a vertical slit in Jayla's throat. A burst of air erupted, speckling his face with blood.

Swiping at his eyes with his forearm, he made out the scuffle of foot traffic on the foyer below. He'd left the front door ajar, and the cops would have seen Dr Hill's body and begun their slow and low search of the house.

'Third floor,' he shouted. 'Unarmed. Woman down. Roll EMS!'

In response, two sets of footsteps pounded up the stairs.

Jayla rattled on the island and he forced her still – 'Sorry, I have to just' – his eyes watering, blinking away her blood. He tried to wipe the crimson wash from the slit for visibility. As she sucked for air, the hole closed again and he parted it with his fingers, readied the metal straw.

Shouting from the kitchen doorway: 'LAPD! Hands hands. Show me your hands.'

Burly cop, pistol raised, aimed directly at Evan's chest.

Behind him, another patrolman shouldered to the jamb, service weapon drawn as well, shiny nameplate reading JEONG.

Evan hesitated, the straw hovering above Jayla's throat. 'I can't.'

Jeong now: 'Back off her!'

'I'm the one who called 911,' Evan said.

Burly cop: 'Back the fuck off and step away.'

They were bulked up in full patrol gear – 5.11 Taclite gloves, Blackhawk flex-cap knee pads, military-grade tactical belt laden with pouches. Flushed faces, adrenaline revving, fingers inside the trigger guards. The standard-issue Smith & Wesson M&P 2.0s in 9 mm had a 5.5 pound trigger pull.

Not a comforting fact at the moment.

Evan looked up at them and put a full measure of calm into his voice. 'If I don't get this straw into her windpipe, she'll die.'

'Hands *now*! Hands!'

A rising heat from Jayla's gaze. A purple splotch of petechial hemorrhage in her right eye, her lips bluing, her gaze going glassy.

'I'm going to do this,' Evan said. 'Please don't shoot me.'

He leaned over, widened the incision once more, and slid the straw in. Though he clamped it at the base to firm it, it still bobbed grotesquely, giving off a whistle.

'Okay,' he told her. 'Breathe slow. Breathe slow. You have enough air now. You just have to catch up to it.'

His hand was drenched red and his sweat-dampened shirt clung to him. He kept his eyes on Jayla's, holding her forehead gently with one hand and the straw in place with his other. Mimicking deep steady inhalations and exhalations until her breathing matched his. Life creeped back into her cheeks, her face.

The cops remained frozen in the doorway.

'Come here,' Evan said to the burly one. 'Take this.'

The burly guy lumbered forward, holstering his pistol. But instead of moving to Evan's side, he grabbed his arm to cuff him, yanking him back. Jayla sputtered and folded upward, the straw clattering to the floor.

Evan stomped the cop's boot, elbowed him in the gut, slammed him into the refrigerator. The cop coughed and came upright, drawing once more and aiming at Evan's chest. Evan stepped off line, knocked the pistol aside with a left-hand kenpo parry, and poked him in the eyes with his right hand. He finished the spin, slamming his back into the cop, banging them both into the refrigerator as he peeled the gun free. Clenching the gun around the barrel, he drew his arm back, ready to smash it into the cop's face.

He barked, 'I'm UC, Robbery-Homicide. Help me help her.'

The cop staggered and sank to the floor. Evan grabbed the straw off the floor, steadied Jayla once more, and reinserted it. The cop strained to grab Evan's leg, tugging him away from the butcher block. Evan kept the straw steady and kicked his foot free.

Jeong hadn't moved from the doorway. He was aiming at Evan but Jayla was between them and his partner was in the kill zone and he stared at the tableau with confusion, trying to piece together what the hell was going on.

Behind Evan on the tile the burly cop coughed and groaned, reaching for Evan again. 'There's no time for this,' Evan said. Holding the straw in place with one hand, Evan placed the gun on the butcher block, crouched, and yanked him to his feet. 'Hold here,' Evan told him. 'And here. Steady.'

The big guy was breathing hard, nostrils flaring. He had a choice between his service weapon and the metal straw. He chose the straw, firming it in place. As Evan drew back, Jayla's eyes darted about, panicked.

'I have to go,' he told her. 'You're safe now. They have you.' She tried to shake her head but he said, 'Don't move. You're okay.'

Jeong had lowered his weapon but not holstered it. 'Show me badge and creds. I have to frisk you.'

Evan wiped his bloody hand on his cargo pants as he breezed past Jeong onto the catwalk. 'Is EMS dispatched?'

'We called it in.'

More commotion below as officers streamed into the foyer.

'Follow me upstairs,' Evan said.

Jeong hastened his pace up the stairs behind him. The third-floor catwalk held a spray of blood and a lump of human matter. Evan crouched over it.

'Oh, God.' Jeong's curled forefinger rose to his lips, pressed to his septum. 'Is that a . . .'

Evan scooped up the hunk of human ear, stuffed it in his cargo pocket, and stepped out onto the balcony.

'You can't touch that,' Jeong said, moving behind him. 'That's evidence.'

Evan leaned over the railing. Nothing below but a puddle of curtain and a plastic trash can dented and toppled from a falling ninja.

Jeong moved next to him and peered over. 'What are you looking for?'

'I need to check the roof. Wait here. Tell backup to hold the front.'

Evan hoisted himself to balance atop the balcony railing, bracing himself with one hand against the overhang.

Grabbing the lip above with both hands, he pulled himself up, his belly scraping along the graveled flat roof.

'Wait!' Jeong called up after him. 'What's your badge number?'

Wind whipping at him, Evan ran across the joined rooftops of the row of town houses. Between them and the neighboring apartment building was a gap of ten feet and a drop of the same.

He had enough momentum for the leap, but the brief flight still spiked his heart rate. Already sailing, no time to think, chill air blasting his eyes and mouth, asphalt shingles flying up at him jaggedly and faster than he would have liked. Bending his knees so as not to jam the joints, he struck hard but left his feet immediately, rolling onto his side and then ridiculously up over his shoulders in a way that would have been more graceful a few years ago.

He sprinted for the far side, where handrails to a fire-escape ladder looped up over the building's edge. A grab and a swing, clambering down, his hands squeaking painfully down the side rails, he slid-fell until asphalt smashed into the tread of his boots. Flashing lights, radio squalls, and siren bleeps issued around the corner from the front of the building.

Getting his legs back under him, he wobbled a few steps in the other direction, darting into the alley. It was blissfully empty.

He'd run less than ten meters when a garage gate rattled open in the building across from the town houses. A black Chevy Suburban reared up the ramp, scraping a wall and spewing sparks. High and menacing on oversize tires, it clipped a row of trash cans, veering toward Evan, a wall of horsepowered metal.

There were two people in the SUV. The driver was hidden

behind windshield reflection, but Evan caught a glimpse of the face of the woman in the passenger seat, balaclava hood shoved atop her blood-smeared head. Her eyes locked on to his, a brief, searing moment of acknowledgment.

The driver completed the turn, filling the alley wall-to-wall, barreling at him.

He had nowhere to go.

16. The Wrath of God

Evan was in a sheer stretch of alley, the truck accelerating. No fire escape to grab hold of. No curb to fling himself behind. No manhole to disappear into.

If he ran forward he'd pancake into the Suburban's grille. If he ran backward he'd be bulldozed before reaching the intersecting street.

The SUV was twenty meters out now, picking up speed.

The driver wore a mesh-back military-green trucker cap with a yellow army star, his teeth a clenched line in an unkempt beard. Despite the starburst of blood at her right ear and temple, the woman in the passenger seat looked as calm as ever.

Now fifteen meters.

Muscles tensed, Evan debated leaping onto the hood, but the truck was sufficiently lifted that there'd be no toppling up and over. His mind spun, grabbing for options that weren't there. It struck him that he might very well die here frozen on his feet like a petrified deer.

Ten meters and quickening.

The Suburban shoved a wall of air before it, gusting against Evan's cheeks, riffling his hair, the V-8 engine growling.

He left his feet, flinging himself down, pancaking to the gritty asphalt, head turned, ear mashed to the ground. He had time to shoot out a breath, forcing every last bit of oxygen from his lungs, collapsing his body like a bellows deflating.

And then it was upon him.

A roar like the wrath of God, fire and fury sweeping

overhead, the hot reek of oil blasting down, his clothes snapping against his body hard enough that it seemed they might tear right off. A screech and a grind as the driver tried to swerve to catch him with a tire, but the girth of the car in the constrained alley allowed scant room for maneuvering.

All at once the world opened up again and there was light and a sky and air to breathe. The SUV had flown overhead with aeronautical thunder and was already rocketing away.

Head ringing, he came up and onto his feet, drawing his ARES and getting off a single shot before the truck hit the street and careened right. The back window absorbed the round, which clacked impotently, the safety glass popcorning.

An instant later two patrol cars whipped by the mouth of the alley, speeding after the Suburban. He heard a burst of automatic fire and then a crash. One of the patrol cars wobbled back into sight in reverse, windshield riddled and red. Drifting lethargically up a curb, it knocked a fire hydrant off its mount with alarming ease and freed a geyser of water into the undercarriage. The vehicle capped the torrent, forcing it to radiate outward like an atomic blast before the mushroom rise.

Evan turned and ran the other way up the alley, ARES swinging at his side. His senses felt misaligned, his breath thundering through him, dampening other sensations. As he passed the backs of the town houses, a tacked-up patrolman dove out of a rear door right on top of him, heel of his hand riding a holstered service pistol, crying, 'Stop – wait – !'

Evan toggled back to nonlethal fight mode, ramming his ARES back into the appendix holster, freeing his hands just in time to catch the cop's gun hand as it rose. A *bong sau / lop sau* trap locked up forearm and wrist, knocking the pistol free. The cop's black-frame glasses made his eyes bulge; he was sturdy and bookish at once, Clark Kent on the juice.

Evan threw an elbow to the chin, not too hard, the cop

staggering back, name tag flashing: GIBBONS. He snatched at Evan's shirt, grabbing a flapping hem, magnetic buttons popping. Evan spun away and out of the shirt, Gibbons falling away with a fistful of fabric, his descent hastened by the weight of his gear. Gibbons's pistol rasped in circles on the ground like a listless top and Evan kicked it across the alley and through the slender mouth of a storm drain. Wheezing and coughing, Gibbons rolled to his side, attempting to rise.

Evan stared at his shirt where it had fallen out of reach. He had to get it back on – he needed its facial-recognition-scrambling properties before Gibbons faced him squarely and captured him with his body cam.

Evan turned to lunge for it, but another tacked-up patrolman banged out of the rear door, stumbling sideways, pistol already drawn and rising. Evan was five meters away panting like a maniac, 1911 strapped to his sweat-glistening torso, an injured officer sprawled at his feet. The patrolman's pistol was still coming north as if in slow motion, the bore now visible. An adrenalized terror flushed his face, pinking up a doughy nose and padded cheeks that still made him look like the teenage kid he'd been a few years prior.

Evan was too far away to engage in hand-to-hand, too close to run. The tiny lens of the cop's body cam glinted, swinging around with the cop's pivot, and Evan jerked to the side, inches ahead of its scope.

The most likely next occurrence was a bullet through Evan's bare torso.

The muzzle almost level, the black circle of the bore waxing to full moon.

There were no good options left.

Evan quick-drew his ARES and shot the young cop in the chest.

17. Green-Screen Hero

Clutching his ribs, the cop left his boots, crashing back into the door he'd issued from. Face purpling, he stood propped against it, weapon tumbling to the side. Then he slid down to a slump, shuddering. Behind the door, sounds of commotion, officers darting to and fro, securing the building. Wouldn't be long before they traced the gunfire to the alley.

Evan darted to the young cop, ripped his shirt open, and tore the body camera free, keeping his face clear.

He'd hit the standard-issue concealable bullet-resistant vest dead in the middle as he'd intended, denting the Kevlar. The greatest protection was around center mass, diffusing the pressure to avoid blunt-trauma injury, and he'd been careful to avoid impact over the heart.

Still the cop wasn't breathing. Head lolling, spread lips quivering, no air moving in or out. The impact had knocked a few years off him; he looked even younger now, a high-school lineman with the wind knocked out of him. Sweat smeared his tight blond hair to his temples, terror emanating off him like heat. Evan shot a glance at his name tag.

'You're okay, Lenik,' Evan told him, tearing at the Velcro straps, loosening the vest. 'Kevlar got you. Just need to catch your breath.'

He tore the vest over Lenik's head, tossing it aside. He was about to begin chest compressions when the young man's lungs released with a screech and he took in greedy gasps of air.

'Good, good,' Evan said, already pivoting away. His shirt

was before him, puddled on the ground, and he swept it up as he rose. Gibbons had just gotten to all fours. Running past, Evan said, 'Sorry,' and kicked out one arm. Behind him, he heard Gibbons's chest slap the asphalt.

Ramming the shirt into his back pocket, Evan sprinted down the alley to the far side of the block, his view rocking from side to side, a nautical effect.

As he spilled from the alley onto the sidewalk, the vroom of an engine startled him into a leaping turn.

The Suburban.

It accelerated off the curb from its tucked-in hideout between a U-Haul and a gardener's truck and plowed into him. He almost managed to clear the grille, but the front headlight clipped him and sent him into a helicopter-rotor spin above the street. As the windshield flew crookedly by, Evan caught a glimpse of the driver's bearded face behind the wheel. Through a haze of motion and pain, he registered the empty passenger seat, the assassin now gone from the Suburban, which meant she was – alarmingly – set up elsewhere.

The landing tore the heels of his hands, his cargo pants at the hip. He tumbled three times across the lanes of the main street, a station wagon stuttering to a stop on antilock brakes, the front bumper giving his cheek a cool metal kiss. The blare of the horn pressurized the inside of his head to the point of bursting.

He popped to his feet and something sliced past him, the station wagon's hood crumpling. A split second later he heard the delayed crack of a sniper rifle. Spinning, he caught a glint of a scope from the low-slung roof of the Burger King diagonally across the intersection, noted the balaclava-hooded head tilted to the buttstock.

The driver of the station wagon was screaming, hands

clamped to her cheeks with Munchian horror. Two toddlers lolled in car seats in the back, drool-slick chins and whale-spout ponytails. At least three different police sirens wailed in the surrounding blocks, their sounds morphing ventrilo-quially off the corridors of buildings.

Evan put distance between himself and the family, run-ning into the open, zigzagging across the street. Sniper rounds chewed the blacktop at his heels, grit pattering against the calves of his cargo pants. He dove behind an empty bus-stop shelter, the supporting wall turned opaque by an action-movie one-sheet featuring an oiled-up green-screen hero. To his side, a graffitied sheet of plywood boarded up an abandoned storefront.

Replaying the sounds in his head, he registered the super-sonic crack of the projectile. There'd been no trailing boom, which meant the rifle was suppressed, giving him less to work with. But the divots in the street, the secondary pieces of dislodged concrete, and the spalling of the projectiles meant he was dealing with a 7.62x51 mm at a minimum.

His mouth was dry and bitter, jaw clenched. Sprawled on his stomach, he hacked and spit, the glob of saliva laced with street grime. Then he risked a glance behind him. Cop cars were screaming up the alley, but the Suburban had embed-ded into the opening, stopping it up, the hood buried in a landslide of collapsed edifice. The driver's window had spi-derwebbed on impact, clouding white.

The crumpled door shuddered once, twice, kicked from within, and then it flew open. The driver in the army trucker hat stepped out and stared across the four lanes of traffic at Evan.

He looked uninjured, unrattled. Lacing his fingers, he thrust his palms outward, and even over the din of the col-lective mayhem, Evan heard the brisk rat-a-tat of popping

91

knuckles. The man's smile was yellow and jagged, teeth missing. His face said this was the most fun he'd had in years.

His finger rose to his ear and Evan read his lips as he spoke into the radio: *Tanner to the Wolf, I've got visual. Behind the bus shelter.*

Rolling to his side, Evan pulled his ARES from the appendix holster and aimed across the street. Panicked civilians swarmed his field of vision, running to safety, abandoning their vehicles. No clear shot.

Through the strobing bodies, Tanner looked at him. And smiled.

An incoming round snapped crisply, and then the bus shelter wall cracked like a wrenched ice-cube tray. Evan's hands stung. It took a moment for him to realize what had happened, that the bullet had penetrated the movie poster and knocked the ARES right from his grip. Above him, the pane held its shape for a single confused moment, unsure which law of physics to obey, and then cascaded down in shards across his shoulders.

He was exposed, his 1911 lying mangled in the gutter.

He moved fast, leaping across the sidewalk, crashing into the plywood covering the storefront. The nails on one side gave, the wooden rectangle rocking inward like a crooked pivot door. He scraped across it, drawing splinters; tumbled into the dusky interior; and landed belly-down on a concrete floor sticky with filth. A big square of a room, perhaps a former lobby.

When he lifted his head, he sensed movement at the desecrated lobby's perimeter. Dirt-blackened faces, glinting eyes, caved cheeks. And the smell – human waste and untreated infection, urine and the vinegar stench of meth. The tilted plywood door had freed a blast of daylight to enter the squat house, and Evan had to blink to acclimate his eyes to the severity of the contrast.

A water leak laid a bruise-colored amoeba across a third of the ceiling, a steady drip tapping a soggy jaundiced couch. Sleeping bags bulging like larvae, a plastic pink child's vanity and stool set, black trash bags and white paint buckets, a row of ragged Christmas stockings nailed to crumbling Sheetrock, red Solo cups, rat nests, a legless teddy bear adorned with a tattered red bra. A squalid underworld less than a hundred meters from Dr Hill's airy three-story retreat. That's what happened when poverty outpaced prosperity, crowding on top of it, leaving affluence nowhere to flee.

The squatters rose like zombies, black maws punctuated by peg teeth, and shuffled into the adjoining room, melting into darkness. The taste of ammonia coated the inside of Evan's mouth, and he coughed hard, trying to clear his windpipe. As he got his hands beneath him, one palm pressed down into something squishy. Shaking the fog from his head, he forced himself upright.

The shaft of light through the mangled doorway laid a spotlight on the rear wall. As Evan rose, his shadow seemed to rise before him, stretching up the crumbling Sheetrock.

Then he noticed the shaggy outline of facial hair, the brim of a trucker hat, a curved spike held in one hand at the thigh, like a meat hook or tent stake.

Tanner standing in the doorway, his form thrown in a distorted shadow-puppet silhouette.

Evan wiped the grime off his hand onto his pant leg, clenched his teeth, drew a breath.

And turned to face what was coming.

18. Back to Lethal

Tanner stepped across the knocked-askew plank of plywood, through the ragged gullet into the onetime lobby, nose wrinkling at the smell. His discordantly pretty amber eyes held the light. From outside came shouts and cries, earsplitting sirens and radio blasts, flashing lights and car horns. Evan hadn't had time to pull his shirt on; he felt it bulging in his back pocket, the tingle of cooling sweat across his bare shoulders.

Once more Tanner pressed his finger to his ear and spoke to the Wolf. 'Through the plywood door. Got him cornered. Any cop comes near, put 'em down.' A pause. 'I know, I know. No loose ends. I got him. Deal with the girl.' Then: 'I said I got him. I don't need backup.'

He hung up, then lifted his hat by the brim, swiped a forearm across his brow, lowered it back in place. Then he and Evan stared at each other. His skin had a sun-battered orange tinge from sleeping on the streets, his face like a pork rind.

'Former army?' Evan said. 'And you're okay killing cops and girls?'

'*Ex,* not *former,*' Tanner replied, relishing the pejorative. 'Chewed on that Afghan dirt, cashiered out, big chicken dinner.'

Big Chicken Dinner: Bad Conduct Discharge. No health care. No pension.

'Plus for two hundred K,' Tanner said, grinning, 'I'd kill anything.'

Wearily, Evan toggled his fight setting back to *lethal* and set his feet.

Tanner sidled toward him, tightening his grip on the spike. 'You look tired.'

'I *am* tired,' Evan conceded. He circled, gauging Tanner's fight IQ.

Tanner loosened his stance, crouching, swapping the spike from hand to hand as he stalked forward. Evan ignored the hands, watched the eyes. A target glance at Evan's gut. That's where he was going. The stake rolled from left hand to right once more. Evan raised his arms in a low-guard position.

And then Tanner lunged.

Rapid prison-shiv stabs straight at Evan's stomach, giving him little to grab at but the sharpened point. Shuffling backward, Evan pounded at the thrusting arm with the blades of his ulnas, deflecting the steel tip barely to one side of his body and then the other. They danced toward the rear wall like fencers – thrust, parry, thrust, parry. When Evan's shoulders struck Sheetrock, he got in a side kick that hit Tanner's right thigh squarely, knocking him back and nearly buckling the knee.

As Evan came off the wall, Tanner reset, wiping his nose and test-bending his right ankle. Then he came again, favoring his good leg, jabbing and jabbing. Evan hammered blows at his forearm just above the wrist, pounding pain into Tanner's limb, deadening the nerves. The forcefulness of Tanner's thrusts diminished, and then he soft-stepped on his injured leg, blading his body just enough to open up a lane.

Evan snatched at him – an arm drag to yank him sideways, clearing a path to take the back. Tanner yelped and slashed at him, but Evan ducked and tied him up from behind. A scrabble of hands led to a belly-to-back body lock, Evan clenching

Tanner's stomach, bending his knees, popping his hips forward, and ripping him off his feet. Arching his back, Evan threw him in a Greco–Roman suplex, twisting him up and over his own body and piledriving him into the floor.

A thud and a bark of pain. Rats squealed and scuttled. As the men tumbled apart, Evan saw that the spike had impaled Tanner's side. Tanner looked down at the metal post sunk maybe three inches into his flesh, the end wagging.

'Wow,' Tanner said. 'That's . . . um . . .'

He pulled it free, let it fall with a clang. Drops of blood tapped the sticky floor. His head dipped down and then back up, and his eyes held the wounded fury of edge-of-death adrenaline. He lunged.

Crashing into Evan, the two going down, clawing and punching, legs wrapping and kicking.

Tanner was skilled but he was losing blood and strength and Evan's sweat-slicked torso made grappling harder. Evan got in an elbow to the temple, slipping behind Tanner and snapping him up in a rear naked choke hold, his arm encircling Tanner's neck and grabbing his own opposite biceps.

Tanner was frantic, ferocious, flailing and bucking. Evan rolled with him across the squalid floor, holding the lock. Tanner's bladder had released, his jeans wet, the hot stench burning Evan's eyes. They smashed into the soggy couch, waterlogged flakes of fabric clinging to Evan's bare back. His cheek rolled through a patch of viscous stickiness. Trash? Blood? Shit? Something bitter had gotten into his mouth and he felt the smell of the place as a paste across his skin.

His OCD flared up hard, but there was no time for it, so he swatted it aside. He was busy crushing Tanner's carotid arteries, cutting off oxygen to his brain. There was no space for disgust or aversion, just each ticking instant and the strain in his arms and the ancient bloody knowledge that after this one of them would be breathing and one would not.

They were spooned together on their sides, grunting, trembling. Evan clenched harder, straining, lactic acid burning in his arms, his legs. He crawled both hands higher up his own shoulders, relieving the strain in his biceps, letting the position do the work. A low clicking noise issued from Tanner's throat.

Outside Evan heard the crack of the sniper rifle – once, twice – and then a screech of tires and a crash.

A shadow flickered across the ruptured doorway, and then a pudgy cop leaned back into sight, staring at them with wide eyes, head tilted to his shoulder mic: 'Moonden requesting backup. Abandoned building across the alley.'

Sweat stinging his eyes, Evan compressed Tanner's throat harder, trying to get it done. The cop ducked inside, running at them, aiming at Evan's exposed back with the S&W M&P 9 mm. 'Stop – *stop*!'

Tanner gurgled, heels scrabbling, wiry hair grinding against Evan's chin. Evan had only a whirligig upside-down view of the cop closing in, finger on the partially compressed trigger. Evan had time for a single stab of cognition – Moonden was at the halfway point of the trigger pull, the center plastic safety feature tab compressed so the entire trigger could move rearward. For a slow-motion instant there was nothing in the world except that finger compressing the trigger, pink flesh turning to white.

Firming his grip on Tanner, Evan spun hard in a crocodile roll, sweeping Tanner over his body.

The gunshot reverberated in the rotting walls, Tanner jerking in Evan's arms, a silver-dollar hole blown through the union of his ribs. Moonden choked out a gasp as Evan shoved the dead body aside.

Back to nonlethal.

Before Moonden could reacquire target, Evan spun on his side and swept the cop's legs. Moonden's shoulders struck the floor and Evan was on him, stripping the service pistol. Knee in Moonden's substantial gut, freeing handcuffs from the leather pouch on the cop's belt, snapping them around the wide wrists. No vest, no body cam – a much-needed break.

Evan leaned close, clicked the push-to-talk on Moonden's shoulder mic: 'Sniper with a rifle on the roof of Burger King. I repeat: Sniper on the roof of Burger King.'

Dispatch came back: 'Bravo Six advises shooter with rifle at Burger King. All units, proceed with caution.'

Moonden's eyes were stunned, water-filled, chalky residue at the corners of his lips. Another of Jack's aphorisms reared up in Evan's mind: *Humans aren't meant to kill other humans.*

Evan spun the officer's pistol home into his own empty appendix holster, rose with a grimace, and nodded at Tanner. 'It's okay,' he said. 'It was a good shoot. He was a cop-killer.'

Rather than risk stepping through the front door, he bolted to the rear of the building. Down a long corridor with ankle-deep trash, past a doorless utility closet turned abandoned meth lab, over a homeless guy sleeping or dead near a mesh security door. Evan twisted the knob, stepped over the body, and shoved out into another alley, congested with trash cans, fire-escape ladders, rusting handrails, cellar doors, and hopper windows peeking up from underground.

The grime of the squat house and Tanner's blood, laid atop his own sweat, clung to him like a second skin. He tugged his shirt from the back pocket of his cargo pants and was about to pull it on when a movement in his peripheral vision froze him in place. At the end of the alley no more than fifteen meters away, a full SWAT crew rolled by, a seemingly endless parade of dark blue utility uniforms toting carbines. All any of them had to do was turn their head and they'd see him there in full sight.

Keeping his eyes on them, he slowly raised the shirt in front of his bare torso, adversarial pattern facing out, and eased toward the opposite alley wall to diminish profile. His boot hit a patch of wet stone.

And then he was tumbling down a brief flight of subterranean stairs, banging through a metal door flecked with patina, spilling onto a sawdust-sprinkled floor. A hydraulic closer cranked the door shut behind him, ratcheting out the natural light and the rising sounds of sirens and officers deploying. A moment later, his shirt floated down to cover his face like a shroud.

He pulled it off.

The place was air-conditioned and mood-lit, cool blue LEDs underlying rows of booze on shelves. A few day drinkers arrayed at a long wooden slab, a female bartender with an unlit cigar in her mouth, a slender bottle of vodka set before her. Just above Evan's head hovered a pair of enormous military boots, the heels hooked on the footrail of a stool.

With a groan, Evan pulled himself to a sitting position.

The bouncer rose from his perch. And kept rising.

His shaved head caught the yellow-orange sheen of the speakeasy's Edison bulbs. At least six foot four, he wore a sleeveless denim shirt that barely accommodated the brawn of his chest and arms. It looked like it would burst Hulk-like from his body if he sneezed.

Evan shoved himself to his feet, drew in a deep breath.

All sets of eyes were on him. No one moved or spoke. Over at the bar, a biker type stared, PBR bottle frozen halfway to his mouth. The jukebox turned over, the opening riff of 'Dirty Deeds Done Dirt Cheap' gaining momentum from partially blown speakers.

Imbibing an excess of Cîroc and getting bounced down a set of stairs by a venerable lady with a cane had left Evan a fraction of a second behind on his reactions. Which might have gone unnoticed had he not found himself targeted by a trained assassin and a colossal manhunt. But that was precisely what he had to be prepared for. Always. That was the responsibility of being who he was, the reason for the perennial roar of the Second Commandment in his head. As Orphan X, he could never afford to be off peak.

He took a moment to reset himself.

The bouncer seemed unwilling to give him much more than that.

The important thing wasn't how Evan got here, shirtless and blood-spattered in an underground bar, nor why he had half a human ear in his pocket, nor why the heavily perspiring bald bouncer proportioned like the Farnese Atlas seemed determined to twist Evan's head off his torso. The important thing, given the size of the manhunt massing for him on the streets outside, was what he did with the precious next few seconds.

19. Howdy, Officers

On the small landing at the base of the stairs, Evan edged around the bouncer. The big man circled, holding him in view, keeping within swinging distance.

The guy had no bulletproof vest, an abundance of fighting confidence, and superior reach. Evan ran a quick calculus; he could clear leather before the bouncer took a swing, but given the tight quarters he couldn't risk being pressed to fire.

'Can I have a second to put my shirt on?' Evan asked.

The guy nodded. Staying alert, Evan tugged the shirt on. The clap of the magnetic buttons was comforting, the fabric sealing around him. The bouncer wore no watch, but Evan noticed that his fingernails were cut more smoothly on the right than the left so: southpaw.

The jukebox run ended, the semi-quiet broken only by the muted sounds of the police response outside. The half dozen patrons watched breathlessly, a panorama of flannel shirts, work boots, and frayed denim.

Evan squared his shoulders, released a breath, gave a faint nod. *Let's go.*

The bouncer reached for him and Evan almost engaged. But the catcher's-mitt hand set down gently on his shoulder.

'You okay, little man?' the bouncer asked. 'Do you need my help?'

Evan stared up at him for a full two seconds. Then felt his muscles shudder loose with an exhalation. He wanted to laugh but couldn't muster the energy.

'Sure,' Evan said. 'Yes.'

'What do you need? Medical?'

'No, thanks,' Evan said. 'Just a back exit out of here.' His gaze snagged on the bartender, the slender bottle set before her. FAIR vodka – made from organic quinoa nurtured by small farmers in volcanic soil high in the Andes Mountains and distilled in Cognac. 'Shot of vodka might be beneficial.'

The bouncer's laugh sounded like a rumbling concrete mixer. He swung his mighty head toward the bartender. 'One pour for the little man.'

The man sipping PBR nodded at the bartender. 'Put it on my tab, Charlie.'

The bartender studied Evan, cigar adhered to her lower lip. Violet eyes bright enough to be contacts, an excess of eyeliner making them pop, a wind chime's worth of thin metal pendants clustered at the hollow of her throat.

She flicked her head at Evan: Approach.

He did.

She grabbed an empty rocks glass and slid it across the fine-grain wood. He caught it with a cupped hand. The bottle followed, purring along the surface. He caught that, too, poured himself a splash of FAIR vodka, and shot it down.

Silky smooth, vanilla and citrus. A fresh green aftertaste reminiscent of jicama lingered for a few delightful seconds.

He set the glass back down. 'Thank you.' The side of his head throbbed; he'd cracked it on the floor when he landed the Greco–Roman suplex. 'May I have some ice for my eye, please?'

She ducked down out of view for a few moments and then rose with a baggie of ice. Sweat glistened at her collar-bone and she smelled of floral deodorant, whiskey, and Havana leaf.

Pressing the bag to his head, he took a moment to catch his breath. The rising sounds outside made him less than eager to step out of cover and back onto the streets, but he'd have to soon enough.

He pointed beside the jukebox at a dim corridor burrowing into darkness. 'Exit that way?'

The bartender nodded.

He tipped an imaginary hat to her and strolled out, the men watching him go.

The narrow hall smelled of beer and urine cakes, its walls clad with framed photos of old Hollywood – Sophia Loren side-eyeing Jayne Mansfield's cleavage, Bruce Lee's chest puffed up like a cobra hood, Veronica Lake sprawled on a divan playing peekaboo behind a wave of platinum. The corridor tunneled the length of the building and then rose in a flight of stairs.

Pausing at the fluted-glass door at the top, Evan dug into a cargo pocket, pulled out the slab of the Wolf's ear, nestled it into the ice bag, and shoved the whole thing back in. Gauzy daylight filtered through the pane, along with the Sturm und Drang of a militarized police force spreading through the surrounding blocks. Shadows flitted by, bodies in motion, and vehicles were still moving on the street beyond, a good sign that the roadblock hadn't reached here yet.

He drew in a deep breath. Exhaled. Waited for a break in the foot traffic. And stepped out onto the sidewalk.

To his right just beyond the purview of the glass door were a full dozen SWAT officers clustered around a parked Lenco BearCat personnel carrier, an old-fashioned paper map unfurled across the armored hood. The sergeant's Oakley Blades shined like a wedge of volcanic glass, his gloved finger stabbed down onto the map. The other men were goggled and helmeted, chin-strapped and geared-up, a war force swathed in darkest blue. There were M4 carbines and Kimber .45s, body armor and ballistic shields with

POLICE block-lettered in white, battering rams and breaching sledgehammers, and a few Heckler & Koch MP5 submachine guns for good measure.

All twelve heads swiveled up at the same time. In the blue mirror arc of the sergeant's shades, Evan saw his own reflection, woefully small.

He cleared his throat. 'Howdy, Officers,' he said.

20. The Roiling Midst

The SWAT team stared at Evan.

Evan stared at the SWAT team.

The sergeant grinned. 'Easy,' he said, lifting his gloved hand from the map. *'Eaasy.'*

Evan stood perfectly still. They all did, too. The wind caught the map and whisked it up into a loop the loop as it neared Evan. For a frozen moment, it floated above the street, trembling in the breeze like a hawk on a thermal.

And then a hole punched through it with a faint *pock* that sounded like a flicked ear.

Before Evan could register the sound, a sniper round burned across the top of his shoulder, fraying the fabric, scorching his skin, and blowing out the fluted glass behind him.

SWAT hit the deck, the men tumbling over one another to take cover behind the BearCat, muzzles lifting to return fire. Their rounds chewed the roof edge of the neighboring four-story, powdering brick.

Evan bolted.

The block was in chaos, every car alarm blaring, headlights flashing. The percussion of the big guns returning fire pursued him, wobbling the store windows in their frames and making the world jiggle. Evan threaded behind a deserted lowrider, tucking in tight to the four-story, taking him out of the Wolf's scope. Radio crackled after him – *'suspect heading northbound'* – and then was lost beneath more gunfire.

He blasted through a florist shop, knocking over buckets

of orange carnations, sliding across a counter slick with cellophane bouquet wrap. Punching out the back door, booking up the neighboring streets. Ford Police Interceptor SUVs and sedans crowded the road with no regard for lanes.

Cops were screaming into radio units and out of loudspeakers. Several faces oriented to him, vehicles peeling out in pursuit. He vaulted a row of hedges, sprinted up the sidewalk, cutting through a park to aim for the tent city beyond.

Ford Interceptors roared after him, tracing the park's perimeter parallel to him at either side speeding to reach the street ahead, their tinted windows dark and menacing. As they cut hard turns and rocketed in like closing curtains, he hurdled a park bench, flew through the narrowing gap of their screeching bumpers, and buried himself in the sea of humanity.

Hundreds of makeshift abodes were scattered along a graveled plain hemmed in by train tracks and the concrete slope of the drought-dry Los Angeles River. Soiled sleeping bags, scorched hot plates, a half-naked man nattering to himself. Trash clogged the makeshift alleys between homes. Mounds of rags and shattered bottles and the high hard reek of grain alcohol. Pots and pans dangled from a clothesline, jangling idiophonically.

Multiple officers had left their cars in pursuit, tracing the ripple of Evan's wake. Barreling down a crammed aisle, he kicked out tent pegs, makeshift domiciles flapping madly behind him, tangling up some of the responders. He cut through a circle of homeless guys sharing a bottle. As one lifted it to his lips, Evan grabbed it and slapped it into the hand of another without slowing. The men turned on one another, yelling and shoving, and he switched direction hard, plunging through a cabana of burlap stretched over a frame jerry-rigged from unfurled Hula-Hoops. The woman inside, ensconced in a beanbag, gummed at a pizza crust, milky eyes taking no notice.

He kept on in a crouched jog, keeping his head low, reading the river of human bodies behind him, the eddies of mayhem, cops flickering into view behind hung sheets, bucking and shouting.

Way at the edge of his peripheral vision, no more than twenty meters away, something drew his focus.

A still form in the roiling midst. The sight brought him up short.

The Wolf, having shed her balaclava and sniper rifle, stood in a small clearing. The breeze riffled her white-blond hair. A clean white bandage, miraculously discreet, swathed her right ear. She stood apart from the commotion all around, distinct from the shadows and clutter between them, bathed in a fall of light that turned her luminescent.

A ripple of her arms and then she was aiming a handgun at his head. Deep blue polished to a near mirror finish. The glint of gold at the trigger and hammer gave it away even at distance as a Manurhin MR73 Gendarmerie, the finest and most expensive revolver ever produced.

Before he could react, she fired.

21. Checkmate

Evan could do nothing more than flinch.

But the Wolf's shot clipped a pan dangling from a clothes-line between them, the spark like a needle to the eye, the ping audible even above the madding crowd. The pan rotated like a spun top, giving Evan a strobing view of her porcelain-smooth face.

There and gone. There and gone. Not a ripple of emotion or anything else.

Panicked from the shot, civilians darted into the line of fire. Evan had Moonden's service weapon drawn and aimed, though it was no match for the Wolf's $3,600 revolver across the fray. People streamed between them, the Wolf whipping into view like someone glimpsed across a platform between the cars of a passing train.

Behind Evan, cops bulled through the crowd, catching up. Civilians clogged the line of sight.

There was no safe shot.

But the Wolf firmed her grip. And fired.

The round clipped the shoulder of a homeless man running by, spraying a fan of scarlet, and then hammered the pan again. The pan flew back, almost taking Evan's head off.

He slammed down to safety, concrete hard against his chest and chin. Over the din he heard the wounded man writhing and screaming.

In the tent across from Evan, a wild woman huffing spray-paint fumes from a paper bag stared at him with red rodent eyes. Crawling forward, Evan plucked the spray-paint can from her side and ran.

Cops closing in now, trampling tents and kicking through mounds of refuse, hot on the scent. Darting through makeshift lanes between tents, Evan came upon a circle of bearded men warming their hands around an oil drum burning refuse. He tossed the spray-paint can into the flames and said, '*Run.*'

They scattered.

He sprinted on.

Ten meters, fifteen, and then – *boom!* – the spray-paint can detonated, the oil drum compounding the metallic scream in its belly. A wave of cops fell back, stumbling.

A rise in the ground bucked Evan above the fray for a moment, and he saw the Wolf thirty meters away, hands in her pockets, strolling swiftly. She glanced over, their eyes locking, her gun hand starting to pull from her pocket. But they both sensed a stampede behind her – SWAT sweeping in from the park, dark uniforms carving through the tents behind her like sharks.

Evan surged over the rise, dropped back out of view, doubled back a few steps, and cut into an even denser stretch of improvised housing.

Softening his footfall, he veered up a narrowing alley, staying low and alert, head on a pivot. Up ahead, a patrolman's shadow fluttered to life, visible through a wall of hung sheets. Pistol drawn. A black outline stalking.

Evan matched him for several steps, tracking him slowly and silently, separated only by the thin sheets. White linen gave way to maroon cotton, the shadow rippling. Rounding the corner, Evan seized the cop from behind, twisting his wrist, threading his own finger atop the cop's through the trigger guard. They swayed together, the gun discharging twice into the ground.

Grunting, straining, they spun in a violent dance, Evan controlling the arm. Up the narrow lane the Wolf floated back into view. Framed by tents on either side, she kept her hands in her pockets, the picture of innocence amid the clamor.

Then her hands blurred, and her gun was out, and she fired.

The cop took the round to his chest plate, the domino effect nearly knocking them over. But Evan wrenched their joined arms north, forcing the shared pistol up, and fired twice at the Wolf.

She dipped low, rolling out of sight, the bullets puffing a mattress stood on end behind her. The cop was wheezing and grunting through clenched teeth.

Evan checked him for blood – none – and respiration – labored but clear – and left him, booking for the heart of the cobbled-together city. More units swarmed the perimeter, headlights skewering tents, engine noise reaching an oceanic roar.

The tents lit up in red and blue, buffeted by the wind, strobing kaleidoscopically. Evan took a step back, crashing into a shopping cart filled with empty cans and bottles. He spun a full 360 degrees. The labyrinth unspooled all around, promising more turns and alleys, dead ends and hidden nooks. Flashing at the edges of sight, officers closed the noose – a glimpse of boots beneath tattered nylon, a peaked police hat floating atop a cardboard wall, a duo of patrolmen plunging behind a row of decaying porta-potties. Two more seconds and he'd be spotted from at least three angles.

Another stumbling backward step brought him into a wider lane forged through the shabby habitat, a cleared thoroughfare atop a stretch of disused railroad track.

An Interceptor sedan flew past up a lane to his side, close enough he could see the gaping mouth of the driver. It swerved toward him, the rear fender clipping a cardboard house and lifting it straight off a frail woman inside sitting on a frayed lawn chair, her filthy skin like a crust.

The vehicle came at him, bearing down, the driver yelling into his radio.

Evan skipped back out of the lane, grabbing the edge of the shopping cart. Across its girth he locked eyes with the patrolmen emerging from the far side of the porta-potties. A few paces behind them stood the Wolf, head lowered, shoulders rolled forward, just another face in the crowd.

Ahead, the patrolmen surged toward him, knocking aside civilians.

Behind, the Interceptor's engine screamed.

Grabbing the cart with both hands, Evan swung it around with a discus pivot, hurling it across the railroad track just in time for the patrol car to pancake into it.

Police airbags were rigged not to deploy for PIT maneuvers and minor contact; to register through the push-bumper assembly, they required a serious front collision.

He got it.

The impact was apocalyptic, an explosion of glass and aluminum throwing a literal cloud of shrapnel over the area. The twisted shopping cart flew up, up, and away like a flung clay pigeon. The bang of the front airbags deploying knocked the driver back in his seat, the autobrakes stuttering the car to a halt.

The driver's door opened and the cop spilled out coughing, his face powdered with sodium azide residue.

Evan hurdled the driver, jumping into the Interceptor and ripping the door shut behind him. Hastened by a flurry of rounds from the pursuing patrolmen, the door slammed in its frame, jarring his shoulder and knocking him on a tilt over the console. He settled back, slapped the locks just as the lead patrolman banged into the side of the car, chest mashed to the pane, hands scrabbling at the handle.

Evan shoved the airbag aside and stomped the gas, four hundred horses roaring to life. The powerful sedan screeched along the railroad track through the rows of tents, shot from a cannon.

Faces and domiciles ripped by as if on a loop. Accelerating, he aimed for the concrete basin of the dry Los Angeles River, using the 101 overpass as a North Star. SUVs raced through the alleys, converging on him, vectoring in from both sides. He goosed the modified 3.5-liter V-6 even more, five hundred pounds of torque smashing him back into the heavy-duty vinyl.

The SUVs poured in at him, push bumpers rocketing for side impact, closer and closer.

He was joggling in his seat, the looming overpass shaking. If he could make it to the river basin he could –

An SUV clipped his rear panel.

Evan's sedan was thrown into a bumper-car gyration, the world whipping by, the hood plowing through a Lego stack of trash cubed like bales of hay, releasing a garbage slick in his wake. The reek of burned rubber leaked through the vents.

Still rotating, the car slid down the slope and launched onto the concrete riverbed before the vast underpass, its sloped foundation pillars burgeoning like mighty oaks.

He stopped spinning in the center of the basin.

SUVs and patrol cars nosed forward, hemming him in from the left side – but at a cautious distance. A steeper embankment to his right. SUVs on the concrete riverbed behind him. A police blockade ahead beyond the overpass.

Evan gritted his teeth, felt the ache along his jaw.

Checkmate.

22. Nowhere to Go

The cops peered out at the Interceptor alone on the concrete plain of the riverbed. None of them dared to breathe. A silent standoff.

Crouching behind the vehicle blockade, a SWAT member shot a nervous glance over at her sergeant. 'We got him dead to rights.'

They stared down at the lone Interceptor, smoke rising from its tires. It was hard to make anything out through the tinted windows or the spiderwebbed pane on the driver's side.

A moment of stillness.

They couldn't get a clear look at the man inside, but he seemed average of size and build.

The SWAT member worried the cross pendant at her throat with glove-thickened fingers. 'Looks like he's surrendering.'

The man in the Interceptor looked over, a flat gaze rife with intensity. It seemed like he was looking right at them.

'No,' the sergeant said. 'He's not.'

The sedan revved. Loud. Louder. A thing of menace.

The roars echoed harshly off the surrounding concrete slopes. The cops jerked back behind their vehicles, staring intently below, awaiting orders to fire.

'There's nowhere to go,' the SWAT member said. 'He's got nowhere to go.'

The engine reached a protracted snarl, vibrating on its tires.

And then the brake released, the sedan fishtailing off the dime, laying down tread in its wake.

It rocketed toward the severe slope of the embankment on the far side, the one leading up to the low overpass.

'No,' the sergeant said. 'Nuh-uh.'

The fastest cop car on the market. Zero to sixty in 5.5 seconds. It could reach one hundred miles per hour in 13.5.

The Interceptor reached it.

Blasting across the concrete straightaway, throwing up rooster tails of grit.

And then it swooped up the embankment, tilting upward, upward, the angle moving gradually toward the insurmountable.

Ten meters up, twenty, twenty-five, its long arc to the overpass losing steam as the hood neared the buttressed edge of the bridge. Could it possibly make the turn from slope to road?

It peaked shy of the mark.

Just three inches.

But three inches in a car skidding up an incline to dodge a concrete bulwark is a lot of inches.

The left front bumper crashed into the concrete barrier guarding the spot where embankment met overpass.

An earth-shuddering crash, explosion of headlight, crumpling metal. The car pinwheeled up onto the overpass, spinning wildly out of view.

23. As Good Once as He Ever Was

Evan whipped across the lanes of traffic, tapped one way by an incoming Prius and then the other by a MINI Cooper. The lightweight collisions were his first stroke of luck in a long stretch or – if he decided to shine a bit of optimism on things – a continuation of the luck he'd been riding since Dr Hill's town house. The smashed Interceptor shuddered to a miraculous halt with cars screeching all around him. His neck hurt and his spine hurt and his hips hurt and his fingers hurt and they all would've kept on hurting if he'd let them.

He'd been trapped like a rat down in the basin, at the edge of his operational abilities. There'd been no contingencies to run, no last-minute physics calculations, not even one of Jack's hoary aphorisms to light the way.

There'd just been a concrete ramp and enough American horsepower to put him within three inches of his goal.

Imperfect, ugly, and painful, but brighter men than him had pointed out that no plan survived first contact with the enemy.

Evan didn't have a moment to catch his breath before he heard the *whump-whump-whump* of the choppers.

LAPD had the most airborne assets of any municipality in the country. At the moment, they all seemed to be headed in his direction.

A swarm of Eurocopter AS350 B2 AStars and Airbus H125s buzzed in from the horizon like angry wasps. Several more hovered over the area of Dr Hill's residence.

Evan stumbled from the wreckage of his car and stepped

into freeway traffic, which had halted around the nucleus of the crash. A few more vehicles skidded in from the periphery, a slick-haired guy in a Tesla braking abruptly, nearly hitting him. Evan came around to the driver's door.

'Thank God,' he said, hooking his hand on the door handle as it slid out. 'You have to help me.'

He opened the door, unsnapped the guy's seat belt, tugged him out, and climbed in. The guy stood there, mouth agape, white teeth shining, a dot of fluorescent-green gum punctuating his molars. Evan took off before he managed to get out a single word.

The scent of AXE body spray permeated the car. An iPhone was plugged into the dash, a podcast of a former SEAL assault team member: '. . . *to change the world, you must be your very best in your darkest moment . . .*'

Already, in the rearview, he could see the helos closing in. He reversed away from the crash site in a modified J-turn and bulldozed west, weaving along the 101, veering to pass cars. Screeching off at Broadway, he sensed the helicopters nearing, the lead bird now out of sight above him. He ripped onto Second Street, oversteering to put the Tesla into a controlled drift. The sideways swoop took a third of the block before delivering him neatly into the gritty east mouth of the Second Street Tunnel. As he blasted through, the world darkened.

Five cars zipped past, and then there was a slight break in traffic coming at him.

He wrenched the wheel sideways, blocking both lanes, gumming up the tunnel. He'd neared the illuminated aperture of the tunnel's west end, flared buttresses wrapping the curved walls like sails.

Horns and screeches and cursing. A Dodge Ram with a camo paint job ground to a halt, its grille a few feet from the Tesla's passenger window.

As Evan hopped out, a burly man sprang from the Ram and charged him. 'What the fuck are you –?'

Evan ducked him without losing momentum and stepped up onto the Ram's runner, hoisting himself into the truck. Reversing a few feet, he knocked into the plumber's van behind, making room. Then he steered forward into the bike lane, smashing through the nose of the Tesla and clearing the way to exit through the east side of the tunnel he'd entered seconds before. The burly guy pursued his truck on foot, screaming, neck flushed with rage.

Evan shot free of the tunnel into a yawn of daylight. The choppers buzzed overhead, a swirling confusion. He held the gas steady and even. An American-flag Little Trees air freshener twirled from the rearview, perfuming the interior with vanilla. The radio display screen showed a country station, a baritone crooning that he wasn't as good as he once was, but he was as good once as he ever was. Leaving the tunnel behind, Evan allowed himself an exhale and gave an amen to Mr Keith.

Blasting along in the truck, he tugged his RoamZone out, thumbed up an EMS scanner app, and jacked the volume high. Words cut through the static: '– *copy that*' – click – '*receiving multiple reports on the incident*' – click – '*EMS Unit Two One en route with police escort to Downtown Medical Center ER*' – click – '*female, approximately eighteen years old*' – click – '*emergency trach, now stable* –

Winding through the uneven streets of Bunker Hill, he rimmed the edge of Pershing Square, zipped past the imposing south entrance of the Los Angeles Central Library, an Egyptian–Art Deco triumph capped with a mosaic tile pyramid.

– click – '*copy Unit Two One*' – click – '*PD has been notified from our end and will meet you there to establish further protection protocols for the victim* –'

Jayla Hill was safe. For now.

He punched the RoamZone to call Joey and – thank God – she answered on the second ring. 'I had my shirt off for a brief stretch of time in downtown LA.'

Joey giggled. 'Say more.'

He gave her the location of the alley and the stretch of streets he'd run. 'No shirt means no facial-recognition thwarting. I need you to carpet-bomb those two blocks – Ring doorbells, surveillance cams, anything that might've caught my face.'

'You got it. Maybe next time you wanna moonlight as a Chippendales dancer you could gimme a heads-up so I can –'

He hung up.

Beelining across the 110 and up Seventh, he neared the edge of MacArthur Park. The home of the West Coast's most celebrated pastrami sandwich flew by on the left, capped with a cursive sign.

At the stoplight at Rampart, he drifted up on a tidy red Jeep and tapped the rear bumper. A woman hopped out, tugging back her corkscrew hair with one hand, almond-shaped eyes visible through tortoiseshell eyeglasses.

He climbed out as well and they walked toward each other.

'Man, this day,' she said. 'You got insurance?'

'I'll leave it in perfect condition,' Evan said, moving right past her. He slipped through the Jeep's open door and took off.

Through the speakers, a new sound washed over him – '*rise unafraid*' – an R&B alto clear as alpine air, soulful and raw. No lights in his rearview, no choppers overhead.

Shooting west to Koreatown, he didn't let up until he banked into a strip mall hosting a so-called Spa Palace. Cars were backed up out of the parking lot, the valets scrambling.

He wedged himself into the line, left the Jeep in park, and

jogged ahead past the impatient patrons. Near the valet booth, a scattering of empty vehicles idled, keys in the ignitions. With the butt of his Strider knife, still flecked with Jayla Hill's blood, he knocked hard on the passenger window of a parked BMW. The car alarm screeched to life. As the valets ducked into the key cupboard, searching for the matching fob, Evan stepped into an idling Escalade tricked out with gold trim, tinted windows, and a dashboard statue of Our Lady of Guadalupe. From upgraded speakers, a funk-rock star was singing that a lowrider knows every street, yeah.

Signaling judiciously, he pulled out into traffic, burying the Escalade in the gunged-up vehicular snarl at Western and Wilshire. Anonymous behind tinted glass and cushioned on smooth shocks, he drifted across the potholed streets of downtown. Drivers bopped alongside him to a symphony of sounds not unlike the ones he'd rotated through in his game of musical cars, and he felt a stab of affection for his adopted home, this ragged, messy city in its full multifarious glory, a tumbled-together mash of melting-pot magnificence. An equal-opportunity carjacker, he'd stolen vehicles across the demographic gamut, though he had to admit that driving this Escalade gave him a special thrill. It would've been a dream ride to the foster kid he'd once been and his pack of fellow savages, running the streets of East Baltimore with empty pockets, a wing, and a prayer.

Dipping south, he carved a circuitous route back to where he'd started. The blockades were lifting, and SWAT seemed to have pulled back, but a few sporadic helicopters still spun overhead. LAPD vehicles grew denser as he neared Dr Hill's neighborhood, but they were mostly running patrol routes, a show of vigilance to reassure residents.

He kept away from the row of town houses, taking an eastward approach to the spot where he'd left his truck. The sun had begun its graceful dive to the Pacific, throwing severe slants of bronze through the patchwork streets, rendering them in bars of gold and gray.

His Ford F-150 waited in a puddle of darkness that had pooled in the narrow run of asphalt between warehouses. One of the rectangular vaults in the back held a change of clothes and a pouch of baby wipes, and he cleaned himself up as best he could and swapped garments, transferring the pouch filled with ice and human flesh to his new cargo pants. Stuffing his grimy, blood-spattered clothes into a foil-lined grocery bag he kept on hand for precisely this contingency, he slid behind the wheel.

Minding the speed limit, he drove home in a haze. The pickup fit him, the seat molded to his body, the steering wheel smooth at the ten and two.

Ignoring the valet as usual, he scooted through the porte cochere, sped down the ramp beneath Castle Heights, and slotted his truck in its space between concrete pillars. Getting out, he allowed himself to experience the sensations in his body. A mistake. He groaned like someone twice his age.

Zippered grocery bag swinging at his side, he headed for the stairs to the lobby. He tried to straighten out his limp and tighten his stomach against the sharpness clutching his lower back.

He'd scraped his chin on the ground flinging himself beneath the Suburban. His ribs ached from something or something else, and his palms and knees were scuffed. Splinters dotted his arm from the plywood door. A bruise bloomed on the side of his neck where it had been caught by one of Tanner's thrown elbows and the dull pain at the side of his head hadn't let go. His tailbone throbbed from his tumble down the stairs to the underground bar, but not as much as his left elbow. The skin of his shoulder burned from the sniper round that had kissed his shirt, and his top vertebrae smarted with a whiplash ache from when he'd rocketed the police car up the pillar to the overpass. His stomach tingled from adrenaline and the shot of vodka. The ice bag sweated through his cargo pocket, numbing his thigh. His skeleton felt like a tower of blocks that a single misstep could bring tumbling down.

And yet a cool blue pilot light flickered in his chest undiminished, triumphant. He felt better than he had after that old dame had knocked him down the stairs. No matter what they'd thrown at him, he'd answered.

And answered.

And answered.

Now he wanted nothing so much as to burn his clothes, take a scorching shower, and drink a gallon of vodka.

After running the deadly Rube Goldberg gauntlet that had taken him across half of downtown, he hoped a seamless route through the battle space of the lobby would deliver him to the elevator with minimal interface with the native hostiles.

As was his habit, he paused before opening the door to the lobby. Deep breath in, longer breath out, seating himself in his alias: Evan Smoak, Castle Heights resident, bland and reclusive importer of industrial cleaning supplies.

He stepped inside.

A mob of Castle Heights denizens clamored around the so-called social area, funneling toward the glass doors to the pool. He was spotted immediately by the imperious Hugh Walters, 20C, retiree and longtime Homeowners Association president. 'He's here!' he exclaimed in a warbling, almost feminine cry. 'Just in time!'

Three dozen Castle Heightsians turned to take Evan in, their faces gaping with excitement.

'Special poolside HOA meeting,' Hugh said. 'I knew you'd make it! I knew you'd make it for the vote.'

Evan had a memory flash of a decorative flyer that had been slipped under his door last week, something about a pending election for new leadership. It had featured jaunty personified images of ballot boxes and the gratified cartoon faces of franchised voters. He'd crumpled it immediately into the trash compactor.

Feigning deafness, he pivoted quickly for the elevator, but a wave of residents swept around him, conveying him toward the pool. Trapped in a miasma of coffee fumes and old-lady perfume, he struggled helplessly against the momentum.

'You won't want to miss this one, Mr Smoak.' Arms akimbo, Hugh waited for him at the glass doors, growing ever larger as Evan was borne forward and delivered sacrificially. 'And given all the last-minute campaigning, I will tell you this . . .' Hugh clutched at his heart with mock breathlessness. 'It's been one *crazy* day around here!'

Evan allowed himself to be jostled out onto the pool deck.

For the first time today, he conceded defeat.

24. A Nightmare of His Worst Imagining

In Evan's absence, perfidy and subterfuge had flourished at the Castle Heights Homeowners Association.

For reasons known only to herself and God, Lorilee Smithson, 3F, had spent her recent cosmetic-surgery recuperation reviewing the HOA bylaws. She'd stumbled upon a loophole that permitted a special election by majority vote for the hotly coveted presidency if an emergency meeting was called on the Castle Heights Cryer, a 'good neighbors' app unbeknownst to Evan until this very moment. Due to a legal oversight, the bylaws neglected to specify either a time frame for the announcement or the minimum number of members necessary for a quorum.

In Lorilee's mind, a scheme had taken shape. And it found fertile ground in the resentment she'd been nursing at Hugh's championing of a no-pets policy that had shut down her weekly sleepovers with her cousin's teacup poodle. And so a few weeks ago, while Hugh was visiting an ailing older brother in Sarasota, Lorilee had called a stealth meeting, which she advertised one minute prior to the event. She'd shown up alone and voted herself president, and Hugh had returned to a nightmare of his worst imagining.

Wedged among fellow residents in strappy lawn chairs and chaise longues around the pool, Evan gleaned this sordid history from cross talk and murmuring.

Mia Hall, the DA who lived downstairs from Evan, and her ten-year-old son, Peter, generally provided the only bright spots at these meetings, but they'd taken a long trip back East for the winter holidays. For now, it was just Evan, deposed Hugh, righteous Lorilee, and the usual menagerie of denizens.

Evan's chair was crammed between 17A, a girthy new resident from Charlottesville named Fred Clutterbuck, and octogenarian Ida Rosenbaum of 6G. Though Ida was cranky and senescent, next to the crone who'd poleaxed Evan with the Switch Stick yesterday she was positively in the blush of youth.

The meeting was barely underway but tempers were already running high. At the outset, Hugh scooted around the pool handing out taupe business cards on fine stock. Gold embossed lettering, raised and smooth to the touch, declared: HUGH WALTERS, HOA PRESIDENT, EMERITUS. This subtle bit of electioneering was shut down after Lorilee cited Code 17.6(a), which forbade campaigning materials within one hundred feet of an active HOA meeting.

She conducted the assembly in a stream-of-consciousness monologue while wielding Boba brazenly in a Tory Burch dog purse. At every turn, Hugh raged Lear-like against her machinations until hushed aggressively by hearing-impaired residents.

Keeping the zippered grocery bag containing his bloodstained clothes between his boots, Evan did his best to maintain a human expression on his face and not commit seppuku with his folding knife. At his side, Clutterbuck kept up a steady grumble of unsolicited one-way conversation, pinning in his belly with his forearms so his love handles wouldn't fall over the armrest into his neighbors' laps. He'd proudly informed Evan that he'd attended UVA in 1969, the last year before women were admitted. He'd played football there and then in the Canadian League, after which he'd run an *extremely* successful accountancy firm in Virginia.

Evan steadfastly refused to engage, holding what focus he could muster on the proceedings.

Lorilee gave a dramatic flourish of a throat clear before resuming: 'For some people like I, empathy is a guiding light. My "why" has always been service.'

Evan thought, *My 'why' is not being assailed by idiotic slogans.* A sentiment best reserved for what Joey called his 'inside voice.'

Ready for her close-up, Lorilee was in a Chanel olive-green leisurewear cocoon wrap and skyscraper-tall Jimmy Choo stilettos. Her collagen-swollen cheeks and tumescent lips were heavily makeupped. 'When I ran, I pledged to encourage a kinder energy in our shared halls and –'

Hugh could no longer contain himself. 'You *didn't* run!' He sprang to his feet. 'You manipulated the institutional mechanisms!'

'It's not my fault you were vacationing in the Gulf Coast when the vote took place –'

'Vacationing! My brother had a life-threatening bout of fulminant colitis, you – you spin doctress!'

'As you can see,' Lorilee said, pointedly stroking Boba's fluffy head and casting a sympathetic gaze at her predecessor, 'our legacy HOA culture could use an update.'

Defeated, Hugh sank back into his lawn chair. Pulling his glasses from his flushed face, he polished the lenses with agitation.

Evan's eye throbbed, and the chunk of ear in the ice bag was melting through his pocket. His gaze found the octagonal sign near the spa with emergency-red lettering: PERSONS HAVING CURRENTLY ACTIVE DIARRHEA OR WHO HAVE HAD ACTIVE DIARRHEA WITHIN THE PREVIOUS 14 DAYS SHALL NOT BE ALLOWED TO ENTER THE POOL WATER. Evan had seen it once before on his 'welcome tour.'

He had never used the pool.

'That's why I'm promoting a new culture based on principles of caring and openness,' Lorilee continued. 'The only rule here is that there are no rules.'

That seemed to irritate the shit out of everyone.

'That's not a rule,' Johnny Middleton said.

Fred Clutterbuck was still yammering on and elbowing Evan's bruised rib conspiratorially, Evan gritting his teeth against the pain. Evidently Fred had had two knee replacements and still had some trouble with his Achilles tendons. He'd been a ball boy for the Braves back when they'd been in Milwaukee but had given up baseball after the selfish players' strike of '94 because who wanted to see millionaires who played a game for a living whine about anything?

Lorilee kept going, full steam ahead: 'Which is why for my first order of business as your new HOA president, I wish to revisit birthday-celebration protocols in the social area.'

'Christ on a stick,' Ida muttered. Her violet perfume was making Evan's nasal passages smolder.

'First of all, if you have a party, please bring enough for *everyone* to partake,' Lorilee said. 'And contribute if asked.'

Evan wiggled a loose tooth, tasted a delicate leaking of blood.

'We've had *lots* of issues in the past about who contributed money versus who ate cake,' Lorilee continued. 'You can't just show up and get a treat if you didn't open your clutch purse. And you *must* pitch in if you want your name on the b-day card.'

'What if we don't know the celebrant well?' inquired the Honorable Pat Johnson, 12F. 'Are we expected to contribute the same amount?'

Boba squirmed free of Lorilee's designer bag and trotted around, sniffing ankles. Hugh stared at the free-range dog murderously.

'That's an excellent question, Pat,' Lorilee said. 'My personal belief at this point in time is that when we're celebrating another trip around the sun for a fellow neighbor, we should all contribute equally. It's part of participating in a community. Don't you agree, Hugh?'

Undercut by his own life philosophy, Hugh nodded miserably. Evan was surprised to feel a stab of admiration for the political predator Lorilee had transformed herself into.

'But I'd like to put it to the group,' she said brightly, 'because we all know: teamwork makes the dream work!'

Debate erupted.

Surreptitiously Evan worked a splinter out of the heel of his left hand. He pictured Jayla Hill writhing on the butcher block, her throat cinched, oxygen just out of reach. The meth-heads in the squat house, their human features worn down to wreckage. All those souls scraping by in the tent city with cloudy eyes and dirt-blackened skin. The splinter worked its way to the surface, and he inconspicuously tugged it free with a pinch of his fingernails.

'So to review,' Lorilee said, cutting in on his reverie, 'the key lessons to remember are: One, make sure no one feels left out at cake time.' She ticked off the points on manicured fingers. 'Two, no squirreling away of corner pieces. And thirdly, let us all reward kindness.' Boba ran over to Evan and yapped at his shins. With his boot, he nudged the little annoyance aside. Boba yapped at him twice, stood up on tiny hind legs, and started licking at his cargo pocket, slick with melted ice and the scent of human meat. Using his index finger, Evan pushed her triangular face away, drawing a nip of needle teeth in response.

'In keeping with my policy of full transparency,' Lorilee forged on, 'I'd like to review the minutes from today's meeting to ensure open channels of communication. But not before a special shout-out to my cousin, Coretta, who designed the lobby centerpieces.'

A scattered round of applause began, but Lorilee shrieked, 'Please snap! Clapping startles Boba.'

With zero fucks to give regarding clapping or snapping, the teacup poodle sniffed at the grocery bag holding the blood-soiled clothes at Evan's feet. When he picked up the bag and set it in his lap, the dog went back to his cargo pocket, lapping relentlessly.

He stood up abruptly, Boba tumbling away from his leg. 'I'm sorry,' he said, too loudly. 'I'm not feeling well.'

'Looks like you've had an accident,' Johnny Middleton pointed out helpfully, gesturing at the wet spot at Evan's pocket.

Before the exclamation could draw the crowd's attention, Hugh cried out, 'But we haven't voted on the presidency!'

Lorilee said, 'In our previous quorum –'

Hugh, once more on his feet: 'A quorum of one!'

'We voted to delay any future presidential vote until the next meeting –'

'Is that a royal "we," you nip-and-tucked nincompoop? Because I'm pretty sure it was just *you* at that sham of a proceeding!'

Lorilee's eyes fluttered from the rebuke. 'Only a misogynist would mock a woman's physical appearance in such violent terms.'

'Misogynist? How dare you accuse me of –'

'Words can't be violent,' Clutterbuck said, with a sudden burst of intensity. 'As anyone who's seen *actual* violence knows.'

An explosion of opinions, buzz phrases hurled from left and right.

When Evan shoved Boba aside with his boot, he felt the

day's damage in his tailbone and lower back, kneecaps and palms, shoulders and neck.

As several residents moved to comfort Lorilee, he slipped away.

Evan set the chunk of the Wolf's ear in a bowl of ice on the poured-concrete island in the kitchen.

Then he burned the blood-spattered clothes along with the foil-lined grocery bag.

Then he burned the clothes he'd worn moments ago.

Then he took an extraordinarily hot shower, finished off with two minutes maxed on cold to reduce inflammation and to encourage blood flow and nitric oxide delivery.

Then he applied two butterfly stitches to a thin gash on the ball of his right shoulder that he hadn't bothered to notice until now.

Then he took five milligrams of meloxicam, washing it down with a half gallon of water.

Then he shook himself out on a mini fitness trampoline, bouncing so gently that his feet didn't leave the polypropylene mat. Shuddering the day out of him, memory shards flurrying in his mind – the shot past Jayla's face, the round to the cop's Kevlar vest, the exploding can of spray paint close to the vicinity of beating hearts and makeshift homes. Making mental adjustments, improvements, searching for errors and near misses that could be made less near next time.

Pretty good, he thought. *Pretty good day.*

The timer on his RoamZone dinged seven minutes, long enough to stimulate his lymphatic system and enhance circulation, and he stepped off the tramp.

He was still very, very sore.

The cycle of pain and healing grew more arduous with the years. He missed his twenties.

Wandering back through the kitchen, he stared at the slice of ear floating on ice like a sashimi delicacy. If he had a flow cytometer, a decent imaging system, microtomes, a mass spectrometer, cutting-edge histology gear, pipette pullers, passable electrophysiological equipment, and a solid analytical-software suite, he could sequence the DNA.

Instead he had a jar of cocktail onions, a rind of sourdough bread, and a bottle opener made from a .50-cal bullet casing.

Plan B then.

Of anyone he'd met, Candy McClure knew the most about disposing of and processing human matter. As Orphan V, she also happened to be the most lethal woman he'd ever encountered, though based on what he'd seen today, the Wolf was in the running. Once blood-sworn nemeses, Evan and Candy had settled into an unlikely and occasional collegiality, communicating only when dire circumstances demanded it. He called her on the RoamZone and told her what he needed.

'Jesus Christ, X,' Candy said. 'I'm not who you ring up when you have a severed ear. Call me when you need to break out of a Siberian prison or something befitting a murderess of my eminence.'

She hung up on him.

He grimaced at the dead phone, set it down, and took another five milligrams of meloxicam. It was above the recommended dose, but he was living life on the edge.

He trudged down the hall at the end of the great room, passing the katana sword mounted on the wall.

As soon as he settled onto his floating bed, exhaustion overtook him. He had just enough energy to text Joey.

Dr Hill was murdered.

An instant reply: wtf?! And then: did u get loco?

It took Evan a full three seconds to process.

Sofia's dog. Loco. Fuck.

Not yet, he typed. Be here at oh six hundred. We have a lot to dig into.

yes sir, boss-man sir. shall i bring u yr caramel macchiato w/ 2.5 sweet n lows?

What's a macchiato?

ur the worst, x

You're the worst, too.

25. Too Tired

Evan stirred in the middle of the night. His calf itched but he was too tired to reach and scratch it. So he lay there and let it itch.

Soon he was asleep again.

26. The Space-Time Shit-Talking Continuum

Evan woke up with hot dog breath in his face.

From deep in his slumber he'd sensed the condo alarm give a personalized alert when Joey had entered, so he didn't spring awake with lethal intent. Instead he opened his eyes groggily to get a fish-eye-lens view of Dog the dog's enormous snout resting on his pillow. Dog's nostrils were shoved up against his own nose close enough that he could feel flecks of moisture across his cheeks with each canine exhalation. The hound grinned broadly, his tail wagging forcefully enough to power a speedboat.

Joey stood behind Dog, fists on hips. From those fists protruded a Milky Way Midnight Dark, a can of Red Bull, a brownie in plastic wrap, and various other snack items. They looked like junk-food fans emerging from her sides. In a feat of incompetence, both Doc Martens were untied. Her T-shirt read: SERVICE DOGS ARE LIKE BOOBS. DO NOT TOUCH WITHOUT CONSENT.

Evan said, 'Subtle.'

Joey glanced down at the block lettering. 'All the old people up in here have no idea what do with that so they leave me and Dog alone.'

'In the wake of a recent coup at the HOA,' Evan said groggily, 'pets are allowed.'

After getting pinballed around Los Angeles yesterday, he didn't want to move, because he knew the kind of pain awaiting him once he did. Plus he wasn't eager for Joey to see his new cornucopia of bruises.

Joey studied him, shaking her head, a grin tugging at the left side of her mouth. ''Member when you got knocked down the stairs by a little old lady?'

He did.

'Know what's a damn shame?'

He did not.

'Well,' she said, 'from coming up on the streets, you get how shit-talk's *supposed* to go?'

He did.

'It's gotta escalate, right? Like you tell the story a little different every time, exaggerate it more and more. But you know what the thing is?'

He did not.

'What happened to you, it's *so pathetic* I can't even exaggerate it. Like if you got beat up by *two* little old ladies with canes that would be *less pathetic* than what you pulled off. So congratulations, X. You did it. You broke the space-time shit-talking continuum.'

Dog lapped at Evan's face until he shoved himself up, sheets across his waist. He felt even more sore than he'd anticipated. His bones ached from the *inside*.

'Shit, X,' Joey said. 'You're all banged up.' Her phone dinged and she tugged it out, checking the text. 'What happened?'

'I escaped a manhunt blockading ten square miles of downtown LA.'

'Huh,' she said, preoccupied, flicking through her screen. A cartoon UCLA Bruin smiled at Evan from a sticker on the back of her iPhone. 'Guess what? I got picked to pledge a sorority.'

It was the first he'd heard her express any interest in the Greek system; she'd been mostly focused on creatively insulting her computer-science professors, whom she ran circles around to their eternal chagrin. Increasingly she'd been cutting out of lectures to audit graduate courses in quantum physics, bioinformatics, and anything else that didn't require her to slow her brain down to a snail-crawl pace. In most regards, Josephine Morales was a difficult human to contain.

Dog lunged up onto the bed, a hundred and fifteen pounds of ridgeback, and settled down into his trademark croissant shape with a harrumph.

Evan said, 'Can you get the damn –'

'A sorority, X!' Joey said, eyes still on her phone. 'It's one of them rich-white-girl ones like from the movies and they're having "diversity outreach."' The air quotes she threw were confused by wagging candy bars and – was that a sack of gummy Coke bottles? 'So it was me and another Latina girl, and a black girl who didn't show up. And these sorority girls, they meet all their brown people on Twitter so they think we're all sensitive and shit! Imagine knowing so few Mexicans that you think we're all woke!' She laughed. 'I mean, with my maunt?' – Joey's mom-aunt, who had raised her before she went into foster care. 'It was all Jesús all the time!' She crossed herself now in earnest. 'She had this one ugly-ass stone Jesús garden statue she refused to get rid of 'cuz superstition, and it got all worn down from the weather, distorted and nasty. It looked like Grimace from McDonald's – the fat purple one, and –'

'I know who Grimace is.'

'Well, ex-*squeeeeze* me, didn't know you'd be pop-culturally literate all of a sudden when usually, you're all like: "What is this information age of which you younglings speak?" Anyhowz –' Her gaze flicked up, caught on his shoulder. 'What's that sorry-ass wound dressing?' Reaching out, she ripped off the fraying butterfly stitches.

'*Ow.*'

'Ow's right. You need proper stitches, not this ragged shit. Hang on.' She disappeared into the bathroom, still talking. 'And these rich girls are so funny, X! They mistake their inside voice for their "speak truth to power" voice so everything's all overly profound and sincere. One of them apologized to me and Silvia – she's the other Latina – 'cuz she was eating a taco! Like it's cultural appropriation and shit.'

Evan heard the secret door to the Vault hinge open, and Joey's words took on an echo: 'And I was all like, I don't apologize to you white bitches every time I drive a monster truck. And they all laughed. They think I'm *funny*, X.'

'I've heard sorority girls are easily amused,' he told Dog, who joined the sentiment with a glance of his red saggy eyes.

'I *heard* that.' Joey emerged with a Navy SEAL medic kit slung over one shoulder. 'Scoot,' she told Dog, who scooted over on the sheets, leaving a liberal trail of slobber.

Plopping down beside Evan, Joey unzipped the kit, flung it open, and pulled out the suture set. She swiped an alcohol pad across his wound without an ounce of tenderness and then pinched the curved needle in the tweezer clamp of the driver and readied the point.

Evan said, 'There's a vial of lidocaine –'

'I couldn't find it.'

'You didn't look!'

'You don't need *lidocaine* for two tiny stitches. When did you turn into such a wuss?' The needle popped the surface tension of his skin and then he felt a burn and a tugging as she threaded it expertly up and out the other side.

'Josephine! What are you using, a knitting needle?'

'Quit squirming. Sit still.' More poking and pulling and surface pain. The emerald glittered in her nose, the diamond pendant at her throat. She smelled like vanilla and Red Vines.

'Dayum, X. You're hella bruised like *everywhere*. What happened to you anyways?'

He winced as the needle dipped once more. 'I escaped a manhunt blockading ten square miles of downtown LA,' he repeated.

'Huh,' she said again, absently. 'And at first I was all like, "I don't need to be your token brown girl for your stupid sorority, right? If all you Mary-Kate and Ashleys are really oh so politically conscious go down to East Los and help the real *Raza*.' She busted out the pristine accent. 'Not Silvia from the fucking Palisades.'

'Or you,' Evan said.

'*Me?*' Joey yanked the needle, the wound cinched shut, and she bit off the thread and tied it off with a few expert flicks of her fingers. She had on her lopsided smirk now. 'I *am* real *Raza*. The Man's been keeping me down my whole life.'

'You're a supervillain hacker with a trust fund,' Evan said. 'The Man *wishes* he could keep you down.'

She slapped a Band-Aid over the stitches with more emphasis than the occasion called for, and Evan took care not to give her the satisfaction of seeing him wince.

Evan gazed glumly at legion shed dog hairs on his sheets. He nudged Dog in the ribs, and Dog flew up with a yowl and hopped off the bed. 'Can I get dressed?'

Joey said, 'Not in front of me, you can't.'

'I wasn't implying –'

She was up once more, heading back to the Vault with the medic kit. 'Hurry up already. We got work to do.'

Once she entered the bathroom, he started throwing on clothes. Her voice boomed out through the secret door to the Vault, which she'd left hinged open. 'But it's kinda fun. This sorority stuff. And I sorta want to belong. But does that make me self-loathing?'

Evan yanked on cargo pants, nearly tripping, feeling a fresh ache in his hip flexors. 'There are lots of reasons for you to be self-loathing,' he said. 'But I don't think this is one of them.'

'Or,' Joey's disembodied voice continued, 'should I get in and do a takeover from within? Turn it into, dunno, a façade for a white-hat hacktivist group. We'd be sinking foreign governments from behind the ivy walls of Slamma Whamma Girlchik!'

He brushed his teeth and hurried into the Vault. Joey finished relacing her Doc Martens and then tossed the medic kit over by the weapon lockers, where it landed in a slump against the wall. He picked it up, zipped it properly, and put it in its place.

Heading back out, she peeled the Milky Way bar and dropped the wrapper somewhere in the air space above the trash can. As it floated wide, he caught it, crumpled it up, and made sure it hit its target.

Grabbing a tissue to wipe chocolate from his hands, he said, 'You would've made a shitty bomber pilot.'

'I looked at all the police reports on Doc Hill,' she continued, logjamming with Dog at the door to the shower before popping through. 'First up, no dog found at the scene. So if Doc Hill had Loco at one point, he's missing now.'

'I need to fill you in on –'

She darted through the bedroom, down the hall, popping open a bag of Lay's Limón chips on her way through the great room. Evan stayed at her heels.

Her words jumbled through loud munching: 'Gun found at the scene was a shit .22, a ghost weapon just like one a yours. Oh – and Hill had a brand-new alarm. But guess what? The panel wasn't connected yet! Dude's the principal deep-learning scientist at Solventry and he didn't hook up the panel!'

As she conveyed another vigorous helping of Lay's to her mouth, a dusting of chips struck the poured-concrete floor. Dog the dog lapped them up vigorously, leaving a mucus smear from his nose. Evan crouched, mopping the slime with the tissue.

'So I'm thinking the killer had no idea the alarm wasn't live and unhooked it for obvious reasons.' In the kitchen, Joey plopped down the sweating can of Red Bull onto the island and herself onto a stool before it.

Evan grabbed a coaster, waited for Joey to take a sip, and hockey-pucked the coaster the length of the island to stop beneath her can as she set it down.

She didn't notice, having moved on to the unwrapping of her brownie. 'I looked into Doc Hill some. Aside from the fact that he was, like, one of the world's leading experts in AI, he seems cool ay eff and from what I can tell he's squeaky clean. Been at Solventry only three months – FreeWillPower, the AI division. What he does there's all secretive and stuff 'cuz Big tech, but it seems to involve bioinformatics. He played with that at his last gig doing medical research at Carnegie Mellon in the throat-cancer ward. That's how his wife died. I guess she grew up in a house with asbestos, hypopharyngeal cancer spread to laryngeal cancer, and –' She performed a sliced-throat, cocked-head gesture, her tongue protruding to complete the Q sign.

Her next brownie chomp freed crumbs across her shirt and the counter, and Evan wondered, not for the first time, if Joey actually had an esophagus or if she just nom-nom-nommed like the Cookie Monster, sending foodstuffs outward. He circled her with a wet paper towel, capturing the crumbs and the splash of Red Bull liberated when she slammed the can down, of course to the side of the coaster. It was probably her second Red Bull of the morning. Or third. Or maybe Red Bull ran through her veins and she was merely topping off her bloodstream.

'There was this interview with him in *Carnegie Mellon Today* and he said when she lost her voice he wanted to give it back to her,' Joey continued. 'AI modeling for vocal restoration. But he didn't get the tech there until after she passed away. It was, like, super emotional to read.'

She finally halted to swallow or draw breath.

And then Evan realized: Her gaze was stuck on the chunk of flesh resting on ice in the salad bowl at the far end of the island. 'Is that a . . . ear?'

'It is.'

She shrugged. 'Okay.' Another bite of brownie, some of which seemed to make it into her mouth. Her attention returned to the ear. She couldn't help it. 'You gonna read me in already? You were all like, "Get here at ass-crack hun-dred"' – she made texty fingers – 'and I've been here for like eleventy hours and you haven't bothered to say anything.' She gestured with her gnawed brownie at the Wolf's ear. 'So. Tell me what happened already.'

He told her.

She listened intently, bobbing her head from time to time. The rate of her chewing even slowed, if slightly. When he was done, she scowled. 'Dayum, X,' she said. 'So you took the ear for the DNA?'

'Yes.'

'How you gonna sequence it? Did you ask your fremesis?'

'Who?'

'Candy. I assume that's who you'd start with. How'd it go?'

'Not well.'

He gave Joey a few seconds of silence to relish that. The

only sound was Dog across the great room still dumbly licking the spot on the floor that Joey had watered with potato chips.

'Can you figure it out for me?' he said.

'DNA sequencing an ear chunk from a mysterious lady assassin?' Joey shrugged once more. For her, shrugging was a language unto itself. 'I'll figure out who to ask.'

'I need you to take point on the canine investigation, too, now, because obviously I have to –'

'"Canine investigation"? Canine investigation! Did you just call it a *canine investigation*? Like phrasing it all formal's gonna sell me on it. "Congrats, Police Sergeant Morales, you got promoted to the *canine investigation*."'

'Joey.'

'"Crack the canine investigation, young missy, and you'll get a star on the wall at Langley."' She was laughing at him, that hair-thin gap in her front teeth on charming display. 'Yes, out of the goodness of my heart I'll help look for a mangy mutt named Loco near his last-knowns but –'

'*And,*' he cut in before she could gain further momentum, 'I need you to find out what you can about Solventry and Dr Hill. Whatever this hit on him was about, it was top-level. The assassin they sent was prepared, well-stocked. Untraceable throw-down gun for the crime scene, long gun from the roof of the Burger King, then she came up with a Manurhin MR73 Gendarmerie in the tent city.'

Joey whistled. 'She got her hands on a Manurhin MR73?'

'Those don't just float around. See what databases you can get into – sales, trades, where they're registered. I know it's a long shot but kick over some rocks.'

''Kay.'

'Also – the body I left behind in the abandoned store near

Dr Hill's town house? I believe Tanner was his name and he claimed to be an army veteran. Dig for any connection between him and the Wolf.'

'The Wolf,' Joey said, trying out the name.

'She's a stone-cold professional.'

'Orphan V level?'

'Orphan V level.'

For the first moment perhaps ever, Joey was silent.

'Taking out Dr Hill was a big move,' Evan continued. 'I want to know everything. His personal finances, extracurriculars, what he was working on –'

'Whoa whoa whoa.' Joey flew up, brownie in hand, and flopped down on the modern armless couch near the heavy bag station. 'You want me to peel back security at Solventry to jump into his workflow? That's like asking me to hack into Amazon's AWS data center in NoVA to find their algorithm for distributing EC2 images across machines.' She snorted indelicately. 'Which I've done. But! It's gonna be full-time. We're talking Red Bull marathon sessions in the Vault.'

Evan pictured Jayla Hill writhing on that butcher block. Now in a hospital room under police guard with an assassin circling the waters.

'Whatever you have to do.' He sank onto the couch next to her, considered the sacrifice of allowing the wreckage of his penthouse at her hands for a greater cause, and forced out the offer: 'Need to stay here a few days?'

Joey finished the last of her brownie, contemplated. 'Well, I've already watched Netflix. Like *all of it*. So yeah, nothing more to do at my place. I can move into the Vault and get it done here. If you're not all annoying breathing down my neck and – and *cleaning* all the time.'

'Give me the sitrep when I get back.'

'Where you going?'

'To see Jayla Hill in her hospital room. She's at the Downtown Medical Center under police protection. Break into the hospital database and put me on the guest list as family. I'll gauge the security and see if I can sneak by to see her.'

'Family? Have you *seen* your skin tone?'

'Say I'm an uncle by marriage. And wipe the record after I'm gone.'

'Which legend you want me to use?'

He thought a moment. 'Marv Miller.'

Resisting the urge to wipe the fresh avalanche of crumbs from the leather cushions, he moved to rise.

'X – shit. I forgot to ask.'

'What's that?'

The words bubbled out through barely contained laughter: ''Member when you got your ass beat by Geriatric Ginny and a folding cane?'

'I thought we were done with this because I broke the continuum.'

'Yeah, well. I lied.'

Evan placed a foot gently on Joey's hip and shoved her off the couch. Cracking up, she brought most of the crumbs with her onto the floor.

It was worth it.

27. Duh

A glossy flyer fluttered beneath the windshield wiper of Evan's F-150. Irritated, he cast a glance around Castle Heights' subterranean parking lot. Every vehicle had been similarly papered.

Plucking the flyer free, he was unsurprised to see Hugh Walters's face peering out from the top like a custom monogram. Part corporate headshot, part Realtor bus-stop portrait, the photo looked as if it had been shot through cheesecloth. Beneath this grinning vignette of solidity, Hugh's myriad legislative accomplishments were bullet-pointed.

- *Overhauled morning beverage selection in lobby*
- *Oversaw transition to 'green' cleaning supplies*
- *Replenished funds for Howdy Nu Neighbor!™ gift baskets*

And so on.

Evan crumpled up the flyer and tossed it at the trash can beside the pillars goalposting his parking spot.

Hugh melted from the shadows near the blue recycling dumpster with catlike guile. 'Mr Smoak!'

The crumpled flyer hit the side of the trash can and rolled to a stop before Hugh's tasseled Florsheims. Evan and Hugh stared at it awkwardly.

Hugh cleared his throat. 'I just wanted to inquire as to whether you had a chance to review my record, so to speak.'

'Yup,' Evan said. 'All good.'

Hugh crouched to pick up the flyer, unfurled it, and

smoothed it against his khakied thigh. 'And to know if I can answer any questions for you.'

'Nope. All good.'

Evan started to climb into his truck.

'It's not just a figurehead position, you know,' Hugh said, his voice growing strident. 'There are real-world responsibilities to being an HOA president. Fire codes to be upheld . . .'

Evan closed the door. Hugh approached, still talking. Due to the Kevlar shields hanging inside the door panels, Evan's windows did not roll down, an inconvenience for which he now felt unbridled gratitude.

A blast of music caused him to start in his seat: *DONCHA WISH YER GIRLFRIEND WUZ HAAAWT LIKE ME?!*

He made a mental note to change the RoamZone's damn ringtone.

With relief he gestured at Hugh with the phone – *Gotta take this* – and clicked to answer. Before he could speak, an impatient eleven-year-old voice asked, 'Well?'

'Huh?'

Sofia asked, 'Did you find Loco?'

Just beyond the driver's window, Hugh's mouth was still moving – *contend with rot and erosion in the roofing underlayment* – and Evan found himself wishing he'd never learned to read lips.

He gestured at the phone once more helplessly and slammed the truck into reverse. 'I tracked him down to a new location and spotted him there but then I lost him again.'

As he squealed into a three-point turn, Hugh remained in front of the truck, pinned by the dueling headlights, lips flapping – *maintenance of the pool filtration system* . . .

'You lost Loco?' Sofia sounded heartbroken. 'How could you lose him?'

'There were some . . . complications.' Evan drove past

Hugh, offering an inane wave and blasting up toward day-light. 'And he scampered away. But now I know what part of town he's in.'

'So are you there now?'

'No. But I've dispatched an associate to stay on it.'

'An *associate*! I want *you*. I called *you*.'

'Which is why I'm overseeing everything.'

'What if he gets hit by a car? Or gets dognapped by a homeless guy who can't afford to feed him? You know the ones who have these starving little pups and their cardboard signs asking for dog food?'

'This associate of mine, she knows how to get into secur-ity cameras everywhere. All over the city. She's going to be searching for Loco in the area where I spotted him. She's the best I know. I'll get back to you as soon as I hear anything.'

'Dad said you could find him. Dad said you could do *anything*.'

Evan cut right onto Wilshire, beelining for downtown. 'Andre said that?'

'Yeah. He gets all braggy about you.'

Evan didn't know what to say. The Fifth Commandment, his least favorite: *If you don't know what to do, do nothing*. He did nothing.

Sofia said, 'I think it's 'cuz . . .'

'What?'

'I think it's 'cuz Dad doesn't have a whole lot else,' Sofia said.

An odd sensation stirred to life in Evan's rib cage. It had scarcely occurred to him what he might mean to his half brother. Or that one could derive pride in a familial associ-ation. He pictured the man who was his father – that loose-limbed saunter, the mirror-gazing, the near-pathological detachment masked in nonchalance – and felt only the opposite. A revulsion at the primordial sludge of DNA he'd somehow emerged from. He caught himself, forced his focus outward.

'You,' Evan said. 'He's proud of you.'

'Duh,' Sofia said, and hung up.

28. No Voice

According to the medical files Joey had hacked into and texted to Evan, Jayla Hill was stable and recuperating in her private room at the Downtown Medical Center. The Wolf's zip tie had crushed her larynx and fractured the surrounding cartilage structures, which meant there was a chance that she might not speak again. She'd been held for additional tests, visited twice by an aunt, her father's sister. No other visitors had been put onto the guest list aside from Evan under his alias.

The police protection was less than exemplary. Two uniforms sipped coffee by the elevators. Another had parked himself with a magazine on a folding chair at the end of the hall near the nurses' station. They'd eyeballed Evan's visitor badge with its green block lettering – CLEARED – and let him walk by with barely a glance.

When he stepped into Jayla's room, he was struck by the scent of fresh-cut flowers from the windowsill. She lay in bed facing away on her side, knees tucked close to her chest. The position – small, frail, childlike – struck a note of quiet fury in Evan. A band of raw flesh wrapped Jayla's neck, visible above the bump of her C2. On the padded guest chair rested an unzipped duffel bag, GRAND ARTS HIGH lettered in teal on its side. A mess of personals were visible inside, no doubt hastily thrown together by the aunt. Bra, shirt, small box of tampons, loose toothbrush. An abundant life reduced to bare functions.

He tapped gently on the open door and she rolled over, her eyes flaring. A gauzy bandage covered her throat in the front, and that blown blood vessel fissured her right eye. Her lips parted silently and she gazed wildly at the door, no doubt looking for one of the cops.

He held out his hands. 'Don't worry. I'm just here to talk with you.'

She shot upright, eyes now narrowing with recognition. Her mouth gaped once more, lips wobbling, and he realized she was trying to talk. Nothing came out but a rush of scratchy air.

'It's okay. I can get you paper.'

Her face contorted with frustration. Her fingers curled inward, hands cupped, and then she flung them out toward him as if ridding herself of something. Then she flattened her hands, her right palm pushing in to slap twice at her left.

At first he mistook her gestures as a display of aggravation but there was a controlled nature to them that snagged a thread of awareness. When Jayla's mother had lost her voice to cancer, her father had devoted himself to restoring it. As a family, the Hills would have figured out a new means of communication.

'Hang on.' Evan stepped closer. 'Say it again.'

The same motions, more vehemently rendered: I don't want paper.

As part of Evan's operational training, Jack had made sure he familiarized himself with a range of languages, including the basics of ASL. Evan wasn't very good at expressing himself in sign but his receptive language was strong enough to follow along.

'I understand,' he said.

She signed at him furiously, her lips moving: Who are you?

'No one important.'

The cops think you did this to me.

He shrugged.

I told them about the lady but they only saw you.

'That doesn't matter.'

Why are there so many cops?

'To keep you safe from her.'

A wave moved across her face, tightening her skin, popping her mouth slightly open – a look of fear so pure that for a single piercing moment she looked like a little girl.

Why does she want to hurt me? Because I saw her face?

'Yes.'

She thinks I can lead the cops to her?

'To her employer. That's what she can't risk.'

Who's her employer?

'I'm going to find that out.'

Jayla chewed her chapped bottom lip. Her eyes were bruised, her skin dry, hair tangled, and she had an over-under look that was vulnerable as hell. She scratched at an elbow.

Why are you here?

'I want to find the lady who killed your father.'

Her eyes welled. With her forehead furrowed, she pounded her palm harder on the syllable, talking the word to life with her entire body: Why?

'So she can't hurt you again.'

Her head pulled back ever so slightly. She looked confused.

Such a bright kid, lobbing one question after another to get her bearings despite everything she'd been through.

Were you there to hurt my dad?

'No. I heard a crash inside. The door was unlocked.'

A nurse passed by the doorway, and through some shared awareness they paused their conversation. Evan noted that no police officer had walked by to check the room since his arrival.

Jayla's motions drew his attention once more: Why did you have a gun?

'I always carry a gun.'

To hurt people?

'When they deserve it.'

When do they deserve it?

'When they try to kill a young woman.'

Like me. Raised eyebrows, head tilted forward. A question.

'Yes.'

A tear rolled over the brink of one eye and tracked down her cheek. She made no move to wipe it. She nodded. Then: Will you get her? The lady who killed Dad? Who wants to kill me?

'Yes. But I need your help.'

Pointer finger to her mouth, then pulling it out and away, then bunched fingers tapping the center of her chest: Tell me.

'Did your father have any enemies?'

A vehement head shake.

'Did he owe any money?'

No. That wasn't Dad. Dad was pay-your-credit-cards-on-time. Dad was get-your-taxes-right. Dad was work-hard-and-tell-the-truth.

'Anything unusual happening in his life? Any changes?'

Work was . . . Fingertips to her temples, rocking the hands slightly.

'I don't know what that means.'

She made fists and pounded her thighs with frustration. Then: *She took my voice. I don't have a voice. I'm a singer and I don't have a voice.*

'I know,' Evan said. 'But I need an answer right now. "Work was . . ." Can you spell the last word?'

She grabbed a cell phone hidden in the sheets, typed on it, and thrust the screen to face him: STRESSFUL.

'Why?'

Back to speaking through her hands. New job. He reported straight to the big boss.

'The big boss? Who's the big boss?'

She typed the name on her cell: ALLMAN. The phone cast aside, signing once more: Dad was a big deal. Tears spilling freely now. He was so smart. Doing big things.

'Like what?'

Dad worked on – she spelled out the letters individually – *AI*. A hesitation. *And* . . . Then she tapped out on her phone: ALGORITHMS.

'What specifically was he doing for Allman?'

I don't know. He didn't talk about it. Then came a flappy hand and finger motion Evan couldn't keep up with, followed by a squeezing motion at the mouth.

'I'm sorry. Can you write it?'

CORPORATE CONFIDENTIALITY. She signed three letters – NDA. Then: I don't know. I'm not into that stuff. I'm a singer and dancer. Like Mom.

The word dancer was beautiful. Her left hand flat, two fingers of her right forked like legs, shaking back and forth above the dance floor of the palm, her head mirroring the movement ever so slightly and with grace. She had tears in her eyes. Mother and father, both gone.

Fiercely: That's all I know.

'Okay. Can I have your phone number?'

A vigorous nod. She signed it quickly and he keyed it into his RoamZone and dialed. Her phone buzzed twice and she stilled it. Now she had a cover telephone number that would forward through to him. They stared at each other. She looked as helpless as he felt.

Dad was gentle. He was kind.

'I understand.'

They said I can't go home. It's not safe. And even if it was, they have to do a . . . Her breath seized in her chest and then shuddered out. She finished the thought: deep cleaning.

'I'm sorry.'

What am I supposed to do now?

For a moment, Evan couldn't find words.

Impassioned slaps of skin, vowel noises from the throat. *What am I supposed to do? He was my dad.*

'Do you have people?'

Right hand, outward-facing fist tracing tiny circles near her jawline, below the nose to indicate the feminine: Aunt.

'Do you like her?'

Her face looked tragic, resigned: Sure.

She scratched at the back of her neck, raising fingernail marks. Evan remembered how his black foster brothers hated when their skin got ashy, the shame they felt attached to it, as if it were their fault any more than the duct tape that had held his sneakers together.

She sat with her shoulders slumped and her bruised eyes. *He was the only thing I had left. I don't even have a voice anymore. He was my North Star. What do I do?*

He owed her the truth. There was nothing else to give her. 'You have to be your own North Star now.'

She blinked at him. Her mouth was slightly agape, and he could see the faint flutter of her heartbeat at the side of her neck. He wanted to fix everything for her. He wanted to tell her it would all be okay.

Without any perceptible movement of her limbs, she slid down once more and turned away.

He withdrew quietly.

Down in the gift shop, he found a bottle of shea-butter lotion like the one Tyrell's sister used back in the day and cut with water to make it last. On the ride up he shared the elevator with a bald teenage boy in a wheelchair. Evan held the door open, but the kid said, 'I got it,' and rolled out angrily.

Back to Jayla's room. She was still lying on her side, her rib cage slowly rising and falling. He weighed the bottle in his

153

hand, thinking twice. What a useless fucking gesture, bringing lotion to a girl who'd just lost her sole parent.

Evan dropped the bottle into her duffel bag along with a burner phone and slipped out.

The chair by the nurses' station was empty. He halted by the counter. 'Where's the cop?'

Chewing the end of a pencil with vigor, the nurse didn't look up from her monitor. 'Bathroom.'

Only one cop remained at the elevator and he was turned toward the wall, on a phone call, joking with someone in a manner Evan took to be flirtatious.

He went down to where he'd parked at a metered space a block away; he preferred to avoid parking lots with their choke points and controlled exits. Sitting behind the wheel of his F-150, he stared through the windshield. A few empty patrol cars remained parked near the ER.

The bad feeling started in his gut and wormed its way outward. The response was half-assed, security theater more than effective protection. LAPD wasn't taking this as seriously as they needed to with a killer like the Wolf out there. He would've felt better if Jayla were in WITSEC. He trusted the Marshals across the board, especially when it came to hiding and protecting people.

But he couldn't exactly call in a security upgrade. Nor could he kidnap Jayla to protect her without bringing on a storm of complications.

For a time he watched people stream out of the high-rise parking structure and into the hospital, limping or wheeling their broken way along, sipping coffee, consoling one another.

He considered various courses of action, disliking each more than the last.

Sometimes there were only bad options.

A decision had to be made, no matter how brutal.

He started up his rig, banked into the parking structure, and rode up to the empty fifth level. The south-facing perimeter looked out through open air onto the hospital. He found a spot across from Jayla's room. After backing in, he opened one of the locked vaults in the bed of his truck and pulled out his Savage 110 Elite Precision Left Hand bolt-action.

Millions of Savage 110s had been purchased off the shelf, so if he ever left behind a spent cartridge casing, he didn't have to worry as much about ballistic forensics. Chambered in 7.62x51 mm NATO, the sniper rifle was good for anything between seventy-five and one thousand meters. Tommy had configured it for a scope – a Leupold Mark 6 3–18x44 with the standard mil-dot reticle that Evan had been using long before it had become an FBI Hostage Response Team standard.

Bellying down in the back of his pickup, he found Jayla through the scope, in bed facing the window. Aside from the steel-cable railing beneath him, he felt like he was floating over the street.

Her eyes were open. A dark spot beneath her cheek showed where the pillow had absorbed her tears.

Putting his RoamZone on speaker, he called the hospital and asked to be put through to her room. When the phone rang, she popped up nervously and stared at it, unsure what to do. It rang and rang some more. Finally she picked it up.

'It's me,' he said. 'You can't see me but I can see you through the window if you'd like to talk to me.'

Her gaze swung in his direction.

'When we're done with this call, power down and throw away your cell phone so you can't be tracked. I put a burner phone in your duffel bag with my number keyed into it. I won't call you until it's safe for you to go home.'

Wait? What?

'Please get beneath the bed. I'm going to put a bullet through the window. A viable assassination attempt will get the feds involved and they'll move you somewhere safe with real protection. And then I will end this.'

Phone pinched between shoulder and cheek, her hands flurrying. *What? No.*

'I'm sorry.'

I'm scared.

'I understand.'

I can't go away. I have no voice. How am I supposed to . . .

He couldn't translate the last words, but he could guess at them.

She was on her feet now, signing furiously. Her little hands, her little face, and that dancer's carriage, shoulders back, proud chest. *I don't want you to do this.*

'I understand.'

I don't want to go away somewhere.

'I understand. Get under the bed now.'

No. No. No no no no no no!

He waited. Her motions died down. Her shoulders slumped, rolled forward. She looked broken.

Her hands lifted halfheartedly, lowered, rose again, hesitated tremulously. *Will you come back for me? When it's over?*

'Yes.'

And take me home?

'Yes.'

She hung up, turned off the phone, and dropped it into the trash can. Then she lowered herself from view.

He checked for pedestrians below, waited two full seconds, and then put a round through the upper left corner of the pane. The glass exploded, blowing across the floor and waterfalling down to the curb.

Within seconds, police officers flew into the room, shouting into radios.

Evan hopped out of the truck's bed, slid the sniper rifle home in the vault, and drove away. When he turned out of the parking structure, backup units were already flying up the street, sirens screaming.

As he pulled onto the street, he hesitated, looking up. His eyes snagged on the fifth level, a chill tightening the skin at the back of his neck.

A black-clad form stared down at him from the precise spot from which he'd taken the shot. Balaclava mask, short feminine build, head cocked.

At her side the Wolf held a sniper rifle, its butt resting on the floor. Her vehicle wasn't visible; it seemed she'd rushed over from another hide.

She'd just missed her shot at Jayla.

They both knew that she wouldn't have time to raise the rifle and find him in the scope.

Plus, given the incoming torrent of PD, she had to get out of there. Tugging off her balaclava, she shook out her ice-blond hair.

She gave him a little salute, two fingers tapping the forehead. *Well done,* the gesture seemed to say. *See ya around.*

He nodded in return and hit the gas.

29. The Full Bezos

When Evan got home, the penthouse was silent, which concerned him.

From the brief foyer, he spotted Dog the dog in a dignified sitting posture, his head cocked. He was staring in the direction of the Velcro wall that Joey had installed against Evan's will when he'd made the mistake of allowing her to oversee a phase of a remodel.

He turned in to the great room and spotted Joey floating a third of the way up the wall, hanging like a painting. Ballooned slightly by her Velcro suit, she'd adhered herself horizontally, cheek propped pertly on a fist, her other hand clutching one of his Ralph Lauren martini glasses, which – he was relieved to see – was empty. From her fingers wrapped around the crystal stem, an unlit cigarette protruded from a slender Bakelite holder. A sequined shawl was draped across the front of her like an apron so as not to interfere with the hooks and loops, and she'd clamped a flapper wig over her hair, which floated unevenly atop her unruly mane like a bad toupee, completing the Zelda-Fitzgerald-sprawled-across-a-divan tableau.

He had no idea how long she'd been there in her suspended pose, waiting for his arrival.

He paused, taking her in. Her eyes flicked to him, but otherwise she didn't move. Her mouth twitched, but she did not break. Dog gave a soft whine like a horse whinny.

Evan walked past her, expressionless.

'Whatever are you doing now, my dear chap?' she asked, in

what he imagined that *she* imagined to be some sort of fancy Daisy Buchanan accent.

'Working out,' he said.

He went into the master suite, closed the door, and tugged on his gear. By the time he emerged, she'd changed costume and position. Now she was angled severely downward with a tailored gray skirt suit jacket fluttering up and pasted to the wall above her, revealing the chubby bulge of the Velcro suit beneath, and a scarf that likewise trailed toward the ceiling. Unfurled to its full length, her hair was pulled upward as well, completing the impression that she was plummeting to her death. Her mouth was open in a silent scream.

The pose was majestic, a piece of living art. It called to mind Kim Novak in *Vertigo*. He'd watched the film with Jack; at Jack's behest, they'd seen most of Hitchcock. Evan wondered if that's where Joey had picked up the visual reference, and a pulse of warmth moved through his heart at the familial overlap.

Dog held his perplexed vigil, his head now tilted in the opposite direction. Joey's former costume was puddled on one of the couches.

Evan headed to the free weights.

'Young man,' she cried in a tremulous voice as he passed. '*Now* what are you doing that you can't help a damsel in distress?'

'Working out,' he said.

'For shame!'

He made sure he was past her before he cracked a smile.

As he hit the bench press, he heard her grunting, the sound of Velcro tearing free, a thump as she hit the floor, and then a quiet stream of Spanish curse words as she tussled with the suit to free herself.

He started doing freestanding handstand push-ups.

It was hard.

Harder than when he was twenty.

Harder than when he was thirty.

Her footsteps approached and then a shadow fell over him. She poked him in the ribs and he collapsed.

'What the hell, X. I hear there's a new app called a sense of humor. Maybe you should download it.'

His muscles took the opportunity to remind him of the wear and tear he'd put them through. He stared up at her face, which glared upside down at him. He noticed now that she'd rouged her cheeks in red circles to emphasize the chill of the suicidal fall.

'A sorority girl might find it amusing,' he said. 'But I'm more urbane.'

'Ur*bane*? More like a hood rat.' She scowled at him but there was mirth in it. She dug a toe into a trigger point in his intercostals with Orphan proficiency. 'And yanking my hair outta Velcro? That shit was painful. Like *stepped-on-a-Lego* painful. And you couldn't even smile 'cuz it's not in your Orphan programming.'

'Allman,' he said. 'The big boss at Solventry. I want to know more about him, too. That is, if you're done playing dress-up.'

'*Playing?* You got *any idea* how lucky you are to have me handling this Sk3wl of Root–plus NSA-level hacking job for you? On a friggin' home visit?'

Her grin was dazzling. Broad nose, full cheeks, dimple in her right cheek – she was so goddamned winning it was nearly impossible for him not to feel affection toward her. And she was beautiful, too, beautiful in a way wholly specific to her, regardless of norms or comparisons, and he wondered if that was what the four-letter word was, when you saw straight down into someone with that kind of clarity.

How different Evan must have appeared in the eyes of the man who was his father. And how different Jacob Baridon had appeared to Evan, with the touch of jaundice in his face and traces of yellow on his teeth. All the human flaws rendered through Evan's OCD, which was powerful enough to drive his whole terrible life but not powerful enough to overcome the purity with which he saw Joey. Joey of the trail of potato chips. Joey of the constantly replenishing mess. Joey of the spilled Dr Pepper and bare feet on his desktop. Joey of the too-loud laugh, the stray hairs in the sink, the heap of dirty laundry. Joey of the blow-the-doors-off-the-car radiance, the twisty wondrous brain. Joey the fierce, proud, vulnerable young woman.

She pinched her lower lip with her teeth, staring down. '*What?*' An accusation.

Evan said, 'You're the worst.'

'You're the worst, too.' She started off. 'I'll see you in the Vault when you're done *trying* to work out.'

'Trying?'

'I hear you grunting with them handstand push-ups,' she threw back over her shoulder. 'Little-boy grunts like you're trying to pull on your socks for the first time.'

And she was gone.

He rolled himself back to a seat and then found his balance on his hands once more. He started another set of vertical push-ups.

It was hard not to grunt.

By half past eight, Joey was sitting all the way up on the sheet-metal desk with her legs bent before her, chin resting on her knees, tapping a gnawed stick of red licorice against her bottom lip. They were reviewing her findings, and she was dead serious.

Or at least as close to dead serious as Joey could manage.

'So here's where we're at so far,' she said. 'The dead vet Tanner? He's a dead end. Fell out of life about five years back, homeless, pops up applying for various VA services here and there. But I doubt I'll be able to connect him to the Wolf and if I can't, no one can. I'm still digging on the weapons front – the Manurhin MR73 Gendarmerie in particular. But as you know, folks buying weapons aren't exactly eager to ensure they can be tracked by databases.'

'And Solventry?'

'Solventry's our Everest. It's like a big-ass umbrella for so many entities that it's not an umbrella anymore, it's like its own complex. Like the Solventry-industrial complex. Get it?'

'Yes.'

'E-commerce obviously and no shit, but we're *also* talking big data, consumer electronics, food delivery, apparel, online pharma, ride share, wearable tech, mortgage sales, robotics, credit monitoring, online payment, game streaming, dating apps, social content aggregators, predictive software, genome kits, health apps, fitness trackers, synthetic media, cloud computing, therapeutics – the full Bezos. Oh, they also own, like, a few hundred daily newspapers – local, national, foreign. And they just spun up a film and TV studio which sounds like a big expense but it's really just a rounding error slash loss leader to open up markets like India, China, and Slovakia for delivering toasters and selling digital storage and all their other services. So, you ask yourself, what do all these ventures have in common?'

'Personal data,' Evan said.

'Yup. Data is the endgame.'

Evan had been sitting long enough that his aches and bruises were starting to announce themselves more vehemently. He held up a finger. 'Hold please.'

He walked out of the Vault and through the penthouse to the kitchen. Moving past the living wall, he entered the small freezer room with its glass walls and centered bar. The chill hit fast and hard, settling soothingly into his lungs. A panorama to the south offered a generous view of Century City's sleek high-rises, each a hive for accountants and lawyers thriving on exorbitant hourlies, doctors tending to the rich and fortunate, and Hollywood agents exacting their tenth of a pound of flesh.

Spaced precisely three inches apart, the bottles represented the finest and rarest vodkas in the world. His gaze settled on one in particular. Ensconced in a black leather case, it came with a small wooden hammer with a brush in place of a claw.

Beluga Gold Line was distilled at the freezing edge of Siberia, three hundred kilometers from the nearest sign of man. Manufactured with hyaline artisanal water for pure-as-the-driven-snow clarity and with coached malt enzymes for a robust profile, it was filtrated with quartz sand and then instilled into a bottle of crystal-pure French glass. Wax poured over mesh wire muzzled the cork: thus the hammer and brush. Each bottle sported an individual identification number.

Along with a rocks glass and two spherical ice cubes formed of distilled natural spring water, he brought the black leather case back to the Vault and sat at the L-shaped desk. Leaving one ice cube in the rocks glass, he set the other atop Vera III's clutch of serrated leaves to water her.

She held it aloft appreciatively.

Then Evan freed the bottle. It was a thing of beauty unto itself, a metal label and a three-dimensional beluga-fish logo adhered to the glass by hand.

'Data is the endgame for what?' he asked, resuming the conversation.

Joey shrugged. 'Allman probably doesn't even know that.'

Slowly, meticulously, he began working on the sealed Italian cork. Gentle taps of the hammer chipped away at the hardened wax, freeing peels and dust. 'He's Solventry's CEO?'

'Founder, visionary, *and* CEO. Dude's worth uh kuh-*billion* dollars. He could, like, buy Argentina.'

'Why Argentina?'

'''Cuz who wants Venezuela right now?'

'I wasn't aware those were the only two options.'

'Plus: steak.'

Bits of wax scattered across the sheet-metal desktop and Evan took care to trap them with a napkin. Joey watched him, one eyebrow hoisted in annoyance.

'What did you find out about him?' he asked. 'Personally.'

'Dude is *secretive*. There's so little out there about him it's crazy. He's not boring tunnels beneath cities. He's not building dick-shaped rockets to go to outer space. He's not dating Belgian nutrition and lifestyle influencers a third his age.'

'Belgian?'

'''French'' would be too on-the-nose.'

'Fair.' The encasement was firm, giving way unevenly, and Evan kept at it with the tiny hammer. Brushing every last clinging speck off the throat of the bottle, he caught them in a cupped hand before moving to a fresh section of wax. 'Jayla Hill said her father reported directly to Allman. That's gotta be pretty rare in a corporate structure as vast as Solventry's.'

'Ya think? That'd be like an Orphan talking directly with the secretary of defense. Solventry has something like eight hundred thousand workers. Not everyone gets to sit on Santa's lap.'

'So whatever Benjamin Hill was on was highest priority.'

'Correct.'

'I have to talk to Allman.'

'Good luck with that. Might as well ask to have high tea with Elon. Or brunch with J. D. Salinger.'

'Salinger's dead.'

'I'm sayin'.'

Still tapping and brushing archaeologically at the bottle, Evan pondered how he might go about getting to Allman and came up snake eyes. 'What'd you find out about Hill's work?'

'Doc Hill's system follows a policy of defense-in-depth . . .' Joey began, her voice slowing as she watched his assiduous advances on the sealed bottle.

Snatching the hammer and bottle from him, she smashed the remaining wax seal with a few vicious strikes. Chunks skittered across the desk onto the floor, a speck of shrapnel hitting Evan just beneath the right eye. Under her continued assault, the extant encasement crumbled across the mouse pad and Evan's lap. She popped the cork, sloshed a finger of vodka into the rocks glass, and shoved it at Evan.

He took it.

Having accelerated the process to her liking, she continued. 'So it'll be an uphill battle to get in. I have to hack through more layers of encryptions and some tricky protocols and this stupid port-knocking thing that just takes longer.' A glance at Evan to see if he was keeping up. 'How can I find language you'll understand?' She contemplated the herculean task of summoning a sufficiently primitive description for Evan to comprehend. 'It's like peeling an onion.'

'What's an onion?'

She glowered at him.

He paired her amused distress with a sip of the Beluga Gold. Faintly medicinal nose, creamy thick body, vanilla undertones, and he swore he could make out a trace of *Rhodiola rosea* extract.

'Plus Hill's access was terminated,' she said, with I-won't-dignify-that-with-a-response haste, 'so I have to restore Active Directory. Big tech doesn't waste time. Two seconds after you get shot in the head, they're shutting down your proverbial cubicle.'

'What about DNA on the ear chunk?'

'I got it to Melinda.'

Evan's trusted forger, Melinda Truong, ran an antique-movie-poster restoration business in Northridge as a cover for her illicit activities. She had more talent, capabilities, and black-market resources than it made sense for any single human to have.

Joey said, 'She needs a day or two but she has backdoor access to all sorts of labs 'cuz Melinda. Also I asked her for help on the Manurhin revolver front since illegally acquired luxury items are her jam.'

'And you're checking on Jayla Hill?' Evan asked. 'The Marshals got her somewhere safe?'

'Put it this way,' Joey said. '*I* can't find her.'

'Good,' Evan said. 'But the Marshals won't hold her forever. She's not a government witness. There's a ticking clock.'

'So we work faster.'

'How about the missing dog?'

'I've been scanning all Web-based surveillance cameras in a five-mile radius around Hill's town house. I'm using facial-recognition software for Loco.'

'Facial recognition for a dog?'

'Yeah, you canine-phobe. Dogs are people, too. I hacked into a DARPA program they're developing to track service dogs and stole their algorithms and training set. So I have that running' – a jerk of her head to the north-facing wall of the

Vault, where avalanches of code thundered ever downward and various progress bars showed various progress – 'because that cloud you've heard so much about is cheap, and spinning up ten thousand machines or so to run my parallelized Erlang cluster saves time, and I'm not gonna be the rusty wheel on a Nowhere Man mission.' With a neat jerk of her head, she cracked her neck and flung the mane of hair above her undercut from right to left, the whole thing like a choreographed dance move or peacock display. Then she gave that high-wattage smile that said she was in her best, easiest self. 'I'm a Mexi*can*. Not a Mexi*can't*. You know it's in my *blood* to do everything better'n everyone else.'

He tilted his glass in her direction. 'Here's to flattering stereotypes.'

She blushed ever so slightly. Hands pressing the desktop, locked elbows shoving her shoulders north, she leaned her head toward him and confessed in a mock whisper, 'I'm not actually all that good at computers, X. I'm just really bad at giving up.'

30. Bad Things for Good Reasons

Aragón Urrea was an unconventional businessman. A man who, like Evan, did bad things for good reasons. At one time from his compound in Eden, Texas, Aragón had run a multibillion-dollar global drug-commerce operation that skirted the edges of international law and occasionally flouted legalities entirely. He'd been called an anarcho-capitalist, a beloved *patrón* to his community, and a drug dealer.

Evan called him his friend.

They came at the world from contrasting angles. They disagreed on more things than they could recount. They lived according to different codes.

And that was the point.

What use was a friend you agreed with on everything?

Some time back, Aragón had tracked down Evan's Nowhere Man phone number in his desperation to rescue his daughter, who'd been kidnapped by a vicious cartel leader. At first Evan had been unsure whether to come to Aragón's aid or wipe him off the map.

It could be good, not killing people. Sometimes you even wound up liking them.

After Evan had helped Aragón restore his family, Aragón had offered him his eternal gratitude and use of his private jets. The latter was a useful perk for someone who preferred to avoid security checkpoints, flight plans, and travel lines.

Sitting halfway up the spiral staircase to the reading loft, Evan dialed Aragón's number now. He'd retreated from the

Vault to get some space from Joey, who was conducting the monitors like Toscanini or Sorcerer Mickey gone mad with power.

The loft pulled double duty as a guest room for Joey. Evan had even purchased skull-and-crossbones sheets for the couch up there, and a dog bed. He didn't have to look to know that Joey had already blown through the space like a tornado, leaving wreckage in her aftermath. Overhead a stray sock was straggled across the staircase's highest step like a dead rat. He wondered at the series of events that could have led to its landing *on the top step of a spiral staircase,* but that level of housekeeping barbarousness was beyond the ken of his imagination.

Aragón picked up after a few rings, his deep voice calling to mind that broad chest, as sonorous as the man himself: '*Mi amigo de borrachera!* How are you?'

'Alive,' Evan said. 'How is Belicia?'

'She is wonderful. If you get through the part of your marriage where you want to kill each other, it can actually be quite enjoyable.'

'A ringing endorsement for matrimony.'

'It has been beautiful all the way through, our marriage. But now it's easier every day as well.'

'That sounds more enjoyable than I know how to grasp.'

'So much brooding, with you, X. You're such an *escandalosa.*'

'And Anjelina?'

A gravelly sigh. '*Mija* is the great joy and terror of my life. She lavishes love upon my granddaughter but she doesn't hold her during the night whenever she cries. They are all about this Dr Spock controlled-crying bullshit.'

'They'll work it out. Besides, no one ever rocked me to sleep when I was a baby and look how I turned out.'

Aragón gave his great laugh, the rolling one that built momentum more slowly than you could almost believe.

Evan allowed a rare pulse of pride that he'd learned to be funny in a different way, using humor more than just as a parry or thrust. *That's what friendship is supposed to be,* he thought suddenly, with the dumbness of a child. *It's supposed to crack you open into new spaces. Like stretching does. And pain.*

'Look,' Aragón said, acquiescing, 'we don't raise polite girls. We raise girls who can be polite when the occasion calls for it.'

'You're raising women.'

'That's right.'

'Women who are worth listening to.'

A long, dry pause. 'Since when did you learn how to have anything to say worth listening to?'

'It's a spell. It'll pass.'

'All right, enough throat clearing, Señor Nowhere Man. Talk. My aunt is "putting dinner on soon" as these *pinche* Texans say, and I'll get an earful of the anger if I'm late.'

'There's a CEO named Allman, founder of Solventry.'

'Haven't heard of him.'

'I need to talk to him. But I don't think I'll get what I want if I talk to him the normal way.'

'Tying him to a cactus?'

'Some variation of that, sure.'

'So you want, what? To have a bocci-ball date with him?'

'I don't know how this works. How to meet with a billion-aire mogul . . .'

'When you're not torturing him.'

'Your words, not mine. Can you arrange something for me?'

'That isn't my world,' Aragón said. 'It is too legitimate.'

'If you had any idea how much dirtier the legitimate guys are.'

'Oh, I do. Those *hijos de sus chingadas madres* have just as much grift and corruption as the streets. The streets are just more honest about what we're doing. That world up there? I don't understand their fancy rules and etiquette. It's all too . . . removed from reality.'

'They make their own reality.'

'Yes,' Aragón said. 'Don't you know any legitimate billionaires who you *haven't* killed?'

Evan gritted his teeth. In fact, a person did spring to mind, a man whom Evan had hoped to avoid for the rest of his life. He was the kind of person you had to look in the eye, and this was the kind of ask that had to be made in person.

'I suppose,' he said. 'But I'll need to borrow a jet. I have to get to the Hamptons.'

31. A First-Rate Mind-Fucker

Southampton's Meadow Lane, called Billionaire's Row for the obvious reasons, ran like a luxurious jetty between Shinnecock Bay and the North Atlantic. Evening darkness augmented the edge-of-earth sensation, giving Luke Devine's sprawling mansion the feel of an island unto itself.

In a rented car, Evan drove past the sign with tartan-patterned letters announcing the estate as TARTARUS, a bit of wordplay from the previous owner, who'd been a Scotsman. The tires crunched across the quartz stone of the circular driveway. Evan parked in front of the unreasonably giant front door and stepped out into a bracing wind laced with salt and seaweed.

He rang the bell, which chimed richly within.

A majordomo in a black suit answered, backed by four uniformed security guards.

'Please tell Mr Devine that the Nowhere Man is here to see him and ask if he'll receive me.'

The majordomo blanched and the guards sidled back a step or two and did their best not to look terrified.

The last tranche of security here had not fared well at Evan's hand.

'Very well, sir,' the majordomo said. 'Would you mind waiting here?'

'I would not.'

The man turned crisply on heel, crossed the vast foyer with its stories-high tumbling-waterfall feature and sweeping staircase. Against the boundless interior, his progress up the stairs seemed comedically slow.

Holding a five-meter standoff, the security guards looked down at their boots or at Evan's and made no move for the handguns strapped to their hips.

A two-minute pause and then the majordomo reappeared, making the same painstaking progress down the stairs and across the foyer.

'He is taking an early supper in the upstairs drawing room,' he said, with a pivot of his slim hips and a flourish of his palm. 'I'm happy to accompany you.'

'I know the way, thank you,' Evan said, brushing past him.

Of all the global power players Evan had encountered, Luke Devine was the most skilled and the most dangerous. After building a fortune as a hedge-funder, he'd used his wealth and connections to spin a lavish social scene into existence around him. Everyone from Supreme Court justices to media moguls to foreign leaders attended his hedonistic affairs, and he caught them in a web of intrigue, surveillance, and black-mail to bind them to his will.

It was Devine's belief that his will led to a greater good. And in fact, he was motivated by some higher calling than merely his own power – pushing through more effective legislation, holding big conglomerates and meddlesome bureaucrats accountable, taking down those he deemed to be bad actors on the global-corporate stage. He thought of himself as doing what Evan did as the Nowhere Man but at a much more important level. He was grandiose, narcissistic, manic, and a first-rate mind-fucker.

Evan might have been the only person in the world who had managed to put Luke Devine in his place.

The drawing room was rimmed with bookcases, wainscoting, and an enormous depiction of Kahlil Gibran above his famous quotation: *Your pain is the breaking of the shell that encloses your understanding.* Devine prided himself on providing pain to those who required greater understanding.

The man himself sat alone facing away at a curved mahogany bar the length of the entire wall. He ate from a silver bowl of snow-crab cocktail claws cracked open to expose a Popsicle bulge of meat. A cuboid of terrine wobbled on a small china dish, and a two-finger pour warmed a crystal rocks glass, the bottle of fifty-five-year-old Yamazaki scotch set beside it, available for replenishments.

Devine didn't turn around. He was diminutive of stature with elegant posture, a tousle of blond hair with the faintest touch of scalp showing through at the back.

'Mr Nowhere Man,' he said, to the twinkling rise of bottles before him.

'How's the Yamazaki?' Evan asked.

'Meh,' Devine said. 'Overpriced.'

The bottle cost $950,000.

Devine neatly lined the edge of a butter knife with a bite of terrine, transferred it onto a wheat cracker, and made it disappear. Evan walked across the drawing room and pulled up the barstool next to him. His lower back complained, displeased from the flight and the previous days' pummeling. His vocation had hastened the inevitable; even on the forgiving side of forty he knew he'd live with some kind of pain every day until his death.

At last Devine favored him with a sideways glance. 'I hoped I'd never see you again.'

'Same.'

'The main course is coming if you'd like to join. What would you like?'

'What do you have?'

Luke looked at him flatly. '*Everything.*'

'That must be boring.'

'Yes. *Yes.* So few people understand that. It's not a position that can be pitied, of course, but it's a loss to have whatever you want whenever you want it. A loss of anticipation, of delayed gratification, of new frontiers. It makes me feel . . . expired. Fat with contentment.'

There wasn't an ounce of extra weight on him. His brain probably burned everything off as fast as he could fill his body.

'I'll have a drink,' Evan said.

Devine shoved back his stool with a chirp against the polished hardwood and circled behind the bar. It was a long way.

He set his palms flat on the mahogany and leaned in, propped on his arms, elbows locked – the classic bartender pose. 'What can I get you?'

Luke Devine was nothing if not polite.

'Let me guess,' he said quickly, before Evan could answer. 'Vodka. Every last time. I wonder what would happen if you drank something different. Would your carefully curated sense of self come crumbling down?' He flashed a mirthless grin. 'Or maybe you just like the taste.'

Evan stared at him.

'What'll it be then?' Devine positioned himself in front of the vodka portion of the shelves, the backlighting moving pristinely through glass and spirit.

'If it'll make you happy, I'll have gin.'

'Gin?' Palm pressed to his breastbone, Devine feigned a swoon. 'Which one?'

'Bobby's,' Evan said. 'With elderflower tonic and a thin slice of orange set on ice. Pour the gin across the orange.'

It wasn't merely a gin and tonic. It was the most

transcendent variation of one. To the dismay of Brits everywhere, the Dutch were the true originators of gin, and Bobby's from Schiedam was the best of them. Full offerings from the Indonesian spice trade – cardamom, cloves, and coriander – balanced with eight separately distilled botanicals. No sugars or extractions to gunk anything up. The elderflower tonic brought sweetness, and the citrus opened the concoction up like a flower. He'd drunk it only once before, in Amsterdam, at a café where he'd sat and lunched while waiting for the uproar to die down across the Herengracht canal where he'd put a bullet through the forehead of an obese Swiss banker and two more through the barrel of his chest for good measure.

Of course Devine had the accoutrements behind the bar. He served up a highball glass sizzling with carbonation. Evan sipped. The combinations of flavors popped off one after another like fireworks before settling into a full – and he cringed to use a vinous term even in his mind – bouquet.

He exhaled, sensed the cool taste on his breath.

'Good?' Devine asked, with genuine interest.

'Very.'

Devine raised his rocks glass and they clinked.

'It's hard,' Devine said, 'to find things that are still thrilling.'

Evan nodded. For a brief moment he didn't dare fully admit that he felt understood in some small, new way.

Men and their strange alcoholic rituals of bonding.

'Have you reconsidered my offer to work together from time to time on problems that require . . . fixing?' Devine asked.

'No.'

'I hope you haven't reconsidered killing me?'

'No.'

'A relief,' Devine said, with an impish twinkle in his eye. 'Why are you here?'

'I need something from you.'

'Ah.' Luke sipped, tilted his head back, let the scotch wash around his mouth. 'Maybe it's *not* so overrated,' he said to the ceiling. Back to Evan: 'Why should I help you?'

'Because I interest you. And what I'm looking into is worth looking into.'

'What are you looking into?'

'Homicidal happenings afoot over at Solventry. Their lead AI guy was killed. Do you know Allman? The founder?'

'Allman.' Devine wrinkled his nose. 'Yes.'

'He's a faceless billionaire. Seems a rarity.'

'Not so rare as you think. There are dozens of them. Pick up a copy of *Forbes* if copies of *Forbes* still exist.'

'I'll take it from you. You don't like him?'

Luke shrugged. 'There are a handful of great billionaires. Brilliant, driven – the ones who actually create something new. Who add a new piece to reality. But usually, with all that wealth? They become solely focused upon maintaining power.'

'Aren't you solely focused on power?'

'Of course. But at least I'm focused on checking that power in others.'

Evan shook his head.

'What?' Devine said.

'Fucking billionaires. You people are the worst.'

Devine laughed a musical laugh. 'It's true. Most are still back on the playground, riding their proprietary machine-learning algorithms like bumper cars, trying to win the game.'

'What game?'

'King of the hill. And a few guys have the biggest cars right now. Musk. Zuck. Allman.'

'And you.'

Devine answered with a wink and held his train of thought: 'COVID, war, locusts – the more bad shit happens, the more money goes to the top. Not because everyone's evil but because that's how the system's increasingly set up. In the past four decades in this country, fifty *trillion* dollars has moved from the bottom ninety percent to the top one percent. And the ordinary folk, all those outraged consumers at home watching their cable news and clicking their Twitter feeds, rubbing their temples with dismay and talking about how it's just so terrifying what the other side doesn't understand about themselves? They don't get it. That's all a distraction to keep that pipeline open, to keep that fifty trillion dollars moving up the ladder. All their think pieces and protests and conspiracies and riots?' He paused for a breath or perhaps not. 'Real power won't be stopped by any of that. Real power is *conducting* all that.'

'What will stop it?'

'Great men,' Devine said. 'Or great women.'

Evan stared at the beckoning bottles behind the bar. He felt exhausted. It was always the same – the same suffering and destruction, the same age-old battles, the same powerful men looking down at it all from on high through the filter of the latest recycled ideology.

'But the hour grows late,' Devine continued, always quick to fill a void. 'It's a widening gyre – the blood-dimmed tide has been loosed, and all that. When we monetize bad shit, we get more bad shit. It's simply too good for the bottom line. And humans don't even run what happens anymore. Algorithms run it. We just exist to service the computers to service the algorithms. Even most of our so-called visionaries.'

'Like Allman?'

'They joke that half of the big-tech founders are on the

spectrum. But some people aren't missing social cues. They just don't give a damn.' Devine thought a moment, the tip of his tongue probing the side of his cheek. 'Some people don't give a damn about anything.'

'I need to get in to see him.'

'Why do you care that an AI guy got murdered? Is this one of your . . . *missions*?' Luke weighted the last word with a touch of disdain.

'He had a daughter. Seventeen years old.'

'You're not getting sentimental, are you?'

'No. Just more selective in where I direct my energy.'

'And you don't want to force your way to Allman because . . . ?'

'I need to talk with him. Freely. I have no idea if he has anything to do with this.'

'And attaching electrical wires to his testicles makes for stilted conversation?'

'Unhygienic, too.'

'I can't just ring him up and ask him to meet with an assassin.'

Evan took another drink of the gin and tonic, the smell of orange rising from the glass. 'So how would you approach it?'

Devine looked flattered that Evan was asking his opinion. 'You'd need a legitimate cover.'

'Like a journalist?'

'Allman would never talk to a journalist.'

'What then? Investor? Insurance agent investigating –'

'*No.* No.' Devine leaned back, lowered his head to think, his smooth face aimed at the empty scotch glass before him. 'It's all ego with people like Allman. It's the only thing left that interests them.'

'It's almost as though you're familiar with the condition.'

But Devine paid him no mind. 'You're a psychology

professor from . . . Harvard. Doing a study on genius. All your subjects will be kept anonymous. For now you're just seeking to understand . . . the nature of genius.' He sloshed another fifty-thousand-dollar pour in his glass and downed it in a single expensive gulp. 'Problem is you don't look like a professor.'

'I don't look like anything. Which means I *can* look like anything.'

'The Nowhere Man. Last time it was a missing young man and woman. This time a seventeen-year-old girl. Doesn't it get boring, doing the same simple little tasks in your simple little world?'

'No.'

'Why not?'

'You wouldn't get it.'

'And why's that?'

Evan let a bit more Bobby's and tonic effervesce its way down his throat. 'You haven't faced it yet. All you children on your bumper cars, playing king of the hill.'

'What?'

'Your irrelevance.'

Devine broke eye contact, busied himself with his glass. It was such a rarity to see him forced to bring down the portcullis. 'I'll make the introduction when you've built an airtight cover,' he said coldly.

Evan finished the last of his gin and tonic and rose to leave. 'That's my next stop.'

32. Unsafe Ground

Rising to deplane the Cirrus Vision Jet at Van Nuys Airport, Evan dialed Melinda Truong.

When she picked up, she was screaming in her native tongue across a not-really-muffled phone, a not-uncommon occurrence at the vintage-poster restoration business she ran out of an industrial park in Northridge: *'That is an intact limited-edition US alternate one-sheet of* A Clockwork Orange*! And you screwed up the color match on* orange, *Vinh! It's literally in the title!'*

Melinda oversaw a hive of male workers, all of whom were entranced by her when they weren't busy being petrified of her. No one could command the elaborate array of tools and technology with her skill, nor could they rise to the level of perfectionism she demanded. And yet they followed her every command with slavish devotion, motivated by no small measure of fear.

In a dark-walled photography room behind CraftFirst Poster Restoration, Melinda ran a second, more lucrative operation. She could forge anything from a US passport to a Flemish masterpiece. He'd seen her mimic everything from holograms to embossments to security key cards using next-gen PKI.

She came back to the phone in flawless English: *'What?'*

'It's Evan.'

A sea change in tone: 'Sorry, *người yêu*' – a term of endearment she reserved for him on occasion – 'you know I'm cranky at the office.'

'Which is why I pretend I don't understand Vietnamese.'

'Let's prolong the charade to protect my delicate sensibilities.'

Nodding his thanks at Aragón's pilot, Evan descended the set of rolling stairs, the night wind biting through his clothes. 'Anything back on the severed ear?'

'Patience, Evan. It's DNA sequencing, not instant ramen.'

'Thanks for working with Joey. She's a handful.'

'Not for me.'

'No?'

'I'm a woman. She's a girl. Game recognizes game, *người yêu.*'

He smiled. 'I have something else I need you for.'

'Here's hoping it's risqué.'

'Building me out a full legend as a Harvard professor.'

Melinda was a hair over five feet, and petite, but her laugh, which came rarely, was substantial. 'I assume you'll need credentialing, published research papers, a spot on the faculty website.'

'I need full backstopping – office line with an assistant, alumni records, the whole nine.'

'Bring cash. The whole nine is expensive.'

'Not as costly as if it's done wrong. Which is why I need you on it.'

'I *am* incomparable,' she mused.

She named her price. It was the cost of a luxury SUV. *Fair,* he thought.

'Joey's read in,' he told her. 'I'll have her text over the details. I'll bring cash now. I can be to you in a half hour.'

'No,' she said sharply. 'Not the office. I've asked to cook you dinner several times. Now it's no longer a request.'

They had never met beyond the empire of her workplace, and it struck Evan that he almost couldn't imagine her

182

outside her warehouse. It would be like spotting a queen bee out of the hive.

'I'll text you my address,' she said, and hung up.

Melinda Truong lived in a pseudo Spanish McMansion in a gated community in Porter Ranch about five miles north of her business. From the curb, the house looked as bland as all the others, which alternated between a half dozen basic architectural plans, each stucco-walled, wooden-shuttered, roofed in terra-cotta.

Evan crossed the xeriscaped front yard to the round-top dark walnut door. Iron strap hinges, speakeasy grille, castle door handle. It was a door not for knocking but for rapping, so rap he did.

An anachronistic electronic hum issued forth, the massive door cracked open, and he stepped through. A discordant fall of natural light struck his shoulders; the sky was open. He was standing not in a courtyard but on a strip of polished black stones that ran like a moat around the actual home before him. As he took his bearings, surprise thawed into wonder.

The entire front of the house was a façade.

The house inside the shell of the exterior had a peaceful Thiền-like quality, with modern concrete walls, frameless panes of glass aligned with the tinted outer windows, gilded wood Buddhist statues, and a variety of water features softened with moss.

A few steps carried him across the moat to the real front door. He rang an electronic bell.

The second door hummed and opened in like fashion.

He entered.

'In the kitchen!' Melinda called out.

Black and brown slippers of various sizes were lined up

on a bamboo mat. He slid off his boots and found a pair that fit. Cheap plastic, no arch support.

Then he followed the voice down a long cool hallway with slate floors and past a sitting room with a polished baby grand piano, recessed lighting, and several striking silk paintings. An open door looked into a powder room animated by a flickering candle. The house was speckless, not a single item out of place, and he felt something inside his rib cage unclench.

Melinda was busy behind the kitchen counter, moving from stove to refrigerator to cutting board to sink in a rotation that held enough of her focus that she didn't bother to look up at him.

'Sit,' she said, shoveling a cup of rice out of a thirty-pound aluminum bin.

There were two settings at a kitchen table surfaced with a disk of concrete.

He sat. A second hall intersected the kitchen, running back to what he guessed was the master bedroom. The lights were dim and pleasing, that portion of the house muted in privacy.

'Can I help?' he asked.

'No.'

Melinda wore bright coral Puma sneakers, and yoga pants with see-through fine mesh stripes on the sides that ran all the way up her hips, disappearing beneath an oversize man's sweater. Her waist-length jet-black hair had been taken up in a long straight ponytail bound at intervals down its length that flicked behind her as she moved. Her face was perfectly symmetrical, her features distinct in the warm glow of the kitchen light.

An altar had been set up in a corner of the kitchen, a diminutive wooden table gnarled with knots and rough with uneven planks, its edges polished by a thousand touches. A white and blue floral ceramic bowl held offerings – apples, oranges, and some vibrant red fruit with bristly, hairlike hides. Incense burned before photos of antecedents in somber poses. Mother-of-pearl tableaus showed mountain-scapes, water buffalo in rice fields, a boy playing a flute. In a small blue vase tilted a miniature South Vietnamese flag, canary yellow with three horizontal red stripes.

Evan breathed the spices and flavors and watched Melinda work.

After a time she brought plates and bowls over to the table, and they served themselves and ate silently. The taste was pyrotechnic, the smell pungent, intense. Caramelized pork belly with mắm tôm – a fermented shrimp paste strong enough to disperse a small crowd. It blasted open Evan's taste buds. He sensed garlic and sugar, Thai chili pepper and minced shallots. The dish was as balanced and authentic as Melinda's forgeries. Chinese broccoli on the side, a scoop of rice.

'It's very good,' Evan said.

'Yes,' she agreed. 'As my *mợ* would say, "not too salty." You have to get it just right.'

'*mợ*?'

'"Auntie." She's the one who raised me here in Westminster.' Melinda gestured at the altar. Among the stoic black-and-whites there were some grainy Kodachrome photos, including one of a vibrant young woman in an A-line dress. 'The mother-of-pearl? That was all hers.'

From the past tense Evan understood that the auntie was gone. He and Melinda had never discussed anything personal. He wasn't good at this part, but he sensed that she might not be either, and that put him a bit more at ease.

She took a gulp from her glass of water and looked at him.

Direct eye contact but not aggressive. Studying him and allowing him to study her. For a time they just looked at each other.

He took another bite. 'Was she your real auntie or "auntie" in the affectionate sense?'

Melinda smiled. 'Asian auntie,' she said. 'No blood relation. Close friend of my mother's.'

Evan started to ask the next question but stopped. Any further headway into her biography was too intimate for him to take point on.

The Fifth Commandment again: *If you don't know what to do, do nothing.*

'Who raised *you*?' she asked.

Evan said, 'Wolves.'

She nodded, respecting the boundary.

They ate for a time in silence, and he wasn't sure if she'd decided to move on from this part of the conversation. Then she set down her chopsticks and straightened them so they were perfectly parallel. 'After my father was killed in the war, my mother ran the black market in forged papers. She was a matriarch in every sense of the word. It's all I know, all I trust. My sisters and I watched at her elbow, cleaned the equipment, ran drop-offs. There were four of us and I was the youngest, so I learned fast. I was doing finish work on documents by the age of five.'

That put Melinda in her mid-fifties now, and yet she looked younger by at least a decade and a half. Something in the heft of her age and the grace with which she carried her experience quickened his attraction to her.

This woman had supplied him with more identities than he could recount, had used her life's skill to wrap him in her protection on mission after mission, to keep him safe when he forged onto unsafe ground. Her work was in her blood. It was her birthright, her inheritance, her identity. The forged documents she made for Evan were more than just jobs; they were gifts of creation and rebirth.

'My *me* – my mom – she worked as a cleaning lady on a US Air Force base. Tan Son Nhut.'

'I know that base.'

'Everyone knows the day Saigon fell, but the day before was the get-out day.'

'April 29, 1975.'

Her eyes gleamed. 'Thirty-six hours to evacuate half a country. My mom planned to get us out through the embassy. But it was chaos. You've seen the footage. People throwing babies over the fence. Paperwork, it was *everything*. But my mom knew even the best papers couldn't get us through that mob. So we stayed at the base, hoping that those nice people she worked for all those years would help. Not that the chances were much better there. The base, runways, and planes had been bombed but there were two cargo helicopters left – tandem-rotor Chinooks. People were screaming and scrambling. We got separated. A soldier carried me. I was seven. He put me on the wrong copter. The second one. The rest of my family was on the first. My mother's friend happened to be on the second one, too.'

'Your *mợ*.'

'Yes. I watched my family in the other helicopter through the open doors as we took off. My mother was reaching for me and her mouth was open in a wail I couldn't hear over the rotors. I'd never seen her cry. Their helicopter went one way, ours another. We landed at Côn Sơn Island off the southern coast. It housed a Vietnamese prison and the prisoners were still there. It was terrifying. The US Navy got us in the morning. On to Guam. From there Camp Pendleton' – a southward tilt of her head – 'in San Diego. Then Westminster.'

'And your family?'

'Years later I found out that their plane went through the Philippines. The records are scarce from there. By the time I was skilled enough to track anything down, I found a death record for my mother. Sepsis. It took years more to get info on my sisters.'

'And?'

'One died, one went missing. One married a Chinese businessman, lives in Beijing, and is unrecognizable to me and me to her.'

There was no grief in her voice, nor was her tone dulled or deflective. There was no emotional ask, no incomplete part of herself that she was looking for him to fill. And he understood that she'd shared these pieces of herself not to elicit pity or cheap condolences but to allow him to know that she had even more strength than he imagined, the kind of strength that demanded respect. He found it breathtaking, that courage to set her full self forward, to require nothing, to fear nothing.

It was a courage he lacked.

He had no idea how to push any of these sentiments into words, to accept and match what she was giving him. 'I'm sorry . . .' A hitch in his processing. What was he trying to say? 'I'm sorry I'm not more forthcoming.'

Her smile was perfection. And it carried a glint of her usual self, devious and unruly and smarter than everyone around her. 'I don't need you to be forthcoming. I know what I care to know about you already.'

'How's that?'

'Women know everything, Evan. Especially about men. We know which men actually like women. Which men respect us. The ones who are scared of us. The ones who are *really* scared of us – the controlling ones. We know who wants us to take care of them. Who wants to save us. Who wants to be our daddy. Who wants to get into our pants. Who wants to make love to us.' She paused. 'Who's curious.'

She watched him and he watched her right back. Over the scent of incense and spice he could barely make out a note of her lavender skin cream.

'Well . . .' Rising, she cleared the plates to the counter, setting them down with a clink. 'It's getting late. I think I'll turn in.'

She breezed back past him and down the dimly lit hall. At the mouth of her bedroom, still facing away, she slid one slipper off with a toe and then the other. She paused by the doorway with her hand on the frame for a moment, giving him a glimpse of her silhouette, then crossed the threshold out of sight.

Evan sat for a moment, feeling her graceful exit in his bones.

Then he walked down the hall to her bedroom.

33. None of Your Business

'Where *are* you?' The sound waves mapping Joey's voice, thrown from the RoamZone's holographic display, danced above the screen like a tiny orange fire.

Evan sat up in the sheets, rubbed his eyes. Gray early-morning light fell through the window at a sharp angle, sliced by the exterior wall of the façade. At his side, Melinda stirred. Quietly he slipped from her platform bed, stepping into his cargo pants.

'Looking into something.'

'O-*kay*. Well, I got a lead.'

Evan tugged on his shirt, eased one foot into a sock and then the other. 'You hacked into Hill's files?'

'No,' Joey said. 'The encryptions are a bitch so I'm still whaling away. I have a lead on the –' Movie Trailer Voice: '"*Canine Investigation.*"' Back to normal. 'The snout-recognition software hit on Loco a few blocks from Hill's town house. Go look for him. I made more flyers and hid them beneath your passenger seat yesterday.'

'What? Why?'

'So *I* wouldn't have to put them up.'

Melinda slid up with a single fluid movement, the sheets mostly coming with her, a wave of loose hair flowing over a shoulder to cover her exposed breast. 'Evan?'

Joey said, 'Who's that?'

Evan said, 'Text me coordinates,' and hung up.

Melinda's eyes glinted like a cat's in the dark. A three-wick candle still guttered on the nightstand of fine ash, casting her in living light. 'Heading out?'

'Yes.'

'I started Thian and his team on building your legend last night, Professor Evan of the Harvard Psychology Department.' She grabbed her phone, checked the time. 'I'll go in and oversee first thing. We should have the digital infrastructure built out by midday.'

Evan would call Devine and ask him to set up the meeting with Allman as soon as possible. 'Excellent.' Starting out, he felt the roll of cash in his cargo pocket press into his thigh and hesitated.

Melinda raised a thin eyebrow. 'What?'

'I, uh . . .' He was at a total fucking loss.

Her lips pressed together with what he hoped was amusement. 'Yes?'

'I have money for you. For the job. But . . .'

'You feel weird about paying me now?'

'Yes.'

'Why? Because it'd make me feel like a whore?'

He held a cautious silence.

Melinda said, 'Does it make you feel like a john?'

'No.'

She extended an arm, hand out, palm up, and beckoned with two flicks of her fingers.

He handed her the roll of cash.

She smirked at him. As he turned to go, she gave him a smack on the ass.

Loco looked fucking crazy.

Evan knew that was the likely provenance of his name, but, still, he was tired of staring at the snaggletoothed grimace, the way his ears stuck out at different angles, the cartoon bite taken out of the left one near the tip. The flyers Joey had made up showed off his damp eyes, wiry hair, and aura of psychotic jitteriness.

Evan had scouted the blocks, checking alleys and dumpsters, stoops and storm drains.

No sign of the ugly little creature.

Plenty of homeless people, though, crammed into doorways and camped out on bus stops. The pandemic seemed to have created even more, flushing them out onto the streets. He remembered reading somewhere that during the shutdown twenty million people had lost their jobs while America's billionaires had made another trillion dollars. Devine's unwelcome voice came to him: *When we monetize bad shit, we get more bad shit.*

Evan stapled the last few flyers to telephone poles and trudged back to the dark street where he'd left his pickup. As he approached, something stirred in the bed of his truck, a human form rising in the morning shadows.

Evan had his hand through his shirt, finger on the frame of his replacement ARES 1911. But the scarecrow silhouette that rose crookedly emanated no threat.

A young man stumbled out of the truck, holding a wool blanket that Evan kept in the back and used from time to time to wrap his long guns. 'Hey, man, don't – don't hurt me. I was just – just having a rest.'

He had a mop of dirty-blond hair, loose curls that wouldn't have been out of place on a surfer. Sweat shimmered on his sallow skin, pooled at the hollow of his throat, and yet he was trembling in the shade. His chest heaved with shallow breaths. He looked to be in his late teens, but he'd worn the tread of his life down hard, black bags cupping his eyes, fingernail marks clawing up his arms, grit at his hairline. One foot was bare; the other sported a dirt-caked sneaker split horizontally at the front, his bare toes lolling forth like a split tongue. Cracked lips, pinprick pupils, and suppurating gums told the tale of opioid addiction.

Beneath the parched skin, Evan could make out his bone structure, the shape of what his features had been. Once he would've been a beautiful kid. Someone's baby boy.

Evan stepped forward and the kid winced, chin tilting down to one side, shoulder rising to block the ear, the instinctive bearing of someone accustomed to being beaten.

After all that had happened in the course of the past days, this small reaction broke something inside Evan.

The kid shuffled back a few steps. One foot was turned inward and dragged when he moved, a lame leg. The busted sneaker scraped the ground, flapping like a half sandwich. 'I just wanted to rest. I didn't – didn't take anything.'

He followed Evan's gaze to the wool blanket in his hands. When he looked up, his eyes were filled with terror. He held the blanket out. He was shuddering. 'Sorry, I'm sorry,' he said. 'Please.'

The tremor in the kid's voice brought Evan back to cold winter nights in the foster home when they used to crack the oven after it was used to try to heat the house some. Two-minute showers, the shampoo watery with dilution, a few ragged shared towels among the whole pack of them. A temptation around every corner – a cash register left unattended, a colorful pill in the palm of a hand, a purse left on a front seat. Most of the kids he'd come up with were dead before twenty, warehoused behind bars, or rotting inside their own bodies, needle stabs between their toes.

What was it he felt now burning through his gut? Guilt?

Guilt was useless and did nothing for anyone, but he couldn't shake the kid's eyes, the way they sagged with defeat, red enough to make the whole world feel like an itch.

Keeping his fearful gaze locked on Evan, the boy turned sideways, bringing visible the patch of dried brown at the seat of his pants. From a five-meter distance, Evan could smell him. His OCD grabbed hold of him before he could tell it not to, urging him to scrub out the truck bed with bleach. He knew he'd do it and he hated himself for it.

Still the kid held out the wool blanket, which despite his fear, he couldn't let himself let go of.

Evan's voice came from some distant place within him: 'Keep it.'

The kid stared at him, trembling.

'Go on, now,' Evan said. 'Go on.'

The kid hugged the blanket to his chest and stepped back some more, dragging his foot, until he vanished into the darkness and there was only the sound of his rent sneaker rasping against the ground, and then there wasn't even that.

Evan stood alone in the narrow street for a moment, collecting himself. Then he climbed into his truck and sat behind the wheel, staring at the graffitied walls, the shattered bottles in the gutter, the sneakers slung up onto telephone lines overhead.

He lowered his head. 'Fuck,' he said.

Then he got back out and wiped down the back of his truck with paper towels and bleach.

The whole family was lined up on Brianna's couch, waiting for the missing-dog report, Sofia taking the spot between her semi-estranged parents. Evan had been summoned by a series of texts from Sofia, the pings coming in one after another with a quickening rapidity reminiscent of the *William Tell Overture*. The younger the person, he'd learned, the more texts they required to communicate a simple thought. Single-word entries had conveyed Sofia's impatience and concern over Loco's ongoing sabbatical, an abundance of feeling adjectives chased by a few solo exclamation points and the odd emoji.

But now Evan was here and they were settled face-to-face. Just him and his client.

'I don't get it.' Sofia wore a long T-shirt hanging down over footed dancer's tights.

She drummed her heels against her backpack, which rested before her at the base of the couch. 'You saw Loco. And then what?'

And then there was a dead body and an assassin and cops and a SWAT team and an all-units response and a sniper rifle and a bridge embankment requiring vehicular scaling and helicopters and a car chase.

'The situation presented more variables than I could control,' Evan said.

Sofia crossed her arms and glared at her father. 'I thought you said he was good at this.'

That seemed to be her refrain.

Andre shrugged uselessly.

'Hey,' Bri said. 'Show some gratitude, child. The man's been working on his own time to find that *pinche perro*. And it sounds like it ran him into some trouble.'

'What next?' Sofia asked.

'We know he's still in the neighborhood where I spotted him,' Evan said. 'We're running canine-detection software on the surveillance cameras around there and he popped up this morning. Healthy and alive.'

Sofia eased out a breath.

'See, baby?' Andre said. 'I told you Evan would figure it out.' He reached across the top of the couch past Sofia and rested a hand on Bri's shoulder. Gently, Bri moved away and folded her hands in her lap.

Andre held his expression but deflated a touch. His hand went to his pocket and came out with one of his AA sobriety medallions, which he rubbed with his thumb like a talisman.

Sofia said, 'How do you know he'll be okay?'

'Baby,' Andre said. 'He'll be okay. He's a survivor, like me and Ev. Hell, even if we wasn't related, we still –'

He froze.

Sofia's eyes had gotten big, and she stared at her father from the left side. Similarly wide-eyed, Bri stared at him from the right.

'Re*lated*?' Bri said. 'As in *related* related?'

Evan felt an overwhelming urge to walk out of the apartment and never return.

Andre shot a sheepish glance at Evan, bobbed his lowered head. 'Yeah,' he said. 'Same mom.'

'When were you gonna inform us?' Bri was suddenly on her feet, fist pressed to a hip.

'Dunno.'

Bri's stare swiveled from Andre to Evan. 'Why didn't *you* say anything?'

'Because,' Evan said, 'it's none of my business.'

'None of your business? None of your business?' She shook her head. 'It's who you are.'

No. No, it's not.

Sofia hadn't moved. She was looking at Evan. 'Really? You and Dad . . . you're . . . ?'

Evan hesitated. Then gave a brief nod.

'What's that make us?' Sofia said.

Jack wasn't Evan's father but was the closest thing he'd ever had. Jacob Baridon was his biological father but nothing else. His mother hadn't been a presence in his life; only in her final days had they forged a few delicate threads of kinship. Evan had barely gotten his head around his relation to Andre, and now he felt the mess of this broken family pulling at him. Sofia's words stirred in his mind: *Dad doesn't have a whole lot else.* This wasn't a language he spoke. There was no Commandment to address this. It was a kind of responsibility he wanted no part of. More important, he wanted it to be no part of him.

'I don't know,' Evan said.

Sofia looked crestfallen. In his peripheral hearing, Evan heard Bri exhale as if in pain, some kind of maternal response he couldn't translate.

From his pants: *DONCHA WISH YER GIRL-FRIEND WUZ HAAAWT LIKE ME?!*

The text alert, too. Cursing Joey, he tugged out his RoamZone.

A message from Luke Devine: Allman has a window tonight. 6:00pm.

And then an address and cell number.

Evan had to prepare for the meeting. He had to find some fresh air. He had to get away from these people and their peculiar needs of him.

He stood abruptly. 'I have to go.'

Andre was looking at him, a bruised stare, his head turned away from the heat of Brianna's judgment. Evan had no idea what to make of all this, why it constituted a betrayal, the stakes. Why did they care? Why should any of this involve him?

'I'm sorry, Bri,' Andre said softly. 'I shoulda told you.' His head still ducked, he found Evan's gaze. 'We shoulda told you.'

Brianna said, 'He doesn't think that.' She looked at her daughter, her brow furled with – with *something*. Like she was feeling her child's pain for her, letting it move through her. 'Look at him. He doesn't care.'

Andre was still watching Evan. His hands were laced at the fingers but parted, and Evan could see the sheen of sweat on the palms, his pleading eyes. 'People are unpredictable,' Andre said. 'You never know when they'll surprise you.'

A heat bloomed beneath the surface of Evan's face. *Anger*. He was using Evan to talk about himself, and Evan didn't appreciate having whatever Andre was driving at put on his own shoulders, too.

Andre kept talking: 'You can't count 'em out. Not ever.'

Sofia remained on the couch, not moving. Her legs dangled over her backpack, zipped together, tiny kneecaps side by side, and she was hugging herself around the stomach as if it hurt.

Evan said, 'I'll find your dog.'

And then he left.

34. Home, Sweet Home

Allman lived in a gated equestrian community at the edge of the west valley. Evan pulled up to the guard station in a Hertz rental befitting a Harvard professor who'd flown in for research and gave his fake name and ID to the guard. After a quick call up to the house, the guard waved him through.

Dirt sidewalks, white rail fences hemming in every last estate, no streetlights. The houses varied from oversize ranch homes to palatial modern farmhouses. Charmingly hokey street signs, capped with a Disneyesque logo of a rider atop a horse, pointed the way.

As he moved farther into the community, it rippled upward into hills and canyons, houses rimming the streets below and twinkling like castles above. Unwilling to forgo the Third Commandment after his adventures with the cane-wielding granny, Evan mapped everything as he drove in. A horse with a pale white face like a sun-bleached skull swung a morbid stare to follow Evan's car as it drifted past.

The same country fence adorned the perimeter of Allman's house, but a few feet behind it, sheer metal plates rose like castle walls, a nearly insurmountable security impediment. Rounded steel pipe topped the unbroken barrier, ensuring that grappling hooks would find no purchase. An imposing solid gate with a brown moss patina blocked the driveway and any view of the house. On an uplit sign sporting the same horse-and-rider logo, the address was lettered along with the house's name: HOME, SWEET HOME.

Evan parked the Dodge Neon, climbed out, and pressed the button on the call box. 'Dr Stanley Leigh to see Mr Allman.'

A voice crackled out: *'Are you going to walk up or drive up?'*

The cameras were well hidden. 'You tell me.'

'It's a bit of a long drive.' Attitude behind the words.

'Thank you,' Evan said, in his best cooperative-professor voice, and retreated to his car. He wore a rumpled suit and a stupid goddamned tie. He required the tie because it fit the costume and had the facial-recognition-thwarting properties of the shirts he generally wore. But he hated it. If his line of work had taught him anything, it was to never intentionally put a noose around his neck. At least he'd adorned it with a pin that he could ram through an eyehole should the opportunity beckon.

When he pulled forward, the gate eased silently aside, revealing a narrow inclined drive lined with funereal cypresses.

He drove up. And up and up.

Allman's house was positioned on a ridge with views on either side. Evan parked and got out. The prime location and panorama cut some of Allman's privacy. Best spots for visibility were a neighboring house to the east, a red barn halfway down the hill, and another house across the canyon with a back deck and an infinity pool.

Clouds boiled up over the opposing ridge, backlit and tumultuous. A scorched violet sangria sky breathed its last breaths. Nighttime had dusk in its teeth already, choking it out. There was electricity in the air, and the sky was vast and dangerous, and somewhere far to the west over the Malibu hills, the tide thrashed against the coast. Alone for a moment on this spot, Evan had the feeling of standing on the planet itself.

Battered soft briefcase in hand, he crossed to a surprisingly run-down house that had no discernible style. A bit of stucco, a bit of decorative stone, the front gardens routed by gophers. A six-foot trench to the side of the porch spoke to halted construction, a decaying cast-iron sewer pipe exposed below. The welcome mat, a triumph of innovation, read WELCOME.

Before he could ring, the door was opened by a well-built man who was insufferably New England handsome. A smugness in the blue eyes, a right-angle jaw, and a chin dimple of Photoshop perfection. High forehead, lanky hair that flopped just so. A broad chest and tapered lats spoke to gym time tailored to appearance. He wore a fucking cardigan.

'My name is Mr Biltmore,' he said, stepping aside so Evan could enter the dimly lit foyer. 'I manage Mr Allman's affairs at the house. But I'm more than some personal aide. I have a law degree from Georgetown, and I worked extremely closely with him at Solventry helping launch several new divisions and making a half dozen acquisitions. He needs me here now and I look after him and I'm quite protective of him.'

Evan appreciated Biltmore's willingness to put his insecurities on such clear display. The guy was up in Evan's space, not enough to be overtly threatening but enough to make the point. He was a good four inches taller than Evan and took up room. Seemed like the toughest kid on his football team, which was plenty tough if you were playing football at a prep school in Connecticut.

Evan tried to think of what a Harvard professor would say. Probably not: *How very nice for you.* So he nodded.

Mail overflowed on a chipped side table, and kicked-off sneakers were mounded mulch-like in one corner. In an enclave off the foyer, a security screen was on display along with a barstool. The vinyl seat bore an ass impression where no doubt Mr Biltmore had perched moments before, studying the footage and stroking his chin dimple. Evan considered the arrogance of Allman to put an executive type in charge of security.

Biltmore said, 'It's my understanding that you're interviewing Mr Allman but will keep all matters anonymous and that you will quote him neither by name nor by station.'

'Nor by anything else that will be identifying,' Evan said, delighted at the chance to add his own 'nor' to the exchange.

Mr Biltmore produced an iPad Air, which he handed to Evan. 'Then you should have no problem signing an NDA.'

Evan peered down at the dense legal text.

'Permit me to help you,' Mr Biltmore said, scrolling for Evan through countless paragraphs. 'Tap to initial here. And here. And here.'

Evan complied. 'This'll just be a general conversation. My past research deals with the correlation between Big Five personality traits and innovative performance. I'm now interested in the question of genius – how we define it, how we –'

'Here.' A throaty voice spoke from behind Evan. 'I'm here.'

He turned.

Allman looked like the frog you'd kiss to get Biltmore.

A tall ovoid face with distinctive sides, like a softened shoe box. Mushy features, cheeks padded with fat, a sheen of sweat on a forehead squiggled with Charlie Brown lines. Above translucent amber rectangular full-rim glasses, bushy brows drew the focus, guarding heavy-lidded eyes that looked to be closed. It didn't help that Allman held his gaze low as if observing a spot on Evan's shirt. He wore a stretched polo faded to a sallow yellow and shapeless sweatpants, the old-fashioned kind with elastic at the waist and ankle cuffs. Chest hair bubbled through his shirt collar, and skin tags sprouted from his neck like ruffles on a bearded dragon. He smelled strongly; personal hygiene seemed not to be a priority.

'Mr Allman,' Evan said.

Allman shuffled behind a dated pony wall made of decorative wood, and it took Evan a moment to realize that he was to follow him. Beyond the foyer was a capacious living room with rumpled couches and coffee tables positioned seemingly at random. Mugs and dishes rested on various cushions, not enough to constitute a full-blown mess but enough to put Evan's OCD on notice. Myriad items were set out of place – a Blu-ray without a case, a tube of toothpaste near the television, a funeral pyre of recharged-too-many-times rechargeable AA batteries languishing beside a smart remote. An uninhabited fish tank burbled listlessly, glass turned opaque with calcium and algae. It was hard to imagine why anyone with Allman's net worth would choose to live like this.

Evan could barely discern the slits of Allman's eyes, and yet the man managed to orient himself in the labyrinth of furnishings, avoiding end tables and love seats, a wakeful zombie. Something about the nest-like mess made it seem as though Allman never left this place. With his technological capabilities there'd be little need.

'Home, sweet home,' Evan said.

'Huh?' Allman sank into a fabric couch, the cushions wheezing. 'Oh. The sign. The house manager chose that for me.'

Biltmore materialized at the edge of the half wall. 'Will there be anything else, Mr Allman?'

Allman waved him off.

Biltmore hesitated before receding. 'May I remind you, Dr Leigh, that you've committed to a legally binding contract protecting Mr Allman's privacy?'

Evan said, 'I understand.'

Once Biltmore withdrew, Allman said, tilting his head, 'Annoying but necessary. You'd be amazed at what we've had to deal with.'

There were three chairs facing Allman. Evan chose the one to the left. Various ancient and exotic items of computer-hardware were scattered around, items he'd need Joey to explain to him.

Evan took out a recorder he'd bought twenty minutes ago at CVS. 'May I record this?'

'No.'

He removed a legal pad. 'Mind if I take notes?'

'Yes.'

Evan had been planning to do neither. But he wanted to make some concessions at the outset to put Allman at ease. Not that he seemed to require comfort. But Evan needed to get into his graces long enough to sustain a conversation; if he wanted to reach the topic of Dr Hill without setting off any alarms, he'd have to arrive there via a circuitous route.

'I'm exploring the nature of genius,' Evan said. 'Particularly how it drives revolutionary technologies that change how humans will live in the world.'

'You came to the right place,' Allman said.

'My research specializes in –'

'Devine explained it to me,' Allman said. 'Go.'

'Very well,' Evan said. 'Your childhood –'

'Mother. Father. Me. They were fine. I'm not interested in talking about it.'

'Okay. How about present family?'

'What present family?'

'Is that something you're interested in?'

'The thing with mate selection,' Allman said, 'is you relinquish more than you get. What can a wife offer me? I don't have a strong sex drive and there's plenty of pornography suited to my needs. If I require more, I can pay for it and not have to give up resources or time beyond the act.'

An empty potato-chip bag was stuck between the couch cushions at Allman's side. Evan could smell the sour cream and onion on his breath.

'Children?'

Allman said, 'I considered whether I care about reproductive fitness – whether my genes survive. But I decided I don't. When I'm gone, I'm gone. And look how illogical society has gotten around kids. I get it, you have them, you want to set them up for maximal success so you can feel good about yourself, like you matter. So we put a moral sheen over the whole enterprise to make ourselves feel worthwhile. But I can't indulge that pretense. I'd imagine if I did have kids, they'd know how I'd view them.'

'And how would that be?'

'As a collection of genes that exist to carry out a specified parental plan. They'd resent it, I'm sure. And who needs someone around resenting you when there's so much to do that's so much more interesting than overseeing a parental plan?'

The door to the kitchen hinged open and a dour woman in a black housekeeper's dress emerged carrying a plastic tray. She crossed to them, balancing the tray with one hand so she could clear a wayward T-shirt and a laptop from the cushion beside Allman. Sag lines tugged the corners of her mouth downward, and parenthetical wrinkles radiated outward from there. Her knees cracked as she crouched to lower the tray. Fork, rectangle of paper towel, breast of chicken precut into bite-size pieces, dollop of mac and cheese, brownie square, glass of orange juice.

The woman drifted away, gray bun wagging mirthlessly. Allman neither acknowledged her presence nor offered Evan anything.

He poked twice at a cube of chicken and then forked a bite of brownie into his mouth, washed it down with orange juice. 'What am I going to do? Teach them things? Show them the world?' He spoke through a half-chewed bite. 'Stuff is just stuff. Travel is just places you're not used to yet. I used to own a yacht – bigger than Geffen's. How many times can you sail to Capri and stare at the sunset? I sold it. The yacht, not Capri. And affection? Affection is just hormones acting on receptors. If I decide I want an oxytocin release, I'll rent a dog for a day.'

Evan wanted to say, *I think I read that in a Valentine's card once,* but decided the joke was unbecoming of a Harvard professor.

Though he was repulsed by Allman, he had to admire the man's ability to bore straight through artifice and convey directly what passed for his internal state. It was refreshing. And – he hated to admit – not unfamiliar. He'd been brought up with a code similar in its soullessness. Only Jack's refusal to perfectly enact the Program's regiment had spared him. Jack had pounded into his head: *The hard part's not making you a killer. The hard part's keeping you human.* That sliver of humanity had caused Evan more suffering than anything else. It had also saved him.

Recent experience had taught him the two were intertwined: suffering and salvation.

Evan cleared his throat with Ivy League aplomb. 'Has your lack of conventional family values benefited you in your work?'

For the first time, Allman looked mildly interested. He shoved the plate away. 'Of course. Other people, they're not real to me. It goes both ways. In your simulation, I could be a tool for *you.* This view, it's not only convenient. It gives me an advantage.'

'Advantage in what?'

'Focusing on my mission.'

'And what is that mission?'

Allman's smile was a creepy baring of the teeth, that of a little boy who'd been caught doing something naughty. He rose, crumbs falling from his lap. 'Now *that's* a conversation worth having.'

35. Stone-Cold Savant

Karissa had turned the round table of her motel room into a workbench, draping a bath towel across it to mute the clinking. Blinds drawn, bed made, water bottles lined up by the TV.

The ritual was soothing, habit pounded into her nervous system from the age of four by her father, a clean-shaven man who loved his freedom and distrusted the government. They'd lived on a forty-seven-acre plot in Idaho with a tribe of fellow-minded citizens. They had no more tolerance for the gun-fetishizing crowd than they did for heavy-handed bureaucrats in DC handing down lifestyle edicts. They kept to themselves, worked the land, paid their taxes, patrolled the perimeter, and never once had a cross word with law enforcement or government officials.

Everyone on the ranch and beyond the barbed wire knew precisely what to expect, and everyone minded their boundaries, and that was precisely how it was meant to be.

When she'd gone into the savage, lawless world beyond at the age of nineteen, she'd gone as a hunter into the wild. Doing all things necessary to secure food, water, shelter, and resources for herself. Life wasn't merely life. It was survival. Life or death all the time.

And her father had made damn sure to raise her so she kept on the right side of that equation.

Her hands moved of their own volition. Unseating slide from frame, barrel and springs set equidistant, the shushing of the utility brush, soft cloth to clear fouling, patch and cleaning rod slid up the bore, lubricate rails and springs, wipe down components, reassemble, check and check and check.

The girl who had seen her face could not hide forever. Jayla Hill was a seventeen-year-old modern girl with all the lack of discipline inherent therein. She'd want to go back to her home, her friends, her phone.

Karissa had been running consistent surveillance on locations familiar to the girl. And she had set measures in place to alert her if the girl went on social media, called her friends or family members, contacted her school, or used a debit card.

It was a matter of time, as inevitable as winter following fall, as inevitable as that groundhog peeking up into daylight.

The instant Jayla Hill's head poked above ground, Karissa would be waiting to take it off.

And Karissa knew that somewhere out in the Angelino night, the man protecting Jayla was preparing just as she was. Maintaining his gear and operational focus, running down leads to get to her. He'd taken Karissa's ear. He'd eluded her scope and a squadron of police officers.

He was a stone-cold savant.

Sure as she was.

He would never stop. He'd have to be put down.

Just like her.

It was a race.

It was survival.

36. Weapons of Mass Communication

Evan rose to match Allman, facing him.

Allman sat back down. After a moment, Evan followed suit.

'Why did you rise?' Allman asked.

'Because you did.'

'And you sat for the same reason.'

'Yes.'

'Why did you pick that chair to sit in? Of the three?'

'I don't know.'

'I do. Check under the cushion.'

Evan reached beneath the cushion, feeling crumbs against his knuckles. A slip of paper brushed his fingertips. He pulled it out. It read, *Dr Leigh will sit here.*

'Go on,' Allman said, his eyes glittering for the first time with something like life.

Evan checked beneath the two chairs to his right. Neither had a note beneath the cushion. 'And I assume there's not a note beneath the chair itself?'

'Correct. It's not a parlor trick. I indicated through non-verbal reinforcement – a tip of my head, encouraging eye contact, which chair you were to choose. Magicians call it a classic force.'

'Hardly shocking,' Evan said. 'That's how social cues work.'

'Are you aware that I've also conditioned you to blink at twice the rate as when we began this conversation?'

The observation knifed into Evan, the first cut of raw

discomfort. Under Jack's direction at the hand of psychologists, he'd been trained as a child – mercilessly – in psyops. He did not like to lose control of his nonverbal tells, and he rewound his body memory and sixth-sensed that Allman was correct. 'I was not.'

'There's an answer for everything. Every human behavior. You just have to be willing to search for it.' Allman smiled his toad-like smile. 'At a certain point, you just sort of know everything there is to know.' He zeroed in on Evan's expression. 'What?'

'I was taught that the point of education is to learn how much you *don't* know.'

'Quaint,' Allman said. 'And outdated.' His digits were wide at the tips, swollen from water retention. He rubbed each thumb across the prints of the same hand as if checking for oil. 'When I was a young man seeking to understand why my mind worked . . . differently, I visited a neuroscientist who put coils on my head to map my brain and send calming alpha waves into my anterior cingulate cortex, which, it turns out, functions at a near-inhuman speed. And I felt better. But I'm primarily an engineer. So I wanted to connect every step of the input and output. To fill in the space between my brain waves and my new sensory perceptions. So I filled in that space. You can fill in anything if you look hard enough. It's just a matter of will.'

'I'm not sure I understand.'

He breathed out through his nose, folded his hands across his paunch, and sank back into the cushions. He looked frustrated. 'I built a brain. But better.'

'Artificial intelligence.'

'A human brain is one point three square feet if you flatten it out. Kind of a circle. Each neural patch, or building block, is a hundred thousand neurons laid six neurons thick. I built a hundred thousand neural patches adjacent to one another. So I have a hundred thousand patches of a hundred thousand neurons in a chip the size of half your pinky fingernail that is programmed to run full speed all the time as opposed to the ten percent humans get from their brains when they're not looking at TikTok and eating snack cakes.'

'And it's capable of filling in the gaps?'

'Yes.'

'Which gaps?'

'*All of them.*'

The words lingered for a moment.

'So we're talking about the Fourth Industrial Revolution?' Evan asked. 'Man against artificial intelligence, machine learning, all that?'

'Oh.' Allman looked almost dismayed. 'You still don't know.' He wet his meaty lips. 'It's already over.'

'What is?'

'The revolution.'

'How so?'

Allman's mouth pursed moistly. 'Imagine if I told you thirty years ago that every American would spend thousands of dollars on devices that remove them from reality, that place control over their persons in the hands of corporations, that cede access to their nervous system, that chart their every location and activity, that invade not just their privacy but the inner workings of their minds, and that they would do so willingly, even enthusiastically? What would our founders say? The framers of the Constitution?'

A coldness pulsed to life at the base of Evan's spine. Across from where they sat was a fireplace framed in cold marble and devoid of flame, which seemed an apt metaphor for something.

'That nondisclosure agreement you signed just now,' Allman pressed. 'Did you read it? In its entirety?'

'No.'

'Do you think anyone reads the consent forms or privacy-policy disclosures when they agree to install software or an application? Let alone vet them through a team of lawyers before clicking "accept"? Do you know how long they are?'

'No,' Evan said. 'No. And yes.'

Allman was shaking with a puzzling kind of indignation, a droplet of sweat at the tip of his nose. Evan wondered how it didn't tickle terribly.

'You feel a twinge of regret each time you click and yet you do it, you override your better instincts because the alternative is inconvenient. So you value laziness over rigor, convenience over responsibility, submission over freedom. And in doing so you consent to cede every last bit of agency I take from you. People today actually believe they're too frazzled and overwhelmed to do any work themselves. More victimized by circumstances than our predecessors when they were winning the West or carving a ranch out of the frontier. Convenience, it will be the death of us.'

'And you profit off that.'

Allman looked at Evan as if he had a low tooth-to-head ratio. 'What else is there to do? There's no un-addicting America now. Or the world.' The more he spoke of the inhuman, the more animated he became. 'Now it just comes down to what it always has, from the Spartans to the Mayans.' A wet gleam of a smile. 'Power.'

'That's all there is? Will to power?'

'That's all there's ever been. I'm only stating it plainly. When you're at the top of the dominance hierarchy you figure out how much you can take and how much you have to give everyone below you so that they don't take up arms or disrupt your system. Anyone who believes they've been socialized out of it is just practicing self-deception. Now we use weapons of mass communication. No different than a nuclear arms race.'

'Right,' Evan said, sincerely.

They were just two men sitting in chairs talking, and yet it seemed a corner of the universe was unraveling in the space between them, providing a glimpse of the abyss beyond.

As the unraveler, Allman had the upper hand, and he knew it. 'You're studying genius,' he said. 'Do you *really* want to know what I know?'

Evan felt a creeping apprehension. *I don't,* he thought. *I really don't.*

He nodded.

Allman's fingers fished around on the plate, came up with a cube of chicken, popped it into his mouth. He breathed audibly through his nose as he chewed, speaking through the meat. 'I have eyes and ears in your phone, in your car, your smart appliances and virtual assistants, in the smart TVs peering into your rooms, the smart fitness mirrors in your home gym, et cetera. From any one of them I can collect over a hundred thousand data points a year and I can weave them together to compile comprehensive data logs for every member of your household. I know your visitors from your doorbell cams, who you talk to on the phone, what you say, what books and articles you're reading. I know when you need to replace the toner in your printer before you do, when you need to reorder paper towels, when the lights go on and off in your house. I know what you look at on any screen and for how long, down to one-millimeter movements of your mouse. I even generate heatmaps of what your eyes focus on at every website you visit thanks to the webcam on your laptop. That eye-tracking tech also tells me when you're paying attention to your boss or spouse or a sales clerk and when you aren't.'

That coldness moved into Evan's veins now, spreading its way through his body. He wondered what else Allman might know about him. And about Dr Stanley Leigh.

He tried to cut in, but Allman kept on with that flat, dead cadence. 'I know when you want me to tell you my widgets or soap bars are environmental or invested in social justice so you can feel virtuous buying from me. I know when you're feeling insecure or agitated or happy based on which phrases you use in your social-media posts, YouTube comments, texts, emails, and podcasts. I know whether you had an aunt hospitalized for paranoid schizophrenia and when you're searching symptoms of depression online. I know who you associate with, who you prefer to see on what day of the week, and which restaurant you're most likely to pick depending on who you're with. I know when you're capable of absorbing a rent increase and when you're at risk of breaking a lease. I know your fertility cycle from one tracker, your bio-rhythms from another. I'm in beta for a contactless heart monitor that bounces sound waves off the people around you so we can access their bioinformatics, too.'

He paused to emit a not-so-muffled belch. His appearance wasn't repugnant because it was some sort of reflection of his moral state. It was repugnant because of how clearly it showed just how little he cared.

'All those fitness apps? Wearable tech? I'm not concerned whether you're healthy or working out. I care about where you are on the map. What stores you're close to and which free Wi-Fi access points you connect to – or even just the ones you walk by. If your blood pressure is high and requires meds. I can alter your movements by recommending different workouts and challenges or pushing promotions for stores you're walking by. I can monitor your sleep, heart rate, perspiration, and target you for which pillow you think you want and what deodorant you believe will make you feel fresh. I can regenerate the same news story for every member of your family using different buzzwords and biases to stoke your respective pain points or proclivities for resentment – and then drive you to fight over it. I can drip drip drip into your social-media feed and a few months later have you enraged over black men kneeling at football games or white girls wearing cornrows at an Ivy League school. That constant anxiety and insatiable anger that you feel? It's by design. It's how we keep you in the desired state of' – Allman's lips twitched as he searched for the word – 'pliability.'

He seemed to have no need to respire; he was like a printer spitting out pages.

'The more agitated you are, the more you stay online and the more we can monetize you. People don't know why they think what they think they think. I tell them. I tell them to stop eating meat or to hate specific public-policy experts. I can analyze your facial expressions when you post or tele-conference and determine everything from mental state to dental health. I can gauge how clogged your arteries are from biomarkers in your vocal register. I know which molar is sore before you've registered it consciously, if it's the mandibular right third or left maxillary second on the left. When you're ripe for blenders, smoothie cookbooks, NSAIDs, Popsicles –'

'Why don't you just tell them?' Evan asked.

'That they have an infected tooth?' Allman blinked at him, momentarily confused. 'Because we're still R-and-D'ing our dental division.'

Evan tried to say, *Oh*, but his throat was dry.

Biltmore stuck his head up over the pony wall. 'Airtight NDA aside, perhaps you want to speak less freely about –'

Allman flared a dismissive hand once more, and Biltmore faded back into obscurity.

Allman adjusted his glasses with a stiff hand, his fingers straight and parallel, the middle one nudging the imperceptibly tilted frame into place. 'Sick and suffering people are valuable, of course, because the ones who have any resources left are price-immune. And I can push them to meds that require *more* meds to manage side effects of the first meds, et cetera. Our subsidiaries lobby to have the prescription process *more* regulated with more "consumer rights" forms which build more and more delay periods into the fulfillment cycles. When we pop people on and off their meds it makes them more susceptible – mental health, physical complications, et cetera.'

'This is all legal,' Evan said flatly.

'Legal *enough*. Or sufficiently hedged against potential settlement damages. Of course Solventry doesn't want people *too* sick. We need functional units.' Allman picked at a string of chicken between his teeth. 'You can't monetize a corpse. We don't want them too unhinged either, since we're boxed out of privatized prisons. For now.' He sighed and sank deeper into the couch. 'So we strive for a sort of unstable stability. It's not a conspiracy because it doesn't have to be. You can no more break free of it than a gazelle can break free of the jaws of a lion. It's the natural order.'

Evan gave his best professorial nod. He felt his confidence falter. And yet. Allman didn't seem to know who Evan really was, which meant there were still limits to his preternatural knowledge. Which in turn meant that maybe Evan – and the world – stood a chance.

'And the media?' Evan's hands felt clammy. 'No one's

found this out, reported it? Hasn't someone put this all together?'

'Didn't you get the tweet?' Allman's smile was a joyless reshaping of his mouth. 'No one cares about anything anymore.'

Luke Devine's voice echoed in Evan's head: *The more bad shit happens, the more money goes to the top.*

'The sick and suffering,' Evan said. 'They're a gold mine.'

Allman nodded encouragingly. 'Want to know who's *really* susceptible to lucrative shifts in consumerism? People in times of disruption. Death in the family, divorce, new move, that sort of thing. And the most valuable of all? Parents-to-be. Pregnant women in particular.' He chewed a thick lip. 'I know when women are pregnant before they do. Shopping habits, sleep disruptions, et cetera. It's obvious really. If you live in Pensacola and buy baggy jeans, sauerkraut, and woven rag rugs in pastel colors, you're eighty-nine percent likely to be knocked up.'

Evan pushed out the words. 'That's impressive.'

'Oh, that's nothing. What's *really* impressive? Making them *want* to get pregnant. To create a pipeline.'

'Like cattle.'

'Yes, but with less methane.'

Evan studied him to see if he was joking. He was not.

'Guide them to scented bath products more likely to stimulate sexual interest. Aphrodisiacal music and entertainment during ovulation cycles. Pairing high-fertility matches on dating apps, et cetera. Everything OKCupid tried to accomplish with those mildly clever quizzes, only I don't ask questions. And that doesn't even get into interpersonal-communication engineering.'

'"Interpersonal-communication engineering"?'

'Are you irritated or overbearing? Should we positively

reward softer, more feminine tones to increase reproductive desirability? It's easy to analyze the emotional content of your conversations – how everyone around you responds to what you're saying. Speech synthesizers and language pattern recognition – emphasis, cadence, modulation, tone, changes in breathing – that gauge hesitations and degrees of uncertainty in your conversations. It has direct business applications, too. You can't imagine how useful it is for algorithmic stock trading. Are employees of a certain company increasingly showing stressed vocal tones or overusing key phrases – "cost cutting," "downsizing" – which can be predictive of corporate underperformance. Think Twitter sentiment analysis but on steroids and on the inside.'

'That's legal?' Evan realized the question wasn't so much a question as an interjected refrain in the epic poem Allman was reciting.

'It's not *il*legal. Try explaining any of this to your average hundred-and-nineteen-year-old senator from a square state. And good luck passing legislation that gets past the libertarian brigade who I fund up the wazoo. So there I am. In your pocket, in your bedroom, in your body and mind. Gauging what mood everyone's in around the kitchen table. And if you're *not* ripe for procreating or inadvertently conveying stock tips – let's say you're sleepy or exhibiting brain fog – perhaps I steer you to order comfort food and watch family programming.'

When he blinked, the slits of his near-closed eyes pulsed like tiny fists clenching. 'On the other hand if you're texting or speaking erratically, should I plug you into a weepy rom-com and a bucket of chocolate ice cream to prime you for your next cycle? We haven't even discussed neurotech yet – brain-sensing headphones, smart contact lenses, et cetera. The key is to keep you inside a little bubble of contentment, outrage, or dismay so I can operationalize you toward maximum profitability. Every time you have a feeling and you're online, someone's making money. And usually it's not *someone*.' His thumbs danced across his fingertips, a rodent-like tic. 'It's *me*.'

Evan's chest felt tight.

Luke Devine had laid out the scheme beneath it all, that fifty trillion dollars flowing ever upward to the top 1 percent. And then to the top 1 percent of that top 1 percent.

Evan couldn't remember the last time he'd felt such a visceral urge to drive his thumb through someone's eye socket.

Allman's face cracked into another of his non-smiles. 'Oh, you all want this. Of course you do or you wouldn't let me do it. You don't want to acknowledge what's happening, not really. If you did, you'd know it already. It's not secret. It's all right there. All you have to do is stop and think.'

'So *why* don't we? Stop and think?'

For once Allman gave Evan's words some thought. 'Because you'd be forced to understand how worthless you are. You're one of ten billion people on this planet. There are a trillion galaxies with a hundred billion stars in each. The odds of *your* being special are spectacularly low. But *I've* managed to load the entirety of human endeavor into a chip the size of a corn kernel so that it can do everything – *everything* – better than you. Then what do you feel? Who are you? You're only confronting what coal diggers felt when the mines closed, what factory workers faced when the assembly lines were boxed up and sent elsewhere to be operated by cheaper and more grateful workers who knew their place. Who cares about your degree from Cornell or your one shitty patent or your ability to compose a symphony? Not when I can make Brahms on demand. Not just Brahms. *My* Brahms. With a snap of my fingers, geared toward all the specifications I've prescribed.'

Allman's shiny cheeks bunched and he showed his small, squarish teeth. He produced a rectangular slate from his pocket, a modern phone unlike any Evan had seen, and held it balanced on the clutch of his fingertips like a waiter's tray. 'You're a monkey, Professor Leigh. This? Is the knowledge of eternity.'

Evan's jaws were clenched, sending an ache through the bone. Snatching the phone from Allman, he hurled it at the fireplace. It shattered against the marble and rained down in pieces. Rising, he hammered a fist across Allman's face, spraying the couch with a rooster tail of blood.

Allman coughed teeth onto the cushions, his spectacles twisted, one metal arm impaling the flesh of his cheek.

'You forget,' Evan said. 'There's always going to be a monkey at the controls. And there's always a stronger monkey than you.'

Evan blinked twice and then he was back and there were no shards near the fireplace and Allman's face was unmarred and he'd never thrown the phone because he wasn't Evan Smoak or Orphan X or the Nowhere Man right now, he was Professor Stanley Leigh of Fucking Harvard and he had a role to uphold despite every last blood instinct coursing through his veins.

'Don't feel diminished by any of this,' Allman said, with impressive sincerity. 'We all seek to be governed, controlled. I don't mean consciously. But we all do. You by me. And me by it.'

'"It"?' Evan asked. 'What's "it"?'

Allman stood and walked to a smudged sliding door that let out onto the rear deck. '"It" is the *next* layer down.'

37. Baby Hitler

Allman stood with his hands on the splintery back rail. The earth sloped precipitously away into woods, no tamed back-yard to speak of. A disused Jacuzzi at the edge of the deck gathered scum, a tornado of mosquitoes flurrying above it. Nothing below but pepper trees, eucalyptus, and oak form-ing a dense landscape that undulated like frozen waves. Way beyond twinkled the second-rate skyline of Woodland Hills.

'I own all that,' Allman said, with a gesture. 'As far as you can see to the next lights. It's quiet here.'

When the breeze shifted, Evan could smell the crispness of the earth, wood and sage, soil and bark. Somewhere an owl hooted and hooted again and was answered by a mate somewhere in the vast darkness.

'What's the "it" that controls you?' Evan asked.

Allman's eyes watered in the breeze. He blinked a few times, his cheeks shiny. 'What I've described to you. The AI. In a few months, it'll be gaming *me*.'

'How?' Evan asked. 'Precisely?'

'Hmm. It tells me trends, things to look at and do. I'm stuck in a feedback loop with it. But increasingly, it's driving the direction of that feedback loop. Understand?'

Evan's stupid goddamned tie flapped in the wind and he smoothed it down, wishing he'd brought a tie clip or chain or whatever Harvard professors wear on their stupid god-damned ties. 'No.'

'All the information I'm gathering? It feeds into a big data farm. And that feeds into my other AI as new training data and then spits out recommendations. So let's just say' – he scrunched his nearly shut eyes, scenario-building – 'Solventry targets heavy people with more junk food because it's an easy sale, right?'

'Sure.'

'Wrong. We do it to push them toward diabetes *while* we're seeking to buy a consortium of endocrinologic health services from apps to meds *and* simultaneously lobbying Congress to widen the prescription parameters *and* shorting health-insurance companies on the stock market. I'm still driving the enterprise. Cool, right?'

Evan debated seizing Allman by the collar and waistband and launching him off the deck. A twenty-foot fall, a forty-degree slope, enough to snap a neck or at least cause permanent mental impairment. Baby Hitler and all that. But yet.

It was legal.

Allman was just playing the game exceptionally well.

Evan cleared his throat. 'Cool.'

'But lately? *It*'s started to drive the enterprise. This month I realized that our automatic stock-trading program had started to invest heavily in caffeine-inhaler vape-pen start-ups all on its own. And I didn't know why. So I searched for other irregularities in the adjacent AIs. Turns out our e-commerce shipping division had begun to create delays of purified water to a specific subset of residences. Turns out our social-media subsidiaries were promoting shorter short-form content that shifted the median duration on our platforms from fifteen seconds to five. Turns out our appliance-development group was receiving machine-learning recommendations to switch to blue-LED light indicators in our smoke and carbon-monoxide detectors. The AIs are playing with each other and feeding off each other. Know what they're doing?'

The breeze blew cool and dry across Evan's face. His lips felt chapped. His stomach roiled. He thought about his tie pin and the beckoning hole of Allman's ear, the tiny bones beyond the paper-thin drum.

'No.'

'Encouraging childhood ADHD.' The moonlight made the narrow slits of Allman's eyes glint. 'Stimulation, dehydration, choppy focus, sleep deprivation. We exacerbate the symptoms in childhood and from there we can move the consumer population on to juvenile-onset bipolar comorbidities.' He moved to straighten his glasses once more, a tremor in his hand betraying the slightest human vulnerability. 'It's beautiful. You asked about my reproductive fitness, what I'll leave behind? It's them. My offspring. They're the future.' His lips parted with a genuine grin, the first speck of humor in his lexicon. 'It's *alive.*'

An unhuman destiny, spun into existence by Allman's prolific mind.

'No one stands a chance,' Allman said. 'Not me. Certainly not you.'

Of all the people, Andre swam into Evan's mind. His words on the tip of Evan's tongue: *People are unpredictable. You never know when they'll surprise you. You can't count 'em out.*

And yet, against all this? The odds didn't merely feel daunting. They felt insurmountable.

Through the muddle of his thoughts, Evan reached for the Seventh Commandment: *One mission at a time.*

He was here because of a little girl and her missing dog.

He was here because of Jayla Hill and her murdered father.

He was here because he had to stop an assassin and whoever was behind her.

At every turn, he'd searched for a detour to steer the discussion toward Benjamin Hill and at every turn he'd felt thwarted. He had no doubt that Allman would snag on any inorganic overture. He needed to figure out how to extend the conversation a bit longer.

Evan put the small of his back to the rail, looking through the smudged glass at the sad house interior. 'Why then?' he asked. 'Why do all this?' He waved a hand, indicating Allman, the estate, the entire Solventry enterprise with its countless divisions, subsidiaries, and artificial brainpower.

'Because I can. It's better for me to control everything than someone else. Why should they? I figured out how. Wouldn't *you* want to control everything?'

Evan considered. He looked inside at the tattered cushions, the dirty dishes set askew here and there. Past the pony wall, that heap of sneakers was visible. It was an arresting image, apocalyptic, reminiscent of chattel trains and smokestacks. 'I would think I would. But if it ever happened, I believe I would realize that it was actually hell.'

'Hell?' Allman seemed genuinely puzzled. 'Imagine an existence in which you had all the leverage. All the time.'

Orphan X thought, *I do.*

Evan Smoak thought, *But it's an illusion.*

Professor Leigh remarked, 'They say if you know too much, you go insane. But I'm not sure that's true.' Evan looked into Allman's reptilian eyes. 'I think maybe you just go numb.'

Allman blinked twice rapidly. A touch of balance restored in their conversational dance.

'Well,' he said curtly. 'You asked about the nature of genius. That's what it is, what it does. Genius alters reality.'

Evan nodded. 'Thank you for your time.'

'If you breach that confidentiality agreement,' Allman said, without malice, 'I will devote my entire arsenal of computational power to destroying you.'

His turtle eyes snapped shut and opened once more and there was barely a difference.

This was a man who could predict anyone. Except Evan.

Living as the Nowhere Man insulated him, kept him outside the data flow of the contemporary universe. He was old-fashioned, analog, uncaptured.

'I understand,' Evan said. 'Now if you'll excuse me, I have to continue prepping for my other interview subjects.'

Allman's fingers shoved hastily at his eyeglasses frame, his squinty gaze averting. 'Who else are you studying?'

There it was. A pinprick opening, the faintest show of curiosity, competitiveness betraying insecurity.

Evan pounced. 'I have to respect confidentiality in all directions,' he said. 'I assume you of all people would understand.'

Allman's head jerked in a nod, his hair rasping the back of his collar.

'Except, I suppose, your employees',' Evan added. 'I'd imagine they'd be bound by NDAs to *you*.'

'My employees,' Allman spit. 'If your report's going to have any worth you should only be talking to visionaries. Which of my employees would you even want to interview?'

'Angela Cheng in artificial neural networking –'

'Competent, not brilliant.'

'Sean Hansen, quantitative methods –'

'Hardworking and versatile but hardly profound.'

'Benjamin Hill –'

'Hill? You didn't hear?'

'Hear what?'

'He was killed.'

'What?' Evan sagged against the railing. 'I had no idea. When?'

'Just this week. They said it was some sort of home invasion but I guess there are complications around it.' Allman shook his head. 'It's too bad.' The human sentiment caught

Evan by surprise, but then Allman clarified, 'Hill's a big loss for us. You can't easily replace someone like him.'

'No? What was he working on?'

'Key AI source code. I can't share anything beyond that.'

'Can you at least explain what that is?'

'How much do you know about autoencoders?'

'Nothing.'

'How much about neural networks in general?'

'Limited.'

Allman pursed his lips, exhaled through his nose. He was frustrated with Dr Leigh's limitations, but it was nothing personal. Evan was frustrated with them, too.

Allman chewed his inner cheek, agitated, his mind no doubt awhirl with ones and zeros and the vexation of having to translate. 'So you've never heard of a generative adversarial network?'

Once again, Evan wished Joey were here. 'No.'

'Then it's too complicated for you to understand.'

'Okay,' Evan said. '"Complications" around Hill's death. What's *that* mean?'

Allman shrugged. 'That's what the newspapers said. Some evidence pointed to irregularities suggesting it wasn't what it seemed. My security is interfacing with the authorities. It's all below my pay grade.'

'Do you think . . .' Evan waved a hand. 'Oh never mind. That's just me being nosy.'

'What?'

'Well, you said he's not easily replaced. Do you think he had any enemies?'

'Him? No.'

'But you?'

'Sure,' Allman said. 'The human race. That's what happens

when you're the leader of it. The race. You're the one in everyone's sights.'

Evan understood better why Allman stayed holed up behind gates, guard stations, and towering castle walls. 'You actually think . . . You actually think someone killed him to hurt you?'

Allman shrugged once more, the same lifeless lift of his shoulders. 'Not me. I don't get hurt. But Solventry, of course. Look. There are people you seek to avoid angering. Murdoch the elder. Ditto: Thiel. But Hill's area of expertise wouldn't directly impact any pies those two have their fingers in.'

Evan saw his eyes twitch with a thought.

The competitor most likely to benefit.

He wondered if he could press with one more question, decided he couldn't. He let the silence work for him.

Allman's wide lips pursed. But he said nothing.

Dr Leigh shuddered off the fearsome thought. 'I'm glad I don't work in that sphere. I hope I'm not interviewing the person who might have had anything to do with it.'

Allman's eyes were suddenly visible. Smooth black stones held in nests of crinkled skin. 'Are you meeting at Youtopia?'

'I am not.'

'Then you should be fine.'

'Thank you.' Evan breathed out a sigh of relief. 'Happy to dodge that bullet.'

He offered his hand.

Allman shook it with an odd clasp, as if he'd never shaken a hand before.

Then he turned and stared out at his land below.

Evan hesitated, then walked back through the sliding door into the house.

Focused intently on the security monitors, Biltmore

pinned down the barstool. Though Evan passed right by him, he didn't look up, a pointed slight.

Evan let himself out. Standing on the porch, he cleared the foul warmth of the house from his lungs. The inhalation brought in the waft of sewage from the trench, hardly an improvement. His brain felt scorched from the conversation, his insides scoured.

Climbing in his car, he tore off the stupid goddamned tie and coasted down the long driveway, darkness enfolding the car. The mighty cypresses loomed on either side, their tops invisible against the night. They might have continued up forever.

Evan tried to contrast Allman's barren worldview with the living realities Jack had tried to instill in him – wisdom, self-determination, and hardest of all, the striving to stay human.

Now it all seemed quaint and outdated, as Allman had said.

Evan's speck of a car drifted down the majestic drive, insignificant beneath the boundless darkness overhead. The sheer gate rumbled aside, and he rolled forward beyond Allman's battlement walls, and then he was drifting through the dreamy wonderland of ranch homes and white rail fences, his gut churning and flipping until he pulled over onto the decomposed granite shoulder, slung open the driver's door, and retched twice, bringing nothing up but a strand of thick saliva that he spit off his lower lip.

For a time he stared down at the dirt and breathed.

When he raised his head, the pale-faced horse was there, giving him a devil stare over the rail fence. But there was no evil in the horse's gaze. In place of where its eyes would be were twinning circles of shadowed nothingness.

38. Whateverthefuck

Driving home, Evan felt the aftermath of the visit with Allman coursing through his veins, toxic and unshakable. The road was dark and the night was dark and the world seemed unsafe, fragile, caught in the clutches of something powerful and unknowable. For the first time since Jack's death, he asked the universe for a lifeline.

Not one second later the RoamZone blared from the glove box: *DONCHA WISH YER GIRLFRIEND WUZ HAAAWT LIKE ME?!*

He pulled the catch, reached for the phone.

Before he could speak, Sofia's eleven-year-old voice spilled out: 'It's Dad,' she choked out through a sob. 'He's missing.'

'Not missing,' Brianna clarified, her voice coming through Evan's car speakers. '*Drinking.*' She'd taken the phone from her daughter and put it on speaker. 'Not that I see why you give a' – she caught herself – 'care.'

Evan had already popped onto the 101, vectoring east toward downtown.

'I can't lose Loco *and* Dad,' Sofia said. 'Something's wrong. He promised he wouldn't drink no more. He *promised.*'

'Yeah, baby,' Brianna said. 'Your father makes a lot of promises.'

Sofia tearfully filled in Evan. Andre called her at eight o'clock every night without fail. It was half past already and he hadn't rung and was not answering his phone.

'And he *always* picks up when it's me.'

'He wants to, baby,' Brianna said. 'It's not about you –'

'It *is* about me.'

'– it's the alcohol. It's what it does to him.' Bri's words had the practiced cadence of a mantra, and Evan could tell she'd spoken them a time or twenty. 'What he *lets* it do to him.'

The thump of footsteps stomping away, and then a door slammed.

The tires of the Dodge Neon thrummed along the freeway. He passed a Solventry box truck, the smiley-face daisy grinning at him cheerily from a side panel.

'Where does he go when he falls off the wagon?' Evan asked.

'Thought it was none of your business,' Brianna said. "Member?'

The worst case hit like ice in his gut – the fear that just as he'd wound forward into the mission, it in turn was winding its way into him. 'Where do you think he is?'

'Now you give a shit all of a sudden?'

Evan felt his teeth grind. 'You called me.'

'No. Sofia did.'

'Then help me help her.'

In the pause, he could hear Brianna breathing.

'Who's On First,' she said. 'A bar, not the joke. Guess where it's at?'

And then she hung up.

Who's On 1st was the arithmetic mean of every dive bar Evan had ever seen. Speakeasy door of distressed wood. Faded brick chipped at the edges and pocked with burns from stubbed-out cigarettes. Alley with standing water in the back. Red and yellow neon glow of a Budweiser sign barely penetrating obsidian-black windows.

Four freeways squared this particular box of East LA, the corner building floating on First Street at the edge of the

Chinese Cemetery. Evan entered to the inevitable Bob Seger song on the inevitable jukebox, the inevitable loners sitting at the bar sipping from timeless brown bottles. Foosball table with broken strikers, dartboard missing chunks of foam, concrete floor tacky against his soles. Emergency door in the back carved with phone numbers and slander, crash bar-equipped for ease of expelling troublemakers. The whole place was a bit larger than a Winnebago and just as opulent.

Evan snapshotted the interior in a single click, a pent-up breath releasing with relief.

There Andre was at the end of the bar, perched sloppily on a stool.

Booze had misaligned his body, hips one way, shoulders the other, torso Slinkying to balance his head. The seats around him had cleared, and the regulars, replicants with denim jackets and chapped faces, seemed plenty happy to give him space.

Evan's relief at spotting Andre quickly gave way to disdain. Andre was a sloppy drunk, and the fact that he was safe only heightened the inconvenience of his idiocy.

Evan walked over to him, his boots knocking the floor. The closer he got the more he drew the focus of the denizens. As he slid into the adjacent stool, the bartender said, 'Your pal's on his last strike. Threw a shot glass at the mirror.' He nodded toward a dent in the wall. 'His aim's no better'n his comportment. One more hiccup, the boys are ready to put him in finishing school.'

'Just do your job and pour, Jimmy,' Andre said.

'That's the last of it for tonight, Andre,' a thick-necked man to Evan's side said. Inexplicably he wore dark Ray-Bans with gold rims, perhaps in anticipation of a solar flare. A rectangular scar at the base of his skull confirmed the provenance of the haphazard sowing of hair plugs filling out his scalp. Aggravated *and* vain made him a threat for escalation. 'I didn't come here to watch you whine.'

'Look what I have for you, Nando.' Andre wagged his middle finger at the guy.

Evan slapped his hand down. 'The hell you doing?'

'Me?' Andre leaned in at Evan, his breath rank with rum. 'You're in *my* bar.'

'Because guess who called me to deal with your drinking problem –?'

'I don't have a drinking problem. I have a drinking *solution*.' Glassy-eyed, Andre waved a hand around. 'My problems are *way* worse than this.'

'And you're helpless before them,' Evan said. 'They're too powerful to do anything about but roll over and let them have their way with you.'

'We can't all be heroes like you.' Andre stretched across the bar past Evan, snatched Nando's pint glass, hoisted it in a toast. 'To Evan the Hero.'

Nando was halfway up but Evan showed him his palm. 'Sorry, sir. I'll get your next round.'

With a glare, Nando lowered himself back onto his stool.

Andre's eyes shone with spite. 'Don't we wish we could measure up to the guy who got saved from the foster home? Mr Detached, silver spoon in his mouth, more money'n he can count. But I'm just one of the little people, Evan. Working three jobs and tryin' to show up for my girl.' He downed Nando's drink. 'And you don't even get it. How much work I – *damn it, damn it* – how much it all is. To *not* drink. To *not* lay down. Even if it don't look like shit to you. All day every day the walls are closing in. Gas prices ticking up at the pump, cutting into my twelve bucks an hour. Fucking groceries. I bought a bottle of Advil the other day for my back – twenty-six ninety-nine. That's, what? Three hours of work less taxes.

For pills so I can keep driving Lyft for another – what? – six months before they replace my ass with self-driving cars or robots or whateverthefuck. It ain't just that I'm not in the game anymore, man. I don't even know what game I'm supposed to be playing.'

He leaned to spit on the floor, a long gooey thread he let dangle from his lips and then fall. Polishing a stainless shaker, Jimmy eyed him warily. At his feet was a corrugated shipping box holding a dozen Kahlúa bottles, the ubiquitous smiling daisy stamped on its side.

But Andre was locked on Evan. 'Know what I tell myself a thousand times a day? "I got this." "I got this." But I don't. I don't got it, man. I don't got anything. And I don't want to admit that, you understand? Even to myself.'

For a long time, Evan stared at him, trying to quiet the seething in his chest. Andre stank of despair. It was hard not to detest him for it. Evan could handle grief – it was an emotion, one he wasn't prone to. But despair, despair was a concession.

'What?' Andre asked. '*What?* Ain't you gonna talk?'

'What for? We already know everything you and I think about this.'

'Yeah? Must be nice having everything figured out.' Andre tried to snap his fingers but couldn't align them. 'Jimmy. Gimme another.'

Jimmy hesitated, hand on a jug of Bacardi. Evan caught his eye, shook his head nearly imperceptibly. Jimmy said to Evan, 'You deal with that then.'

Andre glared at the bartender. 'Don't you listen to him. *I'm* your fucking customer. How many years now, Jimmy? How many years?'

'Too many, Andre.'

Andre threw the pint glass at Jimmy's head.

234

Jimmy ducked, a quick boxer's move, the glass sailing by and smashing against the bar, sending a spray of shards into the drinkers beyond. Everyone was on their feet, Nando closest, Jimmy grabbing something from beneath the bar and vaulting over.

Evan fisted Andre's shirt, shoving him behind him, back-pedaling to the emergency door.

Jimmy's wrist snapped downward and a black chrome ASP telescoped out to baton length.

Nando came in hard, and Evan bladed his hand and jabbed his solar plexus. He coughed out a chunk of air and threw an off-balance swing. With a forearm block, Evan redirected the blow, and Nando's fist smashed into the edge of the bar. He gulped audibly, the pain of impact taking his breath, and dropped to a knee. Jimmy lunged past him, but before he could wind up with the ASP, Evan flicked his boot and swept his ankle, careful not to break it. The bartender hit the deck hard, shoulders slapping concrete.

Beyond the two downed men, the remaining customers shifted on their feet, eyes shiny and alert. But Evan's reaction had stopped them in their tracks. And the cramped space worked against them; they could only come at him in single file.

'We're leaving,' Evan said. 'Let us go. Everyone's gotta wake up and work tomorrow, right?'

He kept squared to them. They didn't agree but they didn't advance either. On the floor, Jimmy hacked a few times and rolled up to lean against the bar, a glob of saliva at the side of his lips.

Evan peeled a hundred from his money clip and rested it on the jukebox. 'Next round,' he said. 'And apologies.'

Reaching behind him for Andre, Evan shoved him again toward the rear door. Andre rag-dolled along, unsteady on his legs.

Another two shuffled steps and a final push slammed Andre against the crash bar and out into the alley. Pivoting, Evan banged him against a dumpster, the metal thundering.

'I'm sick of saving your ass.' Evan's words came hard through clenched teeth. 'You start another fight, you're on your own.'

'That's why I'm *here,* dumbass. To be on my own.'

'You can't just not answer your fucking phone,' Evan said. 'You have a daughter. Your daughter's mom. You have people counting on you.' He was angrier than made any sense. 'Get it together, Andre. People have more to do than clean up after you.'

'You think I don't know?' His lips were wobbling now, his face a confusion of sorrow and rage. 'Your big fucking insights for me? You think I don't know I fuck everything up? That I fucked it up with Bri?' He kept shouting at Evan through a hoarse throat. 'I know, okay? *I* did.' He thumped his chest with a fist. 'I couldn't believe how good she was. That she loved me for me. No way, right? What's the hustle? So I pushed to test it. To see. How 'bout *now*? How 'bout if I'm drunk? How 'bout if I don't show up? How 'bout if I let you down? And again? And again? And finally she said, "Fuck. I give. I give up. I give up on you." And she was right to. And it's not fucking fixable ever, and now and then I want a little rum. I just want a little rum and for everyone to stay the fuck out of my face.' He was cry-screaming, pathetic. 'So get the fuck out of my face, Evan.'

Evan couldn't remember the last time he'd allowed anger to seep through him like this. He slammed Andre against the dumpster again, and Andre collapsed to the ground.

'Happily,' Evan said. 'You piece of shit.'

He walked out of the alley, head down, boots rippling the pooled water, making the heavens wobble. He came around the corner, striding to the crosswalk. His palms were hot and he felt his heart thumping in his chest and he wondered how he could deal with lethal assassins and psychopathic CEOs while barely breaking a sweat and yet this useless drunk, a lost foster-home boy like him, could set his nerves on edge, infect him like a virus.

The Ten Commandments shielded him from letting in weakness, from drowning in shades of gray. He couldn't open the door now. If he did, who else would come through? And how many more complications would they bring?

At a point it was too much. Joey with her needs. Sofia with her shitty little dog. Dr Hill and Jayla. The Wolf and whoever had set her in motion. Allman plotting the digital overthrow of human civilization.

Evan had asked for help but he'd only gotten more mess, more problems, more responsibility.

He halted.

The Dodge Neon beckoned across the street, shiny and clean, a fine escape vehicle.

He pictured Andre as a husky kid back in Pride House, how he'd sit on his top bunk sketching in his notepad, drawing sexy girls and superheroes and Cadillacs, visions of a future where he wasn't someone laid out drunk in the shadow of a dumpster behind a third-rate bar. He thought about himself groggy with vodka on the couch in the Tarzana safe house, Joey storming in with the RoamZone, throwing it at his chest. *It's not just you, you know.* Jack standing amid the Virginia oaks. *What if there's no one to fix anything? Except you.*

Lowering his head, he let a sigh seep through his clenched teeth. Kicked the toe of his boot twice into the pavement.

Then he turned around and walked back into the alley.

Andre hadn't gotten up. He lay crumpled against the dumpster, arms splayed, the puddle soaking into his jeans.

Evan stood over him. Andre didn't stir but his eyes ticked up, the whites shining in the gloom.

'Come on,' Evan said.

'Lea' me alone.'

'Come on.'

Andre's eyes were wet. He sounded like a little boy. 'Fuck you.'

'Andre.'

'I'm not fucking perfect like you! Okay? I didn't get a shot. Didn't get rescued out of the home. I *crawled* out. And I'm still crawling, you arrogant motherfucker. I'm still . . .'

His hands went to his face, trembling, and he was sobbing as openly as a child.

Evan's mouth was dry. He said, 'Andre.'

Andre shoved his hands across his chest under his arms, hugging himself, eyes downcast, shuddering with grief.

'I'm sorry.' Evan's throat was thick. 'Andre.'

Nothing.

Evan put out his hand. 'Brother.'

Andre looked up at him, sweat-damp hair in his eyes, face swollen.

He held out a trembling hand.

Evan lifted him up.

Brianna peered out at Evan through the two-inch slice allowed by the security door latch. She wore a bathrobe, a champagne-colored silk head wrap, and a scowl. She took Evan's measure, undid the door, and walked away, leaving him to follow.

He did.

A fresh humidity from a recently cracked dishwasher heavied the air of the small apartment. There were vacuum lines in the carpet, and the counters were wiped clean, and an insulated lunch bag and thermos rested on a dish-drying mat by the kitchen sink. On the garage-sale desk in the corner, a stapler pinned down a stack of bills that looked taller than a month's worth.

In the corner of the living room, a shrine to the missing dog had been erected atop two stacked shoe boxes. An Our Lady of Perpetual Help *veladora* flickered, giving off a discordant hint of coconut. The candle flame uplit a low-quality printout of Loco's lolling tongue and mildly schizophrenic face.

Brianna turned to face Evan in front of the couch. She didn't invite him to sit.

She crossed her arms, thickened dysmorphically by the terry bathrobe sleeves. 'Well?'

'I found Andre where you said. Got him home. He's okay.'

Her eyes darted away but he swore he read relief in them. She had thumbprint-size bruises beneath her lids, and in the dim light she looked worn-down, single-mom exhausted. 'Was it ugly?'

'Yeah,' Evan said.

A door creaked behind Evan and then Sofia padded out. She wore a lime-green sleeping gown with tutu frills and a matching hair band.

'Is Dad okay?'

Evan said, 'He's okay.'

'Was he drinking?'

Evan looked at Brianna, got back a steely-eyed look. He said, 'Yes.'

'Too much?'

'Yes.'

'That's why he didn't call me?'

'Yes.'

Her eyes glistened and her mouth bunched up with angry determination. ''Cuz he cares about drinking more than me?'

'No.'

'Why'd he do it then? Get drunk instead of calling me like he promised? Like he was supposed to?'

'I don't know,' Evan said. 'People are messy. I don't understand them.'

Sofia said, 'That's fucked up.'

The word in her little girl mouth sounded even more profane. And appropriate.

'Yeah,' Evan said. 'It is fucked up.'

She eased forward on her bare feet one step, two, and then leaned into Evan. Just: tilted until her forehead met his sternum, arms dangling in a zombie hang between them. She wanted something. Proximity? Contact? Comfort?

She'd startled him, his arms floating idiotically up at his sides as if he'd just jumped off a cliff and was readying to flap his way to safety.

Behind Sofia's back, Brianna implored him with raised eyebrows and an emphatic jerk of her splayed fingers: *Do something, stupid.* He felt as men have felt since time immemorial beneath the glare of superior feminine EQ – clueless and incomplete. Resetting, he lowered one arm across Sofia's shoulders and gave the child a pat on her back. It was hard to believe the frailty of her bones beneath the skin, the ridge of the spine, the posterior ribs – like petting a baby bird.

Sofia didn't move. She smelled like shampoo and soap.

'Bed now,' Brianna said, her voice thick. 'Go on.'

Sofia tilted her weight back onto her heels and headed toward her room. She hesitated at the little altar, hit her knees, crossed herself, and then rose and scampered down the brief hall. The door closed, extinguishing the lavender glow of a night-light.

'That dog,' Brianna said, 'he's already dead, right?'

Evan shrugged. 'He's a survivor.'

'Like you. Like Andre.'

Evan shifted uncomfortably on his feet. 'Andre's doing his best.'

'No,' she said. 'Uh-uh. Don't you try'n sell that here.'

Evan said, 'Okay.'

'Let me tell you all I care about now.' Bri pointed down the hall. 'That little girl. Not having her heart broke. Which is impossible. You know why? Because Andre is her father.'

'I understand.'

'Do you?' Her arms were crossed again, her stare hard, accusatory, and Evan understood that he was being asked to answer for something more than himself.

He said, 'Yes.'

Her glare softened, and she loosened her arms and blew out a breath.

'You know,' she said, 'there's a hidden blessing in having someone in your life you can't reach. It humbles you, your arrogance in thinking you could fix everyone if they just had the good sense to listen to you. And . . .' Her lips trembled. 'It gives you gratitude for all the people who *might be* reachable.'

Evan didn't like the feeling of her eyes on him. It felt like a challenge.

He nodded a good-bye and withdrew.

Out in the hall he heard the *thump-thump-thump* of the communal dryers working overtime. He paused a moment and shouldered into the wall, breathing in the relative quiet.

He had no idea what to feel.

39. Wolf-Eat-Wolf

'Who's the visionary behind Youtopia?' Evan asked. The shitty speakers of the Dodge Neon crackled, but the connection held.

Despite the East Coast hour, Luke Devine had sounded perfectly awake when he'd picked up. 'Visionary?'

'Someone Allman would consider a legitimate rival.'

Since he was already downtown, he'd decided to take a spin through Dr Hill's neighborhood on the off chance that Loco had returned to sniff around familiar ground. He laced through the surrounding blocks, scanning sidewalks and alcoves.

'That'd be Nathan Friedhoff, the CEO. Rumor has it he's a bit wobbly of late.'

'Why's that?'

'Too much power can crack a man as sure as too much suffering. Thin line between genius and madness. I could hum a few bars but I'm sure you know the tune already.'

Evan called up Friedhoff's photograph on the Youtopia website. He wanted to see someone who could outcompete Allman on the scale of reprehensibility, someone willing to assassinate competitors with the ease of a Russian *pakhan* and eliminate their children after that. Friedhoff was a slender white guy in a suit and tie. His pose said: whimsical yet competent.

Evan tried to imagine the string of actions that led from this man to Jayla Hill asphyxiating on a butcher-block slab in her own home. Before any heat could gain purchase, the First Commandment backed him off: *Assume nothing.*

He'd get to Friedhoff. And extract the answers he required.

'Friedhoff, he's up in Silicon Valley?'

'No,' Devine said. 'LA, like Allman. Youtopia took over Amazon Studios' old digs in the Santa Monica Water Garden. I heard somewhere Friedhoff bought a designer home in the Hollywood Hills – one of those glass monstrosities.'

'I need to get in with him, too. Same ruse.'

'I don't like taking orders.'

'Want me to fly out, ask in person?'

'No,' Devine said quickly. 'That won't be necessary. Why do you need to see him?'

'He had motive to wipe out Allman's principal deep-learning scientist. Competing technology.'

'Tech is a wolf-eat-wolf world,' Devine observed. 'What'd you think of Allman?'

'Nothing,' Evan said.

'That little?'

'No. I think he *is* nothing. He's a void. He's like . . . evolution. An unthinking force.'

Devine made a thoughtful sound. 'Yes. He thinks that's all any of us are.'

Evan said, 'Friedhoff, ASAP,' and hung up.

The row of town houses materialized ahead, a rise of affluence. Evan drove the Neon right past the front of Hill's place without slowing. No interior lights, dark as a tomb. Vehicles lined the metered street, many with post-market tinted windows. They stretched a full block up to the Burger King.

Looping around, he cut back through the alley where he'd nearly been steamrolled by the black Suburban just three days ago. A grizzly-bear swipe of crumbled stucco marred the east entrance where the SUV had buried itself after it had clipped Evan and transformed him briefly into a human

243

Frisbee. He coasted through the narrow aisle now, headlights picking across the wind-strewn trash, searching out the mangy dog.

The back of Hill's town house floated by on his left, a towering edifice of blackness.

He thought about the row of parked vehicles across from the entrance to Hill's place. Pictured Jayla's curled form in the hospital bed, that bandage across her throat, forcing her to push words out through her hands. *Why does she want to hurt me? Because I saw her face?*

An operational concern tingled to life in his brain stem. He paid attention, excavated it, forced it to the surface.

Parking on a neighboring street, he retrieved from the loadout bag in the trunk a pair of Steiner tactical binoculars equipped with state-of-the-art night vision.

On the building adjacent to Hill's town house, he climbed the same fire escape he'd plummeted down days earlier. Belly scraping across the roof, he combat-crawled toward the edge, inching his way to the brink.

Barely breathing, he lay on his stomach, scanning the parked vehicles, making sure he offered only the faintest slice of profile above the rooftop. There was a beat-to-shit Prius, two Toyota pickups, a half dozen nondescript sedans, a dilapidated Hyundai Tucson, and a Yukon with mud splashed up the wheel wells. Streetlights bounced off the vehicles' windows, turning the panes reflective, hiding the interiors. He paid closest attention to the SUVs.

Ten minutes passed. Twenty. His breath misted faintly in the cold. The night air cooled the inside of his throat. His stomach itched but he didn't move to scratch it. The only way he could get closer to the roof's surface would be if he turned liquid.

He was about to draw back when the window of the Yukon quivered and then slowly eased down.

He caught a round glint – a sniper scope? – and almost jerked back before noting that it was doubled.

A set of night-vision binoculars just like his. Gloved hands curled around the lenses, towhead bangs framing a shadowed face.

He stared through his binoculars down at her.

The Wolf stared through her binoculars up at him.

Lying in wait for Jayla Hill to return home.

Lowering the Steiners, he gave the Wolf a little salute, two fingers tapping his forehead, a match of the gesture she'd given him outside Jayla's hospital: *See ya around.*

The Wolf lowered her binoculars and flashed a smile.

The rising window, a reverse guillotine, claimed her head in a smooth chop. The Yukon rattled to life, screeched out from its spot, and was gone.

40. Permanent Damage

IT'S CALLED THE HOMEOWNER'S ASSOCIATION, the flyer screamed from the door to the Castle Heights lobby. *SO LET'S* ASSOCIATE*!!!*

Standing on the landing of the dim garage, enervated in the wake of Allman's nihilist ramblings, Andre's misery, and the Wolf's competent vigilance, Evan was unsure what he was in the mood for, though he sure as hell knew it wasn't weaponized cheeriness punctuated by an excess of exclamation points.

Smaller lettering beneath declaimed: *Crafts 'n Chit-Chat at the* Rez *of Your Current HOA* Prez*!* Tear tabs at the bottom, scissored into hanging chads, provided date, time, and Lorilee's apartment number. All but one of the tabs had been torn off. Was it possible that a full dozen residents were desperate enough to partake of crafts 'n chit-chat? Or had Hugh Walters ripped them off himself in order to sabotage his nemesis? Either way, the escalating machinations over nominal political control of Castle Heights wore on Evan's frayed nerves.

Setting his jaw, he pressed through the door.

The lobby was tranquil save for the faintest bump of Chicano rap from the direction of Joaquin's security station. As Evan neared, Joaquin tilted forward on his chair and slapped at the radio, changing the station to golden oldies.

'Evening, Mr S.'

As Joaquin adjusted his oversize blazer, Evan spotted a neck tattoo peeking out from his shirt collar. He felt an added measure of respect for the young man. That kind of ink meant Joaquin had some street in him. He'd always played his role here, doing his job and doing it well. Working an hourly wage made it likely he lived in a multigenerational household, maybe with his grandparents, a kid at home, as much an impostor in this world as Evan was.

'Put your music on,' Evan said. 'Until someone complains.'

Joaquin summoned the elevator remotely for Evan, scratched at his throat where the tie chafed. 'Someone already complained.'

'Who?'

Joaquin hesitated.

'I won't rat you out,' Evan said.

'Mr Walters. He, uh, registered his objections when he laid these out.' Joaquin gestured at an array of bright materials resting before him on the laminate surface of the curved reception desk.

Evan veered from his path to the elevator to take a closer look.

Glossy custom buttons featuring a bus-stop-worthy portrait of Hugh Walters's face, along with pens sporting a campaign slogan: *THE RIGHT HUGH OF LEADERSHIP!*

A rare burn of acid reflux singed the back of Evan's throat. 'Good God.'

Joaquin allowed a half grin. 'I just work here, man.'

Evan picked up a pen. Lettered down the tube: *STRONG, STEADY LEADERSHIP.*

The lobby door opened, Lorilee stumbling in from the porte cochere riding a gust of wind. Red, white, and blue balloons bobbled around her, a dedicated micro-cloud. Each one featured her visage, inflation distorting her screen-printed face to even greater rubbery proportion than its Botox-enhanced real-world counterpart. Given the flurry of movement, it took some effort for Evan to piece together the sentence emblazoned across the blue balloons: *LORILEE'S YOUR SALVATION . . . FOR THE HOMEOWNERS ASSOCIATION!* In case the rhymed couplet proved insufficient, the reds and whites featured individual messages: *KUDOS TO YOU FOR VOTING FOR COMPASSION! KUDOS TO YOU FOR VOTING YOUR TRUTH! KUDOS TO YOU FOR DEMANDING THE LEADERSHIP YOU DESERVE!*

There were more kudoses but he'd lost the will to keep reading.

'A sandwich board was too unwieldly?' he said.

'Huh?' Lorilee batted at the balloons, clearing a lane to oxygen, emerging from the hydra-headed confusion. 'Ev! I was hoping you could come to my special –'

'No.' He stepped backward into the elevator, which had swooped down to his rescue. The doors closed blissfully around him, and he exhaled.

A black-and-white version of Hugh's portrait peered out from commercially printed Post-its spattered around the floor buttons: *DON'T FORGET TO EXERCISE YOUR RIGHT TO VOTE AT THE BALLOT BOX THIS SUNDAY!* A green check mark ticked the box next to Hugh's name.

A flute-intensive Muzak rendering of Handel's *Water Music* accompanied Evan and the colorless Hughs up. Evan tried four-square breathing to ease his aggravation.

It didn't.

He strode down the corridor of the twenty-first floor.

A bright yellow advertising hanger dangled from his doorknob.

It featured a glossy rendering of pantsuited Lorilee peering intrepidly into the middle distance, face lit sunnily, hair lifted behind her as if by a headwind. Her fists were set on her hips in a show of resoluteness. Her augmented chest was puffed further with intention, Washington crossing the Delaware. Distinguished script read, *LORILEE SMITHSON. TAKING US INTO THE FUTURE . . . TOGETHER!*

Evan crumpled it off the doorknob and shoved into his penthouse.

Joey was sitting glumly at the kitchen island, thumbing at her phone, Dog slumbering as close to her barstool as he could get.

Evan tossed the balled-up advert into the trash can beneath the coat hangers and trudged in.

Joey barely looked up. "Tsup, X. I'm . . . I have this thing I need to . . .'

Vestigial streaks of peanut butter besmeared a spoon resting on the counter beside her. A half-empty glass of orange juice sat nakedly beside it, not four inches from where he'd strategically positioned the stack of coasters.

He paused at her shoulder. 'Update?'

She had her snout in her phone again, distracted. Evan cleared his throat and she snapped to, setting it down but keeping her hand on it. 'Been in the Vault *literally* all day.' Her phone chimed and dinged with incoming texts, Evan squinting against the distraction. 'Ran into column-level encryption on the Solventry databases – more layers between us and Doc Hill's work. Whatever the hell he was up to, it's buried deep in there. I just popped out for . . . Gonna head back to oversee the cracking of the RC4 private key . . .'

Her phone lifted in her palm once more as if it were controlling her hand, its glow uplighting her cheeks. She shot off rapid-fire replies to texts, one after another: Selfie with her tongue out, hang ten with her hand. Back to a flat expression as she scrolled to the next. Another reply: 😂😂🤣!! Her face didn't change. Another selfie: Eyebrows raised with distress. Sent. Dead-faced text: OMG. LMFAO!

He glared at the phone with enmity, bitterness swirling in his stomach. Allman's words were still roiling around in there, too.

He started to say something to Joey.

Decided against it.

He moved on to the freezer vault, the mist curling up his nostrils, chilling his windpipe, drying the sweat at his hairline. The door closed behind him with an airtight thump, and then it was just him in a glass-encased room with the purest of liquids also encased in glass and spaced at equal distances on glass shelves. And just beyond, through an armor-plated floor-to-ceiling pane, that south-facing view of Century City with its blocky high-rises, empty offices checkered at random with yellow rectangles, windows to the soulless. It felt safe in here, a vodka Faraday cage protected from the signals and transmissions of the modern world that invisibly ruled the air, tentacling their way into screens and from there into brains.

He set his hands on the freestanding bar in the center to breathe.

A craving arose in him to scour his insides, an urge for cleansing warmth, antiseptic numbing.

A tall slender bottle to his left held Smoke Point, a vodka made from smoke-tinged malbec and merlot grapes that had been damaged in the Northern California Glass Fire. An idiosyncratic offering from Hangar 1, it was fruit-forward at first sip but then turned bold, almost aggressive. The distillation process cleared away most traces of flame, leaving behind licorice, pepper, and allspice. He had respect for the vodka and the punishing filtration process it had undergone to transform itself from base matter into pure.

Seeding a stainless shaker with five ice cubes, he glugged in two fingers and shook and shook some more, skin fusing to metal, his palms aching with the cold.

A proper martini glass rested on a lower shelf, frosted to opaqueness. He poured, ice crystals snowflaking the surface. With a steel pick, he skewered a smoked olive, dunked it in twice, and set it aside.

The first sip struck wrong as it sometimes did, a scalding hit of rubbing alcohol. He swallowed quickly, let his taste buds relax, then took a second sip.

There it was, his palate soothed into readiness, the elixir warming his tongue with pleasing viscosity. He could taste the blighted vineyard, strong enough that he'd only be able to handle a few sips.

With his front teeth, he plucked the olive from the pick, chewed, breathed out smoke and salt.

The next taste was perfectly balanced, soothing his insides.

He indulged another sip, let it wash its way down. Then he emerged into the penthouse, the contrast of room temperature sheening his skin with humidity.

Walking over to Joey, he set down his RoamZone on the island and pulled up a stool across from her.

She kept at her phone. 'It's just . . . this sorority thing . . .' Her voice droned off with her attention. 'Been, like, super mixed-signals-y confusing with all this stuff around the rush. Like, they posted a pic with some of the *other* girls from rush but not me. . . .' She zombied out for a few more seconds. 'Dunno if it's, like, intentional. Or just 'cuz. Do they want me? Do they *not* want me? But I don't think it's . . .' *Tap tap tap.* 'I guess at the sorority house it's the Syncocalypse, you know, that time of the month for all the girls living together, so it got all *Mean Girls*-y . . . Trying to . . .'

'Hey,' he said. And then: '*Hey.*'

But she'd glossed over again, trancelike, staring into the void and nervously nibbling a fingernail. He watched her thumbs pecking, the glow reflecting in her eyes, turning them deader yet. ROTFL. LOLOLOL. BWAHAHAHA!

He wanted to shout.

He wanted to shake sense into her.

He wanted to say, *You're deeper and truer than any fake reality found inside that phone. And the fact that you think for a moment that you have to preen or audition makes me murderous with rage at the people who built that device and all the shit that runs on it.*

Instead he said, 'Josephine. Put the phone down.'

He said it sharply.

She looked up. She understood that tone. She put her phone down.

'Sorry,' she said.

'Stop feeding that shit into your face. You're scrambling your hard drive. It's unsat operationally. I know you need to dip in now and then but get it under control.'

She swallowed. 'Okay,' she said. 'It's just, I'm having a problem figuring out how to deal with these kind of, you know, social posts –'

'That's not a real problem. Other people have real problems. Problems they're not choosing to let in.'

She visibly wilted. Seeing her reaction, he rewound and registered the harshness of his words. They were correct but not the best ones. He felt a sting of remorse. But righteous anger, too. Joey was a blazingly capable human and a highly trained operator. Why the hell would she let Allman and a gaggle of sorority idiots into her nervous system?

The too-loud ring tone shattered through his thoughts: *DONCHA WISH YER GIRLFRIEND –*

He snatched the RoamZone. Caller ID showed Jayla's

burner phone requesting a video call. Initiating background filters, he tapped to answer.

There Jayla was in a dark bedroom, staring wide-eyed from her bed. She looked gaunt, hollowed-out.

'You okay?'

A flurry of hand signals. *No. No, I'm not okay.*

'Slow down. What happened?'

They brought in a doctor to see me today. Permanent damage. That's what I have. The zip tie crushed my vocal cords. It's so – A gesture he didn't understand but her expression made clear it conveyed profanity.

'Okay,' he said. 'So it's just a medical problem?'

Forefinger aimed up, scooping the air angrily. *Just? Just?!*

'I mean are you physically safe?'

I don't have a voice. My voice is gone. Index finger in the air making big vehement circles, head wagging for punctuation: *Forever.*

He started to say something, but she was still signing. To his side, Evan sensed Joey leaning forward to take in the screen. She stayed out of frame, shoulders bunched by her ears, eyes shiny with empathy.

I can't sing. I'm not me *anymore. I don't have anyone. I don't have my stuff. I can't see my aunt. They said they arranged to keep me here until Wednesday but I want to go home now.*

Only until Wednesday? He'd have to line out a safe house, which would interfere with his movements and his ability to –

That was for later.

He said, 'No.'

I can't do this alone. I need my bed. Something I recognize. I'm going to tell them to take me home now.

'You can't go home.'

Brow knurled, eyes bunched, right hand to forehead, then

253

flung angrily outward with thumb and pinky thrust wide: *Why?*

'Because there's a hired assassin staking out your house, ready to kill you.'

Jayla ceased her angry gesticulations, shoulders hanging limply, face suddenly bare. Her cheeks trembled and she leaned forward as if she'd taken a blow to the gut.

Keeping out of view, Joey reached over and poked MUTE. 'What are you doing?' she said to Evan. 'You're scaring the hell out of her.'

'She *should* be scared. She's got the Wolf waiting to put holes in her, the Marshals are only giving her five more days, and she wants to put her critical mass on display earlier than that.'

'Okay,' Joey said, 'right. Just remember . . .'

On the screen, Jayla was still hunched over in bed, hugging her stomach, shoulders quivering.

'What?' Evan said.

Joey said, 'She's a kid.'

'She's *your age*.'

'But she's not me, X.'

On the screen Jayla was rocking now, her hands moving repetitively, instinctively. I want to go home. I want to go home.

Evan took the RoamZone off mute. 'Jayla.'

I want my dad. I want my dad. I want my dad.

'Jayla.'

She looked up. Downturned mouth, stretched with sorrow. Her keening made ragged shapes of grief that were hard to hear. He pushed down an internal dial, lowering the emotional content of her sobs until only the other frequencies were audible.

Jayla curled forward, shuddering.

'Stay until Wednesday,' Evan said. 'You need to do that. I'll clear the way. I'll get you to your aunt. I'll get you home. I promise. Okay? Look at me. Look at me.'

It took a moment for her to lift her head, matted hair straggling down across her eyes.

He shaped the word for her, touching his left index finger to his lips then flattening the hand and pushing it down atop his right fist: *Promise.*

Jayla's eyes welled. She looked at him with desperation and hope.

He focused hard on his face, let her in.

A spark of connection he felt through his chest, as a pain in the vertebrae of his neck. He held open. She saw something in him she needed to see, jerked a quick nod, and severed the connection.

The penthouse was suddenly, brutally silent. Alcohol lingered at the back of his tongue, firing his inhalation. He stared at the dark screen.

Joey had blanched. She scratched at her forehead. There wasn't anything to say.

She pushed back from the island, the legs of the stool scraping across concrete. At the noise, Dog curled upward from rump to nose like a bass breaking water, harumphed, and settled down once more. Joey walked back to the Vault.

He sat with his martini glass, two-thirds full.

He no longer felt thirsty.

41. Vivid Reds and Charred Blacks

Evan cleaned the kitchen.

He hand-washed the martini glass, dried it to prevent water spots, set it back in its place. *Didn't you get the tweet? No one cares about anything anymore.* Ran steaming water across the steel pick, put it away along with Joey's cup and spoon, scrubbed the counter down. *It's not fucking fixable ever, and now and then I want a little rum.* Then he wiped down the sink, the faucet, the taps. *I want my dad. I want my dad. I want my dad.*

Using a hand towel, he polished the front of the Sub-Zero, buffing out smaller and smaller streaks until he realized he'd gotten caught in a repetition of the Second Commandment, allowing it to morph into a spin cycle. He set down the towel and stared at the remaining streaks, giving them time to evanesce. Some did.

Not all.

His gaze was still locked on the last stubborn streak on the refrigerator door when Joey came running up the hall from the direction of the Vault.

Inexplicably she was wearing a dress.

It snapped him out of his trance.

Joey: in a dress.

Black and modestly cut but not so modest that it didn't show off her figure. An odd mix of emotions waylaid him – bewilderment, pride in the attractive young woman she'd become, a desire to ensconce her more-shapely-than-he-wanted-to-acknowledge form in a potato sack.

One of her calves was tanner than usual. Could that be – a partially rolled-on stocking? And something wagged beside it, dangling by her ankle. The other shriveled pantyhose leg?

Before he could ensure that he hadn't tumbled through a rip in the multiverse, Joey said, 'Melinda got back DNA on the Wolf. We got her!'

Evan followed her back.

Melinda Truong was up on the big front screens of the Vault, life-size and crisply beautiful. Joey had put visual security filters on, fuzzing everything except herself and Evan into modern art. He paused to try to get his bearings, which proved ungettable.

The floor was strewn with discarded pantyhose, bunched, lined, and ripped. Various cardboard boxes with egg logos were torn open, a dinosaur hatching of hosiery. Against the Vault's masculine concretes and steels, the delicate fabric looked bizarrely out of place. Joey sat on top of the L-shaped table, shoving her bare foot into another pair of nylons. Her toes broke through, an image reminiscent of werewolf transformation. She gave a lupine growl, tossed them aside, and freed a fresh victim from a box.

Evan felt his eyebrows knitting together. 'What the hell are you –'

'Karissa Lopatina, aka the Wolf,' Melinda cut in, never one to waste time. 'Your protégé and I hit it from different angles, pulled together a pretty good picture of her.'

Evan looked at Joey, mouthed, *Protégé?*, but she'd paused from her sartorial misadventures to take note of the compliment and was glowing too much to pay him any mind. On both side walls, her custom cracker ran, targeting RC4's inherent biases, pounding away on Solventry's encryptions.

It looked complicated as hell, the progress bars showing at least another forty hours to get into Hill's files. For now Evan would have to focus on Lopatina.

Which meant focusing on Melinda. He remembered her atop him last night, bare-torsoed, leaning over him. Her lips fuller yet with the added weight of gravity as she pressed her mouth to his. She was so petite and yet she'd been all around him, encompassing him, a whirl of sensation to breathe in. He'd been unsure how their next engagement would go, but Melinda presented now as the stone-cold professional she was. If anything she'd hardened her perimeters in the wake of the tryst. Her clarity set him at ease.

She continued, 'She's been on the FBI's radar for a little over a decade now. Remember that guy who got his head taken off by a Russian 7.62x54 rimmed round in his Super Bowl suite a few years back?'

Of course he did. Nearly impossible to trace given that the Siberian ammo factory pumped out millions of rounds with no traceable taggants.

'The oil executive,' he said.

'Third quarter. Fourth and goal. Two hundred ninety-five meters with a Dragunov SVD. That was Lopatina. A lady who can handle her hardware. Double tap to the chest on the L in Chicago. Car bomb in Dulles long-term parking. Knife nick of the femoral artery in Central Park.'

Internal agency reports, dossiers, and crime-scene photos populated the digital space. As Melinda spoke, Joey clicked through, bringing relevant files to the fore, Lopatina's trail of destruction painted in vivid reds and charred blacks.

'How am I supposed to put these fucking things on?' Joey hissed, her thumbs ripping through the pantyhose. 'What are they, like, designed for butterfly feet?'

'You're asking *me*?' Evan said, out of the side of his mouth.

'Lopatina's not generally so showy,' Melinda continued. 'An accident specialist. Family of five dead in their beds of carbon-monoxide poisoning, private airplane fell out of the sky, a yakuza *oyabun* slipped and fell off a bullet train. Of course, these are just the ones they were lucky enough to tie to her. Who knows how many hits have gone unnoticed?'

'A lot of people have accidents,' Evan said. A ripping sound distracted him, another stocking meeting its untimely end, impaled by an unmanicured foot of Josephine Morales. Evan leaned over once more, whispered, 'Maybe if you don't act like you're punting a football.'

'*You* try ramming your appendage into a spiderweb.'

'Only if the spiderweb buys me dinner first.'

Melinda snapped her fingers at him. 'Hey, *người yêu*! Am I boring you?' Despite the term of endearment, she used the tone generally reserved for her workers. It resonated in his lumbar and he snapped to. 'And you!' Melinda's eyes darted over to Joey. 'What are you doing all contorted on that desk? You look like you're trying to hump your knee.'

Joey colored. 'Nothing.'

'Ask *her*,' Evan whispered to Joey.

Melinda: 'Ask me what?'

'Nothing!'

'Josephine.'

'Fine!' Joey threw up her hands, the latest abused pair of nylons flying overhead. 'I don't know how to put on stockings, okay? No one ever taught me. They keep ripping and tearing and getting streaks and shit and I don't know how to do it. *Okay?*'

'What are you angry with *me* about?' Melinda said. 'I'm not the one dressing you.'

Joey's face softened. 'Sorry.'

'A good rule of thumb, child. If you want help, don't act like an asshole.'

Evan hadn't thought it possible to find a new level of respect for Melinda, but there it was. He felt an internal glow of a sentiment even more specific than schadenfreude, something even the Germans hadn't gotten around to naming yet.

Quieter Joey voice now: 'Okay. It's just . . . I have this dumb sorority event I'm late for already' – an aggravated flap of her hand at her endlessly pinging phone – 'and I don't want to show up looking all *street*.'

Melinda snapped her perfectly manicured fingers. 'Let me see your toenails.'

Joey hesitated. Then held up the offending foot.

Melinda recoiled. 'Clip those nails. That's your first problem. They look *bovine*.'

'Sorry I'm not dipping them in, like, veal milk,' Joey shot back. 'It's not like I have some foot fetish, okay? I mean, feet are for walking. And kicking people.'

Melinda looked puzzled. 'Veal milk?'

'Artistic liberty,' Joey said. 'And your metaphor didn't make sense either. It's not like cows have toenails.'

'No. They have *hoofs*.'

'Gawd, you two!' Joey said. 'Fine. I'll add "supple girl feet" to my vision board.'

Evan: 'Vision board?'

'It's a collage you make to help you visualize what you want your life to feel like. I know it's hard for you to grasp, X, since you just *think* what you want, clench your butt cheeks, and it materializes.'

'Please,' Evan said to Melinda, 'can we ignore and proceed?'

'Go,' Melinda said to Joey. 'Find scissors or perhaps a

suitable machete. Clip them. File them. Then get a fresh pair of stockings. You *tuck tuck tuck tuck tuck* all the way to the toe. And then put them on *very slowly*. If you get a small run, use clear nail polish to stop it.' And then, in the same even tone, 'Can we please get back to the assassin now?'

'Gladly,' Evan said. 'Do you have a closer look at Lopatina?'

Joey brought up a few young pictures of Karissa. Fuzzy childhood Polaroid, a driver's-license picture from when she was sixteen. Smooth, even features, white-blond hair. She looked more likely to sell you Girl Scout cookies than take your head off with a post-WWII Russian sniper rifle, but then again, even psychopaths started out as children. In that youthful face, he recognized the features of the woman who'd cinched a zip tie around Jayla's throat, sent sniper rounds toward his head, given him that dead-eyed two-finger salute. *See ya around.*

'Anything more current?' he asked.

Joey rooted in her pocket, came up with a Swiss Army knife with a scissors attachment, and set to work on her toes.

Atop Evan's desk.

Not wanting to draw Melinda's ire, he fought down an admonishment.

'Intel gets scarce after Lopatina slipped off into the underworld but the girl did her best.' Melinda chinned at Joey.

The girl. That was more like it.

Joey scowled at him before setting down the Swiss Army knife and calling up a few images of Lopatina as an adult. Grainy surveillance shots and a few CCTV angles, not one capturing her face cleanly. Evan studied them and the surrounding crime-scene reports. 'She's well-rounded,' he said. 'Good at distance and up close. Evasion and concealment. Covers her tracks.'

'State-of-the-art gear, too,' Melinda said. 'French Gendarmerie revolvers and Dragunov SVDs. Whoever's putting the steel in her hands might as well be pulling the trigger themselves. A few of my men are seeing if they can backtrace any of the gear now.'

An audible snip sent a toenail clipping airborne, landing on Evan's mouse pad. Vera III looked on with disdain, for once siding with him. He shot eye daggers at Joey until she picked up the clipping, and then got to sawing with the metal nail file.

Back to Melinda: 'Any other leads on Lopatina?' Evan asked. 'Where she's been, where she's heading?'

Joey's teeth pinched her lower lip as she eased a fresh nylon over her foot, guiding it up her ankle, the bump of her calf.

'A few trails led to dead ends in the dark web,' Melinda said. 'Fortunately I have an employee who spelunks in there full-time – it's useful for forgeries, stolen art. He managed to trace some of her activity to a site for contract killers. She's not bitten in a while.'

Joey slid off the table, wiggled the pantyhose up over her knees, gestured for Evan to turn away. He abided.

Evan asked Melinda, 'Do you have any info on her last job? The one before she took out Dr Hill?'

Joey pulled herself upright, tapped his shoulder, threw her arms up in triumph. 'Wa-la!'

He had to concede she looked stunning, black-brown hair tumbling across her undercut, wide smile dimpling the right cheek, tiny emerald nose stud drawing out her eyes, metal-fiber bracelet joined by two magnetized stainless-steel skulls, classic round-cut diamond solitaire pendant resting against her rich brown skin, and the Joeyest pièce de résistance, scuffed Doc Martens into which she'd shoved her elegantly stockinged legs.

His eyes caught on her and she saw them catch and her smile grew wider and he gave her a thumbs-up and turned quickly away before the intimacy between them grew more uncomfortable.

'I can't guarantee it was her last job,' Melinda was saying. 'But her last job on here? She was paid in Bitcoin, which I thought was untraceable, but the girl –'

'The *girl*,' Joey said, her confidence restored, 'has a magical Hungarian hacker who's a blockchain maniac. He sniffed the transaction data, cross-referenced it with KYC information from the crypto exchanges, and identified the wallet owner.'

'Who linked the account to a trust in Wyoming of all places.'

'It's called a Cowboy Cocktail,' Evan said. 'Wyoming's got the strongest privacy laws in the country, basically zero regulatory oversight. Hide a trust inside a tangle of private companies with concealed ownership and you're invisible. Even Russian oligarchs and Argentine mobsters have caught on.'

'Well,' Melinda said, 'the girl's Hungarian is digging for more financial data.'

'Any word on who paid Lopatina?'

'Yes,' Melinda said. 'We traced the payment to a Las Vegas enterprise.'

'What kind of enterprise?'

'Human trafficking,' Melinda said. 'Domestic.'

Evan's jaw tensed, bringing an ache to his molars. He relaxed it. His thoughts tightened into a hard focus. A sudden calmness descended, the tranquility of purpose.

'I'll text you the address of their suspected headquarters,' Melinda said. 'I'm sure you can get some answers from them.'

'Oh, man,' Joey said, 'those poor fuckers.'

42. Any Violent Means Necessary

At first glance, the compound looked like most of the other run-down buildings on the block. Single-level industrial, brown stucco crumbled to reveal cinder block beneath, mission-style roof missing every third tile.

Evan had been observing it through his Steiners for the last hour from the remains of a neighboring attic. The house beneath him had been hollowed out by a fire, the charred wood still holding the chemical reek of meth manufacture. One roof beam had miraculously escaped the blaze intact, giving him a char-free perch.

Michael Way neighborhood, a hotbed of human trafficking, was less than twenty minutes north of the Strip but a world apart. The neon glow of capitalism didn't reach this hood – no whir and chime of slot machines, no European cars polished to a mirrored gleam, no what-happens-in-Vegas tourists jetting in for designer sushi and thousand-dollar handbags.

Instead: hammered-flat land squared in cookie-cutter blocks, brown lawns and dilapidated concrete, weed-infested lots languishing behind chain link. Boarded storefronts, foreclosed apartments, abandoned buildings turned squat houses. On the drive in, Evan had passed a public school that looked like a Third World prison. North Las Vegas PD's Northwest Area Command on Washburn, seven miles away, was loaded up with a half dozen units out front and a well-used paddy wagon big enough to round up a medium-size street gang. With violent crime soaring above the national average and despair running even higher, the neighborhood was a great place to hide a human-chattel operation.

The longer Evan watched, the more convinced he became that the compound was mostly impenetrable. The fifteen-foot-high powder-coated steel fence looked ordinary enough, but a closer inspection revealed anti-climb razor spikes, their angles overlapping like shark teeth. The posts were set in concrete, the sturdy gate barred, access granted only via a video call box. A solid metal front door sat at a slight tilt inside a reinforced frame that strained under its weight. When passing headlights illuminated the few high-set windows, they brought internal security bars visible.

Despite the late hour, a steady stream of men carrying briefcases entered, likely delivering end-of-week cash drops. One of them brought a blond woman in her early twenties, gripping her high on the biceps and steering her with a firm hand. The men looked shockingly ordinary – middle-aged guys with brown mustaches, pleated khakis, and polo shirts bulged over hip holsters. Were it not for the guns, they could have been retail salesmen at a home-appliance store. Evan had expected the usual scumfuck stereotypes to apply – scraggly facial hair, tattoos, weaponized hygiene – but the face of this operation was Hannah Arendt–banal.

The only clear roughneck was the gorilla straining a folding chair on the porch and picking his fingernails with a folding knife like an extra in a Charles Bronson movie. No gun on display, not outside, but Evan had glimpsed bigger hardware behind the door when the others had entered. The surveillance drive-by he'd taken had shown an open parking lot in the back with a few empty trucks. High chain-link topped with concertina wire blocked narrow side alleys clogged with trash barrels and nests of rusting HVAC units.

A proper frontal assault would take a good measure of

planning, a Tommy Stojack gear-assist, and several days of surveillance.

With Lopatina circling the waters and Jayla Hill under time-limited witness protection, he didn't have a few days.

Luke Devine had texted that he was still getting a bead on Allman's rival, Nathan Friedhoff of Youtopia, and that he hoped to line up something concrete for tomorrow. There were arms to twist and cages to rattle and power-crazed tech-mind-eaters to unveil, and the last thing Evan needed to do was waste time dicking around with a bunch of suburban-dad-looking human traffickers.

There was a more direct way in to get the answers he needed.

He figured it was time to take it.

He swung off the beam, punching his gloved hands and steel-toed boots through the fire hose-soaked remaining Sheetrock for purchase. He skidded down, leaving a wake of soggy tracks through the drywall. Coughing out soot, he exited the back of the burn house, moving away from the compound. Then he shot through a side yard, ignoring the homicidal pit bull trying to smash her face through the fence, and popped out another block to the south, where he'd left his Ford F-150.

From the vault of his truck, he withdrew three shitty Nokia phones, a trio of remote-det prepped flashbang grenades, electric caps, detonators, and a pair of zip ties. Sitting in the driver's seat, he peeled off his gloves and tipped his fingers with superglue to smooth away any prints. He blew on them more from habit than anything else. They were dry within seconds.

He proceeded to prep all three bangs, duct-taping each phone receiver to its respective package. Then he pro-grammed the Nokias' phone numbers into his RoamZone, taking excruciating care not to hit the CALL button since he had scant interest in having his ashes scattered across Michael Way.

Still breathing hard. Time to take down his nervous system.

He closed his eyes, let his breathing slow, pieced together what little he knew of the operation and firepower inside the compound. Played through a variety of scenarios. Averaged them out. Zeroed in on an appropriate time frame.

He took his ARES and a suppressor but left his Strider knife behind in the glove box, trading it out for a pair of wire clippers.

He was four steps away from the locked pickup when he halted, picturing that rugged paddy wagon from the police parking lot. Reversing, he grabbed a proper frag grenade from the rear of his rig, stuffed it in his pocket, and headed back out.

Cutting through a different side yard, he approached the compound cautiously from the rear. Low profile, tiny movements, moving from cover to cover. Then into the alleys, clipping through chain-link and sliding the explosives into place. When he was done, he discarded the wire clippers and took a beat to wipe sweat from his eyes.

It had taken nearly an hour for him to get all three flashbangs into position.

He pulled straight out from the rear a solid two blocks before taking a circuitous route back to the front, searching gutters for trash. An empty party-size bag of Fritos had snared in a sewer grate.

Perfect.

He picked it up, ducked into an alley, and used his phone to confirm the precise distance and estimated travel time from the Northwest Area Command to the target compound. After checking the time once more – 11:12 P.M. – he breathed fast and hard, bringing himself to the verge of hyperventilating.

Then he dialed 911.

When the operator picked up, he spoke in a hoarse whisper: 'Help me. I'm – God – there are so many of them. They took my friend's daughter and I went – the address –' He gasped out the numbers between panicked breaths, talking over the operator's questions. 'They tied me up – oh God I'm bleeding – have to sneak out but they're going to – so many weapons, I don't think I can – Hang on, they're coming –'

He hung up abruptly.

He tucked the grenade, his ARES, a suppressor, zip ties, and his RoamZone inside the Fritos bag and finished shuffling up the block to the compound. Just before the gate, he crouched to fake-tie his boot, nestling the Fritos bag in a mound of dead leaves wadded up at the curb.

Then he rose and approached the call box.

Nothing on his person aside from the clothes on his back, Jack's voice like a whisper in his ear: You *are the weapon.*

Clearing his head, he reset the mission.

1. Deal with the human traffickers through any violent means necessary.
2. Find out how they contact the Wolf.
3. Extract any additional information about the Wolf.
4. Kill all the human traffickers.
5. Kill the Wolf.
6. Find out whoever hired the Wolf to kill Dr Hill.
7. Kill *that* person.
8. Do 1–7 in the next five days before Jayla Hill is released from federal custody.

Simple enough. Drawing in a breath, Evan punched the

button by the call box. Across the front yard on the porch, the massive guard paused from his ministrations with the knife, the tip floating just above his thumbnail, and locked on to Evan. The streetlight turned his eyes into flattened pennies. Even at this distance Evan could see the veins squiggling through the sunburned skin of his throat. His shoulders were bunched high around his neck, but he didn't move.

On the call box, an illuminated blue ring encircled the pupil of the surveillance camera. It flickered once and a voice emerged: 'What?'

'I'm the Wolf's rep,' Evan said.

'Who?'

'The Wolf. You've made use of her services.'

'Maybe we have. Maybe we haven't. Maybe we still are.' The present tense was interesting, but before Evan could dwell on grammar clues, the voice asked, 'The fuck are you doing here?'

'She wishes to amend the deal.'

A cough of a laugh. 'Amend the deal? Any deal we do or don't have with her is the arrangement we have. There's no *amending* a deal.'

'You know who she is. You know what she does. I suggest you let me in to discuss this matter before you decide to make an enemy of her.'

A long silence, just the rush of wind through the half-burned house across the street. The razor teeth atop the fence glittered like icicles. From up close he could see that the crumbled stucco of the house was in fact deliberate, accommodating a pair of sawed slits through the cinder block, each just wide enough to fit a muzzle through.

Evan clasped his hands behind him, did his best to look unthreatening. It wasn't hard.

The gate buzzed open.

As he tugged it to enter, the big man on the porch rose. The chair gave a creak of relief. A gold-colored belt buckle spelled JACKO in case he forgot his name while he was taking a leak. The folding knife twirled once around the back of Jacko's hand, and he caught it upside down angled parallel to his forearm, a proper edge-out reverse grip.

He watched Evan's quiet approach, then held up a hand. 'Stop.'

Men like Jacko even *smelled* like alphas. A distinctive musk came off them. Skin of sun-battered leather, stubble coarse as wire. He looked like he subsisted on dried meat and chewing tobacco, like he'd rip your head off and chug mead from your skull.

Evan halted.

They were eye to eye, though Evan had to tilt his head back to meet the man's gaze. A slight twitch of the left eye and the cant of the shoulders gave away the man's favored side.

Keeping the knife, Jacko patted Evan down extensively with his other massive hand, taking care to administer a urology-worthy crotch grope. Then he removed what looked like a fat walkie-talkie from a bag beneath his chair – a professional-grade RF detector. He wanded Evan down head to toe, checking for any wireless surveillance tech.

When Jacko was done, he stepped back without turning around and knocked twice on the door behind him. A heavy clank announced a security bar retracting, and then the door opened with a *foomp* worthy of a submarine hatch.

A fist reached through the gap, grabbed Evan's shirt, yanked him in, and slammed him against the wall.

43. The Holding Pen

A Benelli M1 combat shotgun rose and jammed its muzzle into the soft skin beneath Evan's chin.

Lucky day – M1s were Evan's favorite.

Behind the Benelli, a guy with ice-gray eyes patted Evan down once more and then returned to his gun station at the side of the front door. A matching guard, similarly armed, was posted at the second of the muzzle slits carved through the front wall of the house, the ones Evan had spotted from the call box. A half dozen other men lounged in folding chairs around a pool table, exuding an aura of stageworthy calm. A few had their guns drawn, resting on their knees. The lineup of briefcases atop the green felt were all closed, but a digital currency counter near a corner pocket gave away the game.

Sitting in their midst was the blonde Evan had spotted before, a full-figured woman barely contained by a half shirt and tight black jeans. She wore a vacant, drugged expression and had bruises on her wrists, red spots on her arms, and a raspberry on her chin. A heap of locks pushed high on her head, pouty lips glossed with wet pink lipstick, high-end perfume applied liberally enough that it reached Evan from across the room. He could picture her getting off a bus from Des Moines or Nashville with a suitcase and a proverbial spring in her step. In some other distant context, she would have been sexually attractive, a reality Evan noted and then dispensed with. Something in her bearing, the birdlike perch at the edge of her chair, one shoulder shrugged up as if to defend against a blow, suggested she'd been brought here to be disciplined. Her blasted-wide pupils focused on nothing; she'd gone somewhere else, leaving her body behind to endure whatever it had to endure.

Metal sheets sufficient to deter a volley of RPGs covered the rear door and reinforced the interior walls.

A desk in the back held a flat computer monitor that showed rotating angles of an off-site structure that looked like a repurposed apartment building. The interior cameras showed various hallways, men patrolling them with batons like night watchmen. But that wasn't what was chilling about the hallway feeds.

The doors along the halls had been taken off and replaced with prison bars. Beyond the bars was nothing but blackness. The entire building had been retrofitted.

A holding pen.

Evan at last brought his full focus to the ninth man, the one around whom the room's latent energy swirled. The man had broken the polo-and-khaki dress code, instead wearing a double-breasted dark pinstripe suit baggy enough to indicate abrupt weight loss. Thick black wavy hair without a trace of gray. Sunken eyes magnified by silver-rim glasses, titanium-frame arms denting pronounced sideburns. A slender cigarette holding a good half inch of ash protruded from two knobby knuckles. Above a gaping cuff, a gold Rolex hung loosely around a just-visible strip of hairy wrist.

That was good: Evan needed to keep track of the time.

This man looked connected, a cut above the others. A capo. He nodded at the gray-eyed guard who'd frisked Evan. 'Thank you, Domenic.' The capo's cheeks were concave from illness, and his voice rasped when he spoke. His dark eyes found Evan. 'You say you're a rep of the Wolf.'

From here, Evan could smell his breath. Breath mints covering rot, the reek of necrotic tissue, black spots eating into lungs.

'Yes.'

The capo sipped at his cigarette. His bloodshot eyes watered, showing the hurt.

Behind him the security feeds rotated on the monitors. Evan caught an exterior angle across the blue stucco of the holding pen's front wall. Near the sun-scorched paint of the entry, darker shades of numerals memorialized the spots where street numbers had been pried free. A six? An eight? The feed rotated before he could snapshot the image, and he vowed to catch it when it circled back around.

Besides, he had to focus on the Rat Pack escapee with the dead lungs who was about to threaten his life.

The man said, 'Talking your way in here was the easy part . . .'

'The hard part's gonna be getting out,' Evan said.

The man looked disappointed that his payoff line had been preempted.

'You think I'm playing games?'

'I don't care what you're doing. The Wolf has received an unusual level of law-enforcement scrutiny from the last job she conducted for you. Her determination is that you have loose lips inside your organization. She has handled the inconvenience but it was costly in time and money. She demands a thirty-percent bonus for having to contend with your laxity.'

For a moment the capo's face remained still with surprise, wrinkles fanning outward from his eyes like sun rays. Then he smiled, white caps large in his mouth. Evan half expected a gold tooth.

The capo waved his cigarette, tracing a slender scarf of

smoke around him. 'Her inability to handle *her* business is no business of mine.'

'It is if the problem originated inside your operation.'

'"If,"' he said. 'You come here. You make threats. Over "if."'

The other men kept a dutiful silence while the capo spoke. Past his shoulder, the surveillance feeds rotated around once more on the monitors, and Evan scratched his nose to cover a quick shift of his eyes to catch the address digits. He snagged the first three – *867* – before the angle changed once more.

'It's my understanding that the original agreement provided terms for contingencies like this,' Evan said.

The capo looked surprised.

'You didn't know that,' Evan said.

'My not knowing means the terms do not hold. And anyone in my employ who believed they could negotiate on their own will be dealt with.' The capo canted forward, head slightly ducked, conspiratorial. 'I'm the king of this particular jungle,' he confided, his breath a noxious gas. He wasn't bragging. He was just telling it like it was. 'I only answer to one.'

'God?'

The capo showed his yellowed teeth. 'You could say that.' He lifted a slender finger, tobacco-stained at the first knuckle. 'In this world, I don't handle the trifles. Terms and contracts.'

'Who does?'

The capo looked shocked at the audacity of the question. His eyes flicked toward the building on the monitors, the smallest tell.

Evan pieced together a working theory: Money ran

through here. Truly incriminating matters – kidnapped humans and murder contracts – were handled at the other site.

'Underlings.' The capo waved his hand, and Evan took the opportunity to check the man's watch: 11:17.

'It shows weakness,' Evan said, 'if they're agreeing to terms without your approval.'

'Weakness.' The capo's head bobbed. 'Weakness?' Without looking over, he snapped his fingers in the direction of the pool table. 'Amber. Up.'

Amber's expression did not change. She rose, stumbled a bit, righted herself with a hand on the felt, and then dutifully trudged over. The capo cupped her chin, stared into her face. Her glazed eyes looked back, long lashes blinking.

'At all times, I have a coterie of women who obey me. That isn't status. It's pure *strength*.' The capo was gazing at Amber but speaking to Evan, the effect unsettling. 'I can walk into any high-end restaurant from Beverly Hills to Monaco and if I snap my fingers and ten beautiful women obey, all those beaten-down husbands and dutiful young men see me as an ancient god. Their cells cry out to be freed the way I'm free. I have built an empire around me. An empire I carry on my back. Do you understand what I am telling you?'

'Coercing female companionship isn't my definition of strength,' Evan said. 'I'm old-fashioned that way.'

'Coercing?' The capo laughed his laugh. Evan wondered what his breath smelled like at Amber's distance. She didn't blink, didn't turn away. 'You may be old-fashioned,' the man continued. 'But I'm *primal*.'

Were it not for Amber, Evan would have been bored. He focused on the playing board. One of the men by the pool table chewed gum. Another stroked his mustache. Their muscles were coiled, but they were doing their best to project cool. Domenic was closest to Evan, two strides behind him to the right. The capo's Rolex was momentarily hidden, but one of the seated men had a big-dick diving watch that showed 11:20.

The security monitors continued their lazy rotation through and around the holding pen, not yet back at the angle Evan needed to complete the address. He continued to assemble a picture of the off-site building: Three floors, each patrolled by a single guard. Nerve center on the ground floor – more security monitors, more computer hardware – manned by a single guy with a Benelli. A fifth guard surveilling from the roof, heavy-duty headphones clamped over his ears, bopping away.

'"Coercion" is too weak a word. "Ownership" is more appropriate.' The capo waved his hand, the ash at last falling, scattering across his polished shoes. 'I'm not talking about gutter work, managing lot lizards. No. That's barbaric shit. I own these fine young women. I take what I want from them and when I'm done I sell them to cathouses, individuals, the Mexicans or Armenians who have street operations that require meat, stale or otherwise.'

Evan was tired. Tired of the endless war on corruption, of men doing bad things, of how much work it took to right some small part of any of it. He slid a half step back toward Domenic, closing the distance. On the monitor, the exterior angle Evan needed came up, and he filled out the street numerals of the off-site structure: *86774*. None of the men's watch faces were visible, but Evan knew time was getting tight.

The capo palmed Amber's head like a basketball and pressed it against the wall hard enough that her cheek shoved

276

forward, pooching her lips. He used his right hand, providing Evan a glimpse of the Rolex – 11:23.

Nearly go time.

Amber hadn't made a sound. She didn't even look scared. Nothing human seeped through her numbed façade. She'd been treated like an object so long and so consistently that her outsides had learned to believe it. He wondered if she was still in there, receded behind a thousand layers of scar tissue, and if she'd ever find her way back to the surface.

The capo took the cigarette from his mouth and held it vertically like a tiny chimney, smoke unspooling from the top. Still pressing her head to the wall, he looked over at Evan. 'Eye or cheek,' he said.

Evan didn't answer.

'Since you're so concerned about equity,' the capo said, 'I'll let you choose.'

'What sort of businessman damages his own product?' Evan said. 'If you disfigure her, you just lose income.'

The capo blew a fierce glow into the cherry of the cigarette and hovered it right over her temple. 'If you don't choose, I do both.'

Amber hadn't issued a single noise of complaint but her squirming eye found Evan, the pupil pulling downward: *Cheek*.

Evan said, 'Cheek.'

A sizzle. The stomach-turning stench of burning flesh. Amber grunted but it was without fear or anger, just a response to the stimuli. The Rolex read 11:25. The men around the table were distracted by the spectacle. Domenic's shotgun was at his side, aimed at the ground two and a half feet behind Evan's right boot. The safety was off, bolt closed, so he presumed a round in the chamber.

The capo flicked the cigarette at Evan. It hit his chest and fell to the ground.

'It's funny,' he said, 'that you thought you'd get out of here alive.'

Evan felt the tug of a smile, his muscle memory warming its engines. 'I was just about to say the same thing to you.'

In a single fluid movement, he snatched the Benelli from Domenic's grasp and crushed the guard's left knee with a piston kick. While everyone else was busy being startled, Evan had the barrel up. It was trained on the capo's center mass, but with a shotgun at this range it didn't have to be. The other men scrambled with their pieces, laggards on the draw. The capo shouted '*No!*' and they froze.

It took a moment for the gust of air from the exclamation to reach Evan. It curled up his nostrils, rancid enough to make his eyes water. The second guard was the only one in Evan's periphery, but he hadn't gotten his Benelli to horizontal and couldn't now without Evan taking note.

For a moment everyone remained stock-still.

And then Amber broke the suspension, pressing herself languidly off the wall. Walking back to her chair, she picked her way through the men and sat. The red spot floated beneath her cheekbone, tinged black at the edges.

Domenic's mouth wavered silently for another few seconds. Then he emitted a confused moan. Evan's piston kick had staved in the leg, devastating it. Khaki held the bone, tented up where the shard had shoved through the skin.

The diving watch was at 11:27.

'I'm gonna go now,' Evan said, backing to the door. Now he could hear the sirens, barely audible, maybe four blocks out. 'Stay away from the muzzle slits. If you come out after me, I'll cut you all down in the doorway. Understand?'

The capo's smile had returned, his choppers a polished wedge of insincere mirth.

'You really think —'

Domenic propelled himself off his good leg, lunging for Evan. Without lowering the shotgun from the capo, Evan lashed out with a side kick, driving his heel into Domenic's chin. The guard's head torqued with an audible crackle, and his body hit the floor, convulsed twice, and stilled.

After that the capo didn't see fit to finish his sentence.

Easing backward, Evan reached the door, knocking on it twice to set Jacko at ease outside. Then he jerked through onto the porch and slammed the door behind him. Jacko leapt up from his folding chair, blade in hand, surprise on his face. His arms had snapped into knife-fight readiness — forearms out to present muscle, not tendons — but the rest of his body was misaligned and off-balance.

Evan flipped the shotgun horizontally at Jacko's face. Instinctively Jacko dropped the knife and caught the Benelli with both hands before the barrel struck the bridge of his nose. Evan snatched the folding knife as it fell and drove it straight up through the big man's throat.

It was as messy as he'd anticipated. Jacko flailed back, gurgling. Evan relieved him of the shotgun as he fell over. Crouching, Evan doused his hands in the stream issuing from Jacko's neck and smeared it around his own face. Jacko looked up at him uncomprehendingly, head joggling back and forth on the concrete of the porch until it didn't jog anymore.

Sirens, louder.

Evan backed down the walk and onto the sidewalk, jamming the shotgun beneath the gate to pin it open. After liberating the zip ties from the Fritos bag, he nestled the bag back into the gutter, stuck his hands through the plastic loops, cinched them tight with his teeth, and collapsed on the sidewalk.

Squealing tires, roaring engines, and finally lights as the cavalry blasted around the turn, four police units, paddy wagon, ambulance.

They arrived, pouring from vehicles, weapons out, pouncing on the scene.

'Help me,' Evan croaked. 'Help . . . I called. I called for help.'

A shadow fell over Evan, gloved hands tilting his head, checking for injuries. 'You okay?'

He thrashed his head weakly. 'Yes. My friend's daughter . . . inside. Please . . . careful.'

Medics hoisted him up and pulled him back. He let them, dragging his boots weakly, nearly disrupting the Fritos bag in the gutter. They brought him to the rear of the ambulance parked just out of the line of fire, giving him a quick once-over, and cutting off his zip ties.

'Thank you. I'm okay. I'm okay. There's a woman inside. She's injured.'

'Wait here – wait here.' The medics crept into safe position near the gate, standing by for after the entry.

The cops had cautiously unfurled themselves across the front yard, vectoring at the door, shouting. There were enough to make a shoot-out a bad option.

Evan sat hunched forward, blanket across his shoulders, staring at the back of the paddy wagon about twenty meters away. It was parked across the street in front of the burned house. Jacko's blood dried across the side of Evan's neck, tightening his skin. The Fritos bag was about five meters ahead of him, obscured by leaves. He made no move for it. The timing would have to be perfect.

Across the yard, that massive reinforced front door

opened, the men emerging weaponless, hands held high, the capo coming last. Evan couldn't hear everything he was saying, but the words 'lawyers' and 'regret' carried on the breeze.

The underlings were put down roughly on their stomachs in the front yard, cuffed, frisked head to toe. Then they were brought one by one across the street and loaded into the paddy wagon. Evan watched them shuffle into the vehicle, handcuffs making it hard for them to navigate the big step up.

A female cop emerged at last with Amber and delivered her to the medics near the gate.

The capo remained behind on the front lawn, answering questions and asking a few of his own. He stayed relatively calm, arguing with the cops as they steered him through the gate. They moved him toward one of the police units parked behind the paddy wagon. He bucked a bit, but a firm hand on the back of his head guided him down into the back of the sedan.

The medics brought Amber to the ambulance, and Evan got up to make space for her.

One of the medics said, 'It's okay, pal. Relax. We'll get to you in a second.'

Evan nodded and waited a few feet off the rear bumper. Inching along the gutter, he made his way toward the mound of leaves. Then he sat on the curb, his legs on either side of the Fritos bag. He slid his hand in, withdrew his RoamZone. The phone numbers were queued up one, two, three, ready to dial.

He gauged the scene.

The cops were circled up in two groups, one on the front lawn, the other near the paddy wagon, comparing notes and talking into radios. None of them took note of Evan.

Directly across from him, the capo sat alone in the back of the cop car. His head lowered, shoulders shuddering with a cough.

Then his face lifted and he saw Evan sitting on the curb across the street.

Evan smiled at him.

The capo's eyes were sunken into shadow, but his wiry eyebrows spread in terror and his mouth puckered as well. He started screaming and kicking the barrier between the back and front seats.

Evan pressed the CALL button.

He'd positioned the first flashbang beneath a rusting HVAC unit in the east alley. Metal and mass and a nice tight space to increase overpressure. The explosion sounded biblical, tearing a hole through the side of the structure. The cops crouched or hit the deck, weapons at the ready.

Evan tapped the second button. The other alley erupted before the first explosion had finished reverberating, the threat enhanced by surround sound.

The capo's caved-in mouth stretched wide, his roar lost beneath the detonation. He was jerking his head toward Evan, smacking the side window with his temple, trying to warn the cops. But they were already moving across the street, calling in for backup, jogging up the block to encircle the building.

It was gratifying to see the capo trapped and helpless.

Evan poked his RoamZone once more, and a truck in the rear lot went boom. Cops streamed past Evan, barking commands.

Once they passed, he plucked the ARES, suppressor, and frag grenade from the Fritos bag, and walked calmly across the street.

The capo ceased his frenzy, staring with horror. Given the

man's illness, Evan would have thought he'd have been better prepared for what was coming.

Approaching the unguarded paddy wagon first, Evan slid his middle finger into the grenade ring and pulled it free. The rear door swung open nicely on well-oiled hinges. The men sat lined against either wall, hands cuffed, waist chains binding them to their benches.

Startled faces, mouths shaped in Os beneath those matching mustaches.

Evan tossed the grenade inside. It rattled across the metal floor, knocked the partition wall, and wobbled back. The men stared down in horror.

Evan slammed the door to muffle their screams.

Across the street, the cops were picking through the alleys, assessing the wreckage, clearing the structure once more, spinning around, adrift in confusion and fear.

Evan walked to the parked cop car, calmly twisting the suppressor onto the muzzle of his ARES. His partial reflection in the window showed a mask of blood.

The capo stared out at him, wrinkled cheeks quivering. His cuffed hands rose together and scrabbled against the pane. Then he stopped, cringing, staring downward, terrified to lift his gaze to Evan.

But he had to.

Their eyes met. A pure kind of terror moved behind the capo's eyes, unpolluted by shock. His thick mass of hair shifted on his skull a millimeter or two, his ears sliding infinitesimally back, dread rearranging his features.

Evan lifted his ARES 1911, and the capo twisted his head this way and that, as if he could dodge the inevitable. Evan shot him twice through the face – *pfft, pfft*.

The capo slumped away, face gone, hands clawed and downbent at the wrists.

Evan was around the cop car, across the curb, and into the burned house when the paddy wagon erupted from within. Shrapnel studded the thick metal walls from inside, the giant vehicle rocking on its tires.

Before it had settled back on its shocks, Evan was through the scorched house and out the back, jogging the predetermined route back to his pickup.

44. Objectively More Serious Shit

The nearest address numbered 86774 was 2.3 miles to the north. Sure enough, there was the holding pen, faded blue stucco, three stories high. Evan looped past it twice, gauging the surveillance-camera angles. Then he parked in a blind spot in the rear, tight enough to the building that the guard on the roof would've had to lean way over the edge to see the truck below. Evan had spotted him from a half block over, walking the perimeter with a dancing shuffle, head bouncing to whatever was flowing through his earphones.

He'd be the last to die.

Though Evan figured that the capo and his menagerie of molesters would have disconnected the monitors at the former location before surrendering to the cops, he couldn't be certain. He didn't want to give the law time to put the pieces together and catch up to this location. Which meant moving fast.

He'd just finished wiping Jacko's blood from his face and was reaching for his ARES 1911 on the passenger seat when the RoamZone rang: *DONCHA WISH* –

He stabbed at the polyether thioureas screen to answer, screwed in an earpiece. A glance at the screen showed Luke Devine's caller ID.

'I got you Nathan Friedhoff,' Devine said.

Evan's hands whirred in a tactical reload: touch-verify and extract full mag from concealed pocket behind right hip, up beside partial mag loaded in pistol, eject partial, catch in same palm, rotate palm to shove full mag in, partial load stored in right front pants pocket.

'Okay.'

'It was easier than I anticipated. He sounds like a mess. I'm not even sure he knew what he was agreeing to but he said he'd see you tomorrow at five o'clock.'

Evan checked the action. 'Okay.'

'I'll text you time and address.'

'Okay.'

'That's all you have to say?'

'Yes.' Evan disconnected the call, opened his door quietly, and slid out into the night.

He eased the driver's door back into the frame and leaned against it gently until it clicked closed.

A vent over his head blew out wet-smelling air tinged with mold. The windows of the first floor were boarded up with plywood. There was no sound save the whisper of a weak wind and the white-noise susurration of traffic from Route 95 two blocks to the east. Pressing his ear to the rough stucco, he made out the thrum of an HVAC unit inside and the faint high notes of feminine weeping.

How much disregard and corruption and apathy paved the road to a building like this – smack in the heart of an American state in the twenty-first century – stocked with slaves and walled off from civilization? He thought about Allman streaming digital manipulation into the minds of users, driving them farther and farther from reality. And this place rising before Evan now, erected to feed flesh to real-world desires that had moved farther and farther from any moral bearing.

He wondered how the world could find its center again, let alone hold it.

His jaw had tightened, and he forced it to relax. A few rounds of four-square breathing brought him fully into himself and this moment.

He was here to get information on Karissa Lopatina. To liberate the human chattel inside. And to kill those responsible for their suffering.

Circling the building, he kept tight enough that his shoulder scraped along the wall. Surveillance cameras passed overhead one after another, tilted on metal necks, gazing at the empty space beyond his silent approach.

Setting down his boots with care, he reached the brink of the entrance and peered around the corner. The front door bore two dead bolts that looked freshly installed and a trio of cameras covering the porch. From what he'd pieced together from the prior location's surveillance footage, the building's nerve center was in the first room past the entrance to the right, a shotgun-armed guard overseeing monitors and hardware.

Drawing back to the side of the building, Evan reversed to a high window he'd passed beneath. Sliding window, privacy glass, high-set and narrow – likely a bathroom. Though the pane was opaque, enough interior light streamed through to make clear there was no plywood beyond.

He had to hop up to reach the sill. It gave his fingers a two-inch perch, cramping his hands and forearms as he dragged himself off the ground chin-up style.

His face level, he noted the rusty frame and frayed screen. To free a hand, he jammed his right forearm across the narrow ledge and dug his chin into place beside it. He poked a finger through the screen, jostled the window open a few inches, and then fell back to earth before he made too much noise. The landing jolted his legs. He shook out his hands, then set them on his knees and regrouped.

Another hop, another jostle to the pane, and his hand shot through and caught the inside of the frame. A graceless thirty seconds of squirming and scraping got him over the hump, and then he found himself in a modified handstand on the back of a toilet tank. He eased himself down, retrieved the ARES from his appendix carry, screwed in the suppressor, and exited the stall.

Chipped tile, water stains, four toilet stalls, and a urinal. The mirror had been removed, no doubt to prevent any of the captors from getting their hands on shards. The scent of mold and bleach overlaid the low reek of human waste.

Evan moved swiftly to the swinging door, pushed out into the hall, and literally bumped into the guard on his patrol.

The man drew back, gave a little yelp, the baton dancing on its leather strap around his wrist. Evan shot him in the chest – *pfft* – the suppressed round like a fist punching a pillow. The guard fell stiffly, the back of his skull cracking the floor.

Evan swung to face in the other direction just as the front guard stepped out from the nerve center at the end of the corridor, shotgun rising. Evan dropped to a knee and grouped three shots at his upper torso, the first knocking the shotgun from his hands and ricocheting up into his left ribs, the other catching him in the exposed sternum, the third opening up a red spot beneath his clavicle. When he crumpled to the floor, it sounded like a dropped sack of laundry.

Two dead, three to go – one guard apiece for the upper floors and the hoofer on the roof.

Evan rose.

Prison bars split the black doorways on both sides. The doors weren't pinned open; they'd been removed entirely. It was eerie knowing he was being watched, unable to see what lay out of reach in the shadows.

First he heard breathing.

Then figures melted from the blackness, visible only in

pieces. Stooped forms. Milk-white hands gripping bars. Tangled hair across floating faces.

Mostly women, two or three to a room, but some young men as well.

'It's okay.' He spoke to the nearest room. 'It's over.'

He started for the door to the stairs.

'*Wait,*' a voice hissed from behind him. '*Don't leave. Don't leave us here.*'

'I won't,' he said, keeping on.

Another voice picked up the conversation, a disembodied rasp from the other side of the hall: '*Wait – where are you going?*'

'To kill the others.'

From the shadows of a room ahead: '*No, no, no.*'

It was like having a conversation with a hive. They were all whispering, out of fear or habit but likely both. He understood with a sudden fierce logic that keeping quiet had been beaten into them so deeply that even now they couldn't find their voices in full. The effect was incandescently horrifying.

'I'm sorry,' he said, because there was no other good thing to say in the face of that.

'*Fuck you.*' A croak.

'*– can't leave us, you can't –*'

'*– my insides, they hurt from –*'

He couldn't let their suffering be real to him right now. There was no way to allow that and do what still had to be done.

He shut out the multitude of terrified murmurs, shouldered into the door, collected himself in the stairwell. Leaning into the open well, peering up, scanning the rise over the suppressor-lengthened barrel of his 1911.

Staying on tilt to open his sight line above, he started up.

Loud in his head through the earpiece: *DONCHA –*

He tapped it quickly to answer, spoke as softly as he could: 'Do you need my help?'

'Yes! X! You picked up!'

Joey.

He twisted up the stairs, the ceiling rotating overhead. 'Are you okay?'

'No! I'm at this rush event at the Cheesecake Factory and it's a *disaster*.'

Evan heard a fluttering noise from above and froze, arms tensed. His Straight Eight sights were high-profile so the suppressor wouldn't block them. He aimed at the top rail and waited for another sound.

He whispered hard: 'What do you need?'

'Bad time?'

A pigeon burst into motion way above and he almost put a round through it. It flapped against the ceiling before settling on the rail, its head ducking repetitively, pecking at phantom bugs.

He exhaled. 'Yes.'

'We got here in a big group, and I was flustered because, like, what if I don't know what fork to eat with.'

'Start with the outer silverware and work your way in.' He observed a stab of irritation punch through him. She knew better than to call him with something like this when he was operational. The Fourth Commandment: *Never make it personal.* He gauged the most efficient and strategic path through whatever this conversation was and decided not to blow her up yet. He gave her firmness without showing teeth: 'The point, Joey.'

'Okay so I nervous-went to the bathroom and I'm not used to pantyhose so I didn't know my dress got tucked into them in the back and I walked back out through *the entire restaurant* with my *giant ass* hanging out. On display like a fruitcake –'

He debated commenting that fruitcakes weren't paragons of display-worthy objects but calculated the time cost of the disruption and instead said, 'Talk faster. And shorter.'

'– and everyone in the restaurant saw. Everyone was *laughing* at me. Some nice older lady had to come over and tell me.'

He started back up toward the second-floor landing. 'What do you want, Joey?'

A bit of heat beneath the words now: '*I don't know what to do.*'

Sidling up another step, he breathed out through his teeth, noticed they were clenched again. 'Your alias as a sorority girl is blown. Abort mission, commence exfil.'

'I'm serious. I need . . . I need help, okay? I need help.' The words were hard for her to say. 'I ran back to the bathroom. And I don't want to come out. I can't go back out there.' Her voice quavered – just barely.

That quaver stopped him from saying everything he wanted to say, everything the Fourth Commandment authorized – that he was occupied with objectively more serious shit helping people with concerns that dwarfed hers. For the first time he could remember he hit the brakes before letting the Orphan programming run.

'What am I supposed to do?' Joey said. 'Even the *waiter* cracked a joke about me. What if he makes another one?'

Almost to the landing, trying to focus, to find a way to giving a shit. 'Punch him in the throat and collapse his windpipe.'

'I'm *serious*. What do I do?'

He inched to the door. It had a narrow vertical window of tempered glass. The guard was walking away, about a third of the way down the corridor. No point chasing after him when Evan could just wait for him to draw back into closer range.

He pulled back slightly to make sure he wasn't throwing a

shadow. 'Joey. It's a bunch of sorority girls. You and I – we don't care about this shit.'

His tone was harsher and more dismissive than he'd intended, but given the gap he was trying to bridge he didn't mind.

'What if . . . what if I do? Care?'

Her tone was raw, confessional even, and the admission held too much vulnerability for him to bulldoze over. He scrunched his eyes shut, took a breath, tried to find the right bearings. It was impossible, his responsibilities crashing into one another, distorting priorities, melding two halves of himself that didn't want to meld. Meanwhile the guard's footsteps tapped farther away.

'Diversionary tactics,' he said.

'What?'

'Go back out and make a self-deprecating joke.'

'Like what?'

'You're the funny one,' he said. 'You tell me.'

Off target: index finger straight along the pistol frame, safety back on, thumb on top of the safety. Quick mag check, index finger feeling the nose of the top bullet, confirming rounds left by feel, a tiny, soothing habit. The low capacity 1911 demanded he know precisely how many rounds he had at all times. He reseated the mag with his palm, pulled down on the base plate with the fingertips of his right hand.

'Not right now,' Joey said. 'I'm the sweaty-palms one. And how do I explain why I just *ran off*?'

'Come out with toilet paper hanging from your cleavage and say you had to go back to finish the job.'

High-risk high-reward. He could hear Joey weighing it.

'You have to sell it,' he said. 'Live your legend. You're psyops-trained.'

'Yeah, for *missions*. Not for real life.'

'It's the same thing.'

'What is?'

'Everything.' Evan thought about what he'd had to draw from within himself to get through seven and a half minutes in that double-wide in Texas with the man who was his father. 'Everything's the same thing. Now go.'

He hung up.

The guard reached the end of the hall and turned to head back. A fall of light limned the outer edge of his face, sculpting it, making it specific. A human face. Evan thought about him being born decades ago. Someone had held him in his mewling newness and carried thoughts for his future. He'd had tiny triumphs – a first step, a good grade on a quiz, the first time the right girl smiled at him. He'd had failures. He'd wept and hurt and hardened and driven himself into a hell of bad decisions, until they'd hijacked him, taken him over and turned him into someone who caged other human beings for profit.

Someone who deserved to die.

Pressed to the side of the narrow window, Evan felt the totality of the man walking toward him, walking toward the end of everything he ever was, everything he'd ever known and would ever be. The fullness swelled in his chest, a tangle of thorns, and then he stepped through the door and shot him twice in the chest, and he walked forward with the pistol aimed the whole time and stood over him, stood over this man whose life he had taken.

A whiff of nitrocellulose made stronger from the suppressor buildup, brass rolling on the floor, and the dampness of the air held the next moment in a suspended haze of sensation.

And then the hive hissed back to life, snatches of words flying from the darkness around him. The whispered voices terrified him.

'— God bless you. God in heaven bless you —'
'— you killed him. You finally killed —'
'— so awful, you can't imagine what they do to —'
'Wait. Don't go. Don't go. Where are you —'
'— back, please just come —'

He was irised open, too close to Joey, and he shrank his connection to her into two dimensions and filed it away for later review. Leaving the corpse, he walked back to the stairwell.

The voices kept on and were just as horrific. But they didn't scare him anymore.

As he neared the third floor, the stairwell door opened above, the guard jogged down right at Evan, and Evan shot him in the throat before the guy had an instant to think. The guard slumped over and then scudded down the steps, and Evan shot him once more as he slid past.

Up another flight and then Evan stepped out onto the roof. The last guard was about ten meters away, his back to Evan, standing in place with his head cocked and his hips dipping and his arms slung out, fingers snapping.

Dancing.

His headphones were turned up so loud that Evan could hear their tinny echo despite the distance.

He raised the ARES, thought about the left seventh rib, guarding the heart from behind. If he put the bullet at a slight angle he could dodge the scapula and blow a tunnel through the left lung and heart. But the guy looked young and strong, and heart shots weren't a guarantee of instantaneous incapacitation. Evan adjusted, aiming at the brain stem.

The guy kept on grooving, bobbing on Charleston-wobbly knees.

Evan hesitated.

He didn't like to shoot anyone in the back unless he was

outnumbered. And besides, how do you shoot a guy who's dancing?

He rolled his shoulders forward. Sighed. No longer bothering to set his feet down quietly, he walked over to the man. The guard kept rocking, adding a bit of air guitar now.

Evan stepped in front of him, but the man's eyes were closed and he did a spin move, crossing his feet and whipping around to face in the other direction.

Aggravated, Evan tried to move around him, but now he was making airplane arms and tilt-rocking his way toward the rear edge of the roof.

'Hey,' Evan said. Then: 'Hey!'

What the hell was he doing? Trying to politely interrupt a guy so he could assassinate him?

He raised the ARES. Muzzle two inches from the back of the C2 vertebra.

Now chicken-dance flappy arms. The guy was killing Evan.

He had to talk to him first. Look him in the eye. Maybe Evan could do the whole 'Do I look scared?' speech to elicit a first move.

He lowered his pistol.

The guy swung around in a graceful dance move, feet leading, shoulders trailing his hips. He finished the half pivot and spotted Evan, and his arms flew up in a ridiculous fear display. He gave a high-pitched shriek and then toppled off the edge of the roof.

He fell three stories and landed with a clang worthy of a comic book.

Evan took two slow steps forward, leaning to look over the edge. The guy had landed in the fucking bed of Evan's pickup.

He said, 'Damn it.'

Then he looked up. The rooftop gave him a great sight line across the flatness of the Mojave basin, and that meant the approaching line of flashing red and blue lights about a mile and a half to the north was clear in the pristine night.

Maybe the capo and his khakied henchmen hadn't unhooked the security monitors after all.

He said, 'Damn it.'

He ran back to the rooftop door, flung it open, and leapt down the flights of stairs, his boots rattling the building.

Bursting out on the ground floor, the sibilation of the hive murmuring back to life once more.

'– dead? Are they all –?'

'Will you send help?'

'– why are you why did they why am I –'

Bolting down the corridor, cutting left around one corpse, hurdling the other. He grabbed the doorjamb to the last room on the left and swung into the nerve center. The computer hardware was large and intensely cord-entwined with a jungle of apparatuses, but there were three black cell phones lined up like blackjack cards at the edge of the desk.

He swept the burners into a cargo pocket, ran through the front door, cornering the side of the building just before a wave of headlights lit the stuccoed front from a block away.

A leg crooked a few wrong ways was slung over the side of Evan's pickup bed, the rest of the onetime dancer piled inside out of sight.

Evan said, 'Damn it.'

He flung the leg up over into the bed and it hit the heap of matter on the other side softly and out of view. He hopped into the driver's seat, shot away from the rear of the building, and carved a block-wide U-turn to head back into the fray.

Having a body in the bed of his truck wasn't even the

most pressing reason he didn't want to be spotted fleeing a crime scene. As he waited at a red light, he watched a half dozen police cars whip past, sirens roaring.

He waited for them to pass, signaled dutifully, and then aimed his Ford in the direction of Tommy Stojack's place.

45. Help Burying a Body

Tommy's armorer den fronted as an auto-repair shop. As Evan's wheels popped and crackled across the rocky dirt drive, his headlights illuminated the graveyard of props strewn in the front yard – rusting engine blocks and sedan carcasses and a tractor tire conscripted into planter duty for black mustard weeds. The neon sign over the entrance of the low-slung building was unlit as usual, the cover business perennially closed.

Evan didn't get far before Tommy stepped through the metal door in a pair of cargo pants and a half-buttoned shirt, bowed legs shoved into unlaced boots, an FN SCAR in 7.62×51 in the low carry position in case things sparked off.

He squinted through the headlights, recognizing the truck, and let the semiauto swing to his side as Evan climbed out. Tommy stood there, crooked on his bad hips and bad knees and bad ankles but somehow holding vertical.

Evan said, 'I need help burying a body.'

Tommy rolled his lower lip inward, making his horseshoe mustache bristle, then spit a stream of tobacco juice through the gap in his front teeth. Had he shoved Skoal into his mouth upon being awakened by the surveillance system's alert? Was it part of his routine like stepping into boots and grabbing a carbine? Or did he sleep with his lower lip packed to save time?

He bobbed his head a few times. 'Okay,' he said.

He disappeared back through the metal door. Evan waited

in the cold desert wind. Not thirty seconds later Tommy reemerged, two shovels in hand.

'C'mon then,' he said, in his low grumble of a voice. 'Let's get 'er done.'

46. That Fuckin' Dog

Las Vegas was in peak darkness, the first glow of morning still more than an hour away. Tommy and Evan sat around a fire pit behind the shop. Cedar logs crackled, throwing off a heavenly smoke that brought Evan back to the part of his childhood that was easiest to remember, when he used to take school at Jack's feet in the farmhouse study, the scent of single-barrel scotch mingling with heat of the hearth, just twelve-year-old him surrounded by an empire of books and – for the first time – a limitless future.

There were a million and a half stars overhead, and Evan sipped Kauffman Vintage he'd stashed in one of Tommy's cupboards, and Tommy was gripping a bottle of Angel's Envy in his blocky fist and making quick work of it. Stripped down to undershirts streaked with sweat, they were tired from carving a plot into the hard desert ground, and the alcohol was a necessity to remind them that the world still contained warmth and comfort.

They'd spoken barely a word in the past few hours. It wasn't the kind of work to talk about. It was the kind of work to get done.

And now they basked in a different kind of silence, thawing themselves back to a version of serenity.

Tommy said, 'This all start with that fuckin' dog?'

'Loco,' Evan said.

'You go searching for crazy, you find crazy. That's why generally? I search for bourbon and women who got a liberated relationship with their sexuality.'

'Yeah. It started small and telescoped on me.'

'Mission creep.' Tommy rubbed the back of his neck, his face screwed up with pain. 'I talked to Your Girl Friday earlier.'

Joey.

'That damn school has her off her fighting base.' Tommy took a swig. 'College is for dummies. Makes people get stuck up in their brains too much.'

'She's trying to fit in,' Evan said. 'But she's not built to fit in.'

'That's what I told her. She said next to all them regular girls she feels weird. I said, "Guess what? *Everyone's* fucking weird. Get rid of the weird parts that don't suit you. And keep the weird parts that make you *you*. Then see where the chips fall. That's it." Ya don't need Tony Robbins to spit slogans in yer face to know what's what.'

'What'd she say?'

'That my brusqueness was exceeded only by my ignorance.' Tommy didn't smile, but his cheeks bunched and his eyes gleamed with amusement. '"*Brusqueness.*" See what I mean? Not that I can't keep up. I've read a book before. But "rude" woulda done just fine.' He shook his head. 'College.'

Tommy's stretched T-shirt was one of those commemorative custom jobs the spec-ops guys were always throwing into production. In overly masculine type, someone's initials floated above the crest for the Green Berets: DE OPPRESSO LIBER. And beneath, the date of birth and a date of death bookending a shorter span than any parent would've hoped for.

Tommy fussed with a familiar trinket, a jagged half-moon of metal the size of a poker chip. It was one half of a broken challenge coin, a service-member medallion generally exchanged as a show of respect. As he shuttled the broken half across his knuckles, the stamped words glinted in the firelight: NO GREATER FRIEND.

A damn fine description of Tommy himself.

In all their years, they'd rarely talked about more than guns and matériel, but that subject matter had proven to be a kernel around which they'd grown an understanding of each other.

The flies were buzzing, getting bold at the edge of the fire, and as Tommy rose creakily, he waved a four-and-a-half-fingered hand at them. 'Goddamned sky raisins.' He stood a minute so his warhorse joints, degraded from countless parachute landings and blood-letting clashes, could find equilibrium. 'Gotta take a squirt. See if you can not kill anyone else while I'm inside.'

He lumbered off.

Evan sat alone with the sparking logs and the brilliant desert sky, his thoughts with Jack. And then his mind moved to Jacob Baridon, the man who fathered him, the vacuous nothingness of him, his eyes like inward-facing mirrors that only reflected him back to himself. What had he said when confronted with a person he'd contributed to creating? *I have a girl coming over. Gotta get the tail while the gettin's good.* The obliteration of Evan's imagined father had obliterated a contrast point to anything else. A contrast point he'd never known he'd carried inside him.

His OCD was up.

Everything hurt his eyes, every spot of dirt on his pants, every asymmetrical ridge of sand at his feet, every lopsided log in the imperfect pyre.

Jack used to make him jog in a blizzard. Face chapped, lips cracked, boots chafing, the moistness of his sweat trapped against his skin beneath the claustrophobic shell of a winter coat, marinating him in discomfort. It was awful.

Back then there hadn't been room to think, *Is this too much? Is this too far?* Not when he was being drownproofed or beaten on a training mat or nicked with a Gurkha knife when he parried wrong. And his blood seethed now at the thought of that . . . grooming?

But it hadn't been safe then to question, not for him, not for Jack, and Jack had saved him. And he thought through another filter of reality: him doing that to someone else, someone younger, to Joey. The thought was dizzying, telescoping like the camera in *Vertigo*.

His OCD was up.

It turned the volume high on the dried sweat across his ribs, the wrinkle of his sock in his boot. The strand of hair tickling his forehead no matter how many times he shoved it back. Every little thing assailing him.

Jack had been flawed and human. Jack had loved him and put him through the nearly unimaginable. And yet he loved Jack now as much as ever. Confusing.

Then a voice told Evan that no one gets all the comfort they want in this world, so shut the fuck up and quit whining.

That voice was angry.

That meant it was trying to hide from something.

His OCD was up.

His tongue worked a lopsided bump in his left back molar. He blinked against the grit beneath his eyelids. His –

A crash from inside had him on his feet, even before he heard Tommy's shout of distress.

He bolted into the shop through the slung-wide rear door, ARES drawn, darting through the looming lathes and mills and munition crates stamped with Cyrillic lettering, tread holding firm on the grease-slicked floor.

More sounds of thrashing across the dungeon-lit den,

Evan sourcing it to the bathroom behind the lineup of test-firing tubes. He sprinted over, burst through the door.

There Tommy was, pants slung down around his ankles, toppled over and wedged between the toilet and the wall. He was exposed and the cramped room stank and he was flailing to get back up.

'Get out of here!' he yelled. 'Don't look at me! Don't you fucking look at me!'

For leverage he grabbed at the toilet-roll holder bolted to the wall, but it ripped out and he tumbled back, legs kicking of a piece like a mermaid tail. His other hand clutched the porcelain edge of the bowl and he was more upside down than horizontal and he was stuck and the sight was well past awful.

'Get the fuck out!'

Confused, Evan pulled back. His heart was pounding. He waited at the other side of the closed door. He was sweating, rivulets pouring down his sides.

He'd never been in a situation like this, not once in his entire life.

Through the thin door he heard Tommy struggle and curse and then fall still.

Evan blinked, tried for four-square breathing but there was no breathing through this.

'Fuck,' Tommy said. And then: 'I'm stuck.'

Evan stood paralyzed.

'I said I'm fucking stuck.' Tommy's voice was laced with anger, but there was brittleness in it, too, just beneath the surface, enough brittleness to crack.

'Do you . . .' Evan cleared his throat. 'Should I come back in?'

'What the fuck you gonna do out there?'

Evan drew in a deep breath. Held it. Kept his head pointed

down and angled back. He opened the door. Still looking away, but in his peripheral he sensed Tommy in all his shame and vulnerability.

Facing mostly the other direction, he extended his hand.

Tommy clasped it. Calluses and dry skin, the bite of ragged nails.

The two men almost never touched.

Evan hoisted him up and he came lurchingly, bracing against the wall, and then he was back on the pot and Evan withdrew as fast as he could, shutting the door once more in a futile gesture of privacy.

He walked through the shop, this shop he'd known for so many years. Everything looked different now, imbued with bathos.

He was out the front door, drawing in fresh air, going to his truck, eager to drive away, away, away. He got behind the wheel and skidded out, kicking up clouds of dirt. As the fake auto shop swam into the rearview, an image came at Evan unbidden, that dimple-roofed pink-painted double-wide in Blessing, Texas, as it shrank in the rear windshield, deserving to be left behind.

The Fourth Commandment hammered at the walls of his skull, shouting him into submission – *Never make it personal. Never make it personal.*

One of Jack's Commandments.

But Jack was imperfect and didn't have all the answers, no matter how much he tried to contain the world within rigid parameters to keep it safe.

Some people deserved to be left behind. Others didn't.

And life was more complicated than any set of rules could constrain.

Evan felt himself free-falling through the awful expansiveness of freedom.

His foot hit the brakes.

The Ford F-150 skidded in the loose sand and halted at an angle. Evan was breathing hard.

It took a good thirty seconds of digging for him to acknowledge that he was scared.

Scared to go back. To see Tommy again. To open up what would be opened up inside him if he stepped outside the rules and exposed himself up to all the calamity the world could rain down on an armorless man.

He turned around.

He drove back.

He walked around the unlit shop to the fire.

He was still sweating, so he peeled off his undershirt and sat bare-chested beneath the stars.

Ten minutes passed and then another ten and then he heard the creak of the screen door and then boots shuffling over to him sheepishly, if boots could sheepishly shuffle.

Tommy collapsed into his lawn chair with a groan, the frayed straps groaning along with him, and they sat with the crickets looking at the fire so they didn't have to look at each other. A few clicks of a lighter and then a gust of Camel tobacco joined the cedar smoke.

Tommy's hand swung down, found his bottle. A glug. And then: 'Look, man . . .'

Evan said, 'We don't have to do all that.'

Tommy said, 'Thank God.'

More silence. More sitting. Evan filled the empty space around them and inside him with a bit of vodka.

Then Tommy said, with a flare of anger, 'No one asked you to come busting in there like the Kool-Aid Man.'

'Fair.'

Tommy took a moment to settle back down. Then he

waved the bottle at Evan. 'You're young enough you still think you can beat it. Age.'

Evan didn't agree in full but now was not the time to say that.

'I don't get up no more when it don't hurt. A lot. Ever. What the fuck. You'd think a guy who spent the first haul of his years figuring out how to kick life's ass would get some . . . *concession* at the end before it just breaks you down piece by piece, you know? But no. Just fuck you and your joints.'

They sat and sipped.

'Tommy,' Evan said. 'Quit whining.'

Tommy chuckled some, low like a dog purring. 'If you fall soft, you splat. If you fall hard, you bounce. But after a while you can't fall hard no more. Then what? There's no point, Evan. To any of this.'

Evan let the thought in. Tried to find the right one to send back out. 'If you give up, it's just a fuck-you to anyone who ever cared about you.'

'That's the answer right there, amigo. How many people care about me? How many people care about you? How many people ever really did?'

Once more Evan found himself at the limitations of his experience. If there were words to shape the chaos beyond into meaning, he didn't know what they were.

Tommy gulped down another slug of bourbon. 'That's why we're alcoholics.'

'I'm not an alcoholic,' Evan said. 'I like booze too much.'

'Ain't that some shit an alcoholic would say?' Tommy sucked in a lungful, spoke through the strain of the exhalation. 'You still think you're noble, like I once told myself, back when I blocked out how much of all that was just cover fire for my arrogance. No, not arrogance – it was to distract myself from how tight I was gripping the steering wheel.' He put his hands out, air-steering, cigarette stubbed out of his knobby knuckles, the other fist still gripping the bottle. He looked like an advertisement for reckless driving. 'Then I figured out the steering wheel wasn't hooked up to nuthin', man. It was just a loose steering wheel.' He glanced over at Evan. 'You still think it's your responsibility to fix every damn thing in the world. That's good. But it's just training.'

'For what?'

'For what happens after you learn you can't fix anything or save anyone. All you can do is light a match at a fork in the dark-ass road to show someone a better path that they'll probably not take.'

'There's gotta be something,' Evan said. 'Something you still want to aim at. To leave behind. What do you want them to say when they put you in a casket?'

'"Look,"' Tommy said, '"he's moving!"'

He smirked, flicked his butt at Evan's boots. They sat awhile longer.

'Courage, man,' Tommy said. 'It's for the ignorant. Anyone who's had a taste of what courage puts you at the mercy of? After *that*? They only want *mercy*. That's all I want anymore. Mercy. Lately I been thinking about . . .'

'What?'

'That scared part you build the rest of yourself around so you don't have to look at it. You know that part? Once you see it, trembling in the light of yer, dunno . . . *awareness,* you can never unsee it. But least you know . . . you know it's part of you. Jesus.' He bridged his forehead with his hand, covering his eyes. A dead leaf flew up and stuck in his cuff, a spot of gold. 'I'll tell you what. You get old faster'n you can believe. And you want to get it right. The quicker you can get it right, man. Do it. Because you run out of time. I think about all these rounds I've sent out into the world, how many skulls and chest cavities they've punctured . . . Well, I think about that, I might as well not think at all.' He swung his bloodshot eyes to Evan, gave him a rare glimpse inside. 'Ever again.'

Evan nodded once very slowly, the slightest downward tip of his head so as not to disrupt the course Tommy was charting to wherever he needed to get.

Tommy gestured around with the bottle of amber fire. 'Here's how I see it. When you cash in yer chips? The afterlife is just you frozen at that point in time. All them ghosts you left behind, all that business you didn't settle, all those demons you swept under the rug. They all haunt you. You're suspended with 'em forever.' He was slurring a touch now, a rare ceding of ground to the bourbon. 'So: Clean it up. Clean everything up while you can. Afore it's too late.'

The fire snapped and crackled, and at last Evan felt his body temperature coming down, the sweat cooling across his chest. Tommy was staring out at the night with the glazed eyes of a veteran who had too many memories rattling around in his head.

'You done?' Evan said.

'Yeah,' Tommy said, exhausted. 'I'm done.'

'Good,' Evan said. 'If you can manage to not get any more miserable, when you're old and drooling and worthless, I still might visit you in the nursing home.'

Tommy's mouth bunched, mustache curling up at the edges, and then he spit in the dirt. 'If I let your sorry ass in.'

The first gleam of light warmed the horizon to the east, more a premonition than an entrance. Tommy tilted the bottle, gauging how much bourbon remained, then took a nip. He was still for a moment, and then his broad shoulders started shaking with amusement.

'What?' Evan said.

'When us dudes lose our cool, we think we're Steve McQueen. But we're not. I came at you like a whiny little bitch, didn't I?' Tommy imitated himself in a squeaky voice: '"Don't look at me."'

He smirked some more, polished off the bottle, and tossed it into the flames.

'You were all right, Tommy,' Evan said. 'You were Steve McQueen.'

47. Battle Within

In the morning stillness of the Castle Heights lobby, Evan stood before the closed doors of the elevator. They were appareled in a cling-wrap advertisement featuring Lorilee posed with crossed arms, a Girl Boss CEO. A banner graphic unfurled across her stomach proclaimed, RE-ELECT LORILEE. SERVICE IS MY 'WHY'!

On a yellow Post-it stuck above the word RE-ELECT, a note was jotted in Hugh Walters's proficient hand, reading, *You can't re-elect someone who wasn't legitimately elected in the first place.* A drawn arrow, retraced with a vigor suggesting latent rage, pointed at the slogan.

A pink Post-it adhered above the yellow Post-it read, *What kind of grown man desecrates official campaign materials?*, with an equivalently aggressive arrow aimed at its respective target.

Evan shot a glance back at Joaquin, hoping for a moment of shared commiseration, but Joaquin had dozed off in his chair. After their last exchange, Evan had run deeper background on the kid; he had plenty to be tired about, so he let him rest and turned back to larger-than-life Lorilee.

When the car arrived, the doors parted, splitting her enhanced breasts, a clear design misfire.

Evan stepped through her cracked chest cavity into the elevator and rode up.

He entered his penthouse and nearly asphyxiated on the stench of dog gas, a miasma as palpable as smog.

Joey was perched on one of the black leather couches, bare feet up on the cushion, laptop on her thighs. 'I know, I know. I went to answer my phone and Dog ate my pastor tacos. Then he throoped everywhere –'

'Translate.'

'Threw up and pooped – BUT DON'T GET ALL ANAL. I did a crime-scene-worthy biocleanup 'cuz I knew you'd freak out so it's all handled and just smells bad. That's why I'm out here. I'm letting the Vault air out.'

Shame-immune, Dog the dog rose from his slumber at Joey's side and shook his mighty head, ears snapping like canvas sails against his skull, tattooing a percussive beat.

Evan's eyes were watering. He contemplated various decontamination contingencies.

Dog looked undeterred, licking himself with impunity.

Evan walked around the perimeter and threw open the sliding doors to the balconies, his lungs choking on the fresh air. The sun warmed his face, reminding him just how tired he was.

He came back and sat next to Joey. She was eating ranch Corn Nuts, and bits were stuck in her teeth, and the ranch smelled less like ranch and more like ranch air freshener. A glass of orange juice with ice rested directly on the glass accent table next to the couch. He lifted it, wiped the condensation ring with his sleeve, set it back down on a coaster that happened to be nearby because coasters abounded in his penthouse for eventualities precisely like this. He debated encasing Joey along with Dog in airtight Bubble Wrap but figured that might constitute a civil- and animal-rights infringement.

Joey: '*That's* all you have to say?'

Still searching for the volume control on his OCD: 'I didn't say anything.'

''Xactly,' Joey said. 'You didn't ask how it went. The Cheesecake Factory.'

'Right. How did it go?'

She crossed her arms.

'Skip all this crap and just tell me how it went.'

'Okay. It went okay. I came out and did the whole toilet-paper-décolletage thing and everyone laughed and then it was over.'

She tapped away at her laptop. No eye contact. She was in a mood. She took a sip of orange juice. 'This glass sucks. It's too hard to grip.'

'Joey. What's going on?'

She picked up her phone, caught herself, put it down. She crossed her arms in a kind of pinched hug. Her eyes held irritation verging on fury. And he realized: She was going through withdrawal. From her fucking phone.

She noticed him noticing. 'I'm on it, X. The phone shit. Don't say anything. I'm on it.'

He waited.

Her fingers fluttered. Her eyes were jittery. 'At dinner they was all joking about brands and shopping at, like, Barneys, and I was like, "Isn't that the purple dinosaur?" But for once I said it in my inside voice. But still. I was just sitting there like a dope and I didn't know what to say. I felt stupid.'

'Do you –'

'I don't want to talk about it.'

'Okay.' Evan took the three burner phones from his cargo pocket and set them on the counter. 'I retrieved these from the human-trafficking operation. See if you can get into them to find a line to Karissa Lopatina.'

'That's it?'

'If you want to talk, talk. If you don't, we have work to do.'

'Why don't I just get back in the kitchen and make you a chicken potpie?'

'That's not what I'm –'

313

'And then you can keep ordering me around until I take my confused revenge and get knocked up by a tattooed juvie-offender boyfriend.'

'That'll show me.'

'No one thinks you're funny. I'll get into the stupid phones. And I have to get back to the Solventry hack. My keys are returning garbage when I decrypt with them.'

'You can't get in?'

'*I didn't say that.* The encryption's just really . . . stubborn.' She started grumbling about Erlang programming.

Suddenly he understood her mood more fully. Josephine Morales had met her match. Or was afraid that she had. And she was fighting her way forward into the forest of Solventry's digital security while trying to reset her nervous system from constant electronic engagement.

A battle without. A battle within.

He'd never seen her cowed by a mission. He'd never lived with anyone detoxing from excessive phone use. He'd never had to deal with someone else under his roof while he was supposed to be sleeping and working out and prepping for a mission.

He didn't like it much.

Four days until Jayla was back in the world, released from the Marshals where Lopatina could get her. Seven more hours until Evan was due to meet Nathan Friedhoff, Allman's rival, the man who'd possibly put the Wolf and everything else into motion. If this theory was correct, the execution of Dr Benjamin Hill and the continued terrorizing of his seventeen-year-old daughter were merely collateral damage so Friedhoff could get the upper hand on Solventry in the technology wars.

Collateral damage was unprofessional, imprecise, and unacceptable. It offended Evan as much as it angered him.

He hadn't slept in over twenty-four hours.

Joey and Dog followed him back to the master suite. Once they veered off into the Vault, he stripped down and took a shower so hot it turned his skin pink. Then he dressed, gathered up the heap of dirty clothes, and loaded them into the freestanding fireplace in the great room. From the last purging of worn evidence, a few artifacts remained – the steel shank, toe caps, and lace eyelets from his Original S.W.A.T.s, a Vertex fob watch, a scorched length of zipper. He stoked up a fire and let it roar.

Back to the bedroom, onto his maglev bed, lying on top of the sheets, counting down to sleep from five ... four ... two ...

PROUD OF THE BROWN, THAT'S WHAT WE SHOULD BE!

Rap music pulsing through the walls from the Vault.

He lurched out of bed, through the bathroom, into the still-wet shower stall. Shoving through the hidden door, he saw Joey bouncing her head as she clicked through one of the burner phones from the human traffickers.

'What the hell, Joey!'

Her head snapped up, Red Vine dangling from her mouth, and paused the music. 'I been working twenty-four/seven. I need tunes to power me. You're the one who needed me to move in here to do all this for you!'

Dog was lying on his side, one paw curled up over his face, a pose Evan anthropomorphized into an indication of shared annoyance at the music.

'And guess what, dummy?' Joey waved the burner phone. 'If you'd even bothered to check the phone before giving it to your long-suffering servant, you'd've seen the next hit laid out right here in text.'

'What?'

'There's a text exchange between this human-trafficking douchenozzle and "W." Which your operationally honed brain mighta figured out was the *Wolf*. It *literally* spells out the target, date, time, and location.'

'Which are?'

'Russo Dmitri. Tonight. Ten P.M. Stretch of Sunset Boulevard between Holloway and Larrabee. He's a mobbed-up thug from Sacramento, which has a shit-ton of human trafficking. They want him gone because he's pushing into Reno.'

'How do you know?'

She shoved the phone at him. 'It says right here!'

'Why the location?'

'He travels armored up with heavy security. He's got a meeting with three crime families in a penthouse condo on that block. They want him sniped as he turns in to the parking garage, send a signal to the folks waiting upstairs. Got the license plate of the target car and everything. You want Karissa Lopatina? That's where she'll be.' Joey flipped the phone at him. 'Now quit wasting my time and let me get back to work.'

With a stageworthy pointedness, she screwed in her earphones and resumed her listening quietly.

Having prepped for the evening's encounters, envisioning countless scenarios, Evan sat in the lotus position on a mat in the great room to ready himself for the mission's coming escalation. Veiling his eyes, he prepared his breath for meditation, bringing each inhalation deep into the –

A fucking hair dryer roared to life upstairs.

There was a door to the bathroom up in the loft, but clearly Joey hadn't bothered to close it, so the howl of the appliance cascaded down the spiral staircase into the great room and from there into Evan's skull.

Perhaps this was the meditation then. Learning to focus despite –

Now the hair dryer hit a note of wavering undulation that spoke to forceful fanning. It sounded like a wounded water buffalo.

He rose, heading angrily for the spiral staircase. Joey shrapnel blanketed the top two steps – a shed shirt, a sports bra. The loft was an explosion of Cheetos and magazines and an uncapped lipstick resting atop the pillow on the pulled-out sofa.

At close proximity the hair dryer was deafening. He wondered how Joey hadn't sustained hearing loss.

He knocked on the wide-open bathroom door, and she started, toggling off the dryer.

He said, 'Do you have to blow-dry your hair for nine hours at a hundred decibels?'

'*You* try having lush Latina locks.' She stomped past him into the loft.

'And clean your damn room. How you do anything is how –'

'I *am* doing this anything as I am doing everything.' She hopped onto the sofa, eyed her phone on the sheets, lit up with incoming texts. Then she stopped herself from reaching for it and grabbed a magazine instead, pretending to immerse herself in it. 'And I shall not let you messy-shame me.' A crisp snap of the page. 'Wait. I amend that. I'm *not* messy. I'm just not psychotically OCD.'

'Keep your gear in order. Keep your brain in order.'

She threw down the magazine and hopped back up. 'Oh, great. Just what the world needs. Another white guy in cargo pants barking orders.'

They glared at each other.

Then they cracked up.

317

She walked past him, palm down by her hip for a low-five. 'If you need me, I'll be in the Vault saving humanity.'

Her footsteps pounded down. She'd left her phone behind. Progress.

He stood in the loft, trying to imagine how she could function with all this mess around her. And why he couldn't. And yet here he was, allowing it. Living with it. And still functioning.

His gaze caught on a bunch of magazine tear-outs taped on the wall above the sofa in a collage. Joey's vision board. A shirtless actor with pronounced abs. A glass house in the woods. A brunette singer in thigh-high lace-up boots, sparkly blue shorts, and an American-flag bustier with sequined stars over the right breast. White tropical sand fading into the barely rippled aqua sheet of the sea. And dead in the center, a bunch of smiling teenage girls of all shapes and sizes.

He looked closer. A musical group? A sports team?

And then he realized: It was a group of friends.

Something gave way inside him.

A tearing, a yielding, a struck note that found resonance in his chest, that echoed in the hollow he'd discovered in Blessing, Texas. It was an emptiness, yes, but also a space to hold something new, to hold inside him what Joey held inside herself and to try to feel it as his own.

He sat on the sofa.

He was shocked to realize that his eyes had moistened.

He took a minute to reset himself.

Then he walked downstairs, changed into an outfit befitting Harvard professor Stanley Leigh, and headed back to the Vault.

Joey didn't look up when he entered. Her face was fully focused; she was in her purest state, kinetic and single-minded. Her fingers purred across the keyboard and the light

318

of the OLED screens flowed across her face and he didn't understand the code on the monitors but he knew it was obeying her, that she was conducting.

It was the most in-her-element he'd seen her since the beginning of the damn mission, and he knew in that moment, standing unnoticed in the doorway to the Vault, that by her hand Solventry's encryption would fall.

She barely blinked. Her fingers moved from mouse to keyboard to mouse. Dog slept in the corner, breathing rhythmically. Everything in perfect order.

Evan pictured the phone she'd left upstairs, a portal to the insane, beeping and chiming and beckoning with no one to hear it.

He crossed to one of the weapon lockers and extracted a fresh ARES 1911 and three magazines. He seated the mags one after another, dropping them, loading them, checking for snags and hitches. There were none.

He slotted the pistol into his appendix carry and hid the backup mags in the pockets of his Harvard professor trousers. It was time to go face-to-face with Nathan Friedhoff.

All around Evan, the Vault hummed with movement, scrolling logs, progress bars, and blinking CPU and GPU meters. He started out.

Joey stayed locked in.

He didn't say good-bye.

He didn't have to.

48. The Permanent Hypnotic Drugging of the American Mind

Nathan Friedhoff was a confusion of disjointedness, pacing in the great shelf of a living room jutting out over a sheer cliff in the Hollywood Hills. Evan's faux interview on the nature of genius had been desultory at best. Friedhoff's two teenage daughters had streamed in and out with their faces adhered to their phones, along with a trio of Latina cleaning ladies, and a Slavic manservant of sorts who drifted through at intervals tidying up and then standing obsequiously with his hands clasped at the small of his back awaiting instructions that never came. Friedhoff was too busy pacing to take note of any of them, yammering in circular loops of logic that suggested the need for a med adjustment or shock treatment. No topic was too small for him to opine about, and he ladled out each declamation with theatrical heft as if anticipating its transcription for a *Wired* article.

There was way too much foot traffic in the house for Evan to kill him now, even if he did manage to pry loose incriminating information, so he had to buckle down and see what fuel he might gather for future ignition.

A bar with uplit shelves climbed to a raised ceiling, showing off an array of fine bottles. Friedhoff sipped rum, a substandard spirit, from a rocks glass that he refilled as liberally as if he were pouring apple juice. As the sun dimmed over the thump and pulse of Cahuenga Boulevard way below, he moved to scotch as was befitting the hour.

He swung a bottle of Johnnie Walker Blue toward Evan and then the shelves. 'Want anything?'

Evan remained perched on a barstool with academic delicacy, pretending not to eye the squat bottle of VDKA 6100. Made of only two ingredients, whey and spring water locally sourced near Lake Taupo on New Zealand's North Island, it had been brought to international awareness by an American actor. It was smooth as the action on a vintage SIG P210, and it finished on a note of white pepper along the sides of the tongue.

But now was not the time or place. Friedhoff wasn't just drinking hard; it was the wrong kind of drinking, steeped in grief and toxins. The booze had gone into him, hit bottom, and was now seeping out, clogging his pores, suffusing his clothes, riding his breath.

'No, thank you,' Evan said.

Friedhoff slopped scotch into a glass. 'Johnnie Walker Blue doesn't have the character of a single-malt,' he declared, 'but you can always count on it. Like a top-notch Parisian whore. You get your money's worth.'

Though he was well into his fifties, Friedhoff wore board shorts and a T-shirt with a Pied Piper logo. A glass-fronted mini-fridge behind the bar was stocked full of bottles of Soylent, a trendy Silicon Valley plant-based protein drink, and he wore one of those ridiculous Leatherman Tread multitool bracelets from which you could extract a screwdriver or a hex drive or a heat-pump assembly for your Tesla Model Y. Studiously tousled hair, neatly manscaped two-day growth, boyish wire-frames at odds with the lines of maturity etching his temples – he was one of those boy-men or man-boys who'd never figured out how to grow up and yet despite that or because of it had plummeted into the depths of a midlife crisis.

Luke Devine had hinted about some kind of breakdown, but Friedhoff was even more fragmented and rambling than Evan had anticipated.

He resumed his woe-is-me rant about the technology he'd helped unleash upon the world: 'I wasn't some will-to-power person from the gate, you know? I was a sweet kid who loved coding, who wanted to express himself, to share what I learned with everyone. But it gets into you. Power – the roar of it.'

Time and again, Evan had heard a variation of this speech. Of course it was men like Allman and Friedhoff who did the most damage. The ones with so much to offer who'd fallen into the gravitational pull of their own ego. People who were solely motivated by power rarely got far enough to do real damage.

As Evan sat blinking and pretending to take notes, Fried-hoff slammed back the scotch and moved out to the short balcony that looked down a forever drop to scrubby brush and stone.

'When we started, it was fucking beautiful, man. We were changing the world, creating prosperity, and we were nice to people at work. Everything was possible. Smart prosthetics for amputees, VR PTSD therapy in the meta, AI diagnostics to identify cancer nodules from a voiceprint, low-carbon cities, you name it, man.'

Evan tried to imagine someone this unimpressive building a multibillion-dollar company and then ordering the execution of a key competitor. Nothing seemed real about Friedhoff, but perhaps that was the point. Maybe nothing was real to him outside a screen. Maybe everything was a VR simulation. Maybe he just punched a button on his joystick and deployed the Wolf with a throw-down .22 and a flex-tie sized for a seventeen-year-old girl's neck.

'Now it's all about maximization. Work product. Time. Profit. We measure our workers by metrics of how much they load in our warehouses down to fractions of seconds.

Wearable tech, handheld scanners, performance-tracking software, cameras everywhere, algorithm-driven performance system metrics. Charting time-off tasks like snack and bathroom breaks. I mean, we know the percentage our employees slow down when they're chewing a FreeWillPower bar and the percentage by which they speed up when chewing one of our caffeinated Youtropical bars. I think: How did we get here? And then I remember: I aimed at this. *I* did. And now . . . what if it's too late?'

'For you?'

'For *everyone*.' Friedhoff slumped into a stool, despondent. 'There's no going back.' He spun his glass on the bar and then spun it again. 'We can't put the tech back into the box. When I was in college I used to bike through the rain. To read fucking Kierkegaard. In a library. That was open all night. Real-world dedication, right? And me, I'm a shitstain on the heel of what my grandfather was. And these kids now? Who we're creating? Who we already created? And are powerless to stop? They're so . . . softened in luxury. Eroded. I have two daughters, man. If I admit what I've done to them? To the kids of this world? If you teleported me in from a few decades ago to behold my work? Faces stuck to screens, anxiety skyrocketing, FOMO and body image, the permanent hypnotic drugging of the American mind. No – *global* mind. Not anymore. I'm out, man. I'm out.'

'What does that mean?'

'I don't know.' Friedhoff's eyes held equal parts remorse and pleading. 'I'm tired of being disgusted with myself. Like a lot of people. But the sin I carry, my burden, it just seems . . . *heavier*. Our way of life is dying. Human life. And I helped oversee its demise. The singularity's bearing down on us like a freight train.'

And so you had one of the world's leading AI experts killed, Evan thought. *To slow it down a little.*

'What sin?' Evan asked. 'What do you mean by "sin"?'

'Just the stuff I've done,' Friedhoff said vaguely. 'To people.'

He grabbed at his hair, made a fist atop his forehead. A man barely holding it together.

'How do we stop it?' Evan asked. 'The freight train?'

'They have too much power, man. *We.* We have too much power. And the laws can't catch up. We need, dunno. An overthrow. A revolution. A coup. Something . . . drastic.'

Were these really the pioneers at the helm of our uncertain future? In Allman, an ambulatory left prefrontal cortex? And a third-rate Peter Pan philosopher in Friedhoff?

'It's your belief that we need to halt AI at any cost?' Evan asked carefully. 'Even violence?'

Friedhoff's eyes jerked from his empty glass to Evan and then quickly away. 'Who knows,' he said softly. 'Who knows.'

He was sufficiently muddled with guilt and booze that Evan decided to take a more direct run at the object of his curiosity.

'Solventry,' Evan said, 'they're one of your competitors, right?'

'Sure,' Friedhoff said. 'They're everyone's competitor.'

'I interviewed a man named Dr Benjamin Hill for this study. Are you familiar with his work?'

'What is this? Why are you asking me about Hill?' The words came faster, a staccato beat of paranoia.

'The genius study,' Evan said.

Friedhoff's daughter drifted in from the back hall. She wore a flowing white dress with a gauzy wrap across her shoulders. Straight blond hair parted in the center, 1970s long, round pale face with light freckles. Her phone cradled expertly in the palm of her hand, the light shining up at her pale green eyes. 'Dad? Dad?' Her gaze didn't lift from the screen. 'The Wi-Fi's out. I'm streaming a thing and I can't ... It keeps glitching.' She moved forward, bumped into the couch, readjusted course without lifting her eyes.

'I'm busy, June,' Friedhoff said. 'I told you I'm in a meeting.'

'Daddy?' The younger daughter floated in from the kitchen. Dark curly hair, crop top showing a pierced belly button. She held an iPad before her, thumbs tapping away. 'Can you reboot the server? I'm Snapping with Peyton and it just went out. Can you –' She stumbled over the edge of the rug, kept her footing.

The girls stood there, swaying, eyes locked on their screens, a bizarre walking-dead effect.

'I taught you how to reboot the router,' Friedhoff said. His face had darkened, brows heavying over his eyes. He watched Evan differently now, with suspicion.

'Yeah,' the daughters said in unison, 'but you're better at it.'

Friedhoff reached out and grabbed Evan's forearm, not gently, his words delivered on a current of alcohol. 'I don't understand why we're discussing Solventry.'

Evan said, 'My subject pool includes –'

'Oh wait,' June said, dreamily. 'It's – hang on – it's coming back online ...'

'I got it,' the younger daughter intoned. 'I quit out and then reloaded ...'

The teenage girls stared at their screens, swaying slightly on their feet like anchored kelp. 'We're good,' they said in a single voice. 'We're good now.'

June stood mesmerized by her phone. Her little sister didn't so much withdraw as rewind out of the room.

Evan looked down at Friedhoff's hand clamped on his

arm. Friedhoff followed the stare, noticed what he was doing, and let go. He covered with a nervous laugh.

'That's it,' he said. 'I think you should leave now.'

'Thank you for your time.' Evan rose.

As he started out, he felt the heat of Friedhoff's glare at his back. Beside the couch, June blocked his way to the foyer. Her iPhone video was going full blast, an electronic beat underscoring a flurry of fast edits.

'Excuse me,' he said.

She didn't look up.

Blading his body, he slipped past her and moved to the front door.

She didn't seem to notice.

49. The Second-Best Sniper Hide in the Kill Zone

Evan was set up in the second-best sniper hide in the kill zone. A seventh-story corner office at a fifty-meter stagger across the street from the condo building that was Russo Dmitri's destination. Based on the text from the recovered phone, Evan knew that the Wolf's bullet was going to arrive in the one-block span unfurled below him.

He'd borrowed this particular office because of its open sight lines and wide vantage, its outswing casement windows, and its gauzy voile roller shades that hid the reflection of his sniper scope. He had *not* chosen it for its witty poster art ('You Can't Deposit Excuses!'), nor the ponderous heave and groan of water cycling in the fish-tank-for-one (red veil-tail betta), nor its Air Wick Freshmatic dispenser (Hawaii scent).

Though he intended to observe and then track or approach Karissa Lopatina, he'd brought his Savage 110 Elite bolt-action. In the event that she made his position and sought to engage, he didn't want to find himself having brought binoculars to a sniper fight.

In the unlit office he lay flat on his stomach across a folding table two meters back from the open window and lowered blind. For the past forty-five minutes he'd moved little more than his eyelids. In his thirteenth year, he'd been taught by a marksmanship instructor to hold prone sniper position for as long as was demanded, to move in inches per hour when the necessity arose. Breathing in air perfumed with papaya and hibiscus, he let the reticle creep across the entire area of operations – curb drains and lampposts, windows and parked cars, rooftops and awnings – and land once more on the sniper hide he would have chosen himself if he were the one who was going to execute Russo Dmitri.

The double billboard was perched on the roof of Book Soup across the street from the bleached-yellow extant signage of the old Tower Records. The billboard's two faces were separated at an angle, meeting at one end like a chevron, providing an isosceles triangle of protection within. A perfect view to a kill.

Currently empty.

He'd identified the hide for the same reasons Lopatina would. Given Dmitri's likeliest route, the perch provided the straightest line of sight to his vehicle for the longest window of time before its planned turn in to the parking structure. It would widen the Wolf's range to between seventy-five and four hundred meters, though if he were her, he'd take the shot at the closer end. The dual billboard had a platform as well as plentiful scaffolding beneath, opening up multiple routes across the adjoining roofs and down. The billboard faces would tamp down the echoes and mask the muzzle report, which would buffalo the shotlocs – shot-locator microphones – that the last mayor had ordered built in to most telephone poles. Lopatina would make use of a Killflash ARD honeycomb mesh cover to mute any glint of the scope and supersonic projectiles that would emanate hard-to-trace shock waves. The rounds would be machine-turned, differentially tempered, barrier-blind solid copper projectiles with hardened tips to get through a windshield and body armor with little difficulty. Hanging a wind flag would be too conspicuous, but there was plentiful lightweight debris blowing in the gutters to give her whatever cues she needed at this distance.

Yes: The billboard was the best position for the shot.

Which meant he'd wait here in the runner-up spot, patient as a mantis.

These blocks of the Strip were one of Los Angeles's pressure points, an epicenter wired to the life of the city. The bookstore's sign glowed in red and yellow neon. The billboard threw a spa-cool blue light. Car headlights washed across bars and restaurants, across decked-out hipsters and past-their-prime rockers. The thump and pulse of unseen dance floors set dark-tinted windows vibrating, throwing back wobbling reflections of cars and streetlights, rendering them aquatic.

A squiggle of movement along the sidewalk caught his attention, a FWIP scuttling underfoot, largely ignored by passersby and partiers. The delivery robots had become part of the scenery here, like parking meters and trash cans, just one more piece of the urban landscape to step around.

He'd unclipped his fob watch and placed it on the table in front of him next to his RoamZone. The Vertex clockwork was originally commissioned for ordnance timing by the British War Office during World War II. Its luminescent hour markers and hands showed 9:13. Another forty-seven minutes until Russo Dmitri's approximate arrival.

Evan felt his first ping of uncertainty. He'd anticipated that the Wolf would have been in position by now.

He waited and waited some more.

The facing billboard read, NO PATIENCE REQUIRED. SAME DAY DELIVERY.

He tried to think of anything of enduring worth he'd ever gotten that hadn't required patience.

If he hadn't been watching precisely the right spot with 4X thermal night-vision magnification, he would not have seen her.

A flicker within the darkness. A gloved hand gripping a piece of scaffolding. A flash of a masked face. A ripple of altered shadow.

And then a quarter-second blink of visibility as she strobed across a shaft of ambient light and out of sight behind the V of the billboards. He'd caught only the quickest glimpse of the sniper rifle at her side, but that was all he needed.

A Savage 110 Elite Precision bolt-action chambered in 7.62x51 mm NATO and enhanced with a Phoenix-S clip-on thermal scope – just like the one in Evan's hands. But hers looked to be a right-hand bolt-action to his left.

A mirror image.

Since she was a pro, she wouldn't be recoil-averse, but the Savage 110's adjustable stock could be suited to her petite stature, and as a common rifle it was suited for a shoot-and-dump. Rewinding the mental snapshot he'd taken of her, he noted the titanium tube extending the muzzle. His guess was a SureFire suppressor pinned in place; the Wolf wouldn't mess with a cheaper variant that screwed on and off while also screwing with the ballistics.

The tip of a barrel eased into visibility, protruding from the slender vertical gap at the nearly joined seam of the billboards and giving him a second glimpse of the Phoenix-S thermal in front of a Leupold scope.

Lopatina was looking down at the area of operations through the same thermal optics through which he was observing her. For a still moment, the executioners watched their respective targets, taking in the world through matching filters – a poetic observation he chose not to dwell upon.

The tip of her rifle withdrew slowly, steadily, and then she was entirely invisible once more. Shooting farther back from the aperture would hide the minimal muzzle flash and degrade the sound signature even more.

She was gone.

Motionless, he watched the billboards enfolding her and the strip of darkness through which she aimed. No muzzle, no shadow, no movement.

When the wind shifted, he thought he caught a dissipating puff of her breath.

Together and apart, they waited for Russo Dmitri.

In keeping with the First Commandment, *Assume nothing*, Evan had drilled down on the target and found him to be the bona fide mobster and human trafficker the texts had described.

He felt delighted to have the opportunity to not intervene in his execution.

The RoamZone hummed softly in front of him, caller ID showing Sofia. He clicked his earpiece. 'Go.'

'Huh?'

'Sorry. Yes?'

'Someone saw Loco! I got a call from the flyer. They said he was over at –'

'Text location.'

'Please please please call or come over after you check no matter how late.'

'I have to go.'

'Wait! Have you heard from Dad? I've called him a bunch and –'

Evan said, 'I'm sure he's fine.'

'I didn't ask that.'

Smart kid.

Evan said, 'I'll contact you later,' and severed the call.

The night air leaked around the edges of the roller blind before him. The fish tank gurgled. The Hawaiian mister misted.

For a solid twenty minutes he watched the seemingly

innocuous billboards and the street below. Barely moving, barely breathing.

And then he spotted it.

A Lincoln Town Car on the approach. As it coasted west down the waterfall of the boulevard, he picked up the license-plate number designated over text. When the car stopped for the light at Holloway, Evan got a good look at the bodyguard driver. Teardrop tattoo by the eye, pistol bulge where a deep-concealment underarm holster would be. His blazer and button-up puffed out over what he guessed was Level IIA body armor, helpful against a 9 mm or a .45 ACP but not so much against a Savage 110 bolt-action with AP projectiles.

The familiar clarity of anticipation came on. He was aware of the soft cadence of his heartbeat and his breath pressing his lungs outward.

His body anticipating the shot as if he were the one taking it.

The light changed.

The Town Car coasted forward.

Evan was the devil on Lopatina's shoulder or she the one on his and he stared through the same scope and watched the kill zone through the same optics and waited for the bodyguard to be put down by the same sniper rifle he held in his hands. A surreal sensation shifted outside and within him, like a virtual-reality game in which he was playing someone else or she was playing him.

The vehicle closer yet, nearing the turn in to the office building's parking garage. One man in the rear seat behind the driver, just a shadowed head and torso conveniently outlined like a range target. The Town Car changed lanes, the passenger vanishing from the sight line, hidden behind the driver and headrest. Crosswind looked to be low.

If it were Evan, he would take the driver first. Given a

conventional windshield and a bit of luck, there was a chance to get it done in one, sending a round straight through the driver and into the target. If not he'd anticipate that the organic shrapnel would spook Dmitri from the car.

He'd just decided where he'd place the shot – just beneath the driver's collarbone on the left side – when the windshield shattered and a hole appeared in the man's chest as if Evan had thought it into existence.

The Town Car veered calmly out of its lane, slowing.

Karissa would be transitioning to the second shot now, working the bolt. As clearly as if he could see through the billboard, he envisioned her behind the rifle, butt seated at her right shoulder, head on slight tilt, dominant right eye not leaving the eye box of the scope.

Evan eased his own scope to the left rear door, anticipating Dmitri would make a panicked run, and sure enough he did.

Evan swept the Leupold and Phoenix-S to follow, reticle bullseyeing the bulge of flesh at the back of Dmitri's shaved skull – primary target acquired – and then there was a puff of pink mist, the trailing crack of a supersonic bullet in flight. As Dmitri crumpled, Evan had to double-check that his finger was still outside the trigger guard. She'd even fired to the same rhythm; it was as though Evan had shot the man himself.

The car slowed, dribbling against two cars parked at meters, then rode up onto the curb and smashed into the newsstand in front of Book Soup.

Dmitri was laid out dead in the middle of the street. A girl in a latex dress froze in the crosswalk and screamed, box clutch purse jerking on its baby straps. Traffic veered and stopped and honked and the rest of the block lurched into frenetic action, pedestrians running to safety, others sprinting to help.

Evan looked back at the billboards just in time to see Lopatina's black-clad form swing down on the scaffolding, launch itself onto the roof, and vanish over the lip to the adjoining building.

He traced her anticipated movement. Though his scope was pegged on the sidewalk below, he almost missed her.

She emerged from an alley one block over wearing a fitted red dress, sleeveless, with a high-low hem that showed off the fronts of her thighs and swooped down in the back to kiss her calves. She held a sequined black purse just large enough to contain a Manurhin MR73 Gendarmerie revolver. Red-striped white Adidas sneakers filled out the look and were better than pumps for fleeing a crime scene should the need arise. Her calves were defined, ankles strong, trained for impact.

Crossing the street, she buried herself in a stream of pedestrians, so there'd be no neutralizing her at the moment even if he hadn't planned to follow her to bigger fish.

He hoped to see her move to a vehicle or parking structure.

Instead she drifted across Larrabee Street and pushed through glass-fronted swinging doors into an elegant restaurant. Now he understood the red dress.

She'd left her Savage 110 behind, and he did, too. Double sniper rifles would pretzel the crime-scene investigation, but there was nothing he could do about that.

He grabbed his fob watch, took the stairs down, thumped out through a rear door he'd left unlocked. The night was filled with excitement and energy, the air wavering at a dog-whistle vibrato.

He ignored the commotion, the incoming cop cars with sirens, the onlookers clustering at the street corners in herds for safety. Moving across one street and then another, he waited for the crosswalk light to change, the murder two blocks back fading into lesser consequentiality.

Forging across Sunset, he moved through the glass front doors that Karissa Lopatina had stridden through just minutes before, giving the maître d' a polite nod.

Her red dress grabbed the focus of the restaurant – hiding in plain sight. She sat at the bar, facing away, her sneakers just reaching the foot bar of her stool. Her bare shoulders were on display, and they were feminine and powerful, athletic.

Evan walked over and sat down at her side.

50. Every Fucking Girl Bean Beetle Ever

Evan and Karissa Lopatina sat elbow to elbow, looking at each other in the mirror behind the bar. She wore a designer Band-Aid decorated with roses over her right ear where Evan had shot her. She had a fantastic body – not the way men bandied about the expression, though she was appealing as well, but fantastic anatomically. Lithe and muscular, compact biceps, tapered lats, breasts like muscled plates of armor. She had tall towering cheeks with Eastern European cheek bones, and her other features were plain and symmetrical, beautiful by default because there was not one damn thing wrong with them.

She was self-contained and self-possessed and seemed to require nothing from the world.

He knew he would kill her if he was good enough to get the upper hand. She was fully embodied in her power and menace, as much as Candy McClure, and to not engage her with lethal force would be an insult to everything she was and everything she'd fought to become.

The bartender approached wordlessly and set down a linen coaster.

They had the VDKA 6100 Evan had wanted earlier, so he ordered it now as a lowball on a block cube. A rocks glass was more solid, a better weapon than a thin-stemmed martini glass.

Perhaps for the same reason, she'd ordered similarly, a whisky highball. He could smell the peat on her breath and something deeper than that, a pheromone underlay that was attractive and menacing, a great cat in her lair.

'I always liked my ears best,' she said to the mirror and herself and no one in particular. 'The lobes.' She shook her head, eyed the Band-Aid in her reflection. 'Vanity.'

'I felt that way about my collarbone,' Evan said.

A ratchet wrench had broken it in Bulgaria, a fight in an automobile shop that had rendered a Russian spy dead and Evan's clavicles forever asymmetrical.

Lopatina took a leisurely sip, set her drink back down. 'So,' she said. 'Are we going to do this then?'

Evan kept an eye on her hands, the purse resting three inches from her right pinky. 'What's that?'

'Talk. If you wanted to shoot, we'd be shooting.'

'I don't suppose you'll tell me who hired you to kill Dr Benjamin Hill.'

'No.'

He tasted his drink. The vodka was as smooth as he recalled, zero burn on the swallow. He caught that hint of white pepper, though it was more subtle than he recalled.

'How about you?' she asked. 'Why are you here? Who's paying you to give a shit?'

'No one.'

'Goodness of your heart,' she said.

He thought about grinning. 'What's left of it.'

'Friend of Hill's?'

'Nothing like that,' Evan said. 'Nothing personal.' What did that even mean anymore? The Fourth Commandment, blurred into irrelevance. 'The girl. You tried to kill her after you killed her father.'

'Right. And jaguars hunt newborn impala lambs. Mother bears eat their cubs if they can't find food for them. Then there's bean beetles.' She sipped her whisky, set it back down. 'The males have these nightmare penises. Covered with hard sharp spikes that anchor the males during sex. They also scrape out any sperm of a rival male who might've gotten there first. But there's more benefits, too. The spiked mace club, for lack of a better word, is good for vaginal tearing. Not sure how much time you've spent considering bean-beetle ejaculate –'

'I'd put my knowledge at dilettantish.'

'– but there's a chemical in there that boosts female fertility so all those lacerations help get it into the female's bloodstream. Then if all goes right and she's not savaged by another male in short order, the scar tissue clogs her up so she can't mate with anyone else. That's not some of them once in a while. That's every fucking girl bean beetle ever.' Karissa skewered a floating lemon wedge in her water, took it off the pick with her incisors, then sucked the bitter. 'God made all that. Or nature did. Made me, too.'

At last she looked over, hazel eyes flecked with green regarding him over those defined cheeks. A forbidding gaze, her face an inscrutable cliff face against which you could throw yourself for eternity and never find a handhold. She was precisely what she was and nothing else, nothing more.

'It's the way of the world. And me, Hill, Jayla? We're the least of anything.' Her eyes stabbed over at him in the reflection and she seemed to notice he looked unimpressed. 'I know, I know. It's hard to take a woman who thinks this way. We have to dress it up, dress it down. Waxed and shaved, delivered with a smile, close the door when we pee. You have no idea how much more we see and know. How much we have to civilize ourselves for you to tolerate our power. But then? I realized what *men* are holding themselves back from being also. It's equally fearsome. And awful. We are so alike when we are willing to be what we are.'

Evan sipped, let the cold sting evaporate on his tongue.

He made his gaze soften and leaned closer. A fraction of a fraction. An invitation to keep talking.

She did. 'Once in a blue moon, I used to wonder: How much did the world damage me that I think this way? No, not *think*. *Perceive*. And then I realized. It's not about damage or– or trauma. No. I was *designed* this way.'

The bartender brought over a steak fresh from the kitchen. Center-cut filet, charred edges, side of creamed horseradish sizzling on an oven-heated plate. He receded, leaving them wrapped in an aroma of deliciousness.

'You want to talk about justice and morality and seventeen-year-old girls,' Karissa said. 'But I don't care. I don't. It's all too fucking complicated to figure out what's right. So I go back to nature's rules. You know – the real ones. I kill. And I feed myself well.'

She sliced off a cut of beef, swiped it through horseradish, popped in her mouth. Her jaw worked methodically. She looked gratified by the food – not the pleasure of an epicure but the relish of a predator refueling itself for the next hunt.

'There's no point in talking,' she said, through a slightly full mouth. 'There's nothing to talk with me about.'

Evan felt the heft of the lowball glass. Gauged the best angle to her thin temporal bone. Her hand was curled around her glass. He noted her eyes; she was gauging the same. Behind him he heard the tinkle of flatware and the hum of excited conversation. Not the time. Nor the place.

'Okay,' Evan said, pushing back his barstool to rise. 'Next time we'll just get to the shooting.'

51. A Window to Another Universe

Loco's last-known was an alley a quarter mile east of Dr Hill's town house. En route, Evan tried calling Andre twice, but it just rang and rang and dumped into voice mail, which was full. He knew if he stopped by Andre's he'd find an empty house, and he wasn't eager to undertake a bar hop just to bounce his half brother off another dumpster.

He was angry.

The alley was dark, clogged with trash and forsaken homeless encampments. Evan parked on the street and searched on foot, his flashlight picking across ripped nylon tents, stained blankets, soaked shanty walls built of Amazon delivery boxes.

He heard movement down at the end, a rustle of what sounded like a paw against an empty beer can.

The beam darted across an overturned shopping cart and found a pair of eyes in the depth of the alley.

A coyote.

There was a tuft of fur stuck to his claw.

He looked well fed.

Brianna's living room.

A few minutes past midnight.

Sofia was next to her mom on the couch, shoulders hunched with anticipation, her palms pressed together and smashed between her knees. Brianna sat sideways, stroking Sofia's hair, but Sofia paid her little mind. She was all in on Evan.

It was Saturday night, but Evan had a feeling Brianna would've let her daughter stay up late even on a school night to hear the update.

Awkward on his feet, he was unsure how to begin.

Fortunately, he didn't have to.

'Loco's dead, isn't he?' Sofia said. She refused to lift her gaze.

'Likely,' Evan said.

Bri looked at him sharply. What was wrong with his answer?

Sofia rocked herself a bit and then stood up, her hands stretching into starfish and then clenching into tiny fists. To her side, the shoe-box shrine to the homely dog endured, the *veladora* low on wax and incandescence, guttering to an end. On the other wall hung a framed travel poster for Paris, one of those bright retro numbers with the tip of the Eiffel piercing a cabaret moon. According to Andre, Bri and Sofia had never been east of Las Vegas, the poster like a window to another universe.

Sofia's face broke. The fierce, ugly beauty of pure grief. 'You said you could find him.' Her voice, blurred through a constricted throat.

Evan said, 'I know.'

'You *promised*. You *promised* you could find him.' Moving to anger but it was weak cover for what was beneath. '*Everyone* promises. Everyone –'

A breath screeched in horribly and then she was sobbing. She came at him, struck at him weakly, miniature fists smacking his stomach, his chest. 'Where's my dad? Where's my dad? I wish my dad was here!'

'I know,' he said.

'Okay,' he said.

'I'm sorry,' he said.

She kept striking him and Bri watched from the couch, there were tears on her face, and there was not a goddamned thing either of them could do.

'I want my dad!' Sofia shouted. 'I want my dad!'

Evan put his hands gently on her shoulders as her punches grew weaker and weaker and then she was crying into his chest messily, fingers clutching his shirt.

'I know,' he said. 'I know.'

52. The Waiting Nothingness

Evan sat in the darkness of his parked truck with his hands on the steering wheel. Smooth resin against his palms. Press of fabric against his legs, lower back. Cramp high in his shoulders, knitting up the base of his neck.

He tried to breathe his way back into himself, back into a state of the world he recognized enough to operate efficiently in.

DONCHA WISH YER GIRLFRIEND WUZ HAAAWT LIKE ME?!

The ringtone. Still had to change it.

He reached in his cargo pocket, withdrew the phone.

Joey.

He said, 'Go.'

'The mission just got a whole bunch easier.'

She texted something over to him with a ping. A video.

'A confession. Well, not a confession. But a smoking gun. No – more than that. Caught on film. Leaked by an anonymous worker. Case closed.'

'Okay.'

'This wraps it up with a bow,' she said. 'But I'm gonna keep whacking into Allman's Solventry files. I'm making good headway. And now it's personal.'

'Okay.'

He hung up. Played the video.

YouTube, 1,495,993 views.

Nathan Friedhoff in what looked to be an empty conference room, glass walls, a massive *Citizen Kane* table, and a whiteboard wiped clean. The angle suggested that he was being filmed through the camera of a laptop that had been left on the table.

He was partially turned away, speaking in a hushed voice into what looked like a burner phone: 'Yes,' he said. 'You're greenlit for Dr Hill. Usual fee. Nothing that can trace back to me or this company. Cut with wide margins.' He hung up the phone, cupped his hand over his mouth, tugged down so the edges of his eyes sagged. He looked deeply upset, on the verge of screaming or sobbing or vomiting.

He took two deep breaths, screwed a calmer expression onto his face, and exited the conference room.

Evan refreshed the video.

It had crossed the 1.5 million mark.

He turned the engine over, slotted his pickup into drive, and headed for Friedhoff's place.

Nathan Friedhoff was in his bathroom, leaning over the Carrara marble of his ex-wife's vanity, staring at himself in the mirror. It was as though he'd never seen his face before. He regarded his features as if he hadn't looked at them every day of his life, as if they belonged to someone else.

His eyes had flattened; they looked beady, untrustworthy. When his face contorted in grief, the crow's-feet forged down into his cheeks and he saw a premonition of what he would have looked like as an old man. What he'd done he'd done for the right reasons. He'd started out with good intentions. At bottom he was an engineer, a maker of things. He'd brought new technologies and capabilities to the world, and maybe some of them could still be used for good, to stop the avalanche he'd helped create.

'You're a good man,' he told himself in the mirror. 'You're a good man.'

He almost believed himself.

His phone rested on the marble by his hand, teed up to the poster frame of the video of himself ordering Dr Benjamin Hill's murder. Already it was storming through the World Wide Web, the children atwitter on Twitter.

He picked the phone up. His portal to his work, his life, the universe.

He dropped it on the matching marble floor. The screen shattered pleasingly.

On numb legs, he walked out of his master suite. Down the hall. His daughters were up – did they *ever* sleep? – the bluish glow of screens casting a faint light on June's partially opened door.

He stepped inside.

His daughters lay side by side on June's bed, head to feet. London's legs stretched up the headboard, June's bare feet nestled into the fluffy duvet by her sister's head. They held their phones up above their faces, watching blankly, and he could see the reflection of the screens in their pupils.

'Girls,' he said. And then: '*Girls.*'

'Uh-huh?'

They were nested together as if in a pod, plugged into different existences, the phones leeching their attention. He wondered how long it would take for the leaked video to penetrate their virtual realities.

'Don't believe . . . whatever you're gonna hear.' His voice: wobbly, thin. 'There's just, some work stuff, a work matter, and I want you to know . . . just don't believe everything.'

'Okay,' June said.

London: 'Mmm-hmm, Dad.'

Shouldered into the doorway, he looked at them. They did not look at him. He'd never felt so disconnected from his life. It was as if he'd been unplugged from the world.

'I . . . I love you girls.'

'Me, too,' June said, her voice on autopilot.

London's thumbs clicked and clicked, her tongue testing the point of an incisor.

There was nothing more to get here, and it was his fault both intimately and karmically.

It didn't matter anymore. Nothing mattered anymore. Anything was what anyone could make of it.

He withdrew quietly.

The living room was dark and empty, the bar shelves unlit, staff gone for the night.

The sliding glass doors to the narrow balcony were open. When he'd bought the house he'd felt a rush of power at the view he would own. Out across Cahuenga Boulevard, the 101, and Universal Studios, above and beyond the concerns of all those stars-to-be, just him in the rarefied air, an overlord to an unattainable city.

Now it all looked tawdry and polluted. He wondered at another life on a farm somewhere, a speck-on-a-map town where folks left their doors unlocked and rose with the sunrise for real work that put dirt under their nails.

A string of flashing lights beelined up Cahuenga.

Red and blue.

The police cars turned off, heading up the canyon.

To him.

He was standing on the rail now. If he kept his arms wide, it was surprisingly easy to balance on his bare feet. The drop was severe, seventy-five or so feet to a stretch of sandstone and shale.

He'd read about people who'd wound up quadriplegics after failing to calculate properly. But he was an engineer at heart, driven by numbers and angles.

If he led with his head it would definitely get the job done. He just had to hold his nerve for two, three seconds.

The red and blue lights tilted up the hill toward him, vanishing behind a fold in the canyon. For a moment there was just the silence of the night and the whistle of the wind.

He steeled himself.

And let his weight pull him forward into the waiting nothingness.

Evan neared the turnoff to Friedhoff's place, but cop cars barred the street. News helicopters circled overhead, spotlights stabbing the hillside. He slowed down, prepared a U-turn at the sawhorses, a tired-looking cop waving him to move it along.

He slowed by the dirt shoulder where a collection of lookie-loos had gathered, their cars slanted this way and that. They looked young, fingernails on the cutting edge of Hollywood, primed for gossip and insider knowledge. They were on their phones, comparing notes, watching footage.

Evan rolled down his window. 'What happened?'

A long-haired guy with surfer muscles swayed his focus from his cell phone to Evan. 'Youtopia dude killed himself,' he said. His breath carried a tinge of bubblegum and pot. 'Jumped off his balcony. Crazy shit, man. Hit like a water balloon.'

Evan nodded once and drove home.

53. Cracking the Motherfucker

The next morning, Joey shook Evan gently awake. She'd been hacking away in the Vault last night when he'd crashed and evidently had spent the night in there working. He was so tired he hadn't alerted to her entering the bedroom. Or had he subconsciously recognized her footprints, a domestic patter he knew to be safe?

If so: weird.

'X, Melinda needs to talk to us,' she said.

He rolled off the bed, set his bare feet on the floor. He was wearing boxer briefs, so he kept the sheets wrapped around his waist. For once, Joey was not in a joking mood.

'See you in there,' she said. 'Hurry.'

He threw on clothes and padded back to the Vault. It carried Dog's warm canine smell, musk and popcorn. Only seat in the room was the solitary chair behind the L-shaped desk. The Vault was a cockpit for one, even if he trusted Joey to fly from time to time.

Slurping the last of a Big Gulp, Joey gestured for Evan to sit.

He took the chair.

Melinda was writ large over the videotelephony program. She was in the back room of her warehouse, the windows blacked out, standing in front of a desk scattered with counterfeit passport stamps. In a construction tool belt she wore an Olympos double-action airbrush, its grip padded with proprietary pink tape, and she had a war-paint streak of periwinkle below her left eye. Her hair was straight and neat, and she looked sharp and alert to the point of perfection.

'The girl's Hungarian blockchain expert and my dark-web specialist put something together,' Melinda said.

No foreplay, no flirting – she was in full-blown work mode. As Jack might remark: *La donna è mobile.* Evan found her focus remarkably attractive.

He rubbed sleep from his eye. 'What?'

'It wasn't just one payment to Karissa Lopatina. Three payments routed sequentially through the same channels on the same day. Bitcoin to the Wyoming trust.'

'Friedhoff paid for three hits, not just the one.'

'That's the working theory.'

'Date?'

'November 9.'

'Three days before Hill was murdered.'

'Correct. Which means two hits are outstanding.'

'Well,' Evan said. 'Hell.'

The last thing he needed was another pair of executions out there floating.

'With Friedhoff dead,' Melinda said, 'you'd better stop the Wolf now. Those contracts were paid in full and are pending.' A landline rang and she picked up the heavy black handset, barked something in Vietnamese, and hung up. 'I have to go. A client found a 1933 style-A three-sheet for *King Kong* in a vintage trunk from the era. The gorgeous girl needs some love and patching and Nguyễn started in with the wrong vintage paper because that's how Nguyễn rolls.'

Evan said, 'Right.'

'As for the Gendarmerie revolver and Lopatina's other gear, my men have come up empty. As you know, weaponry isn't our strong suit. But my dark-web expert is finishing his forensic deep dive on Lopatina's engagement with the contract-hit site. I'll circle back if he extracts any other useful data points.'

Evan said, 'Okay.'

'And if not,' she said, 'perhaps we can have another meal soon.'

Maybe *la donna* wasn't so *mobile* after all.

Evan said, 'Okay.'

Melinda killed the connection.

Evan stretched out his arms, his shoulders. He needed a cold shower to wake up. Vera III looked not particularly sympathetic.

He took in the rest of Joey's work on the walls. Machines pounding away at firewalls, an array of exploits trying to burrow past various routers and servers.

In addition, she had Nathan Friedhoff's leaked video up, using machine learning and CV algorithms to scan him and everything around him, rendering every contour and line as a digital wireframe. Beside that window was some kind of social-media account for Jayla Hill.

He looked over at Joey. She was eyeing Jayla's image, chewing on the end of a pen.

'What's up?' Evan asked.

Joey shook her head. 'Was just thinking about her. How much it would suck getting your voice taken away.'

Evan waited.

'I mean, I was sitting here all stupid-nervous about this sorority thing I have tonight – disco bowling, lame, right? – and I kept picturing her alone with a bunch of deputies in some safe house and what she's feeling like right now about the rest of her life. I have a hard enough time figuring out how to find my voice sometimes out in the world and I *have* my voice.'

He waited some more.

'Have you heard her voice?'

'No,' he said. 'I never did.'

'You know how some people have their personality in their voices? That was her. She had a really cool husky voice. She was a singer. And that bitch took it from her.'

Evan looked at the screen – jaylahillsingergurl at TikTok. Jayla wore braids with a headband, a few decorative beads thrown in the mix. A PLAY icon rested in the middle of her chest.

Evan reached over to the mouse and clicked.

Jayla sang.

An R&B number he didn't know but her voice had grit and texture and she could reach down for a kind of power that seemed beyond her or anyone's years. He felt the music through his whole body, and when she finished and the video froze once more, her voice reverberated around the Vault like a memory, which was all it was anymore for Jayla and everyone else.

It seemed a crime against humanity for Karissa Lopatina to have taken it from her so ignobly.

He didn't feel like talking, and Joey didn't feel like talking, so at last she said, 'C'mon, Dog, let's go potty,' and the big ridgie heaved himself to his paws and they padded out of the Vault together.

Evan stared at the OLED screens wrapped around him. He had to get to Lopatina again any way he could. The money trail had been run down as far as possible. He'd intersected with her at the only juncture points he could predict. What other angles were open to him?

He thought about her ghostly form behind the billboard, a figure of smoke and stealth, how he'd barely glimpsed the bolt-action and Leupold scope that were a match for his own.

There. He could push harder there.

He brought up the video-call software and dialed Tommy.

Three rings and then the feed blinked on. Tommy at his kitchen table, spooning oatmeal into his face and reading a spec sheet for Black Hills ammunition. He looked more banged up than usual. 'Your ugly mug's about the last thing I need to see first thing in the morning. Better be important.'

'I want you to help track down an assassin I'm circling. She uses top-tier gear you might be able to source to a black-market dealer or something.'

Tommy rubbed his neck, grimaced, then palmed a few Advil into his mouth and washed them down with coffee. 'I don't track down other folks' deals. I *make* deals.'

'I know, but my other contacts hit dead ends.'

'What gear we talking?'

'Specialty stuff from Manurhin MR73 Gendarmeries to Phoenix-S thermal scopes to Dragunov SVDs. I'll text a list of her tools so you can ask around.'

'Right.' Tommy leaned forward to reach for the sugar, wobbly in his crouch. A squint gathered up the folds of his left cheek as he braced against the ache of his joints. 'I'll do some sniffing. Never know who's who in the zoo.'

He swiped for the pot of sugar and missed, tilting back decrepitly. And fell out of his chair. Not a heart-attack tilt but a wood-splintering, screws-breaking, eyes-flaring, what-the-fuck tumble.

For a moment he was gone from sight. There was just the surface of the table and the upended bowl of oatmeal drib-bling sludge onto the wood. Then a four-and-a-half-fingered hand gripped the edge and Tommy pulled himself back up, standing at a tilt. He kicked the unseen wreckage of the broken chair away, scooted over a new one, and sat once more.

For the first time in a long time, Evan looked at him as if he were someone he'd only just met, noting how heavily age hung on his features – the sun-beaten skin, the liver spots on a cheek, the puckers at the edges of his mouth. Tommy wasn't just an old warhorse, he was an old guy, and yet he'd never seemed that way before.

'Not a word,' he said. 'I'm fine.'

'Tommy, you might want to get –'

'*What?*' His baggy eyes held embarrassment as well as an uncharacteristic sharpness. 'Doctors poking and prodding at me so they can tell me what I already know? That my joints are shot to shit and pretty soon I won't be able to wipe my own ass?'

'You can still –'

Tommy cut him off: 'Tell me more about this assassin broad. If you want me to play errand boy, I need some situational awareness.'

Evan took a moment to reset. 'I surveilled her yesterday on a job.'

'Who'd she take down?'

'Human trafficker.'

'What's her name?'

'Karissa Lopatina, aka the Wolf.'

'Copy that,' Tommy said. 'I'll see what I can root out.'

His wide callused thumb stabbed at the phone, and the screen went black.

Evan sat for a moment parsing this recalibration of Tommy Stojack. His friend. Slowed by the ravages of time, countless wartime injuries nipping at him like a pack of wolves. Evan, too, had only so much time, and there was so much work to be done before he could rest.

He stared at everything rendered on the walls of the Vault. So much interstitching data, overlapping trails, and loose ends straggled out across the screens. Despite Friedhoff's death, the mission wasn't over. Jayla, a front-row witness to the Wolf's face, would be out of federal custody in three days and back in the crosshairs. Melinda was running down anything else from the dark web. Tommy was backtracing the Wolf's weapons. And Evan had to figure out who the two outstanding targets were and intercept them before Lopatina could put a bullet through their critical mass.

He closed his eyes, drew in a deep breath. Not one second passed before the First Commandment sailed in and smacked him in the face: *Assume nothing.*

Of course.

Lopatina's not generally so showy, Melinda had told him. *An accident specialist. Who knows how many hits have gone unnoticed?*

A moment later, Joey entered, treat in hand, Dog the dog hopping alongside her like a skipping schoolgirl. 'Sit,' she said, and Dog sat.

Evan said, 'Come,' and Joey came.

She dropped the cube of dried liver for Dog, then stood behind Evan and stared at what he was staring at – the same confusion of nothingness. 'What?'

'Can you get into HR? For Solventry?'

'Human Resources? Uh, yeah. Already in. It's just a stupid SaaS I hacked ages ago.'

'Can you check if any Solventry employees have died since November 9?'

Joey's breath came over his shoulder – Red Vines and Dr Pepper. He waited for the dime to drop. It did.

Her voice, slowed with the epiphany: 'You think she might've *already* committed the other two executions.'

'The First Commandment.'

'Of fucking course.'

She nudged him aside and he rolled in the Aeron and she hit her knees and her hands blurred across the keyboard, and the screens danced and obeyed like virtual puppets on virtual strings.

Three names of the recently deceased came up.

Martin Quinn, Warehouse Shopping Fulfillment Advocate.

Peter Savodnik, Public Relations Intern.

Anwuli Okonkwo, Senior Software Engineering Manager.

'Let's look at causes of death,' Evan said. 'Solventry has eight hundred thousand workers. Some folks are gonna die for normal reasons.'

Joey's hands were at it again, a profusion of databases sprouting before him – the Los Angeles County Department of the Medical Examiner-Coroner, the Register of Cremations, the Office of Decedent Affairs. 'Quinn died in a . . . autoerotic self-asphyxiation mishap. Gross.' Another flurry of fingers, the Das Keyboard thrumming with the sound of a heavy rain. 'Savodnik died of pancreatic cancer. Hard to fake. And Ms Okonkwo . . .' The windows leapt and loaded. 'Accidental drowning in her bathtub.'

She cocked a skeptical eye at Evan. 'Quinn and Okonkwo.'

'Seems likely,' Evan said. 'So let's go with that for now. Question: Why would Friedhoff want to pick off more Solventry workers?'

'From what you told me about what Allman's up to,' Joey said, 'I can't see why anyone *wouldn't* want to kill his employees.'

'But why these ones?'

'So Friedhoff's feeling the heat of competition,' Joey said. 'Or he's trying to slow the progression of the technological monster he helped build and unleash. Then he performs some targeted strikes on his biggest rival to slow them down, too.'

'Why?'

'To make sure Youtopia, his own company, leads the way with more, dunno, moral responsibility or whatever compared to Allman. To give humanity a fighting chance against AI.'

Evan said, 'A warehouse worker?'

Joey said, 'Maybe Quinn had an unusual skill set or something. I don't know.'

'Can you reach back further? The past year?'

'To see who else at Solventry might have "accidentally" died?'

'Maybe this wasn't Friedhoff's first foray into targeted strikes on Solventry's personnel.'

'I can do that,' Joey said. 'And I'll be into the internal network by day's end so we'll know exactly what Doc Hill was up to.'

That would work well. Evan had to cycle through his safe houses and make sure they were lined out in the event that Jayla Hill landed in his lap before this was over. It took some prep to 2.0 a witness-protection plan, and he didn't want to get caught scrambling. Plus he had to attend to a personal matter.

He checked his Vertex fob watch, gauged the necessities he needed to handle. 'Day's end? You sure?'

Her phone dinged in her pocket. She took it out, turned it off without looking at it, and set it facedown on the sheet metal. Focused.

'It's a self-imposed deadline,' she said. 'But I'm over it. I'm cracking the motherfucker before I head out. That way I can disco-bowl with these Karennials in peace.'

'Meet back here at seventeen hundred for a sitrep,' Evan said. 'Let's break this open.'

54. Nowhere Anyone Wants to Be

Evan's safe houses were scattered across Greater Los Angeles, and it took the better part of the day to service them properly and make them look lived-in. Changing automated sprinkler and lighting schedules, bringing in mail, moving vehicles from driveway to garage or vice versa. Some of the surveillance cameras had gotten glitchy, so he worked through the bugs and upgrades to make sure he'd have eyes up on everything should the need to stash Jayla arise.

He hoped everything would come to a head before that.

Around 2:00 P.M. he started in on what he'd been putting off. The search for Andre. To begin with, he hit Who's On 1st, drawing semi-hostile eye contact from the regulars and Jimmy the barkeep.

'Seen Andre?' he asked.

'Not since you bounced him outta here,' Jimmy said.

'Know any other hangouts he likes?'

Nando was there with his gold-rimmed Ray-Bans, hunched over his pint glass. 'HMS Bounty on Wilshire.' He kept his back turned, showing that rectangular scar at the base of his skull where hair plugs had been harvested. 'The Living Room on Crenshaw.'

Evan started to withdraw.

'I been where he is.' Nando still didn't turn around. 'It's nowhere anyone wants to be. I hope you find the poor bastard.' The day drinkers looked down into their glasses and waited for Evan to leave.

The other two stops proved equally fruitless.

It was nearly three o'clock by the time he swung by Andre's little house in El Sereno. It had been destroyed once and rebuilt cheaply but sturdily with insurance money. Evan walked around the xeriscaping, peering in windows. Blinds drawn, house dark.

He tried the front door. Unlocked.

He stepped into the triangle of light thrown through the doorway, his senses assailed by the thickness of unscented air. Trash and old food, the sickly-sweet smell of spilled booze.

A number of empty boxes in the tiny living room bore the Solventry logo, that inanely smiling daisy logo. Liquor boxes broken into bottle-size sections by corrugated-cardboard dividers. Spilled across the couch, a mound of bills and other unopened mail. Evan clicked the light switch, but nothing happened. Electricity turned off. He tried once more, the familiar futility of the gesture bringing him back to his Pride House foster-home days. Darkness then, darkness now.

Pressing on to the bedroom, Evan found Andre passed out on his bed. Jeans and work boots on, a Carhartt jacket, sprawled on his back, snoring. A half dozen empty bottles of rum on the floor and windowsill – no, seven. Among fast-food wrappers on the desk, a sketch pad showed Sofia, beautifully captured in pencil and then scratched out with heavy scribbles.

Evan stood there for a long time.

When he stepped forward, his boot knocked over a handle of Bacardi. A loud clatter, but Andre didn't stir. Some of the packing material was wadded up on the floor, that grinning daisy patterned across even the Bubble Wrap and carton-sealing tape, the brand omnipresent, tattooed onto the face of the world everywhere he looked.

Evan shook his half brother once and then a few times more.

There would be no waking him.

Evan checked his vitals, thumbed up his eyelids. Steady pulse, pupils dilating. Andre was fine. At least in one regard.

Evan tugged up the blind and cracked the window, a tired breeze displacing some of the staleness. He found an empty McDonald's soda cup on the floor, rinsed it out in the bathroom, filled it with water, and left it on Andre's nightstand.

He rolled Andre onto his side in case he threw up, propping him in place with a brace of pillows.

Then he left.

As he neared his pickup, he stopped for a moment, breathing out the despair that had curdled inside him when he'd stood in that unvented bedroom.

A few intrepid weeds had shoved through the sidewalk seams, flowering in yellow, bees lazily browsing their offerings. The sun lay heavy and pleasing across his back, and he felt its warmth as if he were a child again, eleven years old on that ragged East Baltimore park back when there was all the time in the world to do nothing but feel the sun and to watch the bees do their bee business among the flowers, and he was present now, not present strategically and alert to threats, not present as a Zen state of mind for internal hygiene, not because he was living up to Jack's laws or to anyone or anything else, but he was present because now he couldn't help but not be, because it was true. And he was there, despite everything, just him in the sunshine.

A rattling announced itself behind him. A FWIP motoring along the sidewalk, delivering its next round of goods. Its six rugged wheels managed the terrain expertly, navigating the delivery robot across a mini sierra of concrete cracked by tree roots. Same aquatic-blue design, same cheery neotenic flower, *FreeWillPower!* scripted across the side in whimsical white cursive.

Feeling the heat of the sun come up through the soles of his boots, Evan watched it approach. As it passed, he kicked it. Hard.

It tumbled over, falling into the gutter, wiggling helplessly like a beetle flipped on its shell. Evan felt a ping of cheap satisfaction.

Then a prong emerged from the roof, pressing into the ground, forcing the delivery robot up off its back. It righted itself.

The all-terrain wheels rippled as it pushed itself once more up onto the sidewalk.

Undeterred, it continued on its way.

55. Psyops on Hugh

The subterranean parking garage beneath Castle Heights was Evan's favorite part of the building. Concrete and oil, fat pillars, dim overheads throwing scant light. It felt honest, utilitarian. Plus he always felt at ease moving through terrain with shadows and multiple positions of cover.

He spotted movement inside a white Tesla near the stairs to the lobby.

Lorilee.

She hadn't noticed him, not yet. Her face was puffier than usual and she held a balled-up tissue in her fist, which she pressed to her mouth.

He was struck immediately by a deeply ingrained instinct to avoid her. If he walked up the ramp, he could circle through the porte cochere and enter the lobby through the front door.

He stood unnoticed in the shadowed space between lights. Fighting with himself. He checked the time. Forty-five minutes until his meeting with Joey.

He could spare a moment.

He didn't want to.

But he could.

Lorilee tossed aside the tissue and put her hands on the steering wheel. She looked haggard, hollowed out. No theatricality, a rarity for her.

Forty-four minutes now.

Damn it.

He tried to find that part of himself he'd felt on the

sidewalk outside Andre's house, to forge the connection from himself to himself, but the signal kept going out – it was so goddamned temperamental – and he thought what the hell, he'd go over and try his imperfect best.

She was too buried in sadness to notice his approach. With a single knuckle, he tapped. She glanced over, lowered her eyes, and then the automatic doors unlocked with a click. He went around and sat in the passenger seat.

A watermelon air freshener stuck in the vent made the car smell like a cheap cocktail. There was a tissue box on the console and a nylon trash bag mounted behind the headrest and a rubber container at Evan's feet that held water bottles and protein bars and an assortment of over-the-counter allergy and pain meds. It felt less like a vehicle than a mobile drugstore.

Lorilee patted his knee with the hand that had previously held the tissue, and he noted the spot on his pants for later disinfecting. 'Thank you for checking on me, Ev,' she said. 'This damn campaign . . .'

Her Botox had been recently and robustly injected, and her face was stretched out of shape enough to resemble that of a great cat, adding a surreal tinge to his entrapment.

'Do you actually care,' he asked, 'about being HOA president?'

She shook her head immediately and then shook it some more.

'Then why are you running?'

Her face pulsed like a fist, a spasm of shame, and she plucked another tissue from the box and held it to her trembling lips. 'Do you remember my last boyfriend?'

'No.'

'The juice-bar entrepreneur?'

'No.'

'Built guy in his late forties, wavy black hair?'

'Lorilee,' Evan said. '*No.*'

'Well, the breakup was hard on me. At my age . . .'

Her age was a closely guarded secret, preserved by a cadre of plastic surgeons, dermatologists, and dieticians. She might have been late forties or well into Social Security. Evan had of course noted her birthday once in the files he meticulously maintained on all Castle Heights residents, but he'd made a chivalrous effort to forget it.

'. . . you see all the loneliness ahead,' Lorilee continued. 'And I didn't take very good care of myself after he left me. I . . . ate more than I should have. And, well, it showed. In my figure.'

Evan hoped there would be some way to accelerate this excruciating rollout of information. 'Okay.'

'And one morning I was taking the trash out. To the chute. And Hugh was on my floor overseeing a baseboard repair in the hallway with two young male workers. And they were rushing by with their tools and equipment. And Hugh said to me . . . he said, "God, Lorilee. Get out of their way. You're taking up the whole hallway."'

Voicing the slight brought the humiliation into her body anew, and she cried some more, but Evan didn't mind, because it wasn't performative. It was pure, a letting out of something that needed to be let out, and while he couldn't empathize with her, he identified a green shoot of sympathy.

'So you ran him off the HOA?' Evan asked. 'Over *feelings*?'

She nodded into her tissue.

A tactical overreaction. An unnecessary escalation. And a waste of resources.

Jack had built the foundation of Evan's worldview – mortal stakes, mission imperatives, military history. As always he struggled to lasso all those lethal factors and translate them to this other world of quotidian social interactions. No one had ever taught him to break down the walls within himself. To let all parts of himself talk to all parts of himself until every-thing achieved internal consistency. Hard objectives versus soft-power considerations, force versus mediation, aggres-sion versus deescalation, strategic alliances versus enemy engagement. Maybe the same evaluations held whether you were infiltrating a human-trafficking compound or waging a battle for the scepter of the homeowners association.

'He made me feel so . . . worthless,' Lorilee was saying. 'Or maybe he didn't *make me* feel that way. Maybe that's what I am. And he just reminded me. But he didn't have to. Not that way. Women need to take in emotional information at a . . . remove. So we can let it in on our own time. Men are so appallingly *direct*.'

'Only some,' Evan said.

'What?'

'Men. And women.'

'Are you being politically correct?'

'What?' His first-ever feeling of – what was it? Social mor-tification? 'No!'

'So I decided not to react like a woman for once. I handled it like a *man* would.'

'You're running psyops on Hugh?' Evan said. 'To get back at him?'

'Psyops?'

'A full-bore assault to run him off the HOA.'

'That sanctimonious little man deserved it.'

Surreptitiously he checked his fob watch. Joey was wait-ing, and there were executions to untangle and an hourglass running on a seventeen-year-old girl and a capable assassin waiting in the wings. He rubbed his face. 'Okay,' he said. 'Now what?'

'That's the thing,' Lorilee said. 'I was going to post about him and all this . . . bad behavior.'

'Post?'

'On social media. And the Castle Heights Cryer.'

Evan said, 'Oh.'

'So his friends and family and neighbors and former colleagues can all see him for who he is.'

Hugh Walters, sixty-eight-year-old widower, father of two, retired senior accountant at a midsize firm. Evan pictured Hugh at the receiving end of online asymmetrical warfare designed to inflict maximum reputational damage.

'Is that who he is?' Evan asked. 'Or is that the worst of him?'

'I don't know,' she said. 'That's why I'm sitting here. I wrote it all up but I can't click *post*. I keep thinking about that one time after Ida was attacked and he was so protective wanting to make sure the building was secure and we were all safe. And I thought about what it will do to him if I send this. It'll seal my reelection. But then I realized I don't even really care about being HOA president.'

'It is an awesome, awful responsibility to destroy a man,' Evan said.

'It's just a tweet. You make me sound like some kind of vigilante.'

Evan took a moment with that one.

'And besides,' Lorilee said, 'Hugh has plenty of money. He'll be fine.'

'It's not about him,' Evan said. 'It's about you. If you wreck him, make sure you want to carry that. Because you'll have to live with it.'

'With what?'

'With the winning. Let's say this diminishes him. You and he live together in the building. You'll see each other all the time. In the elevator. At the mail slots. Plus if you win you'll have to actually run the HOA.'

She breathed wetly. 'So what am I supposed to do?'

'Open negotiations.'

'Talk to him?' she breathed. 'Oh, Ev. Would you?'

Would *he*?

There was nothing he wanted to do less. Before he had time to clarify, she clung to him and wept with relief.

After a moment, he told himself to lightly pat her back.

And then he did.

Evan moved through the lobby swiftly. Joaquin had Neil Diamond on the radio and looked as miserable as anyone his age would feel listening to Neil Diamond.

At the elevator, Evan stood eye to eye with Lorilee's augmented bust on the cling-wrap advertisement until she peeled apart, breasts widening. Then he rode up to the twentieth floor, doing his best to ignore the fluttering Post-its and flyers. Coming in hot down the hall to Condo C, he banged on the door.

When Hugh answered, he didn't seem to read Evan's mood, stepping back to welcome him in. 'Mr Smoak! So glad you swung by for a confabulation.'

He led Evan through the impeccably neat condo to two feminine love seats and a rose-colored couch with rolled arms and pronounced piping. The place bore the design imprint of Hugh's deceased wife – fake plants, pastel watercolors on the walls, chenille throw blankets with excessive fringes – and Evan thought about him living here alone for the past decade and change, maintaining the condo and his wife's memory in frozen suspension. The plastic fronds had been dusted and wiped down to hold a shiny luster and the blanket was perfectly folded over the back of one of the love seats, forcing Evan to imagine the grown man before him tending to these silly items with honor-bound constancy.

Election merch was fanned in neat display atop the brass-framed glass coffee table. Hugh gestured at the *RIGHT-HUGH-OF-LEADERSHIP* offerings. 'Would you like a bumper sticker?'

Yes, if he could put it over Hugh's mouth.

'Walters,' Evan said instead. 'Sit down.'

Hugh sat.

Evan followed suit, the fringes of the blanket tickling the back of his arm. Taking a deep breath, he laid out the Lorilee perspective as best he could, painfully navigating the melo-dramatic minutiae. Hugh listened intently, his owl eyes pronounced behind black-frame glasses.

When he finished, Hugh's face had taken on a sheen of sweat. 'Ridiculous!' he said. 'So *this* is how she reacted? Seizing power? What did she say I said again?'

'"Get out of their way,"' Evan intoned, feeling absurd. '"You're taking up the whole hallway."'

'Well.' Hugh's glasses slid down his nose, and he knuckled them back into place. 'I would never mean it that way. It most certainly wasn't about her weight.'

'It's still a piggish way to talk to a woman.'

Hugh looked down at his hands, studied his wedding ring. Evan glanced at the bank of silver-framed photographs on the mantel, Hugh and his bride through the years. He'd always known that Hugh's wife had died, but he'd never con-nected the fact to Hugh's emotional life. He considered it now – Hugh's fussing over pointless regulations, the endless interactions over heating vents and pet regulations, all to stave off loneliness.

He wondered why loneliness was such a fearsome thing to so many people. That they couldn't sit in it, learn its contours. It was that fear that let in assholes like Allman and Friedhoff to fill the hunger with empty calories until everyone was stuffed with emptiness instead of loneliness.

'Look,' Evan said, 'you need to clean it up with her so that she can feel vindicated and declare some sort of internal victory. And then you can take over the HOA again so the rest of us can be spared around-the-clock electioneering and get back to our lives.'

Hugh's eyebrows were thick and blunt where he'd clipped them. He spun his wedding ring a few times and nodded meekly.

'And Joaquin,' Evan said.

'What about Joaquin?'

'The kid's a single dad, works two and a half jobs, has a special-needs boy at home and a dad in an Alzheimer's facility. Leave him the hell alone about what kind of music he wants to listen to sitting in a starched uniform ten hours a day at twelve bucks an hour.' There was no anger in Evan's voice. It didn't tick up a decibel. 'Got it?'

Hugh swallowed. 'He doesn't make twelve dollars an hour. Minimum wage is fifteen fifty.'

'Less taxes,' Evan said.

'Well, I didn't consider that. Okay. Maybe if I ... regain the presidency we can give him a raise.'

Taking out his RoamZone, Evan texted Lorilee to come up as they'd arranged. Not two seconds later there was a knock on Hugh's door; clearly she'd been lingering outside in anxious anticipation.

Hugh rose. As Evan followed him to the door, his Roam-Zone rang: *DONCHA WISH* – He grabbed it. Joey.

'X. Where are you?'

'There in five.'

He hung up. Hugh was staring at him with an eyebrow cocked.

'Sorry,' Evan said. 'Ringtone. Long story.'

Hugh answered the door. Lorilee stood with her arms crossed over her chest, puffing herself up for the encounter. 'I'm so happy you agreed to stay, Evan,' she said. 'It's important that you're here. It makes me feel so much safer.'

'I actually have to –'

'Ms Smithson,' Hugh said, his voice low and gentle. He removed his thick glasses and polished them on the hem of his shirt. From a photo on the side table, his wife observed mutely. 'I'm very sorry for how I spoke to you in the hall. I didn't mean it how you took it, but it wasn't very . . .' A slight wobble in his voice. 'It wasn't very gentlemanly of me. And I am . . . I am ashamed of how I spoke to you.'

Lorilee blinked a few times rapidly. 'Well,' she said. And then: 'Well.'

Undone, Hugh stared at his tasseled loafers.

The rims of Lorilee's nostrils reddened. She uncrossed her arms and then crossed them again. Her cheeks were flushed, and she looked vulnerable and open. She looked like a little kid.

She tipped her head with an affected formality. 'Apology accepted,' she said. 'Mr Walters.'

Hugh lifted his gaze, and there was relief on his face, not for the HOA or the election, but as if he'd been let off the hook for something within himself, something he was dreading to have to live with. That great hungry need, the need to

369

be forgiven. He'd wanted it so badly, it seemed, that he'd been unable even to acknowledge it.

'Really?' His voice was dry.

She nodded. She was holding her breath. A tear leaked from one eye, cutting a swath through her makeup foundation.

Hugh was a fit man for his age, but even so he stood a touch hunched at the shoulders. He gathered himself up now. 'Perhaps you'd like to come in for a cup of tea?'

'I'd like that,' Lorilee said. 'I'd like that very much.'

She breezed past Evan in a waft of Chanel No. 5, and then they were moving to the kitchen. Utterly forgotten, Evan stood there a full two seconds before finally snapping back to his senses and splitting for the stairs.

When he made it through the penthouse and stepped into the Vault, he was still shaking off his confusion, but Joey bounced up from the chair, startling Dog and Evan both, and said, 'I cracked it, X! I cracked *everything*!'

56. Skinlift

Solventry's inner workings were exploded across the OLED screens of the Vault, and Joey was talking fast, even for her.

'So Doc Hill's work at Carnegie Mellon – 'member?'

'Bioinformatics,' Evan said. 'AI modeling for synthetic vocal restoration.'

'Which involves source sequencing, expression editing, pose editing, expression plus pose plus blinking editing, punctuation imitation, tonality, speech and movement patterns –'

'Joey, slow down.'

She was dressed nicely in anticipation of her outing – jeans, black button-up shirt, touch of makeup – and she was chomping on caffeinated cinnamon gum with caffeinated vigor.

'What's the logical extension of all that?' She gave him a split second to respond. 'Okay, okay. Just – *watch*.' She clicked on the screen, and Evan appeared on the facing wall of monitors.

'Hello,' Screen Evan said. 'This is my KINDER profile. It's, like, ironically named Tinder for killers. My hobbies include vodka and the fetishization of sharp objects. My likes are: control. And, uh, control. Dislikes: wrinkled sheets, out-of-order books. Wow. I sure sound like a loser.'

The deepfake was semi-convincing, but there were modulation issues, his hand motions glitched in a few places, and the background ate slightly into the side of his neck, a green screen-esque effect.

'This is a shitty version,' Joey said. 'I literally made this off a single freeze-frame of you I pulled off your internal security cam when you stepped through the door twenty seconds ago and one recorded sentence.'

Evan rewound to answering his phone downstairs. 'When I said, "There in five."'

'Yes. I wrote out the dialogue and off it goes. The new machine learning *insanely* reduces the amount of video required to make a skinlift. It can be used for everything – porn featuring your favorite celebrity, spreading disinformation from the mouths of world leaders, bringing back Elvis for a movie. You can make anyone say anything. And? Hill created a video deepfake AI that is literally indistinguishable from reality. Even to me.'

Evan gestured at the image of him up on the screens, his mouth frozen half open. 'Then why do I look so shitty?'

'Aside from the obvious jokes, because this is a beta version, not the deepfake perfection that Doc Hill created. Where is that deepfake perfection, you ask? Doc Hill stole all his code, corrupted his files, and wiped the program from Solventry. Just before he was killed. *That's* why Lopatina tossed Hill's place after shooting him. It wasn't just cover to sell a home invasion gone awry. She was searching for the code.'

'Oh,' Evan said. And then: '*Oh.*'

Joey watched him, humming with heightened focus.

'And he wiped the program from Solventry because he'd discovered from the access records or whatever that Allman had used it outside of protocols,' Evan said.

'Yes.'

'Illegally.'

Joey's eyes shone. 'Witness.'

Another click brought up the leaked video of Nathan Friedhoff in the conference room. A flawless reality, sunlight and shadows and organic movements. Every fold of his crow's-feet, every stray hair and mannerism in ultra high definition. There were crumbs on the conference-room table and a perfect reflected glint off the burner phone at his cheek. The words came perfectly modulated: 'Yes. You're greenlit for Dr Hill. Usual fee. Nothing that can trace back to me or this company. Cut with wide margins.'

'Watch *this* now.' Joey brought up the wireframe, zooming in on Friedhoff's face and the phone pressed to his cheek. 'That's a TrakLess T81.' She scanned over to the interior glass wall where Friedhoff's reflection was weakly captured. Then she tapped the mouse, enlarging the mirrored phone, enlarging it some more, and then sharpening the image with an AI de-blurring tool. The pixels bled away, dissolving into clarity. 'See that MEID on the back of the phone? Right above the barcode?'

There it was in the reflection, a Mobile Equipment Identifier rendered faintly in the plastic, coaxed to visibility by the glint of sunlight off the phone.

'Guess what? It doesn't exist. The last digit was altered. Which means that phone doesn't exist. Which means?'

Evan said, 'That Friedhoff doesn't exist.'

'That's right. Not that iteration of him.'

They stared at Nathan Friedhoff on the wall before them. Flesh and blood, ones and zeros.

'One motherfucking digit,' Joey said. 'And you know what? Next time there won't even be that, 'cuz if I figured this shit out, you can bet your ass AI has by now, too.' She jabbed her finger at the screen. 'If not for that single number, this happened. Friedhoff made this call. It's indistinguishable from reality. That's not playing God. That's *being* God.'

'We were focused on Friedhoff knocking out the competition. But it was Allman.'

'Right. Youtopia's synthetic-media division is still zeroing in on the perfect deepfake. They're a few steps behind but closing the gap. It's all in the internal emails.'

'What about Martin Quinn? And Anwuli Okonkwo?'

'I did some deeper digging. Turns out Quinn was stockpiling weapons. And Okonkwo had a brother who owed a lot of money to the wrong kind of people. But it's not just them. In the past eighteen months, there are nine suspicious deaths. "Accidental."' Her pronunciation evoked air quotes. 'I've been digging through internal comms with HR and legal and I think I figured it out.'

'Say more.'

'All those machine-learning algorithms? Allman's AI? It's reading everything about everyone. Which means it can *literally* predict the future. A worker at high risk of committing a workplace shooting, like Quinn. An employee likely to commit embezzlement, like Okonkwo. A secretary considering filing a big-ass #MeToo lawsuit. Someone primed to become a corporate spy and leak sensitive tech. Allman can identify them in advance before they do anything. And cancel them. Predicting future behavior. It's not science fiction. It's now. It's real.'

'Real,' Evan said.

Dog stood and shuddered off his sluggishness, freeing a mist of shed hair. He padded over and sat beside Joey. The three of them stared at the tableau of Friedhoff in the conference room, a man who wasn't a man greenlighting an execution that he didn't greenlight. A deception so bold and mind-bending it felt almost satanic. All as cover for a CEO killing his employees because a computer program predicted they might cause trouble for his corporation in the future.

In the face of it, there was not much man or dog could offer.

57. Removal of Troublesome Personnel

For some reason, Evan was not surprised that Allman answered his own cell phone. Evan stood on his east-facing balcony in the Angeleno night, breeze in his hair. Twenty-one stories below, cars streamed up Wilshire Boulevard, high beams animating the asphalt in a pale champagne wash. In the distance, downtown thrust jaggedly into a hazy swirl of moonlit clouds. Glowing windows delineated the skyline and punched through the dark of night as well as the invisible buildings holding them aloft.

'I know who you are,' Evan said.

A long pause as Allman breathed wetly. 'And I know who *you* are, Dr Leigh,' he said.

'I'm surprised it took you this long.'

'Me as well. Turns out there are advantages to your staying offline, no digital signature, et cetera. Your cover was good, I'll give you that. But not as powerful as my digital progeny, who revealed the study on genius – and you – to be a sham. AI pattern recognition of the destruction you've left in your wake – weapons abandoned, operations raided, tactical maneuvers – matched you to past Nowhere Man operations with 99.893 percent accuracy. Only one question remains. Why are you interested in me?'

'I know what you did.'

'Perhaps less vagueness.'

'You had Hill executed and pinned it on Friedhoff. The woman you hired was willing to take out Hill's daughter, too, just to keep it clean.'

'Okay,' Allman said, unruffled. 'Fine. But let's at least be honest. That's just an excuse for you to try to stop me. What this is really about? Is the power I have and the fact that you don't want me to have it.'

'No,' Evan said. 'It's the girl. And her father.'

'But that can't be,' Allman said. 'That doesn't make any sense. They're just . . . a rounding error. It's so much less than everything else.'

In the neighboring building across the street, a little boy sat at an upright piano, practicing. His legs swung beneath the stool, too short for his feet to reach the floor. His father was in the kitchen hovering over the stove, poking at pots with a wooden spoon.

'I know,' Evan said. 'But it's real. I can touch it.'

An even longer pause. 'You're upset,' Allman said. 'Emotionally.'

'Not emotionally,' Evan said. 'Deeper.'

He could practically hear Allman trying to process what he was being told, cogs and wheels grinding, searching for a different gear.

He knew the feeling.

'Okay,' Allman said. 'I can fix this. I will cancel the upcoming measure on the Hill girl. And I'll give you the assassin lady.'

Evan said, 'That's not enough.'

'I understand. I understand now. I won't do it anymore.'

'Do what?'

'No more rounding errors. No more removal of troublesome personnel.'

'That's not enough.'

A slight whine, tempered by impudence: 'I said I won't do it anymore.'

'I heard you.'

'Killing me is a measure to ensure that I won't erase other people. But now I won't erase anyone else.'

Allman's tone was shot through with spoiled disbelief that he couldn't talk or negotiate or think his way around Evan. That Evan existed in a world he'd dismissed as irrelevant. The real one.

Evan said, 'It's too late.'

'But that's not fair.'

Evan brought his hand to his forehead, felt the warm pressure of his palm. The wind riffled his hair, cooled the sweat at the hollow of his throat. Was this really a conversation he was having?

'What's the point of it going any further between us?' Allman asked. 'I said I was sorry. I said I will leave the Hill girl alone. I said I won't do it again. I give up. You win. What's to be gained by your coming after me?'

There was no way to explain something like that and especially no way to explain it to someone like Allman.

'It's merely a waste of resources,' Allman said. 'Yours and mine. You playing offense, me playing defense – and eventually I will play offense, too. There's so much work to be done in the world for you and me. There is nothing here for either of us or the world to gain. Our conflict over this matter is resolved, concluded. I concede defeat and agree to your terms. Why be enemies?'

He was like a child. A broken child.

'I'm sorry you don't understand,' Evan said. And he meant it.

'And you will be sorry,' Allman said, 'that you don't understand me.'

Evan hung up the phone and breathed, felt the coolness in his lungs.

For everything Allman had created, there was a nothingness

377

at his core. And that nothingness stretched out its tentacles through a billion screens, wound its way around the bones of anything it touched. And squeezed.

Such bleakness. Such nihilism. And a predatory avarice as limitless as the World Wide Web itself. Evan couldn't act on any of that.

But he could act for Benjamin and Jayla Hill.

He looked out across his city, all those people driving home and working late and settling into their evenings, wrapped in the comforts of the modern world.

For a brief private moment alone in the darkness, he wished he could be any one of them.

58. Dirt-Diving

Joey came in sometime past two o'clock and started when she saw Evan sitting at the kitchen island in the darkness.

'X! You okay?'

'Yes.'

She sloughed off her jacket, let it hit the floor behind her, and trudged over. She pulled up a stool. 'No vodka?'

'No vodka.'

'Why not?'

'Preparing.'

'Oh,' she said. 'It's like that now.'

'It's like that,' he said.

'When's it going down?'

'Tomorrow,' he said.

'Wow. So you're sitting here dirt-diving it in your head?'

'Yes.'

She let out a breath just shy of a sigh. Her shoulders were slumped, rolled forward, and her cheeks looked heavy.

Evan said, 'How'd it go at the disco bowl?'

Joey placed both palms flat over her face and rubbed. When she lowered them, her makeup was smeared as if she'd been crying. Her features were full and open, and the solitaire diamond pendant glittered at her throat as if floating, the platinum filigree chain invisible in the semidarkness.

'We was out at the bowling place and there were some frat guys there and one of them got all gropey with Silvia . . .'

'Yeah?'

'So I punched him in the throat.'

'In the throat?'

'Uh-huh. Dropped him. And the cops came and since I'm a university girl student they were all like, "Do *you* want to press charges against Chet?"'

'His name was Chet?'

'What? *No.* Can you imagine, though? If they'da caught us on the street? Chet would be pressing charges on *my* brown ass.'

She drummed her bitten nails on the island, chewed her lower lip.

'How'd that go over with the sorority girls?'

'X.' Joey shook her head. 'Those girls, they talk a big game about empowerment and shit. But when you *do* it? They're horrified. They said . . . They said I'm not Chi Phi Alpha material. Not up to their "standards."' She threw angry air quotes. 'They looked at me like I was some other species. Except one of them.' She smirked her evil smirk. 'Blond girl from Brentwood. Ms Girl was all like, "Don't worry about it. We all want to *be* you."' The smirk faded. 'So. I won't be invited back.' Her cheeks were glittering. 'It's so stupid, I know. And – if I tell you a secret you can't use it against me, got it?'

'Copy.'

'I wasn't even sure I wanted to join the stupid sorority anyways. I just wanted to prove I could get in. That I could be *asked* in. I think . . . I think I just wanted to prove I could belong somewhere. That I could be an ordinary person. But I wanted to be the one . . .'

'To make the choice.'

'Yeah.' Her nervous drumming stopped. 'Pathetic, right?'

'No.'

It took a lot for her to force the question to the surface: 'Why not?'

'Because it's brave,' he said.

'Rushing a sorority?'

'No.'

Joey was waiting, not patiently.

He tried to figure out the words but they all sounded wrong. He remembered pulling over on that dusty Texas road and vomiting the bile out of him.

He said, 'To risk getting hurt in a way you don't know how to defend against.' A pause. 'Yet.'

The faintest upward tug at her lips. She blinked a few times, wiped at her cheeks. 'Could you get me a glass of orange juice?'

He poured her a glass, dropping in a few block ice cubes. He eyed the stack of coasters on the island, didn't make a move for it. A show of faith, bringing her a sweating glass, setting it down bare on the poured-concrete surface.

'Listen . . .' he began, not gently, but not *not* gently either.

'I need to move the hell out of here before we kill each other?'

'Yes.'

'Gimme the stupid coaster.'

He slid it across to her. She set the glass on it, dead in the center. Cracked that gap-toothed smile. 'You're the worst, X.'

'You're the worst, too.'

59. A Trained Assassin Maneuvering with Ninja Dexterity

Karissa Lopatina knew he was coming.

Given the security stations, police patrols, and surveillance cameras that limited mobility around and within the gated community and Allman's own towering sheer walls topped with anti-climb razor spikes, she figured the Nowhere Man would take a sniper's approach.

Which is why she'd set up in an overlook position on the dense and wooded hillside stretching down the west side of Allman's estate. Two-thirds up the slope just above a red barn, she was bellied onto the warped plywood ledge of a long-abandoned tree house. Prone position, the leaf-strewn wood hard against her knees and elbows, eye to the scope. She'd replenished with a fresh Savage 110 from her stock, the thermal upping the rifle's weight by a touch over a kilogram, and she'd turned down the gain so she'd give minimal reflection back off her eyeball. The load was a 168-grain round with enough foot-pounds of energy that even if she missed the precise mark she'd take off a limb and he'd die by exsanguination.

For additional concealment, she lay under sniper's camouflage mesh treated with Armus active IR camouflage that hid her IR and thermal body signature. A rucksack to her side held three CamelBak bladders filled with performance fluids to keep her electrolytes and blood sugar at the right levels, the thick plastic tube resting an inch below her chin so she could corral it into her mouth when she required hydration. She'd urinated once already right in her cargo pants, fighter-pilot diapers absorbing her DNA. The dampness was an irritant in the coolness of the night but nothing she couldn't manage.

She'd been set up here long enough for the front half of her body to start flirting with numbness, and she alternated tensing and relaxing individual muscles to stimulate blood flow without having to move. The lack of streetlights and traffic signals in the neighborhood conferred a denseness to the night, a robe of black wrapped around her perch. Foliage and treetops shaded her further into the hillside, shearing the faint starlight into camo splotches laid across her hide.

She'd advised Allman to keep inside away from the windows, a command easy enough for him to oblige given that he cloistered in the carapace of his house like an eel in a reef. She'd arrived eighteen hours ago, cloaked in the pre-daybreak gloom, in order to scout the surrounding terrain. Moving slowly between positions of cover, she'd assessed the vantages, calculating angles to Allman's HOME, SWEET HOME from 360 degrees and rank-ordering every last line of fire.

She'd thought one step ahead of the Nowhere Man, choosing the second-best sniper hide overlooking the location from which he could have the best angle on Allman. When he appeared, she'd have a clear field of fire on him.

Then a single shot would get it done.

There was only one problem, of which she was unaware.

Evan was already set up at the *third*-best hide.

Without moving his head, Evan surveyed the artificial lighting of the back deck on which he'd taken up position across the canyon from Allman's house. A solar-powered LED topped each post of the railing, though he remained safely in shadow. It was a hair past midnight, which meant there'd be no change in the automated lights for the foreseeable future, and he had six hours and twenty-seven minutes before day-break would shift the optic landscape.

He was coming for Allman. Lopatina knew he was coming for Allman. And he knew she knew that he was coming for Allman.

He'd entered the neighborhood through the adjoining upper Las Virgines public preserve over a stretch of low residential fencing and moved from yard to yard, dodging the security cameras of the rich and famous. He'd dropped a rucksack of gear behind a hedge of aggressive needle-bearing yew bushes at the base of Allman's fence before withdrawing to his current position.

Now he was beneath the pergola to the side of the infinity pool, wedged in a body-size gap behind an elevated wooden Jacuzzi and the edge of the deck. He lay at a slight angle, his legs atop a nest of flex PVC piping from the heating unit, and his torso, arms, and rifle flat on the composite planks.

He'd been in position for nearly thirty-eight hours, in which time he'd observed hikers and cars and couples out for walks, a pack of coyotes pawing silently across a horse trail below, a western spotted orb weaver spinning a perfectly symmetrical web not two meters from his face, and caught fleeting glimpses of a trained assassin maneuvering with ninja dexterity between spots of concealment. The Wolf had given him virtually no chances for target acquisition; he'd charted her course by the almost imperceptible movement of waving branches and dirt trickles. A few hours ago she'd settled invisibly into a hide in the area he'd anticipated – a maw of darkness atop a dilapidated tree-house platform on the facing slope.

At this distance, the four-inch gap in the rails beyond the tip of his muzzle gave him enough horizontal movement to cover the field of fire.

Evan was draped with active IR camouflage sniper's mesh glazed with active nanoformulated coating to mask his IR and thermal body signature. Tommy had even applied the Armus semiliquid polymer-based paint to the entire rifle and suppressor. Only two parts couldn't be coated and concealed – the suppressor's muzzle and the huge hemispherical objective lens of the Phoenix-S, polished to a mirror surface and tuned to gather thermal radiation that the human eye cannot see. He'd take great care not to allow either to come visible to Lopatina's vantage. As long as he stayed still and concealed, his position would remain unknown.

From what he hadn't seen, the Wolf was shielded in like fashion, so the only advantage he had was the angle. He was ready. He just needed to pin Lopatina down precisely.

Six hours and twenty-six minutes. Now it was just a matter of self-discipline and patience. He had to end the Wolf tonight. There was no margin for error. Tomorrow Jayla would be released from federal protection into the wild.

The earth rotated and Evan along with it. A wispy claw of cirrus clouds dragged its nails across the gibbous moon. The night was so quiet he could make out the whisper-soft feathers of an owl swooping low overhead.

And then the RoamZone went off, its screen lighting up to *DONCHA WISH* –

A half second later, Lopatina's projectile hit directly in the center of the Nowhere Man's thermal optic and then crashed through his dominant left eye into his skull, blowing out a fist-size chunk along with secondary fragments of the optic.

60. Shut Up and Hold Me

Moments earlier

Evan centered the reticle of his Leupold scope in the middle of the dark mass where he expected Lopatina to set up for her shot.

Frozen in predatory stillness, he thought in biology.

Breathing in a four-square cadence to lower his heart rate. Blinking at regular intervals to clear debris and flush the ocular surface. Attuning himself to his heartbeat so he could gauge the nearly imperceptible pulse in his fingertip, pressed to the side of the trigger guard.

But the critical mass of Lopatina's body was still invisible to him, swathed in IR-masking camouflage that disclosed less of her body's heat signature than the throw from an earthworm or a bird dropping. He estimated where her head and torso would be, approximately two to two and a half feet behind the polished objective of the Phoenix-S clip-on thermal. He had to determine precisely where her vital areas were. And there was only one way to do that.

In the hide that the Wolf was zeroed on, Evan waited patiently, not moving a millimeter, barely respiring. Ten meters to his side, a broomstick handle duct-taped under a cardboard mailing tube protruded through the deck railing, the convex mirror of a lady's purse compact makeup pushed into the forward end of the tube. To complete the tableau, Evan had duct-taped a mannequin's head to the right side of the decoy rifle and scope. And he'd shrouded the whole apparatus in the Armus IR coated camouflage – except for a two-inch gap in the treated fabric directly in front of the mannequin's face. One foot in front of that plastic face was an encrypted burner phone with the screen facing upward, programmed with the most annoying ringtone he'd ever heard.

Evan triple-checked his math. One meter from the end of the Wolf's SureFire suppressor to the trigger guard. Fifteen centimeters farther to the nexus of spine and skull. Ten centimeters back from there and fifteen centimeters down pulsed her ascending aorta beneath the left scapula.

He slowly reached inside his chest pocket and pressed his RoamZone to dial.

The screen of the burner cell flickered for less than a second before the Wolf reoriented, her first round smashing through the mannequin's left eye.

From Evan's vantage through the Phoenix-S thermal, the hot gases that could not be contained by her SureFire suppressor vented into the cool predawn air, a conical mist.

He waited. Let her cycle the bolt-action and recover her sight picture. Her body would settle into the same position from which she'd sent the first shot.

He waited another 1.5 seconds.

Took the slack out of the trigger.

Calm-as-death inhale.

Smooth exhale.

Waiting for the space between the muffled thumps of his heart.

Steady even pressure, the trigger releasing at the bottom of the exhalation.

The crack of the projectile going supersonic.

The muffled push of butt plate into his shoulder.

The stock jogging his cheek against his molars.

And then she was lying sprawled atop the plywood sheet, spun onto her back into a fall of ambient light, blood pumping from the union of her arm and shoulder. He sensed a flash of movement as her sniper rifle, a match of his own, tumbled from the tree house.

He had another clear shot at her chest, but he wouldn't need it to end her.

She was already dead.

Groggily she pulled at what looked like CamelBak tubing, looping it around the gushing mess of her shoulder and tugging it tight with her teeth. But the entry wound was right at the shoulder; there was no proximal spot on the limb to tourniquet and therefore no point.

When he rose, his joints burned, lactic acid rushing out as the blood flow worked in.

He slipped over the railing, slid down one of the deck's support posts to the square of concrete footing, and then stepped off onto the steep, ivy-tangled hillside.

He headed across the canyon.

From the base of the tree, he could hear her gurgling.

Lengths of two-by-fours had been hammered into the venerable trunk, forming a crooked ladder up to the tree house.

He climbed.

Her breathing grew louder as he pulled himself up toward the hatch cut into the platform. Then he was through.

Through his SOCOM-spec BNVD-31 unfilmed white-phosphor night-vision goggles, her blood pool reflected bright, almost white. He clicked the goggles off and locked them up against his forehead.

Karissa Lopatina was still on her back, and the blood slick had spread around her, and in the moonlight it shined up a dark reflection of the wind-played branches bobbing above.

He stood over her.

Her teeth were chattering, but she focused her voice. 'Nice . . . shot.'

'Sorry I didn't get you clean.'

'It's done.'

'Yes.'

'You . . . got me . . . let's . . . skip . . . small talk . . .'

'Okay.'

'Might as well' – her lungs seized up, her head tipping upright and then thunking back down – 'pleasant . . . as possible . . .'

'Okay.'

'Can you just . . .' She rolled her head toward him and her eyes pulled up to white and then came back online. '. . . just . . . shut up . . . and . . . hold me?'

Evan stepped across the puddle of blood to her intact side, lowered onto his knees, and eased down beside her. She was shuddering.

She turned slightly, groaning with pain, and seated her back against him, two spoons nested together.

She clutched his forearm and shuddered some more, all her muscles trembling.

'Just want . . . warm . . .'

They lay there together. It didn't take long.

Her breaths grew quick and shallow, and then came a terrible rasp. Her left knee bent, her boot scraping, and then the leg kicked long.

She wasn't shuddering anymore.

He extricated himself and stood over her for a moment.

Those pronounced cheekbones, the cool-blond hair, that plain even-featured face. It was hard to imagine the manner of brutality she'd been capable of.

He climbed down the tree and started for Allman's estate.

61. Shhh Shhh Shhh

Scaling a fifteen-foot-high powder-coated steel fence topped with anti-climb razor spikes presented a trying but not insurmountable challenge.

Adhesion-based climbing devices for sheer walls were generally insufficient outside of science fiction. Fortunately, a Silicon Valley biomimeticist with whom Evan had violently collided on a past mission had started several relevant projects with DARPA which Evan had kept tabs on. One such enterprise produced suction paddles that replicated the feet of geckos, which have millions of tiny hairs around each toe. All those fine hairs create van der Waals forces, where atoms in close contact create an attraction. At the moment, Evan was interested in neither geckos nor Dutch physicists, but he needed to get over the wall and would take any help beast or man saw fit to offer.

The paddles he was currently clinging to were lined with nanoridged silicone skin. They were connected to foot stirrups that, when engaged, evacuated extra air from the suction cups above, enabling stronger adherence. Tommy Stojack, purveyor of rare and distinctive tactical gear, had sold Evan a beta version of the contraption that had been liberated from an Arlington lab by a disgruntled engineer.

The device was unwieldy and ridiculous-looking, like a jet pack worn on the front side. Under cover of darkness, accompanied by mechanical hisses and vacuum pops, Evan humped his way up the wall. Strapped to his back was a tightly rolled three-foot length of high-pile carpet.

Nearing the top, he set his boots in the stirrups, hung from a paddle with one hand, unfurled the carpet beside him, and then slung it up over the spikes. It took some wriggling to free himself from the straps, find new handholds, and leave the clunky contraption behind. Once he squirmed up and on top of the fence, he reached back to release the last suction cup, which gave way with a cephalopodic pop, and the unit fell back into the hedge of yew bushes.

He slid over the fence to the other side, bringing the carpet with him. It dragged in his wake, sliced into neat ribbons by the razor spikes.

From his cargo pocket he pulled out a flashlight. Its diffuse filter ensured he was throwing a sufficiently subtle glow not to flare the surveillance cameras even as he scanned the darkness to spot their glinting lenses.

He needn't have worried; they were predictably positioned among the cypresses along the narrow drive. Keeping to the landscaping, he climbed his way up.

No camera on the porch. Allman's crew probably figured that between the medieval wall and the bevy of cameras, no one could get here unspotted.

Evan scratched gently on the door with his fingernails like a branch in the wind or a horror-movie slasher.

A moment later he heard a stool squeak back and then footsteps tap across the foyer.

The movement of the door was smooth and easy, no indication of any fear behind it.

That came more directly a second later in Mr Biltmore's widened eyes.

He blinked it back, down, away, and then his smug jaw set once more with the conviction of a man who'd been given every last thing he'd wanted from the world. He crossed his arms and widened his stance, taking up more space like an agitated sage grouse.

'I know,' Biltmore said. 'You're thinking another fucking white-collar guy who thinks he's tough. But I don't *think* I'm tough. Sixth-dan black belt in tae kwon do, trained at the same dojo for eighteen years.'

'Where?' Evan asked.

Biltmore faltered. 'Encino.'

Evan kicked him in the dick.

Well-placed, and the toes of his Original S.W.A.T.s were steel-lined.

It was crass and he knew it, but the guy had left an open lane as wide as the Chunnel and it would have been a disgrace to the Gods of Fighting for Evan to have shirked his moral obligation to capitalize on it.

Biltmore made a noise like an old door creaking open, his legs zippered up, ass sticking out. Then he toppled over.

Evan zip-tied his wrists and ankles together, hauled him up, dragged him across the threshold, and slung him into the sewer trench to the side of the porch. An audible clang as he ricocheted off the iron pipe below and then there came a groan, a muffled sob, and then silence.

Evan went back inside.

He stood in the security alcove, surveillance cameras feeding him live footage of various angles around the property and inside every room in the house. Convenient.

Evan stared at the image of himself in the security nook, his face fuzzed to an unidentifiable mess by the adversarial pattern of his shirt, lab-designed to confound capture. Body of a man, face of a ghost.

The Nowhere Man. Aside from him, only one person appeared to be on premises, a lump beneath the sheets in the master bedroom.

Evan glided back through the house.

Same unvented smell of crusted food, old sneakers, dusty furniture. Piles of batteries. Solventry delivery packages, piled three high, lined an entire side of the hallway.

The door to the powder room remained ajar, showing a half-squeezed toothpaste tube and a capless deodorant stick set on a marble sink basin. A wet vacuum cleaner lay on the carpet of a guest room, dissected as if for an autopsy, a plastic tank of moldy water set where the head would be. Heaps of framed art rested atop the unmade bed.

Evan had the sense of having entered an animal's den. It felt strange peeking into the intimate cubbies where life was unglamorously lived, where hours dragged into seasons, where an organism labored in the service of basic functions – hunger, respiration, self-care. This house wasn't Allman's reality. It was an inconvenience to which he had to acclimate his body so he could exist within the virtual world he'd engendered, a binary landscape of ones and zeros that matched the pattern of his own mind's eye, that required neither nuance nor the moral shadings of human intelligence.

Evan kept on.

Double doors at the end of the hall, one open forty-five degrees.

Sensing no trap, he slipped through into the darkness of Allman's bedroom. The air felt thicker here, hard to breathe.

He could hear the man wheezing beneath the covers.

He drew closer.

Allman lay beneath the blankets, a CPAP contraption strapped to his face. It regulated his breathing – the wheezes Evan had heard from the doorway – but Allman snorted over it, sleep apnea fighting the machine at every turn.

One shoulder was hunched up into view, showing

old-fashioned blue pajamas. His cheek and the side of his neck sparkled with sweat – a hot sleeper.

His nightstand held well-used laptops, a half dozen of varying sizes stacked like coasters, and an eye-dropper bottle missing its top.

Evan halted at the foot of the bed and stared at the slumbering form before him, this man devoid of anything Evan could recognize as human.

Evan turned off the CPAP machine.

Allman stirred. He clutched at his mask, sliding it free, tufts of sweat-greased hair shoved tectonically this way and that from the straps.

'Biltmore? Biltmore?' Allman pushed himself upright with a groan.

His face caught a band of shadow. Evan could discern only the outline of his head and shoulders, but he sensed the muscles tense, a sudden stillness.

'Oh,' Allman said. 'Oh, no.'

'I'm sorry,' Evan said.

'No,' Allman said. 'No.'

He scrambled off the bed, tangling in the sheets and hitting the carpet with his palms. 'I don't understand,' he said, rising. 'I don't understand why.'

Evan said, 'I know.'

Allman shook off the sheets and stood before Evan, his eyes darting to the doorway, but there was too much fear. It had overcome him. He wouldn't bolt. He knew it was hopeless.

Beneath the wild tangles of his brows, those heavy-lidded turtle eyes bunched once, twice. They would have looked closed were it not for the faintest crescent glimmers of awareness seeping through. His chest was jerking violently, the skin tags around his neck bristled darkly, and he smelled powerfully of body odor and sleep breath, and Evan was repulsed by him, but not nearly so much as he was repulsed by what he had to do.

Because Evan finally saw Allman for what he really was: a child, a fat kid set apart from everyone else by cues and mores he couldn't grasp and a brain that didn't work like anyone else's. A scared little boy who'd built the controls to a universe of his own making, a universe into which he could disappear, a universe in which everything made sense to him. And this world out here was filled with nothing more than avatars, players who could be deleted from the game at will.

Allman's knees buckled, but he held upright. He was sobbing soundlessly, mouth ajar, jagged teeth exposed.

'I'll make it gentle,' Evan said.

Allman couldn't form words, but he nodded once and then again, his mouth frozen in an awful shape of grief.

Evan took him by the shoulders, the pajamas wet to the touch where he'd soaked through them, and turned him gently around. Allman meekly complied.

His head was still bobbing, but no noise came out of him. Only now, staring at the back of Allman's head, did Evan notice that Allman was shorter than him by a good five inches. He wondered how he'd failed to observe that during their last visit.

Evan let the age-old instinct guide him, arms slithering around Allman's neck, clamping the head, tipping it forward so his throat met the V of Evan's forearm and biceps.

And then he squeezed.

'Shhh,' he said. 'Shhh shhh shhh.'

Afterward he lowered Allman to the carpet, his thick form puddling.

In the process, Allman's leg had kicked the nightstand,

knocking over the small plastic bottle. Evan picked it up. It read: FOR SENSITIVE EYES.

He set it back on the nightstand.

He made it out of the bedroom, down the hall, onto the porch, and past the trench, where he could hear Biltmore's labored breathing. He made it down the long narrow drive with the van Gogh cypresses thrusting overhead from either side. He made it out of the gate, which acquiesced to a manual touch of the control box, sliding aside. He made it from front yard to side yard to horse trail to backyard.

And then he leaned against a disused stable and vomited a few times in the packed dirt.

He'd never thrown up after a mission.

Not since his very first.

A hose lay coiled snakelike in the dark. A wrench of the rusty handle freed a healthy torrent of water. He washed away his waste in the dirt. Squatting in the moonlight, he drank from the hose, spitting to clear his mouth.

Only now did he remove the RoamZone from his pocket. The number of Jayla Hill's burner phone was the top entry, teed up and waiting.

His thumbs wrote out the text: It's safe now.

All these years into his strange and solitary existence, these were still the best three words he had to offer another person.

He stared at them for a long time.

And then sent them off into the ether.

62. Need No Praise

Luke Devine called the RoamZone at seven o'clock the following morning.

'I introduce you to two billionaires and they both wind up dead!'

Evan said, 'Sorry about that.'

He'd already been up for two hours, had worked out and meditated, and was poking at the remains of last night's fire, in which he'd burned his clothes. Joey and Dog were gone, the penthouse tranquil. He felt glad to have Allman and Solventry in the rearview, happy to return his attention to concrete matters within his singular control. Sleep, muscle, focus, ashes.

Devine's anger was paper-thin, a veneer to his fluster. There was nothing even a man of his empire-moving influence could do. Evan knew where he lived. And Devine did not know where Evan lived.

One of Jack's Unofficial Rules – Evan's favorite – sprang to mind: *Need no praise*. If Devine was smart, he'd have been one of the faceless billionaires he'd described. If he truly deserved the power he wielded, he wouldn't have needed so much damn credit for it.

'I offered you a partnership once,' Devine said. 'This doesn't feel like a partnership. This feels like you using all of my resources and offering nothing in return.'

Evan said, 'Huh.'

He hung up, stood, and stretched.

His stomach told him it was time for breakfast.

63. Vicarious Loneliness

Eight days later, Evan fulfilled the promise he'd made to Jayla, driving over so he could walk her into her town house for the first time since the Wolf had nearly succeeded in strangling her. Released from her unofficial WITSEC, Jayla had been living with her aunt until the forensic-cleaning crew could render her place livable once more. Though her aunt was planning to move in with her, Jayla had told Evan that she wanted to see her place alone first.

Alone meaning just with her fear and with Evan.

He hadn't seen her since the hospital room, and the sight of her waiting on the porch caught him off guard. She was scared, shoulders tensed and lifted, one toe pressed to the concrete stoop, twisting into the concrete like a drill bit.

He'd taken the usual precautions before approaching, surveilling the surrounding blocks and leaving his truck parked a quarter mile away in an alley.

As he walked up, she jerked around, an arm rising to cross her chest defensively.

He stood a good distance back from the porch and let her acclimate to the sight of him.

She caught her breath, then gave a flip of a salute from her forehead: *Hello.*

He said, 'Ready?'

She nodded. Only now did he notice that she had her key out. She was gripping it in her fist so it protruded between her index and middle finger, a makeshift weapon.

Unlocking the door, she stepped into the vestibule.

Same side table, same hanging Tunisian tapestry, same inoperative alarm panel stuck back into the wall, its clipped wires dangling.

A few hesitant steps brought them to the brink of the vestibule, the town house yawning wide and upward. Those imperial staircases mirrored each other, fallopian tubes scaling the yawning hollow.

It had been cleaned up.

Some pieces of art had been reglassed and rehung; others were missing, their ghostly outlines preserved in negative space outlined by sun-faded paint. The cushions of the sectional had been replaced, but the Berber carpet beneath was missing, likely stained beyond repair.

Its absence seemed to draw even more attention to the bare spot where Jayla's father had lain dead. Evan pictured him vividly. Zip-tied hands purpled from lack of circulation, stubbed up at the small of his back. Head twisted to one side, blood seeping from his parted lips and the hole atop his head. That fluttering eyelid.

One step ahead of Evan, Jayla had frozen, staring at the same spot, seeing the same thing.

He stood silently behind her.

Several minutes passed, and then several more. She did not move.

At last she let a breath shudder out of her and moved forward. Evan flanked her, giving her room. They developed a system without words, Jayla leading the way into rooms only after checking that he was at her back.

She pointed at places she wanted him to clear – beneath beds, behind couches, in the umbra thrown by a front-load dryer. He raked aside shower curtains and checked cabinets big enough to hide a human. They moved meticulously, silently through the entire town house. Space by space, Jayla reclaimed it as her own.

They'd just finished the top balcony from which Karissa Lopatina had launched herself when the doorbell rang.

Jayla halted, seized up by fear once more. She signed too quickly and Evan had to ask her to go again.

I don't know who that is. My aunt said she would wait in the car until I texted her to come.

'I'll check.'

Jayla kept at his shoulder all the way down the stairs. He moved her out of the sight line before stepping into the vestibule. A cautious peek through the peephole showed Joey waiting on the porch, holding a flat box the size of a hardcover book.

He'd told her he was coming over.

As he opened the door, she peered past him. 'Where's Jayla?'

Evan stepped aside.

The two young women met in the vestibule, Jayla's brow wrinkling with confusion.

'Hi,' Joey said. 'I'm a . . . colleague of his. I guess you'd say a technology expert. I'm, um, real sorry for . . . everything you . . .'

Joey lost her footing. Was it her nerve? Did she question her right to offer condolences? To connect? She stood there with her thoughts tangled in her throat.

Jayla was watching her, still confused. In the strained interlude, Evan caught a glimpse of the awkwardness Joey must have had on inadvertent display during the sorority outings. He thought about how uncomfortable she must have felt at that restaurant, that bowling alley, and how much she'd held back within herself until she'd finally punched a deserving dickhead to self-sabotage her way out of there.

Joey was never this ungainly around him; she was different with him, freestyle Joey in all her awful glory. It struck him like an epiphany, allowing him to see in new colors what intimacy might mean.

Leaning slightly, he nudged Joey back to life.

She reanimated: 'Anyways, I, um, I brought you something.'

Awkwardly, she proffered the box.

As Jayla took it, her features smoothed, eyes enlarging. A softening.

She lifted the lid.

Nestled inside was what looked like a choker necklace made up of matte-black disks. The most prominent one was centered on the chain like a pendant, aligned with the others but slightly bigger.

Jayla looked up, confused. Her hand rose to the hollow of her throat, where a lightning bolt of scar tissue split the skin above her larynx.

Joey said, 'Can I show you what it does?'

Jayla looked at Evan, her eyes scared. He gave a subtle tip of his head.

And then Jayla nodded at Joey.

Joey moved behind her, cinched the choker into place, and adjusted it by carefully feeling around Jayla's throat. She seemed to be getting the central pendant into a precise position.

'Okay,' she said, when she was done. 'Say something.'

'I can't.' Jayla's hands flew to her mouth. She'd spoken the words in her own voice. Her eyes were brimming and her face was contorted and then she shook out her hands as if flinging water from them. 'I can't . . . I can't believe it.'

She sounded just as she had on the TikTok video Joey had found, her voice husky, textured, singular.

'This is what your father was working on at the throat-cancer ward at Carnegie Mellon,' Joey said. 'For your mom.'

Jayla's face trembled.

'Most tracheoesophageal prostheses have crappy sound,' Joey said. 'That's why he was combining technologies and rendering voices with AI. I took yours from the videos you posted and it extrapolated from there.'

'How . . . how is this possible?' Jayla's hands were in front of her mouth, as if to catch the words as they came out.

'It reads vibrations of your throat like an electrolarynx and anticipates from the movement of your facial musculature how you're shaping words with your lips.' Joey tapped the choker gently. 'It's your own voice. No one should ever take that away from you.'

Jayla hugged her. When she pulled away, she started to sign from habit, caught herself, and spoke: 'Best Thanksgiving present ever.' Her words were tentative, her voice still on training wheels. 'Thank you . . . friend.'

Joey's lower lip wobbled, so slightly that no one in the world could have caught it. Except Evan. She hardened her face, held herself together. Took an extra beat before speaking.

'The future's gonna be amazing,' Joey said. 'Don't let anyone scare you into thinking otherwise.'

Evan noticed that he had receded a few steps, as he often did when emotion got palpable.

His shoulder brushed the alarm pad, jostling it from its uncertain perch on the wall mount. When he caught it, the plastic casing came apart. He held the pieces in his hands. It had cracked open to reveal something within.

A hard drive.

No doubt containing Dr Hill's perfect deepfake code, the IP he'd stolen back from Allman. It had been right there all along, the perfect hiding place.

The sight of it stole Joey's attention immediately. She stared at it, her face serious, and then held out her hand. Evan looked at Jayla. Jayla took the hard drive out of Evan's hands. And set it in Joey's.

'I'm ready now,' Jayla said, her cadence finding a more natural rhythm. 'To be here.' She looked surprised every time she heard herself talk, and she paused to grin, the effect charming. 'Because of you.'

Evan didn't like this part, when gratitude was aimed at him, making his face sit heavy on his skull like a mask. He struggled to receive it.

'How can I possibly thank you?' she said.

This was the part he didn't mind, when he asked them to pass the baton and in doing so to complete their transition from being pursued to searching out another human in desperate need.

'Find someone else facing the level of trouble you were in, someone being terrorized by another person, and give my phone number to them – 1-855-2-NOWHERE.'

Jayla's long lashes flared wide. 'And then what?'

'And then I'll help them. Like I helped you.'

'That's it? That's all you want?'

'Yes.'

'That doesn't seem like much.' Her voice, it still sounded like a miracle. 'I mean, to repay you. For everything.'

'You can see what I don't. Different kinds of people, vulnerability, suffering. That's what I need.'

'That's an awful thing to need.' She said it with no judgment. Just empathy. 'But I will. I'll do it.'

404

He nodded.

It was. It was an awful thing to need. An awful thing he required to be what he was.

Joey tapped the hard drive against her knuckles, supremely distracted by what she held in her hands. When Jayla glanced down to text her aunt on the phone, Evan slipped away with Joey.

They crossed the street, started down the opposite sidewalk.

He said, 'What you did for her back there –'

'I'm gonna get on this right away,' Joey said, waving the hard drive.

She looked worn out. Her eyes were lowered, her manner curt. It had taken a lot for her to decipher and navigate a situation like the one with Jayla. In some ways it was easier for her to give Jayla her voice than to find her own, and he felt a sudden fierce vicarious loneliness for what Joey could manage for others versus for herself. And a pride for her trying.

He started to say something, but she cut him off again: 'I'll let you know once I'm in.'

She walked away.

He stood a moment watching her go, the sun warm against his face. Way up the street a FWIP rattled along, skillfully circumventing a battered gray tent stuffed in a doorway, a homeless man's abode.

Movement drew his attention back to the town house. Jayla on the porch, greeting her aunt. The woman had arrived with plastic grocery bags lining her arms, elbows bent to sustain the weight. Jayla made a move to help but the woman shook her off, wobbling past her niece into the house.

Jayla hesitated on the doorstep, fingertips touching the choker in seeming disbelief. She hadn't shared her voice with her aunt, not yet. Right now it was hers and hers alone.

Her eyes lifted and she caught sight of Evan across the street. Traffic had picked up between them, but they could still see each other clearly through the flow of cars.

Jayla flattened her fingers, touched them to her mouth, and then tipped her hand toward Evan.

He signed back: *You're welcome.*

Jayla spun gracefully on her toe, a dancer's turn that reminded him of Sofia, and eased back into the town house. The door closed behind her.

Lost in thought, Evan walked the seven blocks back to his truck. There it was in the shadows of an alley, parked next to a dumpster.

An ugly little dog with stiff hair and crazy eyes stood with his grimy little paws submerged in a puddle. He sniffed twice at the ground, rat nose quivering, then looked directly at Evan.

Holding the stare with his bulging eyes, Loco lifted a hind leg and urinated on Evan's tire.

64. A Place He Didn't Belong

Brianna's apartment smelled of turkey and mashed potatoes and gravy and green beans and rolls and pumpkin pie. The cornucopia of scents hit Evan halfway down the hall as he marched with Loco tucked beneath his arm.

The dog alternated between licking himself and trying to bite Evan's face.

He reached the door and knocked twice gently.

Loco's lips wrinkled back from his snaggled teeth and he nipped at Evan's chin.

Bri opened the door. Her penciled eyebrows rose up toward her hairline and stayed there. 'Really?' she said. 'Oh my goodness. Oh my goodness.' Then: '*Sofia!*'

Scampering footsteps, and then Sofia careened around the corner from her bedroom and Loco caught her scent and clawed viciously to escape Evan's clutch, scraping his stomach. He dropped the dog, who fell and landed with feline grace, the first blip of elegance Evan had seen from the creature. Then Loco rocketed to Sofia, scaled her leg, scrambled into her arms, and froze beneath her chin as if he had suddenly fainted and been delivered into nirvana.

There was crying and hugging and kissing and licking and all order of cloying emotions. Evan lifted his shirt to examine the puffy red claw marks that had been raked across his abdomen. Watching her daughter roll around on the floor with the dog, Brianna held a tissue to the edges of her eyes and shook her head with grateful bemusement.

'That stupid mutt,' she said to Evan. And then again: 'That stupid mutt.'

Finally the celebration wound down and Sofia got up, Loco nestled into her arms, snoring audibly.

'I can't believe it,' she said. 'You found him.'

'He found me.'

'Cause for celebration,' Bri said.

Sofia chewed her lip and looked down at her bare feet, her mood shifting.

Evan said, 'What?'

'Dad's missing again.'

He looked over at the dinner table laden with food. Three place settings waited. Now he understood the aura of punctured hopefulness.

'Want me to find him?'

Sofia shook her head, then dipped her face to kiss Loco. He snarfled and went back to sleep. The tip of his tongue stuck out, a pink tab against his wiry beard. She set him down and he staggered over, asleep on his feet, and collapsed by the ridiculous shrine that had been erected in his honor.

'But . . .' Sofia looked across at the dinner table.

Evan thought: *Please don't ask.*

'There's a extra seat,' she said. 'You could use it.'

He felt the familiar tightness in his chest, a cramping of walls closing in, the age-old challenge of holding himself intact in a place he didn't belong, a place that he'd always thought hadn't wanted him any more than the man in that double-wide in Blessing, Texas, had.

What if there's no one to fix anything? he'd heard Jack ask. *Except you.*

Sofia stood with her feet pushed heel to toe at ninety degrees, dancer's fifth position. Despite her perfect posture, she was nervy with anticipation, humming beneath the skin.

Evan forced the decision, gave the slightest nod.

Sofia's eyes found a kind of light he hadn't seen in them before. It had taken so little to give her so much. People could be shocking in their simplicity.

She raised her tiny fist, aimed the knuckles at him. 'Uncle?'

He thought of the man who was his father staring at himself in the mirror, flicking his hair this way and that, trying to hide his thinning spots.

He thought of the man who was his father saying, *This is where you tell me who your mom is.*

He thought of the man who was his father.

And then he didn't.

He stared at Sofia's proffered fist a moment longer.

And then bumped it.

65. Together

Joey had the windows open in her apartment, but still it smelled like a convenience store – candy and soda, the after-glow of microwaved burritos. Dog lay sprawled across his luxury bed, his head flopped onto the floor at a strained uptilted angle as if he were a heron swallowing perch. Except for the regular thwaps of his tail against the wall every time Evan made eye contact, he looked dead.

Evan stood inside Joey's circular desk beside her gamer's chair. Scattered across the surfaces were speedcubes solved and half solved, wireless keyboards, Big Gulps at various life stages. Spread across the stacked monitors were the contents of Dr Hill's hard drive.

The hard drive itself hadn't been named. In place of a disk name were emojis of the three monkeys of lore – see no evil, hear no evil, speak no evil. Symbols for willful blind-ness, deafness, and muteness seemed appropriate in the face of the power that the code could unleash.

Deepfakes perfect enough to bend reality.

He and Joey had been at it for at least an hour. Weighing what to do, flip-flopping positions, devil's-advocating them-selves into a Prince of Denmark standoff.

'Who the hell are we to make the choice to hold it back?' Joey asked again.

'As good as anyone else,' Evan said.

'They'll just re-create the tech,' Joey said. 'Someone else's gonna get it perfect. Youtopia is only a few months behind and from what I've seen, there are at least three dozen other entities pushing toward indistinguishable skinlifts.'

At Evan's behest, she'd opened the project, broken it down into its separate components, and readied its release onto open-source repositories across the dark web.

With one click of the mouse, he could send it out into the world.

Or drag and delete the files forever.

He thought about heads of state making declarations of war. Spouses screaming incriminating information. Children stripped down for whatever use anyone wanted to make of them. A perfect deepfake was a genie unbound. It made anything possible.

In the past he'd collided with a Silicon Valley visionary who'd designed a digital conscience able to make decisions to kill in order to remove the moral burden from soldiers – as if the moral burden wasn't the last damn thing tethering humanity to the cost of killing. Now he'd stared face-to-face men like Allman and Friedhoff who dared to nudge AI into full sentience. Creating conscience and sentience made them – truly – Godlike. But Evan saw nothing in them approximating the wisdom of Gods in any creation myth he'd read from any culture that had survived long and well enough for their origin story to reach him.

Highlighting the software, he dragged it over the virtual trash can.

Hesitated.

'At a minimum, this'll delay it getting out,' he said.

'What's the point?' Joey said. 'Doesn't it have to get here and fuck everybody up for anyone to learn what to do about it?'

'Maybe a few years of peace.'

'Months,' Joey said.

'Even so. Maybe, I don't know . . .' He laughed.

'What?'

'Maybe humanity'll get wiser in the interim.'

Joey cocked her head, looked up at him over the bulge of her shoulder, amused. To the side of the mouse pad, her phone chimed, and without breaking her focus on him she reached over and shut it off. 'I know, right?' she said. 'This shit is *weighty*, X. Along with the rest of everything else that's coming.'

'Yes,' Evan said.

'But in the face of it? We can't only be cynical. That's just another cheap trick.'

He nodded. 'We've been here before. Humans.'

'Not *here* here.'

'Right. But in just as stark a place. It's not like Hitler had AI technology. Or Stalin. Or Mao Zedong. And they had their people brainwashed and locked up. To break free?' He shrugged. 'It's the same challenge. No matter the era. No matter the technology. It just comes down to the man.'

'Or the woman.'

'The individual.'

'So that means . . .'

'We give it to them. Democratize it.'

Joey nodded. 'Crowdsource the countermeasures.'

'At least everyone'll have the same fighting chance.'

He moved the files back to the desktop.

Hovered the mouse over the UPLOAD button.

'Are you sure?' Joey asked.

'Of course not.'

He thought about what Jack would do. Tommy and Candy. What Aragón's slant on it would be – and even Luke Devine's, though he mostly detested the man. Then he closed his eyes,

412

exhaled deeply, and scattered their voices to the wind. There were no rules for this, no commandments.

At the precise moment he'd made up his own mind, Joey rested her hand atop his on the mouse.

Together, they clicked.

Epilogue

No Please

Evan had entered a rare pure phase of mindfulness meditation. Cross-legged on his floating bed, eyes veiled, a full awareness of every last –

DONCHA WISH YER GIRLFRIEND WUZ HAAAWT LIKE ME?!

That goddamned alert.

Half drunk with endorphin release, he grabbed the Roam-Zone from the comforter beside him and asked 'Do you need my help?' before realizing it was not a call but a text.

forgot 2 tell u i left a gift 4 u in the vault

Okay, he texted back. And then: Change my ring and text alert remotely.

kewl kewl i'll dig thru some classic Menudo 4 u

I don't know what that is but no please.

He slid from the bed, set his bare feet on the poured concrete, and stretched deeply, feeling his back pop. Then he padded through the bathroom, passing through the secret door in the shower and into the Vault.

Vera III was floating.

Just like his bed, her tiny white pod had been hoisted magnetically. Above a small electronic base she rotated, a perfect rosette atop her multicolored glass pebbles. Her fleshy leaves splayed outward in a roller-coaster display of fun. She looked like she was having the time of her life.

He walked over to his L-shaped desk and sat before her. She spun and spun, free of gravity and earthly concerns.

Her floating bed delighted him. The perfect gift.

He was rising to go when he saw a new alert for his account: the.nwhr.man@gmail.com.

The email was from Melinda Truong. The subject line read: *FINALLY SOURCED KARISSA LOPATINA'S ORDNANCE SUPPLIER.*

Crouched a few inches above his chair, he felt it come on at the base of his spine, premonition tightening into dread.

And somehow he knew.

He sat.

Melinda's words returned to him from back when they were first building a profile on the Wolf. *French Gendarmerie revolvers and Dragunov SVDs. Whoever's putting the steel in her hands might as well be pulling the trigger themselves.*

Instinctively Evan's hand had moved beneath the sheet-metal desk to the saw-toothed piece of metal he kept resting atop the computer tower by his right knee. His fist clenched around the memento as he stared at the unopened email projected on the wall before him.

The information was coming to him whether he wanted it or not and more senses than he had were telling him that this was not information he wanted. He saw everything with a sudden horrid clarity, the identical weaponry, how the man had literally fallen out of his chair when Evan broached the topic with him. It felt inevitable, yes, but also as shocking as anything he'd encountered in his three decades and counting.

The metal piece was biting into Evan's palm. He pictured its missing half, lit by the fire pit: NO GREATER FRIEND.

Loosening his fist, he stared down at the half-moon of the roughly cleaved challenge coin: NO WORSE ENEMY.

Broken and shared many years ago. Call and answer, two parts of the same whole, equal sides of a balanced equation.

He set down his half of the coin on the mouse pad. Stared at the unopened email with its unwavering subject line promising the name of Karissa Lopatina's ordnance supplier.

It presaged a conflict of the worst kind. Maybe even a war.

It took a moment for his hand to obey him and move to open the email.

There it was in black-and-white.

Thomas J. Stojack.

Acknowledgments

Great thanks to:

Jim Keller, my favorite stunt pilot, who happens to be the world's most wondrous computer chip designer. He and Bonnie also make okay kids.

Van Lai, for sharing with me the texture of her own background so I could in turn share it with Melinda.

Al Gough and Miles Millar, who planted the seed of an idea for Melinda's past.

Luis Urrea, for providing me with ongoing insight as well as unimprovable cursing-in-Spanish lessons.

John Rogers, who lent Joey (a version of) his motto: '*The future is cool. Don't let anyone frighten you into thinking otherwise.*'

Michael 'Borski' Borohovski, for continuing to supercharge Joey's brain in ways I cannot.

Kurata Tadashi, for providing Evan a brilliant, meticulous continuing education in weapons and tactics.

Dr Melissa Hurwitz and Dr Bret Nelson, for helping me inflict injuries in violation of the Hippocratic oath. And yes, for sometimes helping me treat said injuries as well.

Philip Eisner, for his friendship and delightfully dark imagination.

Terry McGarry, for bringing Second Commandment-level copyediting expertise.

Lisa Erbach Vance of the Aaron Priest Agency, CEO of Orphan X.

Stephen F. Breimer, my lawyer of nearly three decades, and Keith Kahla, my editor for fifteen books. Gentlemen, you've given me so much.

Angela Cheng Caplan of Cheng Caplan Company, my manager who has expanded my creative scope in ways delightful and surprising.

Caspian Dennis and Rowland White, for overseeing Transatlantic operations.

Andrew Martin, Sally Richardson, Jennifer Enderlin, Kelley Ragland, Martin Quinn, Hector DeJean, Paul Hochman, Grace Gay, and the sales team of Minotaur Books, for making me the beneficiary of more hard work and creative talent than I can enumerate.

Louise Moore, Mubarak Elmubarak, Jennifer Harlow, Ciara Berry, Christina Ellicott, Anna Curvis, and the sales team of Michael Joseph / Penguin Group UK, for making me feel as at home in the UK as I do in America.

My parents, Alfred and Marjorie, who poured the foundation beneath me and gave me the tools to build upon it.

Zuma and Nala, my glorious Rhodesian ridgebacks, endless feedback loops of positive emotion, and perennial providers of oxytocin.

Natalie Corinne, for ever bending to the light.

And Delinah Raya, for being the light to which I bend.

Orphan X will return in

NEMESIS

Coming Spring 2025

Read on for an exclusive extract . . .

—

'A stellar series, and the stories get better with each instalment' *DAILY MAIL*

We'd love to hear what you think of the Orphan X series!

Use the hashtag **#ORPHANX** and tag **@MichaelJBooks** and **@GreggHurwitz**

NURTURING WRITERS SINCE 1935

Prologue

Meet-Cute

Fifteen Years Ago

Tommy Stojack.

The guy's name is everywhere, a hushed referral at an ammo trade stall, a proper noun rising above the buzz at the Green Beret Foundation booth, a fleck of sea-foam shot from the swirls and eddies of the churning crowd on the convention floor. It is a secret handshake, a dropped name to prove bona fides, a password to a private club.

Depending on which snippet of conversation is trustworthy, Stojack either gunsmithed at the local police range, *or* he ran the veterans' parade, *or* he demilitarized obsolete and surplus munitions at the Hawthorne Army Depot, *or* he'd bare-assed the Ward 5 councilman at last year's city meeting for cutting survivor benefits for the spouses of firefighters. The valets joke about Stojack's filthy rig, and the bartenders compare notes on his generous tips.

Evan does not know the man nor has he come here looking for him, but his situational awareness demands that he take notice. He's been trained to read the street wherever he goes, to assemble unofficial dominance hierarchies in his mind—which warlord oversees which zone of rubbled mountainside, which bureaucrat requires a palmed-off wad of yuan in a well-appointed consulate office, which oligarch demands more elbow room in which forgotten corner of Eastern Europe.

Muscle memory pounded into his cells from the age of twelve, when Evan had been taken from a foster home and ensconced in the dark arts of the Orphan Program, a full black operation buried so far beneath the DoD that its protocols never glimpsed the light of day.

A throwaway child brought to the water's edge of his American promise, a promise that receded from him when he bent to it, a promise that is his to uphold, if not for himself then for others.

Like the other products of the Program, Evan had been a clean asset with no familial or community entanglements. Any record of his brief pitiful existence had been wiped from the databases. His face was unknown, his biometrics uncaptured. As the twenty-fourth recruit, he'd been assigned the matching letter of the alphabet for his operational alias.

X.

It was stamped on him, his alias, the cruel power of his own nothingness. Two bloody strokes against oblivion, the awesome, awful power to obliterate.

They'd turned him into an expendable human weapon deployed around the globe to complete missions unsanctioned under US or international law. If caught, tortured, or killed, he would be neither claimed nor missed.

His mind is a treasure map of buried bodies, verboten knowledge sufficiently radioactive to overthrow administrations and unleash wars. Which makes him all the more dangerous to the Powers That Be since he'd fled the Program, slipped off the radar, and rebooted himself on the left coast under a new alias as an importer of industrial cleaning supplies. A great number of powerful men would sleep more soundly in a great number of soft beds could they ensure that Evan joined the legion of corpses he'd put six feet under.

They'd already executed Jack Johns, the handler and father figure who'd raised Evan from the age of twelve, training him in isolation aside from myriad subject-matter experts brought in to augment his instruction. Jack had been the first person to treat Evan as if he had inherent worth, a dizzying concept that even now as a young man Evan struggles to embrace.

Early on, Jack had told him that the hard part wouldn't be making him a killer. The hard part would be keeping him human.

Turned out the *hardest* part was to contain both warring directives inside one person.

Recently Evan had chosen to disappear from his countless enemies by hiding in plain sight, tucking into a penthouse lair in a residential tower on Los Angeles's Wilshire Corridor. Step by step he'd been surreptitiously hardening his sanctuary—replacing the windowpanes and sliding glass doors with bullet-resistant Lexan, upgrading the Sheetrock to five and eight-tenths commercial grade, hiding a steel fire core in his front door beneath wooden laminate matching the other residences. Wanting further protection from snipers, explosives, and prying eyes, he'd been seeking some sort of discreet-armor shades for his windows and glass sliders. That's what had brought him here to the SHOT Show, the world's biggest trade exhibit for firearm manufacturers and aficionados of tactical products.

The second floor of the Las Vegas Sands Expo and Convention Center is where most of the action is. Partitioned into conference rooms, exhibit spaces, and booths, it features cutting-edge law-enforcement and military gear alongside the most ridiculous shit on earth.

Spray-on thermal camouflage. A brassiere holster designed to nestle an inverted pistol between the breasts. Kevlar inserts for school backpacks. Exoskeleton therapy machines. Sniper cartridges machined into bottle openers. Concealed-carry leggings for women. Challenge coins of every unit and branch of service. Mylar-coated tents. Key chains and bumper stickers and beverage coasters.

Not a beer coozie lacked a logo.

Evan moves anonymously among the sixty thousand attendees. Surveillance cameras, Las Vegas Metro, and other eagle eyes are on the lookout for Chinese spies, Turkish peddlers of subpar ordnance, and entrepreneurs willing to bend FARA regs past breaking point.

To thwart facial recognition he'd mashed dental wax around his molars, which gives him a movie-star jaw that makes him—amusingly—better-looking than he is and pleases him in an odd way he finds mildly confusing. He is easily overlooked, average size, average build, not too handsome, and he is dressed to blend in further. Worn blue jeans, olive-drab jacket, desert-tan combat boots. He'd infused a sloppy smoker's stench into his outfit with the ceremonious wagging of a cigarette. John Deere cap slung low, the white netting yellowed by last night's application of olive oil, several spins in the microwave, and a dusting of sand taken from outside this morning's breakfast-burrito joint, a crooked shanty that had likely since collapsed.

Testosterone hangs musk-heavy in the air. There are cargo shorts and Oakley Blades, drugstore perfume and décolletages aplenty. The big draws are Marine Gunnery Sergeant R. Lee Ermey at the Glock booth; Duane Dwyer talking chisel pike blades, karambit knives, and Zen Buddhism; and celebrity booth babes over at Dillon Aero autographing calendars featuring twelve months of provocative poses and pistol clutching.

Grabbing a bottled water from a vending machine, Evan pauses near an overladen table to take a few sips. His elbow knocks over a sturdy police boot of suede leather and nylon. He picks up the boot, gives it a flex. Stitched heel and toe, rustproof hardware, nonmarking rubber. He notes the name.

Original S.W.A.T.

Continuing on to various vendor booths, Evan makes inquiries about discreet-armor window shades, but the pickings are slim. He receives a special invitation to a conference room on the third floor, but the only offerings there are knockoff habergeon silliness out of Bangalore and aluminum idiocy better suited to Renaissance cosplay than mil-grade defense.

As he withdraws, he hears a two-pack-a-day voice floating out of an adjacent conference room: '– swear to Christ amen, you lot are rock-chewing stupid. Who in the good Lord's name puts a Pic rail foregrip on a cut-down Kalashnikov twelve-gauge? It'll cheese-grate the flesh right off yer dickskinners.'

Passing the doorway, Evan slows to peer inside. He catches a glimpse of a hefty man in a beat-to-shit red trucker cap facing away, cocked back in a chair at the head of the conference table, boots of aforenoted Original S.W.A.T. make propped up on the surface. The man's quarter profile shows a sun-beaten cheek pouched with chewing tobacco and a downstroke of what looks like a biker's mustache. Arrayed around the table, a half dozen suits from a gun manufacturer stare at the man with submissive chagrin. The decaled espresso demitasses before them look all the more delicate contrasted with the thirty-two-ounce paper cup with coffee bleeding through at the seams set beside those sturdy Original S.W.A.T.s.

Before Evan can hear more, someone heels the door shut.

That name again.

Tommy Stojack.

Evan hears it this evening as the punchline of a bar story told through a smoker's laugh. And not three minutes later on the lips of a middle-aged woman wearing swaths of too-broad aquamarine eye mascara, whispering in a manner that suggests carnal knowledge. The guy is low-profile, hard to spot, just like Evan. But unlike Evan, he is woven into the fabric of a community in a way that Evan finds perplexing and intriguing.

Evan sips an insufficiently shaken Grey Goose martini at the cocktail lounge of the newly constructed Palazzo next door to the convention center. The couple beside him are having a meet-cute over a spilled Amaretto sour, a beverage sufficiently cloying in its liqueur-and-simple-syrup stickiness to double as a tool for enhanced interrogation.

The marzipan smell is making his nasal passages throb, so he leaves his barely touched drink and a hundred-dollar bill on the bar and takes a long, circuitous route toward his room. The Third Commandment, pounded into his head by Jack: *Master your surroundings*. He notes the location of the cameras overhead and searches out alternate means of egress – a swinging door to a restaurant kitchen, a service elevator, a side door between the Grand Canal Shoppes that lets out onto an alley.

As he starts to withdraw from his quick check of the alley, a commotion near the loading docks at the far end catches his attention. A man wearing a chef apron drags a little girl toward a parked car in which a woman in a housekeeping uniform waits angrily. He is shouting at the woman in Spanish as he approaches, gesticulating angrily, and she is shouting right back at him. From what Evan can hear, he gleans it is a custody handoff. The father tugs his daughter like a rolling piece of luggage; she stumbles alongside him blankly in her Frida Kahlo crown braids, stained Disney princess gown, and scuffed sandals.

She clutches a stuffed-animal elephant, ragged gray with a striped blue shirt and red bow tie – a business-casual pachyderm.

When the father jerks the girl up to shove her into the car seat, the stuffed elephant falls into a puddle. He and the mother are too busy screaming at each other to take note.

Though the girl can't be older than three, she secures her own chest buckle and then stares longingly through the half-rolled down window at the fallen elephant beyond. Soaking up water on the asphalt, it looks woefully post-apocalyptic.

In the threshold of the doorway, Evan hesitates a moment longer, watching.

The parents keep bickering but he senses the argument contains more bitter exhaustion than threat.

The girl doesn't cry and her expression remains blank but she reaches her hand out the window toward her stuffed elephant, fingers splayed.

A movement by the loading dock draws Evan's focus. A broad guy emerges from the shadows. He is spry on his legs but his gait shows hints of damage in the knees and hips, a waiting arthritic future.

Unseen, he ambles over and picks up the stuffed elephant. Evan can't make him out clearly, not from this distance, but he can see a biker's mustache and catches a glimpse of hound-dog eyes beneath the ragged brim of a trucker's cap.

The man hands the stuffed elephant to the girl through the rear window, musses her hair, and withdraws into the darkness from which he'd come.

Locked in their feud, the parents don't even notice.

The next morning is range day, where Evan hopes to suss out a new supplier of custom 1911s. He doesn't get five strides in when he spots a guy with media credentials firing a full-auto 5.56 with one hand while filming himself with a selfie stick in the other.

He exfils immediately.

Back at the convention center, he resumes his search for discreet window armoring. Threading up the broad central aisle of the Sands Expo ballroom, he takes in the sundry tactical offerings.

A guy decked out in an army Fifth Group beret-flash T-shirt sits in a large exhibitor booth. A snazzy presentation video on a suspended flat-screen behind him shows a computer-rendered simulation of the seemingly impossible – a .50-cal sniper round with embedded reconnaissance capabilities. Fire a shot over a target and the round itself records telemetry, land contours, temperature, wind speed, and air density, and then feeds them back to an encrypted militarized tablet.

'Think of the private-sector applications,' the guy is saying. He has late-stage Elvis's gut with none of the latent grace. "We're open to series-A-round investments now, slugs of twenty-five kay." He wears a sheathed Yarborough combat field knife adhered to his belt and a name tag identifying him as ROBBIE OLSON. 'The tech's only a few years out. We're talking a ten-, twenty-ex ROI *at least*.'

As would-be investors crowd in, Evan eases away across the aisle. Before a smaller group, a grizzled vet in an Eighty-Second Airborne shadow cap is showing off a lightweight collared long-sleeved shirt. The shirt has show buttons atop hidden magnetic ones that part without hesitation when you go for your holster, allowing you to draw straight through your shirt. He has the move down well, part frontier gunslinger, part carnival barker. Tucked into the side of the stall, Evan watches a few times, running mental calculations. The magnetic buttons would be useful, giving him an extra eighth of a second on the draw. In his world, an extra eighth of a second meant he'd get to keep more of his blood inside his body. He notes the shirt's make and designer, vowing to return when the line dies down.

An eruption back at the big exhibitor booth draws his focus. A military-aged woman wearing a black headscarf with a red flower is jabbing a finger at the screen and shouting in heavily accented English at Olson, the portly guy from Fifth Special Forces. 'This was mine,' she says. 'This was *my* idea.'

'I told you yesterday, I'm doing business here,' Olson says. 'This is how capitalism works in the civilized world.'

'I understand how capitalism works. *And* engineering – better than you do.'

'Yeah? Where's someone like you learn engineering?'

'I studied at Erbil Polytechnic –'

'Erbil Polytechnic?' A braying laugh. 'You're a regular Bill Gates then, huh? Look, consider your sweet ass *lucky* to be here on a special immigrant visa instead of cowering beneath a heap of rubble back in Buttfuckistan. SIVs are a privilege. They can be revoked. One phone call.' He snaps his fingers. 'Don't poke a sleeping eagle, little girl.'

'You stole from me. The telemetry algorithms. The whole idea.'

'How'm I gonna steal anything from you? I barely remember you.' Olson makes eyes at the crowd. 'Some third-rate translator.'

'Not just a translator.' Her eyes are on fire, her cheeks flushed, and finally Evan places the accent as Kurdish. 'A warrior.' She turns to the onlookers. 'I fought by his side.'

Enduring in the battle zone between Turkey, Syria, Iran, and Iraq, the Kurds are as tough as any people Evan has encountered. American foreign-policy jackals had been spurring them to conflict against whichever neighbor they deemed inconvenient, arming them in proxy wars and pledging alliances they never backed up when the time came to honor them. The Kurds had been betrayed by America at nearly every turn – seven times in the past hundred years. Not by the quiet professionals in BDUs but by orders initiating from the five-sided building in Arlington. There was an old Kurdish proverb Evan related to all too well: *No friends but the mountains.*

He had seen the rot in the military-industrial complex from the inside, up close enough to know the Kurds were still being used every bit as roughly as he and his fellow Orphans had been. He feels the sting of his own complicity as a cog in the wheel of empire, of the blind adamance of his own youth, of the blood he's spilled in the name of causes he does not understand. Still he musters hope that the best and the brightest will do right by the Kurds whenever the time comes for the United States to withdraw from Iraq and Afghanistan.

The conflagration at the exhibit booth rages, the woman now talking to the crowd as well: 'When ISIS was stealing stolen oil from the fields of northern Iraq? *We* were the ones shooting armor-piercing incendiary rounds from .50-cal Barretts to light up their tankers.' She gestures at Olson. 'While these *sagbab*s were back in the green zone soaking their pedicures.'

Olson is on his feet, leaning over the table, jabbing a finger at her. 'You'd best get the hell out of my sight. You don't question a Green Beret's honor on his own land.'

A ripple of hostility moves through the throng, a few men nodding in agreement. A familiar red trucker's hat pokes up into view at the back of the group, but an instant later it is gone.

The woman's face is set with calm fury, her gaze locked on the man. She refuses to step back. Evan eases close enough to hear her say, '*Hezar heval jî hindik in. Yek dijmin pir e.*'

She turns and walks away, her expression holding strong, but Evan catches a glimpse of the shaken young woman beneath the surface. In a rare flash of empathy, he can see that she feels demeaned. Treated like an expendable thing. That flicker behind her face finds resonance with a part of him long-and deep-buried, a part he's walled off under muscle and callus because he is too weak to have done otherwise.

The crowd parts for her, giving her wide berth, several folks still glaring.

'The hell's that gibberish she's babbling?' Olson says.

As Evan floats past the table searching for that trucker's cap, he translates in a low voice: '"A thousand friends are too few. One enemy is too many."'

'A threat?' Olson says. 'That bitch threatened me.'

'Oh, calm yourself, Robbie,' someone says as Evan moves away.

'Fuck you, calm down. She comes in here lying about me, showing me up in front of my clientele.'

Olson is still ranting when Evan turns the corner and gazes across the breadth of the second floor, still trying to spot the man in the trucker cap.

Currents of people sweep past him in both directions. The floor is packed; footfall and voices and laughter echo off the tall ceiling, the convention center seething with life and movement, a carbonated fizz.

A sharp voice cuts through the commotion behind him – '*warned* you not to stir the pot' – and he whirls in time to see Olson slam into the Kurdish woman from the side, banging her into the crash bar of a metal door and propelling her into a back hallway.

433

It is no more than a blip, the passersby still passing by.

Evan walked the rear halls yesterday. He knows them to have spotty surveillance cameras. And he knows that's why Olson had pressed her into them, removing her from view.

He is hustling, moving fast enough to catch the door before it swings shut.

He slips silently into a wide corridor crowded with shipping cartons, empty weapon containers, a few haphazardly parked forklifts.

The conflict has moved about fifteen meters down the hall, Olson and the woman partially in view squaring off between two pallets stacked high with crated gun racks. Olson grips the woman by the wrist, flinging her against the wall. As she wrenches her arm free, he cuffs her with an open palm.

A grown-man slap with grown-man weight behind it snaps her head to one side, knocking the headscarf askew. As Evan runs toward them, the woman drives into Olson with a knee in the crotch, slamming him into a pallet. Several of the heavy crates spill, crashing thunderously to the floor. As the gun racks topple, they reveal another man beyond approaching quickly from the opposite end of the hallway. Just a silhouette, but Evan recognizes the gait and the red trucker cap at once.

Olson howls, shoving himself off the crumbled tower of crates and ripping from his sheath the combat knife, which he holds in an expert forward grip.

Evan is still eight and a half strides away from the fight, the man in the trucker cap farther than that on the other side and moving slower.

Olson lunges at the woman's throat, a skilled thrust that leaves little but the blade to grasp.

Five strides out, Evan braces himself for bloodletting, and then the woman's hands move in a skilled parry and then the knife is out of Olson's hand and spinning around and then it

434

is embedded at an upward tilt between his ribs at the dead center of his torso and he is standing stock-still and shocked and already dead though his brain doesn't know it yet.

He slides diagonally to the floor, legs limp, torso flopping, head smacking tile.

No movement.

Evan comes to a halt behind the woman.

The man in the trucker cap stops behind Robbie Olson's corpse.

They stare at each other.

The first clear look Evan gets of the man. Sagging eyes held in measured pouches. Biker's mustache touched with gray. T-shirt featuring a bald eagle clutching Old Glory in its talons. Left forefinger blown off at the first knuckle. A combat veteran's face, a face that has seen things not easy to see but has come through still capable of holding emotion.

The woman is breathing hard. She looks at her hands as if they've betrayed her. Her pleading eyes go to the other man, standing protectively over Robbie Olson's body, and then they find Evan. 'You saw. You saw he tried to kill me.'

The hallway is tinged with Lysol, axle grease, sweat turned acrid by panic, and exposed organ meat.

It is a serious smell.

It is a serious situation.

'What's your name?' Evan says.

'Deijly. I am here on a visa. For my service. I am not American. They will not believe me. No one will believe me.' She fights down a tremor in her voice. 'Will you help me?'

Before Evan can respond the door bangs open behind him and two uniforms from Vegas Metro trot over. In the lead is a young kid with a blond starter mustache.

'The hell was that crash? Sounded like someone touched off a Bouncing Betty in here. You'd better –'

He comes around the fallen crates, spots the body, and freezes.

His partner takes his side, thumbs hooked through his belt loop. He has a seen-it-all face aged up with crow's-feet and graying sideburns. His name tag reads CARR.

'The *hell*,' the younger cop, ID'd as MCCLOSKEY, says. 'The hell went down here?'

Deijly makes a small noise at the back of her throat. The air conditioner hums overhead. Sounds from the convention floor wash through the walls at them.

They all look at one another, a Mexican standoff without the benefit of any Mexicans.

Evan breaks the relative silence: 'Guy was showing off his flashy edged-weapon moves with a Yarborough combat knife. Tripped on the edge of the pallet there, went down with the crates, and impaled himself.'

A long silence. McCloskey sucks his teeth. Carr blinks and blinks again. Both cops' gazes shift simultaneously to the man in the trucker hat.

Evan follows their stare. Deijly keeps her eyes lowered, afraid to look up, her heartbeat showing as a faint flutter at the hollow of her throat.

The man's eyes are unreadable. He looks down at the corpse, rolls his lips, making that mustache dance. He smells of tobacco, coffee, and cigarette smoke.

The silence lasts maybe five full seconds but feels a great deal longer than that.

Then the man sighs. 'I go back with Robbie Olson forever and a day, but we all know that boy's corn bread ain't done in the middle.'

McCloskey clears his throat. 'You're telling me that he tripped and fell exactly so? I mean, forensically, that angle of entry indicates –'

'"Forensically"? "Angle of entry"? Son, you're talking chicken to Colonel Sanders. How many knife fights you been in?'

'Uh, I'm not saying –'

The man points at McCloskey with the stub of the finger severed at the knuckle. 'I ain't big on stupid, McCloskey. I knew your old man back before he knew how to field-strip a .45. So let's not start dick jousting, not when you're bringing a pencil to a bazooka fight. Robbie Olson played *Enter the Dragon* to impress the young lady here and Darwin had something to say about it.'

Carr covers his smile with a fist, gives a faint cough. Deijly doesn't move, doesn't lift her gaze, but Evan hears the soft hiss of an exhalation through her teeth.

'Now let Carr here teach you how to handle an accidental death,' the man says. 'Same as I taught him when he was fresh outta the academy.'

McCloskey looks at Carr.

Carr gives an amiable shrug. 'You heard the man.'

'Okay,' McCloskey says. 'I'll need to take statements from everyone present for –'

'They don't need to give statements. I just did. You want a character reference from your captain?' The man pulls a barely intact flip phone from his pocket and wags it. It looks like it might disintegrate. 'He's at his boy's high-school graduation today but if he don't answer, I'm happy to call the missus to pull him out by the ear.'

McCloskey looks down at his polished boots. 'No, sir. That won't be necessary. Of course I trust your word and your . . . your experience. I didn't mean to imply –'

'Don't bother with all that,' the man says. 'I'm immune to charisma.' He squats beside Olson's sprawled form and rests a hand on the corpse with surprising gentleness. Evan is caught off guard seeing his baby-blue eyes mist. 'Goddamn it, Robbie,

437

you fool,' he says, quietly. 'It was your own damn fault. Your own damn fault.' He bridges his eyes with thumb and that stub of a forefinger for a moment and when he lowers his hand, his eyes are deep with grief. 'How the hell am I gonna break this to June Lynn?' He looks up at Carr, gives a snap of his head. 'You know where to find me when you need me.'

Carr taps his forehead with two fingers, an affectionate salute.

The man in the trucker cap turns to the woman. 'Ms Deijly,' he says, with a perfect pronunciation, 'I'm sorry you had to witness that.' He proffers an elbow, and she takes his arm with a trembling hand. At her side, he leads her out like a gentleman.

Evan nods at the officers and follows.

They move past a few more pallets and forklifts and step through an outer door into an empty alley wide enough to be a street. The sun lays itself across their shoulders, locking their shadows underfoot.

'Thank you,' Deijly says, her voice hoarse. 'Thank you both.'

The man nods. 'What kinda fool picks a fight with a Kurd?'

She smiles but it is fleeting. She rubs the back of her neck.

'You okay?' Evan asks.

'Fine. What do you say? "Dinged my bell"?'

'Close enough,' Tommy says.

'And I hit my hip pretty hard.' She rubs her thigh, pauses at the feel of something, then reaches in her pocket.

She pulls out a challenge coin broken in two from the force of her hip striking the wall. The halves glitter in her palm.

The top half reads: NO GREATER FRIEND.

The bottom: NO WORSE ENEMY.

438

Two raised ledges had once intersected at ninety degrees, dividing the coin into quadrants, but the metal disk has snapped horizontally, leaving a V to embrace the upper words and a caret angled down like a lampshade across the lower phrase.

'From my time in the fight.' She peers down at the pieces thoughtfully. 'I want you two to have it.'

She hands a half-moon to each of them, the pewter interior showing at the rough edge.

Gifting a token from her elite military unit is a show of great respect, and Evan and the man in the trucker hat receive the gesture as such.

She hugs the other man quickly and then gives Evan a peck on the cheek. 'Sometimes help is where you least expect it.'

She walks away.

Evan and the man watch her go. She does not look back. Reaching the end of the alley, she turns out of sight.

The man shifts chewing tobacco around in his cheek and spits a brown stream through the gap in his front teeth. 'I had McCloskey's asshole knitting a sweater back there.' When he grins, his eyes gleam. 'He's an okay kid. He'll be all right.' He produces a card from a cargo pocket, offers it to Evan. 'Never know when you might need a friend.'

The jagged piece of metal is heavy in Evan's hand: NO WORSE ENEMY.

'I don't have friends,' Evan says.

'Well, lookee here. The first true lone wolf ever to walk God's green earth.' He shoves his card into the pocket of Evan's jacket. 'Why don't you keep it for when you're stuck and need to make bail. What's your name, young man?'

'Evan.'

'Evan what?'

'Just Evan.'

'Ain't you fancy. One name, like Madonna and Elmo.' A wink. 'Heard you were having some trouble locating armored shades worth a damn thing.'

'How'd you hear that?'

Those hound-dog eyes twinkle again. 'Never know who's who in the zoo.' He starts up the alley and Evan holds pace at his side. 'The chain mail here at SHOT Show's about as useful as tits on a bull. I got a vendor outta Scandinavia, weaves sheets of it, tiny interlocking rings of unobtainium. Hell, you can even order it in harvest gold or avocado green.'

Evan's nose wrinkles at the thought.

'Or periwinkle. We'll get you hooked up, son.' The man slings his arm across Evan's shoulders, an easy, affable gesture. No one has done anything like that to Evan since his foster-home days and even then rarely. Evan suppresses his instinct to underhook the arm, gable the shoulder, take the man to the ground. 'Bet we could square you away on some hardware, too. You look like a 1911 man, that right?'

Evan feels . . . What is it he feels?

Warmth?

He pulls away, turns to face the man. He tells himself to proffer his open palm and then he does.

The man shakes with his intact hand. 'Tommy Stojack.'

His palm is as callused as Evan expected.

Side by side, they keep on up the alley, a wide stripe of sunlight illuminating the way.

'Like the gunrunner said, "I think this is the beginning of a beautiful . . ."' Tommy pauses, spits another stream of brown juice. 'Well, whatever the hell you wanna call it is just fine by me.'

1. What Tommy Had Done

Fifteen Years Later

Tommy Stojack had supplied weapons to a psychopathic female assassin called the Wolf.

That's what Tommy had done.

The Wolf had been at the center of Evan's last mission. The Wolf had attempted to kill Evan with a .357 Magnum revolver and a Savage 110 sniper rifle and an SUV with an unyielding front bumper. She had shot a father in the head in his own home and had tried and tried again to put a sniper round through the critical mass of his orphaned seventeen-year-old daughter after failing to garrote her with a zip tie. Through all of that and more, she had been armed by Tommy.

That's what Tommy had done.

The man who'd coaxed into Evan's stone-hardened heart the first faint heartbeat of trust since the death of Jack Johns.

The man who'd shone a ray of friendship into Evan's shadow-eclipsed soul.

The man with whom Evan had walked the past decade and a half at some distance but together, who'd manufactured his guns and field-tested his weapons and provided crotchety remote backup on his missions.

A dead father. An orphaned seventeen-year-old. A betrayal of what Evan had thought was a shared code.

That's what Tommy had fucking done.

Since Evan had deserted the Orphan Program, he had operated as the Nowhere Man, a pro bono assassin devoted to helping the powerless and terrorized. There'd been precisely one person he'd been able to count on for the entirety of that time.

Not anymore.

At the moment it was less than helpful for these thoughts to be cycling through Evan's head with white-hot OCD compulsion. Not when he was nestled into bushes outside a heavily armed Hancock Park house nearly big enough to be called a mansion, his face darkened from a loam paint stick, superglue glazing his fingertips to obscure prints, suppressed matte-black ARES 1911 in hand.

This was not the time to be musing about Tommy. Or the weapons he'd supplied to the Wolf. Or the purpling face of Jayla Hill, the seventeen-year-old Evan had held in his arms as she'd gasped for breath. Or the slit through Jayla's trachea, the splatter of blood across her face. Or the fact that his own supposed friend had indirectly broken the Eighth Commandment: *Never kill a kid,* and directly violated the Tenth: *Never let an innocent die.*

Evan had already scaled the spiked wrought-iron gate and waited now tucked into the shrubbery, twenty-four meters off the front of the unlit house-mansion, twenty-three if the Angeleno darkness had screwed up his internal range finder. Night blooming jasmine perfumed the air and as anyone familiar with night-blooming jasmine understood, 'perfumed' wasn't too fancy a word for it.

A crunch of movement issued from the blackness of the wraparound front porch. Evan thumbed off the ambidextrous safety, but he couldn't make out the source and couldn't risk reaching for his night-vision headset. Three hours ago, as dusk had filtered into nightfall, he'd surveilled the property from atop a telephone pole one long block over. He noted the movements of each of the four hired

442

guns – which one walked with a shuffle of the left foot, which one took smoke breaks every quarter hour, which one scratched at his dandruff, which one was close protection. For obvious reasons, Stavros's house-mansion was under extra-heavy security tonight.

Evan's brain clicked back to Tommy. Certainly Evan had other associates with shady intentions and deadly intent. But they'd never crossed his missions. People had been murdered on Evan's watch with Tommy's weapons. Was he supposed to just forget that? Was he supposed to make this the only time in his life he didn't trace a threat to its source and uproot it? If he allowed a crack in his code, he'd have no idea what else might leak through, widen the gap, and surge into a torrent.

The snick of a match on the porch.

Evan waited.

The flame flared and rose.

A glimpse of downbent face, the crackle of a cigarette breathed to life.

Then just the cherry floating in total darkness five feet and eleven inches off the ground.

Evan lined the high-profile tritium Straight Eight sights ten inches below—*pfft pfft*—and the cigarette twirled away in a streak of sparks and then came the pleasing sound of crumpling meat and laundry hitting wooden planks.

He rolled from cover, tucking up against one of the porch columns, a fluted Ionic monstrosity befitting the home of a shipping magnate with deep syndicate connections and delusions of Old Country grandeur. A slight lean gave Evan a decent vantage of the bowed balcony rails directly above.

On the last mission, Evan had saved Jayla Hill despite Tommy's best hardware and the Wolf's best efforts. Every time he finished a mission, he asked the person he'd just helped to find someone else in dire straits and to pass on the number to his encrypted phone: 1–855–2-NOWHERE.

That helped his clients transform from being victims to becoming rescuers.

In less than two weeks, Jayla had identified his next Nowhere Man mission. On a follow-up visit to her otolaryngologist at Cedars, she'd come across a distraught woman, Neva Alonso, surrounded by police officers in the lobby of the pediatric ward. Neva had been hysterical, barely able to render a report.

Jayla had waited, followed the woman home, earned her trust, and passed on the secret phone number.

So here he was.

Fully operational, in the red-hot center of a mission, and yet his mind remained stubbornly fixated on Tommy. These past weeks, Evan had forgone comms with his former friend and ally, performing his own weapon checks, oiling his Strider knife, cleaning his pistols, running bore brushes down his shotgun barrels. Though he field-tested his magazines regularly, it was time for a fresh batch, but he'd put off heading to Tommy's armorer den in Las Vegas to pick them up.

He'd been avoiding Tommy's face, knowing the unspoken conflict between them would ignite when they next squared off. Evan had countless skills for countless varieties of conflict and clashes, but with – what was it? intimacy? – in the mix, he was unsure.

Or afraid?

Afraid of what?

Of how he might *feel*?

How ridiculous was that?

From above came a creak of decking and then the *scritch-scritch* of the dandruffed guard. A shadow moved into view, the guard resting his hands on the railing, and Evan leaned out further from the preposterous Greek column and fired upward.

Against the faint backlighting of the stars, he saw a spray leap toward heaven. A grunt, a topple, and then the guard piledrived into the hydrangeas by Evan's feet.

At some stage of the last mission, Tommy had known that his hardware was putting Evan's clients at risk, that his specialized weapons had even been used in multiple attempts to kill Evan.

And he hadn't spoken up.

That was a declaration of war by omission, wasn't it?

Evan was inside the house-mansion now, having used a diamond pick to make the spool pins of the front-door lock dance into alignment. Instead of a foyer, there was a gallery lined with resin sculptures of Greek gods, Poseidon featured most prominently as befitted the owner's profession and ego.

Evan had just drifted inside; he hadn't checked corners.

He did so now, a full two seconds too late.

This level of distraction was untenable. It put the current mission in jeopardy of failing.

Dark of face, firm of grip, he drifted through the gallery, the gods flanking his progress from either side.

Stavros would be awake and waiting.

Tonight was his big night.

Two guards remained, one tall and slender, the other tall and as wide as a deep freezer.

Evan heard footfall in the adjoining hall, the padding of boots. Radio silence of the first two guards must have drawn notice. The steps were inconsistent, one crisp, one shushing across the Thassos marble in a slight limp. The slender guard, then.

If Tommy had in fact declared war by omission, that had to be answered, didn't it? Evan had to confront him no matter what emotional complications that might produce.

In the middle of the gallery, he struck a flawless isosceles stance, raised his ARES, and waited for the lanky guard to limp into his sight. A few more steps and he surged into view, his head framed beautifully by Hades' two-pronged staff. Evan took a micro-moment to appreciate the Jungian synchronicity of dispatching a man by shooting him through the bident of the god of the underworld. Then he exhaled smoothly and pressed trigger—*pfft*.

Moving swiftly now, Evan swept past the guard as he was still falling, dumping another two rounds into his chest—*pfft pfft*—for good measure.

Six rounds burned. The ARES held eight in the mag and one in the chamber. Evan had Stavros and the deep-freezer guard left. Stavros would be easy given his state, but the big man's muscle mass would eat up rounds. While the 1911 had decent stopping power, Evan couldn't let his luck ride on three bullets.

His Original S.W.A.T.s skimmed silently across the marble. Hustling up the next hall, he extracted a full backup mag from the concealed pocket at his right hip, lifted it adjacent to the still-loaded partial mag, and ejected the partial into his waiting palm.

It snagged on the lip of the well.

A slight hitch on the drop, which from feel and habit he guessed was caused by a tiny burr lifted from the top right corner of the magazine tube between the catch notch and the top opening.

A half-second delay.

A half-second was the difference between this side of the dirt and the other. One of Jack's Unofficial Rules stood Voltaire on his head: *Good is the enemy of the great.*

Feet blurring, breath low and steady, Evan stripped the mag free and instinctively added the repair to a mental task list: *Replenish mags from Tommy.*

The thought escaped him before awareness could catch up but when it did, it came like a gut punch.

His weaponry was a part of him, and that meant Tommy was a part of him, too. And now he'd have to lop that part off and trust someone else to supply and service his weapons. For Evan, trust was not easy.

Three-fourths of a second had passed now. He was unsettled but could not spare a moment to reset himself.

Head down, swapping the clean mag, shoving it north.

His momentum carried him around the turn toward the back hall of the house, and his gaze rose from the union of his fists around the Micarta checkered grips and aluminum receiver, noting only now, too late, the massive form before him aiming a double-barreled sawed-off shotgun directly at his forehead.

Evan froze, pistol still aimed ineptly, unforgivably, somewhere at the junction of the ceiling and the wall at his ten o'clock.

Evan said, 'Oops.'

The big bores of the twelve-gauge gaped at Evan. The deep freezer grinned, gave a quick jerk of the barrel. 'Why don't you step into Stavros's office? He's waiting for you.'

Stavros looked like hell.

Baggy jaundiced skin, a prodigious gut that bulged outward to sit heavily across his thighs, ankles swollen to bell-bottom proportion. He sat stuffed into a distressed leather armchair, wearing it like a carapace. He was shirtless, his hairy torso mottled with blots and bruises, too-small athletic shorts showing the marbled wreckage of his legs. Dry flaky skin, bright yellow sclera, white paste gumming at the corners of his mouth.

The office smelled of stool, sweat, and urine. Photographs in dark wooden frames wallpapering the room showed Stavros in younger days and slighter form beside various leaders and celebrities, the one constant his open-mouthed 'this guy' finger point at his companions. Medical supplies were scattered everywhere – snapped-off latex gloves, bedpans, vials and orange pill bottles scattered across the leather desk blotter at his side. Syringes overflowed a red sharps container. IV in his arm, oxygen feeding his nostrils, rattling breath finding resonance in the bulging prow of his chest.

Across from Stavros, Evan sat in a much smaller chair. The guard loomed at his back, from time to time tapping the nape of his neck with the shotgun muzzle, no doubt concerned he'd be forgotten. He was standing so close Evan could make out the tip of his size-sixteen boot.

Stavros's voice came as a great-cat purr. 'Who are you?'

Evan shrugged.

The guard prodded the back of Evan's head with the shotgun.

Evan said, 'No one.'

'And yet you know me.'

Again Evan did not answer. Again he was prompted by steel.

'Yes,' he said.

Stavros's amused rumble of a laugh deteriorated into a coughing fit. 'You come here in judgment.' A wave of his monstrous hand to Evan's 1911, which the guard had placed on the desk at Stavros's side. 'With your little gun.'

'It's not *that* little,' Evan said.

'I am to assume you know about tonight's proceedings?'

The Strider knife in Evan's front left pocket pressed into the top of his thigh. The deep freezer had been overconfident in his girth, shotgun, and frisking abilities. 'I do.'

'And you find it' – Stavros's tongue poked out, tasting the air – 'distasteful.'

'"Distasteful" is too meek a word for what I think.'

'Hardly worth making a fuss,' Stavros said. 'Nice room upstairs, well cared for, won't know a thing. I'm not a savage.'

'No?'

'You hold that I am not within my rights?' A wheezing breath. 'My name, it is derived from *stauros,* the Christian cross on which Jesus Christ was crucified.'

Evan said, 'Wow.'

Stavros crossed himself Orthodox-style, right to left, thumb joined with the first two fingers, the others close to the palm. 'That means I am worthy of making sacrifices.'

'Ah,' Evan said. 'An allegorical interpretation.'

The retort brought another tap of the double-barreled shotgun from behind. Evan let it tilt his head more than necessary so he could steal a glance back. The tang-mounted safety was still engaged.

Stavros flared sausage fingers. 'I am also immensely significant in my own right.'

Evan said, 'Huh.'

Stavros tried to lean forward but his gut would not allow it and he settled back, winded. 'Do you have any idea how powerful I am?'

'Yes, I do,' Evan said. 'You're the third-most-powerful person in this room.'

He waited for the shove of the muzzle into the back of his head.

There it was, right on cue.

He seized the barrels with his right hand, jerking the shotgun aside as he rolled off the chair, left hand already grabbing for the Strider, hooking the shark fin atop the blade on the corner of his pocket to snap the blade open.

The guard stumbled forward, his substantial weight tugging him into a fall, and Evan cleared the chair away with a kick and stabbed him three times up the right side through the rib cage—*tap tap tap*—hitting a trifecta of key organs.

The guard hit the floorboards hard, leading with his chin, which knocked him out cold, a stroke of compassion since it would have taken his brain at least a few excruciating minutes to figure out what had happened.

Evan stood facing Stavros. 'Now you're the second.'

Stavros gasped and tilted forward, trying for the 1911 on the desk.

Evan watched him.

Stavros's catcher's-mitt hand knocked the pistol farther away and he tumbled from the chair onto the beautifully woven kilim. His face mashed into the earth-toned wool, the fulcrum of his enormous distended belly tilting him forward onto his chest. He made muffled noises into the carpet.

He lay there, suffocating, his chest unable to expand beneath his own crushing weight.

Evan reclaimed his ARES. Crouched near Stavros's head. He'd managed to tilt his face slightly so one straining eye peered pleadingly at Evan.

He wheezed into the carpet.

That yellow eye stared at Evan.

Evan stared back at it.

It blinked and blinked, tears clinging to the lashes.

A subconjunctival hemorrhage leaked through the sclera, red bleeding through yellow.

Stavros was trying to speak but his lips remained mashed to the floor. He made a sputtering noise and then was still.

Evan rose from his crouch.

He walked out of the study and through the quiet hall-ways to the base of the cherrywood stairs.

The doorbell rang – the Westminster Chime melody. Classy.

Evan walked back through the gallery of tacky statuary and opened the door.

A nervous man in blue scrubs stood on the porch. Late-middle-aged, round glasses, old-fashioned doctor's bag. At his side stood a burly nurse a decade younger with a septum pierce and buzz-cut hair died in orange and purple swirls. Behind them a mobile medical Sprinter van idled.

To the side of the porch, barely visible in the darkness, the leg of the fallen guard poked up barely into view among the hydrangeas. This amused Evan darkly.

'Listen,' the sweaty little doctor said, 'get the others. We have a lot of unloading to do and we still have to prep and sterilize the theater.'

Evan shot him in the face – *pfft* – swung his arm a foot and a half to the right, and shot the nurse through his gaping mouth – *pfft* – and chest for good measure – *pfft*.

Leaving the door ajar, he withdrew once again to the stairs.

At the base, he drew in a deep breath. He reloaded the 1911 with a fresh magazine and then gingerly unscrewed the still-warm suppressor and secured it in a thigh cargo pocket. With one fluid motion, he swept aside his shirt with the base-plate of the ARES magazine, seating the pistol into the appendix carry holster and securing the shirt's magnetic buttons *click, click, click* as he had thousands of repetitions before.

He ascended to the second floor.

Walked quietly along the corridor.

The third door on the left was locked. From the *outside*.

He hesitated, unsure what he might find within.

Steady breath in, steady breath out.

He unbolted the door and swung it open.

The room was jarringly bright and nicely decorated. A queen bed with a princess canopy and a yellow and blue quilt. A cheery circular rag rug. Dolls of all shapes and sizes, a rocking horse, and a plastic kitchen with play pots and pans.

A girl sat in the middle of the rug, playing with Lincoln Logs.

Querida Alonso, eight years old, universal blood type negative, healthy two-pound liver just big enough to harvest.

Neva's daughter.

'Querida?'

She looked alarmed.

'Oh,' Evan said. 'My face. That's just makeup. Like baseball players wear.'

Querida nodded. Smooth skin, big brown eyes, her hair taken up high in a ponytail spout. She was wearing a yellow dress two sizes too big for her.

'May I come in?'

She nodded again.

Evan took a few slow steps forward. The girl did not flinch.

He nodded at the Lincoln Logs. He kept his voice soft, so soft. 'What are you building?'

'My house,' she said.

Evan took another step toward her and lowered himself onto his knees, making himself smaller. 'Are you okay?'

The girl shrugged. 'I miss Mamá. They said I had to come here. Like for camp. They said this is what she wanted. But I don't understand why she didn't just say so herself.'

'I don't think this is what she wanted,' Evan said. 'I think it was a misunderstanding.'

The girl added some green split logs to the roof.

'Did anyone hurt you?'

She shook her head. 'But they won't let me leave. Or call Mamá.'

She had matching dimples in her cheeks and her lashes were long and curled. He pictured the man lying downstairs on the woven carpet, a man who'd been ready to absorb this child, to slice her open, part her out, and discard what was left so as to leave no evidence.

Evan's distraction had nearly left her to that fate.

His focus, judgment, and gear had been compromised by his rift with Tommy.

If he'd wound up with his gray matter spattered on Stavros's office wall, it was one thing. But what his failure would have cost Querida and Neva was unacceptable.

Observing the girl's delicate wrists, the way she chewed her bottom lip with focus as she lowered another plastic log into place, he replayed the closeness of the miss. On his knees before her, he felt penitent. This child deserved perfection from him.

That was it, then.

He'd deliver this child to her mother. He'd ask Neva to find someone else to pass his number on to, someone else in need of the kind of help that only he could provide.

And then?

He'd deal with it.

He'd deal with Tommy.

'Your *mamá* sent me to get you,' Evan said. 'Would you like to leave?'

A vehement nod.

'I'm gonna ask you one favor, okay? I want you to keep your eyes closed until we are out on the street.'

'How'm I supposed to know where to go?'

'I could hold your hand. Or I could carry you.'

She scrunched up her face, thinking. Then she shot her arms up, straight at the elbows.

Something twisted inside Evan's chest, drawing pain.

He scooped her up.

She closed her eyes and nuzzled into his side, legs clamped above his hip, arms around his shoulders, forehead at his neck. He kept his forearm beneath her bottom. Her breath came feather-soft against his oft-broken collarbone.

He moved smoothly down the stairs.

Eased around the fallen guard in the hall of statues.

The front door remained open as he'd left it.

Holding Querida tight, he knuckled the keypad button mounted by the sidelight window. Out in the darkness, the wrought-iron gate started to rattle open.

He stepped over the body of the doctor, toed the nurse's arm out of the way, and carried the girl to safety.

He just wanted a decent book to read ...

Not too much to ask, is it? It was in 1935 when Allen Lane, Managing Director of Bodley Head Publishers, stood on a platform at Exeter railway station looking for something good to read on his journey back to London. His choice was limited to popular magazines and poor-quality paperbacks – the same choice faced every day by the vast majority of readers, few of whom could afford hardbacks. Lane's disappointment and subsequent anger at the range of books generally available led him to found a company – and change the world.

'We believed in the existence in this country of a vast reading public for intelligent books at a low price, and staked everything on it'
Sir Allen Lane, 1902–1970, founder of Penguin Books

The quality paperback had arrived – and not just in bookshops. Lane was adamant that his Penguins should appear in chain stores and tobacconists, and should cost no more than a packet of cigarettes.

Reading habits (and cigarette prices) have changed since 1935, but Penguin still believes in publishing the best books for everybody to enjoy. We still believe that good design costs no more than bad design, and we still believe that quality books published passionately and responsibly make the world a better place.

So wherever you see the little bird – whether it's on a piece of prize-winning literary fiction or a celebrity autobiography, political tour de force or historical masterpiece, a serial-killer thriller, reference book, world classic or a piece of pure escapism – you can bet that it represents the very best that the genre has to offer.

Whatever you like to read – trust Penguin.